M000165621

Angus slammed the book shut, making her jump, then sat in his chair, turning his attention to other papers on his desk. Confused Morag didn't know what she was supposed to do.

'Am I dismissed, sir? Have I to pack my bags?' she asked.

He looked up at her and smiled. 'Well, that is up to you. If you want your mother and father to stay on in their cottage then I suggest you do not lock you bedroom door tonight. If I do find it locked then I will expect to find you gone by tomorrow night and your parents out of their house by the end of the week.'

'Sir!, she protested, then turned and walked to the door. He rose from his desk and put his hand over hers as she turned the knob.

'Morag,' he whispered gently. 'Be sensible. I am showing you a very pleasant way out of a difficult situation.'

Anne Vivis was brought up in Fife, Scotland, where all her books are set. *The Rowan Tree* is her third novel; her first two, *Daughters of Strathannan* and *The Lennox Women* are also available from Mandarin. She now lives in Warrington, Cheshire.

Also by Anne Vivis
and available in Mandarin

Daughters of Strathannan
The Lennox Women

Anne Vivis

The Rowan Tree

Mandarin

A Mandarin Paperback
THE ROWAN TREE

First published in Great Britain 1994
by William Heinemann Ltd
This edition published 1994
by Mandarin Paperbacks
an imprint of Reed Consumer Books Ltd
Michelin House, 81 Fulham Road, London SW3 6RB
and Auckland, Melbourne, Singapore and Toronto

Reprinted 1995

Copyright © Anne Vivis 1994
The author has asserted her moral rights

A CIP catalogue record for this title
is available from the British Library

Printed and bound in Germany by
Elsnerdruck, Berlin

This book is sold subject to the condition
that it shall not, by way of trade or otherwise,
be lent, resold, hired out, or otherwise circulated
without the publisher's prior consent in any form
of binding or cover other than that in which
it is published and without a similar condition
including this condition being imposed
on the subsequent purchaser.

Had we never lov'd sae kindly!
Had we never lov'd sae blindly!
Never met – or never parted,
We had ne'er been broken-hearted.

Robert Burns

ONE

Ben Ochrie Strathannan, 1902

Thirteen-year-old Morag's teeth chattered convulsively. Shivering she hauled her threadbare blankets up and wound them tightly round her thin shoulders then squirmed more deeply into the lumpy mattress, drawing her icy feet up under her nightdress. But it was no good. She was still too cold to sleep.

From the other side of the loft she could hear the noisy, regular breathing of her three younger brothers, twelve-year-old Davy and the twins, Iain and Billy, who were almost eleven. She knew they would be snuggled up together, like puppies, and envied them. Last winter she would have nestled in beside them without a second thought, but she was too old for that now and self-conscious about her budding body. In any case it was too cold to creep all the way from her own bed, down the rough ladder, across the ten feet of cottage floor, past her parents' bed and up the ladder to the opposite side of the loft where her brothers slept.

In fact the loft was nothing more than two rough planking shelves, set under the roof on either side of the cottage, giving just enough room for a couple of mattresses. In summer it was unbearably warm and stuffy. In winter it was bitterly cold. In any season, if the wind was blowing from the wrong direction, the peat smoke billowed back down the inefficient chimney and gathered under the roof in noxious clouds.

1

Wrapping the blankets round her, Morag sat up and peered into the darkness, clicking her fingers softly. Immediately there was a soft whining noise followed by the rapid patter of paws on wood. The draft of cold air stirred up by Corry's swishing tail brought fresh goose bumps to her skin. She put out a hand and a damp nose muzzled into it, snuffling with pleasure. 'Shussh, boy. Shussh . . .' Morag told him gently, praying her sharp-eared father hadn't heard the dog's excited scramble. He didn't approve of her petting the animal. 'Poor boy,' she whispered in his silky ear. 'You're as cold as I am.' It couldn't really be true. Corry was a working dog, a hardy, black and white Collie, used to being out on the hillsides in all weathers and well protected by his thick, double coat. 'Come on then,' she said, patting the blankets. Corry needed no second invitation. With a delighted whimper he dived under the covers and settled against her legs, only his pink muzzle poking out. Already Morag could feel his heat spreading into her chilled limbs.

When next she opened her eyes it was still dark, but that was normal at this time of the year. The dog was gone, off with her father to do a day's work on the hills.

Morag sat up, fully alert now, sensing something different in the air. Tensing herself against the cold she threw the blankets back. Grabbing her flannel petticoat she dragged it frantically over her naked body but not before the sharp morning air had bitten into her bare skin. She let her breath out in a long shiver of white vapour, hurriedly pulled on her brown woollen dress and poked her frozen feet into sturdy, battered boots. Her toes were painfully cramped inside the coarse leather but she knew better than to complain. The penalty for that, which had been paid by each of the children in the past, was a week without footwear of any kind and no sympathy for the cuts and bruises which resulted.

Without the benefit of a mirror she dragged a comb through the tangled, mass of wild auburn curls which tumbled almost to her waist. When it was as tame as she could make it she bundled it into the nape of her neck and tied it with a strip of fraying, green ribbon which was two shades lighter than her eyes. That done, Morag slid down the ladder into the one room which served all their domestic purposes.

The cottage was dark, as it always was when she rose, but this morning it was a different kind of darkness. Running to the window she rubbed at the glass, letting the warmth of her hand melt the frosty coating. Even when the ice was melted the whiteness remained, a translucent, shining mass which completely covered the small window allowing only a tiny amount of light to filter into the cottage.

'Snow!' she cried, excitedly.

'Aye. Snow,' Annie McDonald said wryly, turning from the peat burning fire where she was stirring porridge thick enough to plaster walls with. 'Come and get some warm food inside you, lass.'

Annie was a strong, proud woman whose trim figure, gentle beauty and health had all survived the rigours of bearing seven children, three of them now dead. Nor had the hardships of life on this hill farm managed to destroy her spirit. Despite her husband's low earnings, the fact that almost everything they wore was old before they got it, Annie refused to think of herself as poor. Her few bits of furniture were polished into gleaming submission and the cottage was cleaned and swept until it would have shamed many a more wealthy woman.

3

Even at this hour of a bitter morning Annie's fair hair was pulled back into a tidy bun, her face still glowed from the freezing water she had washed in and her hands and nails were immaculately clean. Her clothes, though old and much repaired, were spotless. That she successfully maintained these standards for herself and everyone in her family was a minor miracle in a house where there was not even running water.

Morag took the bowl her mother offered. 'We'll not be able to get to the school in this,' she asserted happily.

'A good job too,' her mother retorted, turning away to hide the smile on her face. 'It's already after nine, you'd have been gey late.'

'It's not my fault! The snow's over the window. I thought it was still night,' Morag defended herself stoutly. 'Is it deep?'

'Up to the roof at the back,' Annie answered, her pale, blue eyes already shadowed with worry. Snow meant weeks of cold isolation and the lurking possibility of hunger. The thaw, when it came, would bring dampness as well as coughs and colds for everyone. Even the children would lose their sense of wonder if they couldn't get down to the village, if the peat didn't last. But it would be cruel to spoil her daughter's pleasure in it just yet.

Annie's husband, Coll, was a shepherd on Arneil's farm on the very border of Strathannan. It was here that the fertile floor of the strath narrowed to meet the hills of Perthshire as they crept over the county boundary, bringing with them a taste of the real highlands. The cottage, nestling in a sheltered fold on the side of Ben Ochrie, at the end of a steep, two-mile trail from the village of Pitochrie, came with the job. With hills which were very nearly mountains at its back and the strath

4

below, the setting was magnificent. Beside the cottage a wide, peaty burn, flowing straight off the hills, tumbling wildly over rocks, sparkling in the shallows and eddying into deep, dark pools, gave a constant source of pure, sweet water and a strictly illegal supply of salmon and trout. Further down, where the burn flowed into the River Annan, stood a sizeable patch of woodland, big enough to hide a rabbit or two as well as the man who was poaching it.

Arneil's farm was part of the Fraser estate. The laird, Sir Angus Fraser MP, was more often in London than in Strathannan and was content to leave the running of his estate to his manager, Rab Bannerman. A straight-talking but reasonable man who had known poverty at first hand, Rab couldn't bring himself to grudge a hard-working family man like Coll McDonald the odd fish or rabbit. So long as no one was greedy and no one shot the grouse which were reserved for the pleasure of Angus Fraser and his London friends, he turned a blind eye to a bit of poaching.

This morning, well wrapped against the cold, Rab set out from his home in the lodge house of Pitochrie Castle, Fraser's grandly named tower house. As surprised by the unexpectedly heavy snowfall as anyone, he was anxious to see that all was well on the Fraser property.

There were two farms on the estate, one on either side of the River Annan. Ewart Morrison worked the swathe of lowland on the southwest side of the river, running dairy cattle and raising crops. The cattle had long been brought into the barns and the snow would have little effect on them. If the milk wasn't collected for a day or two old Morrison and his wife would simply make butter and cheese, a contingency plan they put into effect nearly every year, though seldom as early as

5

this. Rab knew he need not concern himself with their welfare. But Arneil's farm was a different matter. Here they had only a narrow strip of fertile land on the opposite side of the river. Within a hundred yards the ground started to slope up into the hills and was fit only for sheep. Dod Arneil himself was an old man, stiff in body and slow of mind. His one surviving son, Charlie, had never been strong and was unable to walk more than fifty yards before being forced to stop and gasp for breath. He did his best to take a hand in the farm but responsibility for the flock of sheep which roamed the braes rested with Coll McDonald.

And more than likely Coll would be out there this morning, thought Rab, scanning the whitened hillsides for any sign of his closest friend. Even now, after a lifetime in hills and mountains, the sheer beauty of a fresh snowfall awed him. The storm had lasted from early afternoon until dawn when a plunge in temperature had crispened the powdery surface. Now everything was perfectly, eerily still and silent, waiting, while the sky overhead lowered with threatening greyness, promising yet more snow before the morning was out. Frowning, Rab looked for the McDonald cottage, usually just visible from here and only found it by patiently identifying the still visible landmarks. The single tree, gnarled and frosted, which was in the centre of the saucer like indentation on the hillside – appearing now as a blue-grey shadow – and, beside it, the dark slash where the burn still flowed through the ice. Camouflaged by a complete mantle of snow the cottage itself was almost impossible to see, even to someone of Rab's experience, until the faint haze of grey smoke from the chimney caught his eye.

Like him, Coll McDonald had spent most of his life in

6

the hills and was well used to weather like this but Rab knew that the suddenness of this storm would have caught even Coll unprepared. No one had expected such a severe storm in October. As late as noon yesterday the weather had been normal for the season. Then an abrupt change of wind and an ominous build up of cloud had warned the weatherwise of what to expect. All through the afternoon and into the evening, long after the first flakes had flurried down, Coll's piercing whistle had echoed round the braes as he and his dog worked to bring in the scattered sheep, his job made almost impossible by blizzard conditions. Rab knew there hadn't been time to get them all. This morning Coll would be back on the hillfoots, desperately trying to dig out buried animals before another fall made such work impossible.

Rab shaded his eyes and squinted at the hillside, searching for the black dots which would be Coll and Corry, then listened, hoping to catch the sound of Coll's voice which sometimes carried right across the floor of the strath. But there was nothing. Rab rubbed a hand over the thick, black beard which hid his craggy face and emphasised the piercing blue of eyes which were set in a web of lines. A shower of frost fell from the coarse hair on to his thick jacket. Again he scanned the slopes for any sign of his friend, his eyes watering with the intense cold.

Half an hour later Rab was on the trail which led up to the cottage, feeling his way carefully, knowing that to stray off the track could be to tumble into one of the many clefts which marked the hillside. As he walked he constantly probed the ground ahead with his long stick, testing its firmness before trusting it with his weight. In places the snow came halfway up his calves and he knew that on the exposed hillside there would be drifts many feet deep.

It was more than an hour later, and he was panting with exertion, when he reached the cottage. Coll's lads had already cleared a path to the door and were working with spades and shovels to dig out the drift which piled to the roof at the back.

'I'm thinking you'll be doing it all again tomorrow,' he greeted the three boys, nodding at the sky which was now a leaden grey. They groaned with good natured resignation. 'But it beats going to the school, eh?' he laughed.

'Keep to it, lads. You've not got time to blether.' Annie said as she ushered him inside. 'What are you thinking of, Rab Bannerman?' she asked. 'Why in God's name have you come away up here in this weather? Come along in and get yourself warm.'

'I came to see if I could give Coll a hand,' he told her with absolute honesty but they both knew the second, unspoken, truth was that he was as concerned for her as he was for Coll, that the attraction was mutual. And they both understood that nothing would ever come of it. Annie loved Coll and Rab would no more betray a man who was like a brother to him than he would harm a child.

'It's taken me the best part of two hours to get here,' he admitted. 'I didn't think it would take so long but once J was halfway there was no point in going back. Has Coll many sheep out there?'

'Aye. Too many,' she sighed. 'I'll not rest till he gets home.'

'How long has he been gone?'

'Two hours before first light, as soon as the snow stopped.'

Rab pulled his watch from his fob pocket. Over six hours. He looked at the sky again and felt a flicker of unease. But Coll was an experienced shepherd and knew the hills hereabouts better than anyone.

'Maybe I'll just have a wee look. Och, see! There's Corry!'

The black and white dog followed half a dozen saturated, exhausted sheep up the path past the house then set to barking as he rallied the animals outside the stone pen. The boys ran, ploughing thigh deep through the snow to dig out the gate and open it just wide enough for the animals to be chased in.

'That's a canny animal,' Rab said, admiring the beast's skill.

'Trained by a canny man,' Annie laughed. 'I swear if anything happened to that dog, Coll would mourn him like a human. Here Corry,' she called when the last sheep was safely penned. The dog bounded over to the house, panting but wagging its tail in pleasure. 'Good boy. Here,' she filled a bowl with the left-over porridge. Corry wolfed it in two seconds and went to scratch at the door, impatient to be let out again.

'Look at him! Just dying to get back to Coll. Wouldn't you have thought he'd have had enough?' Annie asked. 'Well, at least I know Coll's all right.'

As they watched the dog churning off through the snow in search of his master a huge flake of snow drifted slowly to the ground. A second later another one followed it. Rab was back outside before Annie could stop him.

'Wait. You can't walk all the way back to Pitochrie in this. At least have some broth to warm you.'

'Save it. I'll be back. And that husband of yours with me,' he said, taking Coll's spare crook and hanging the

9

coil of rope from behind the door over his shoulder. Then, walking as fast as he could, he followed the dog's tracks through the snow before the new fall could obliterate them.

Coll lay flat on his stomach peering over the edge of a small gorge. It was easy to see what had happened. The rift in the hillside was narrow and almost completely closed by over-hanging snow which had given way when the animal stepped on it. No matter how he stretched his crook Coll couldn't reach the sheep which stared back vacantly. There was nothing else for it, he would have to go down there and drive it up the slope himself. First he knocked the loose snow away from the edge, then slipped and slithered towards the sheep, grateful that the chasm wasn't as deep and dangerous as some on the hillside. Using his crook he grabbed the animal by its horns and pulled. The beast gave a bad-tempered bleat and wrenched its head free, seeing absolutely no reason to move. Losing patience Coll called Corry away from guarding the half dozen sheep he had already dug out of various places in the last four hours. The dog knew what was expected of him and plunged eagerly down the edge of the cleft, positioning himself behind the sheep. Encouraged by the barking Collie, the sheep launched itself at the steep sides but lost its footing and tumbled down again.

'Nip. Nip,' Coll ordered the dog to do what was normally forbidden.

As exasperated as his master, Corry was only too happy to obey and snapped angrily round the sheep's legs, nipping the skin lightly. Terrified but hampered by the weight of its saturated fleece, the sheep ran at the banking. Coll moved in behind, got his shoulder under its rear end and heaved it unceremoniously over the top. The sheep trotted off to join the others, totally unconcerned.

'Good boy, Corry,' Coll heaved himself back over the ledge and rubbed the dog behind its ears. 'Off you go now. Take them home. Home boy. Home.'

Corry turned intelligent, questioning eyes on his master, as if reluctant to leave him out here alone. Coll smiled. The dog was exhausting itself controlling the sheep they had rescued. Best to send him home with them. Annie would give him some food and send him back. 'Home boy,' he repeated, more sternly this time.

The dog whimpered its disagreement but turned and nudged the sheep before trotting obediently away.

Coll watched him go, taking a minute to chew on a lump of the thick, congealed porridge from the tin in his pocket and enjoy a swig from the flask of cold tea hanging from his belt.

Coll was an impressive sight as he waded through the snow. Six-feet-four inches in his stockinged feet, red-haired and loud-voiced, he was a well-known and respected figure for miles around. The common belief that shepherds care little for the company of other human beings found its biggest challenger in Coll McDonald who liked nothing better than an evening at the local inn, in the company of his best friend, Rab Bannerman.

A man given to deep thought, a listener rather than a talker, when Coll did have something to say it was generally worth hearing. There were many people in upper Strathannan who wondered why such an intelligent man should have to make a living as a shepherd. Few understood that to deny Coll the freedom of the hills would be like cutting his heart out. As long as his conscience

11

was clear, his wife and children were healthy and his friendship with Rab Bannerman was intact he would ask little more of life.

Coll walked with confidence as he made his steady way over the hillside searching for the tell-tale depressions where the breath of a buried sheep had melted the snow above its head. Often he stopped to drive his stick gently into the snow where it had drifted enough to cover an animal. Years of working in the hills had made him familiar with every small depression, every sharp boulder, even when they were covered with snow, and he knew the most likely place for the dozen or so animals which were still missing was in the gullies, like the one he had dragged the last beast from. They went there for shelter then found themselves trapped.

He rounded the edge of Ben Urquhart and plodded on, sure most of the sheep would be in one or other of the small gorges up here. He went more slowly now, aware that the ground beneath the snow was uneven and dangerous, disguising gullies and clefts which could break the leg of an unwary man.

A quarter of a mile further on, the ground dipped sharply, disappearing into what Coll knew to be a steep-sided glen. Coming as close to the edge as he safely could, Coll looked down into a deep, snow-filled chasm, hoping to see some signs of trapped animals, but found nothing. Cold now and tiring rapidly he glanced at the sky and knew there was another storm about to break. He had no desire to be caught in the open when it did. Feeling a sense of failure he decided to follow the glen down the hillside and then start for home.

Sheep were hardy beasts and had been known to survive for days in air pockets under snow drifts but he knew his animals were likely to die if he couldn't find them today. Coll was not overly sentimental. He had no compunction about snaring a rabbit for the pot or even selling a salmon to raise money for clothes for the bairns, but these stupid, docile creatures were his responsibility and to lose even one was a personal failure.

The glen's precipitous sides fell thirty feet to where an icy mountain stream rushed between sharp boulders and snow-covered banks. Coll crouched on the edge, looking round one last time. As the first flakes of the threatening storm settled on his sleeve, sudden movement, deep in the bottom of the glen, caught his attention. There, huddled on a ledge under the overhanging bank, on the far side of the burn, were three sheep, almost indistinguishable from the snow. Without hesitation Coll dropped to his backside and slithered down the sheer slope. The icy stream was littered with rocks and he crossed it with relative ease. The animals, frightened by his approach but having nowhere to run to, turned in tangled circles. Coll waited patiently until they had calmed a little then deftly hooked his crook into the horns of the nearest animal and pulled it steadily forward, forcing it across the water. It came nervously at first but as soon as the other bank was within reach, leapt nimbly into the snow there. Coll pulled himself up the steep banking, using rocks and stunted trees to steady himself and, crook still in place, hauled the animal after him. It slithered precariously but then hauled itself over the top. He repeated the whole process with the second animal but already the banking was dangerously icy. After twenty exhausting minutes Coll succeeded in dragging himself and the panicky animal over the edge.

The snow was now falling thickly. A less experienced man might have found what shelter he could in the glen and waited, hoping for the snow to stop, but Coll knew the temperature would plummet at night, and probably kill him. His only chance was to start off for home now, before the weather got any worse. Grimly he looked down at the sheep still trapped on the ledge. It regarded him with a helpless, uncomprehending stare. Five minutes later Coll had the animal across the burn and was attempting, with a mixture of pushing and pulling, to get it to the top of the icy slope. Twice the animal's front legs collapsed and it slid backwards on its knees, taking him with it. Each time he managed to hold it, to get it moving again. Fifteen minutes later the exhausted animal finally got its front legs over the lip of the chasm, its hind legs scrabbling frantically for enough leverage to propel itself over the top. Wedging himself as firmly as he could, Coll put his back into the sheep's rump and heaved, bracing his legs and feet against a snow-covered rock. At the moment when he was exerting the most pressure, when the animal finally began to move forward, his feet slipped. He kicked wildly, searching for grip then flailed desperately for something to grab hold of. Above him the sheep scrambled frantically then gave a panicked scream as it plunged down the banking. It landed with a splash in the water, then lay absolutely still, its neck broken.

Coll caught at a scrubby tree but the branch snapped in his hand. And then his body was tumbling down the rocky slope, lurching thirty feet to the floor of the glen where he landed with a sickening thud, crashing his head against a boulder. He too was absolutely motionless, the blue-white, jagged ends of shattered bones poking through the ripped fabric of his trousers, just above the knee. Blood seeped on to the snow, staining it crimson. Already the snow was settling over him.

On the edge of the glen, Corry ran wildly up and down the bank, whining with frustration. Every two or three yards he picked up his master's scent but it was getting weaker all the time as the snow settled on it. Finally Corry found a place where the man's smell was mixed with that of sheep. Yapping in excitement he threw himself down the banking and landed almost on top of Coll. Snuffling gently he poked his damp nose into the man's cold face, prodded him and licked his ears. But Coll was past response. Crying, panting with distress, the dog settled in the snow, his front paws and head on his master's chest and settled down to wait, the velvet brown eyes deep, dark pools of sadness.

Rab knew that to go any further was tantamount to committing suicide. But he forced his aching body to go on, propelled forward by something that was neither instinct nor feeling, just the absolute certainty that Coll was in trouble of some kind. There was no other reason for him to be out on the hillside in weather that would drive any sane man back to his own fireside. Only when he reached the edge of Ben Urquhart without finding a trace of his friend did Rab seriously consider turning back.

He stood for a moment to catch his breath and rest his aching legs. The snow fell silently, steadily, with no trace of the blizzarding winds which had been behind last night's fall. Everything was still, shrouded in unearthly silence. For the first time in his thirty-seven years, Rab felt the fear of absolute loneliness. As much to shake it off as anything else he put his hands round his mouth and roared.

'Coll! Coll! Answer me, Coll . . .' The sound seemed deadened by the snow. 'Coll!' he roared again. Every nerve in his body told him his friend was out here still.

Common sense said it was possible, even likely, that they had passed, unnoticed in the snow. But surely the dog would have found them ...

The dog! Rab turned suddenly, his back to the strath below him, and looked up the side of Ben Urquhart. There it was again! The distant, unmistakable sound of a dog barking.

'Corry!' he called, ploughing on towards the glen which dissected the hillside. 'Corry!' If Corry was still on the mountainside then so was Coll.

Again the dog barked, more clearly now.

Rab struggled on through ever deepening snow, the feeling in his feet and hands quite gone. 'I'm coming, boy,' he called out to the dog every minute or so, using the barks to guide him until, at last, he was at the edge of the glen.

Corry was very close now but when Rab looked down the side of the Glen he could see nothing. 'Where are you, boy?' he called softly and was rewarded by the dog suddenly leaping up the bank and scrambling to his side. Corry yelped and barked, jumping and circling. Finally he nudged Rab from behind to make him go in the right direction. Rab looked at the slope and knew he had little chance of climbing up unaided once he got to the bottom. While the dog barked impatiently he secured one end of the rope round the bole of a tree and used it to steady himself as he made the steep descent.

The dog slithered past him and ran to stand over his master.

Coll was almost entirely covered in snow now, only the place where the dog had been lying was clear. Rab saw the dark stain of blood before he saw the gaping wound. Stunned by the horror of it he simply stared. Corry's urgent barking brought him back to his senses.

A close inspection showed the bleeding had stopped. Taking advantage of Coll's unconscious state Rab strapped the broken limb to his friend's crook, binding it with the end of the rope. That done he turned his attention to the deeply depressed gash running across Coll's temple. By the time he had cleaned it the light was fading fast. Rab knew there was no hope of getting Coll home that day.

The glen was deep and rocky with one or two stunted trees clinging to its banks and at the water's edge. As gently as he could, Rab moved his injured friend into the most sheltered place he could find, against a huge boulder. In his pocket he still carried yesterday's daily paper, something he habitually took to Coll whenever he went up to the cottage. By good fortune he had forgotten to give it to Annie. Rab crumpled some pages and applied one of his matches to them, feeding small twigs into the flames one by one and blowing gently until, after ten minutes, he was able to add some larger ones, praying there was enough dry wood to make a good blaze. They smoked and crackled but finally caught. Carefully Rab added more, not taking his eye off the fire until it had a steady, red heart, knowing that this grudging source of heat could mean the difference between life and death for him and his friend. As soon as the orange flames started to send out warmth the dog dropped down beside it. Within five minutes the air was reeking of steaming fur.

Rab gathered more sticks and built up the fire until he had a fair blaze going then dragged Coll as close to it as he could. Coll's breathing was soft and regular but every so often he moved restlessly, obviously in pain. Exhausted now, Rab led Corry to lie close against Coll's uninjured side then he too laid down, sandwiching the tired animal between them for warmth.

Some time during the hours of darkness the snow stopped. Rab, who had spent most of the night keeping the fire alight, finally allowed himself a couple of hours sleep, buried into the dog's flank. He woke gritty eyed and cold just before dawn. Beside him, Coll was still unconscious but alive.

As soon as it was light enough to see, Rab fashioned a rickety stretcher from branches, lashed together by their two belts, Coll's muffler and the bits of string he had tied round the bottom of his trousers to keep the snow out. It was unsatisfactory, too flimsy to last, but would have to do until they got out of the glen.

The rope which Rab had lashed round the tree at the lip of the gorge before climbing down was stiff with ice. With difficulty he tied it to the end of the stretcher before starting the arduous climb out of the glen, using the rope to help him. At the top he untied the upper end of the rope, looped it round the trunk and prepared to haul his friend up.

Coll was a big man, almost two stones heavier than Rab who measured his progress up the bank in inches. When the makeshift stretcher finally slid over the lip of the bank, Rab was almost at the limit of his strength.

It was twenty minutes before he felt sufficiently recovered to start the long trail back to the cottage. Using his penknife he cut the rope and used it to strengthen the stretcher. Ominous drops of fresh blood were staining the snow under Coll's leg. Coll himself was still insensible but tossing restlessly and groaning in pain.

Rab supported the injured limb as well as he could then, draping the rope over his shoulders, he harnessed himself to the stretcher and began to drag it over the snow.

Beside him Corry ran in circles, alternately barking and whining. Rab managed a grim smile. 'Well you've a better brain than me, lad,' he said to the animal. 'You've been trying to talk sense to me for the last hour, haven't you?' He bent to fondle the animal's ears, tucking Coll's soft leather tobacco pouch under the dog's collar as he did so. 'Don't you be losing that, lad. Off you go then. Go home, Corry. Go home.'

He watched the dog streak off across the hardening snow then bent his back and hauled again at the stretcher. He knew he was reaching the end of his endurance. Blood pounded behind his eyes, colouring everything he saw in red mist, and his legs were buckling. He kept his head down and trudged on, not daring to look up because when he did, everything spun and he was in danger of collapsing. His chest hurt, as if there was a lump of lead under his ribs, his shoulders were chafed raw with the friction of the ropes, and his feet and hands were numb. Behind him a scarlet trail of blood marked their progress through the snow.

Rab had long passed the stage of consciously seeing his direction. He kept going by concentrating only on each heavy footstep. He didn't see or hear the dog until it sprang on to its hind legs and shoved him over. Once in the snow he didn't have the strength to rise again. When Corry licked his master's face Coll groaned, a sound full of unbearable pain, and Rab choked back tears of failure.

'Never mind, boy. You did your best.' He fondled the dog with clumsy, nerveless hands, understanding that it too had been prepared to die for Coll. It had been too much to ask of the dog.

'Come on, lad. Let's get you to your feet. Lean on me, I'll support you.' The words seemed to come from a very

19

long way away but Rab was vaguely aware of strong arms lifting him, of the smell of whisky under his nose, the burn of it in his throat.

'Coll?' he mumbled, trying to turn round, impeded by the weakness in his head.

'He's being taken care of.' A familiar voice, fuzzy and distant, echoed round his head. 'He's lucky to be alive. He'd have died for sure if it hadn't been for you, lad. Take it easy now.' But Rab was past listening, his knees gave way and he crumpled silently into the cushioning snow.

Annie sat in her window. Beside her the oil lamp burned like a beacon. Over and over again she told herself that Coll was a shepherd, a man who spent nearly all his waking hours outdoors, on these very hillsides. He, more than anyone, knew how dangerous they could be. It would have been foolhardy to risk crossing the hillfoots in this weather, and plain common sense to seek shelter overnight in one of the little glens which fractured the slopes. He had done that before. But never in weather as harsh as this. And where was Rab? Had he found Coll? The questions rolled round and round in her mind.

All night Annie watched the snowflakes swirling down until the cottage again rested in an undulating sea of pristine whiteness. About four o'clock it stopped. Gradually the clouds cleared and the moon shone down with eerie brightness, throwing shadows over the braes like a weak winter sun. Annie looked out of her window with silent tears streaming down her face, hypnotised by the cruel perfection of it all.

When day finally came the sky was a clear, dazzling blue and the snow glistened with the touch of frost. Stirring at last from her seat she busied herself with

20

mundane chores, heating the porridge, giving the boys their breakfast, setting a kettle to boil on the trivet. When the men came home they would need something hot inside them.

'Mammy?'

Annie jumped. She hadn't heard Morag get up. 'Wash your hands, lass,' she said automatically. 'I'll have your porridge ready in a wee minute.'

'Has Daddy not come home yet?' Morag asked, already knowing the answer. For hour after hour she had lain and watched the oil lamp shining on her mother's worried face. She must have dozed off just as day was breaking though. She hadn't even heard the boys get up.

'No, lass. Not yet. It was gey bad again last night. O'er bad for him to come home. He'll have taken shelter in one of the wee glens. He'll likely be home before long.'

'Aye . . .' But Morag didn't sound convinced. 'You don't think he's hurt himself?'

Annie winced then steadied herself. 'No, lass. I don't think that. If your Daddy was hurt would Corry not have home to fetch us?'

'Aye! Of course he would have. Corry came back with the sheep already, didn't he?'

'Aye. He's a fine dog.' And would not leave his master's side unless Coll told him to go. If Coll was hurt, lying unconscious somewhere, Corry would stay with him. Annie felt dizzy thinking about it. 'Here, lass,' she called, anxious to keep herself occupied. 'Get your porridge now.'

'Mam! Mam!' Iain and Billy yelled in unison, as they so often did, bursting into the house bringing snow and slush with them.

'What? What is it?' Annie span round, for once forgetting to chide them for the mess, expecting to see her husband walking towards her, her heart hammering with relief. But there was nothing, just endless snow.

'It's Corry! Look!' Billy was jumping with excitement.

The dog raced across what was normally a vegetable patch, scratched from the stony soil in front of the cottage, and hurtled through the open door. Exhausted he threw himself at Annie's feet and lay there, panting and whining.

'Well, boy?' Morag asked, fondling his ears. 'Where's Dad?' There was already a tight feeling in her throat. 'What's this?' she whispered as her fingers found the tobacco pouch which had slipped round his neck, out of sight.

'Oh God!' Annie stared at her daughter. They both understood the message. 'Feed him. Get him dry and warm again. He'll have to lead them to your Daddy.' Annie shouted her instructions from the snow outside, already on the way to the village for help.

'Good boy. Good boy,' Morag said, stroking his muzzle, her tears mingling with the snow in his coat.

Annie saw Corry sliding down the slopes almost half a mile away, a tiny, circling dot. Behind him more dots, too far away to see the details.

It had taken her over an hour to slip and slither down the hill to the village. A bare thirty minutes later four men were already climbing up through the Fraser estate, on to the hillside, nearer to Ben Urquhart and, hopefully, closer to Coll and Rob. Another three men had gone ahead of her to the cottage to collect Corry, knowing the dog would guide them to Coll if the first party couldn't find him. Annie followed them back up the hill. And then there had been an agonising three-hour wait.

The dots on the distant slope disappeared. She knew she wouldn't see them again until they crested the rise, less than a hundred yards from her front door. She banked the fire, feeding it with the few lumps of precious coal sent up to them by Fraser last Christmas and hoarded ever since. Then she fed the wood-burning oven, not caring that there wouldn't be enough fuel to bake bread tomorrow. The oven brought a rare heat to the cottage. The bent metal chimney ran though the roof, heating the air as it went. If Rab or, God forbid, Coll was hurt, they would need warmth to recover. And good food and warm drink . . .

'Mam.' Morag gently removed the water bucket from her mother's shaking hands. 'They're here.'

For one awful moment Annie didn't want to look. She wanted to stay here, make some scones, knead some bread, scour the table. Anything. But then the dog burst into the cottage, barking at her, almost as if he knew what she was thinking.

She wiped her hands on her pinafore and turned, steeling herself for the worst. 'Sweet Lord,' she whispered, staring at the stretcher, seeing Rab who was being half dragged through the snow. Now she was running. 'Dear, sweet Lord.' The wound on Coll's leg was obvious, gaping, crippling. The huge purple dent in his temple even more ominous. 'Bring him in.'

Silently they filed into the house and settled the still unconscious man on his own bed. Annie, faced with an emergency, was calm now and practical. Tenderly she bathed the wound, wiping away the dirt with a clean cloth and water from the kettle. But that was the limit of her capabilities. Coll's horrific injury could not be healed by the pulling, straightening and splinting which had worked on Davy's arm. Coll's bone was splintered,

the spongy pink marrow exposed, the break too complicated for anything but the best doctor. A hand fell on
her shoulder and she turned a hopeless face to Rab.

'I'm sorry, lass. I found him, fallen to the bottom of
the glen. It wasn't easy, pulling him out. It can't have
helped him.' His voice shook with fatigue.

Annie stood, feeling great tenderness for this man
who had been her husband's true and faithful friend for
so long. 'You brought him home, Rab Bannerman. You
risked your own life to go after him. He'd have died but
for you.'

'He once saved my life. I owed him no less,' he said,
his mind slipping back in time.

'You would have done it even without that and well
you know it,' she murmured.

'Best get him down to the village,' someone said.

'NO!' Annie was appalled. 'You can't take him down
there. He's not fit to be moved.'

'It's his best chance, lass,' Sandy Chisholm insisted. 'He
needs a doctor. Old Doctor McEwan is not fit to climb
away up here. He'd not manage to climb this brae even
in good weather. And Jim Kineil'll not make it up here
with his horse and cart either. We'll have to make him
safe on the stretcher and carry him down.' Even as he
spoke the men were fashioning a more sturdy pallet
with planks from the loft. As soon as it was finished they
lashed Coll to it and left, carrying him as tenderly as a
new-born child. Annie stood in the doorway, watching,
her face the colour of churned snow.

'Go after them, Annie. He'll need you with him.' Rab,
recovering his strength but not yet able to face the extra
two miles to the village, was behind her. 'Away you go.
I'll stay with the weans until you're able to come back.'

TWO

Annie paused and wiped sweat from her brow. 'One more good heave and that should do it,' she gasped to Morag. 'One, two . . .' With an enormous effort they managed to throw the largest mattress aboard Jim Kineil's cart. The table, chairs, tin bath and the heavy kitchen dresser were still waiting to be loaded.

'Could you not give us a lift with these?' Annie turned in exasperation to Jim Kineil who was amusing himself by watching their struggles from a rock at the side of the burn.

'Aye, well, I could,' he said, scratching his head and sauntering over. 'But it'll cost you another bob.'

'A shilling! I'm paying more than enough for the hire of your cart, Mr Kineil. A decent man wouldn't stand and watch women struggle,' she retorted, knowing full well that he was taking advantage of her.

'If the cart's not to your liking best take your stuff off, hen, and I'll away home.' Who did this woman think she was, talking to him – a man well set up in his own business – like that? And her little better than scum. Her husband nothing more than a shepherd even before his accident.

'I have paid honest money for the hire of this cart, Mr Kineil,' Annie said, facing him, her hands on her full hips. 'Money which I understood included your services.'

25

'And so it does,' he smirked. 'For without me how would the cart have got here in the first place? And how would it get back down the hill?'

Morag knew her mother would never lower herself to have a shouting match with this arrogant man and felt her own temper rising. 'With a beast as poor as that one, Mr Kineil, it's a miracle the cart got here at all. With or without you,' she said, placing herself firmly at her mother's side.

The horse was the sorriest-looking creature she had ever seen. Turned loose to roam the hillside, it chomped the short winter grass greedily. Lumpy ribs showed through a rough, ungroomed coat and its back was ridged with suspicious scars. Its whole appearance was one of miserable defeat.

Kineil snorted his indifference then turned his back on them and walked over to the burn where he lit a cigarette.

It was well after midday before they got the cart loaded.

'Hurry up, lads. Put those pots there, where they'll not fall off.' The last thing Annie wanted was to lose her precious belongings over the edge of the hill as the cart jolted down the path to the village.

The boys stowed the last of the family's possessions then wandered off to sit moodily on the wall of the sheep pen. Morag slumped dejectedly under the rowan tree, her back against its trunk. Through tear-glazed eyes she stared out over the hills, trying to commit every single detail of the view to her memory. Annie walked slowly back into the bare house. Although she had done it ten times already she opened the oven door, checking that the inside was clean. Then she ran a finger over the edge of the grate and felt the peats, piled beside it, making sure they were ready to burn. At least Teg Robertson and his family would find the place ready for them tomorrow. Blinking back tears she went back into the sharp January air and pulled the door closed behind her.

'Right lads,' she called.

They came sullenly, as if it was her fault they were leaving.

'Where's Mr Kineil?' Annie asked.

The boys shrugged.

'Mr Kineil!' she called, thoroughly irritated now. 'Morag. Do you know where he is?'

'I've not seen him since this morning.' Her red-eyed daughter answered. Annie sighed. 'If we don't get away from here soon we'll be working through the night to unload the cart. You laddies get that poor horse over here. I'll find Mr Kineil.'

'No. I'll go,' Morag volunteered, suddenly realising that her mother seemed exhausted.

Kineil wasn't difficult to locate. His loud snores echoed through the clear air as soon as she rounded the side of the house. She found him propped unevenly against the inside wall of the outhouse, sound asleep. Morag snorted her anger then kicked out at his behind with her solidly booted foot, unbalancing him. He opened a bleary eye and glared at her.

She glared right back, her red hair adding to the impression of barely controlled anger. 'My mother's waiting for you, Mister Kineil. If we don't leave soon it will be dark,' she said with cold fury.

'Wee bitch,' he hissed, scrambling to his feet. 'I was just getting myself out of the cold,' he mumbled, following her to the waiting cart.

'Cold?' She rounded on him furiously. 'I am not cold,

27

Mr Kineil. None of us are. But then, we've all been working.'

He muttered away to himself while he got the horse securely between the shafts. As soon as the beast was settled he leapt on to the cart, reins in hand, and perched his backside on Annie's prized kitchen dresser.

'Get off!' Annie ordered, standing in front of the horse so he couldn't move away.

'I have to hold the reins. This is the only place to sit.'

'Get off of my good furniture,' she repeated, anger glinting from steely eyes. Silently Annie's family surrounded her in a display of complete unity. The boys, all big lads, like their father, seemed intimidating, threatening. The red-headed girl was worse, anger radiating from her like a well-stoked boiler. Secure in the strength of her family Annie McDonald met his eyes in a calm challenge. With the speed and agility of a scared rabbit, Kineil hopped over the side of the cart, dropping the reins. Annie was quick to pick them up.

'That poor beast will have enough to do with that weight behind it going down the track and I didn't pay for you to ride with my furniture while I walk.' She flung the reins back at him. 'You can lead your horse, Mr Kineil.'

Annie had known they wouldn't be able to stay in the hillside cottage which was needed for the new shepherd and had feared they would be put out on to the street. It was thanks to Rab Bannerman that they still had a roof over their heads. The Fraser estate had several empty cottages on it, the better of which were used as extra accommodation for guests in the shooting season. Rab had only managed to get them this one because it was in such a run-down condition. Angus Fraser, always eager to make an extra shilling or two, had been willing enough to collect rent on a building which would otherwise have cost him good money to repair.

If Annie had had any tears left to cry she would have wept them when she first saw her new home. Situated on the far side of the village, towards the castle, down a rough forest track which became a quagmire each time it rained, the grey, single-storey house squatted, lonely, dark and dank, in a small clearing. The estate worker who had been the last human to inhabit the place had moved out five years ago and it had been unoccupied ever since. It was so damp that black mould coated every wall. The roof leaked, the wooden floor was rotten and the windows had long ago been broken. The outside privie was overgrown and rank, and the range was solid with neglect. The garden was almost indistinguishable from the woodland which was reclaiming it.

Rab patched the roof, glazed the windows and used the wood from the loft in the shepherd's cottage to repair the floor. The boys cleared the overgrown garden ready for digging and seeding as soon as spring made her appearance. With Rab's help they felled a tree which was pushing its branches through the broken windows. Then it had taken Annie and Morag three weeks of scrubbing, rubbing and white-washing to make the place barely habitable, walking down from the hills each morning and back at nightfall.

Despite all that, Annie was forced to admit that her new home was more convenient than the shepherd's cottage, especially with Coll the way he was. Here there were three rooms, a stone-built shed and a washhouse. Unlike the garden up in the hills the soil here was dark and rich, promising decent vegetables, something they would be grateful for now that Coll could no longer earn a living wage. And, for the first time in her life, Annie had a decent pair of sinks in her scullery and the novelty of pumped water to one of them. She was even beginning to appreciate the range which heated the rooms, dispelling the damp which Coll's health would no longer stand. And there would never be any shortage of wood to fuel it, or the open fire.

Surrounded on three sides by dense woodland, the cottage was situated on a bend in the woodland path. From her front door Annie could see straight down the track, through a tunnel of dark foliage to where it divided, half a mile away. To the right, another half mile on, was the village; to the left the castle. By following the overgrown pathway which went past the back fence it was possible to get to the village in half the time but Annie didn't think she would ever pluck up the courage to tackle the dense undergrowth alone.

The whole place felt oppressive. Even the birds sounded different here, muffled by trees, hidden by ever deepening, ever shifting shadows. But, she told herself sternly, this was home and they would all just have to make the best of it.

Exhausted by the business of flitting, the children were already asleep, the boys revelling in the novelty of a room of their own. The main room which contained the sinks, the range and most of their furniture, was more than big enough for them to live in, even with Coll's bed in the corner. He would be warmer in here. The enforced inactivity had gone to his lungs, making him cough. And in this room he would still be part of the family. Until night fell. Then he would be alone. Sharing his bed was no longer possible. Any movement caused him agony so she and Morag would share a mattress in the tiny front room.

30

Annie's head dropped towards her chest. She jerked up with a start, realising she had fallen asleep where she sat. She was so tired she barely had the strength to rise from her chair. The wind soughing through the trees sounded eerie, unnatural. She shivered and decided to go to bed before she let her imagination get the better of her. She was overtired, that was all. There was no oil for the lamp, no candles, and no money to buy more, so she was forced to grope her way round the unfamiliar room in darkness, disturbing Corry when she blundered into him in the darkness. He whined, sounding as unhappy as she felt.

'Poor boy,' she fondled his ears, knowing he was as disturbed by the change as any of them.

Morag didn't stir when her mother crept into bed beside her nor did she hear the long, sobbing sigh that escaped Annie's lips. Annie clenched her teeth and swallowed the tears of despair, telling herself she still had so much to be grateful for. Four strong children, a home, her health. And her husband – the stranger who now lived in Coll's body.

She was grateful to Rab for taking Coll to his own house while they moved. But tomorrow he would bring his friend to his new home for the first time. Annie dreaded that moment, knew Coll would hate it. And how could they ever survive now that Coll was unable to bring in a wage? How would she manage to live with the bitter, angry man Coll had become?

'Would you like some more tea, Coll?' Annie asked, keeping her voice cheerful.

Silence.

'Coll . . . ?'

Corry, who was stretched across his master's one re-

31

maining foot, lifted his head and looked at Coll with tragic eyes. Getting no response he flopped his head down between his paws, sighed and went back to sleep.

Iain and Billy surged into the room, arguing cheerfully as they came.

'Stop that bloody racket!' Coll thundered, his red face outshining his hair.

The boys exchanged apprehensive looks then subsided into silence.

'Get your porridge then off to school with you,' Annie said gently. At least she didn't have to worry about them on the steep hillside path now. The boys loved the woods and turned their daily walk to school into an ongoing adventure.

As soon as they left, Morag, who now stayed at home to help her mother, made her way to the washhouse to set the copper boiling. While she was out Annie saw to Coll, washing him and shaving him as if he was a child.

'You should try to get up today, Coll,' she said as she towelled him dry.

'What for?' he demanded, jerking away from her.

'Because it is a beautiful day. You could sit outside, in the sunshine. You should see the way the sun comes through the trees.'

'Bloody trees! Why would I want to look at trees?'

'It will do you good.'

'It will get me out of your way. Why don't you just say what you mean?' he asked bitterly.

'NO!' she retorted hotly. 'I thought it would make a change for you.'

'If you want me out of the house, then you'll have to move me. I can't walk.' It was almost triumphant the way he said it.

'You can walk! You just won't try,' she accused him

angrily. 'You have an artificial leg but you won't even try it. You have crutches but you won't use them. You don't have to stay in that bed . . .' Annie caught herself just in time, stopped herself from pouring out the anger, the resentment, the bitterness she felt for this hostile, selfish man.

They both knew there was no reason for him to be confined to bed, knew that with effort and perseverance he could learn to walk again, might even find work of a sort, could be a true husband to her once more. And there was nothing she wanted more. Her chest tightened, filling with the tension and frustration of knowing that any further accusation from her would only provoke Coll into one of the vicious, vindictive diatribes she dreaded. Outpourings of filth and obscenities, words which he had never used before his accident. Terrifying, violent attacks when – before she learnt to get out of his way – he lashed out at her, hitting her, throwing himself out of bed and on to the floor in paroxysms of rage.

Annie wandered out into the early spring sunshine, not able to trust herself to stay silent, anxious to get away from the sight and sound of her crippled husband. She had loved Coll so much, had been content to know that he loved her and had never asked for anything more. And now? Now there were times when she hated him, or what he had become.

Annie understood that it wasn't the injury to his leg, horrific though it was, that was the cause of Coll's problems, but the head wound, an injury which had seemed of secondary importance at the time but which had taken the man she loved and turned him into a monster. No one could offer her any real hope. It was possible that Coll might wake up one morning, fully restored to

33

his old self, to the intelligent, gentle man she had married. A man who had never raised a finger in anger against her or the children. But it was much more probable that he would never recover, that he would gradually get worse.

'Annie?' The deep, soft voice broke through her misery.

She raised her face and did her best to smile. 'Rab.'

Rab saw the lines of tension in her face, the shadowed eyes. 'Take yourself off to the hills for a couple of hours, lass. Or down into the village, have a blether with some of the women. I'll stay with Coll.'

It was tempting. Even though there was no one she could call a friend in the village, the women were unfailingly polite and it would make a pleasant change even to bid good-day to a fresh face. 'I can't, Rab. He gets angry even when I go to the shop. I have to send Morag.'

'You shouldn't let him get away with it. You have a life too,' he said.

'My life is here, Rab, with Coll.' How could she tell him how terrified she was of Coll's jealous rages.

He sighed. 'I know, lass. I know. But I would be more than willing to sit with him.' Even though his old friend steadfastly refused even to look at him. 'Just to give you a wee break.'

She shook her head.

'All right. But if you change your mind . . .'

'Who's there?' Coll's angry voice seemed to jar the walls of the cottage. 'Who are you out there with, woman? Get inside. Get back in here.'

'It's me, Coll,' Rab yelled, following Annie into the dark interior of the house.

'Rab's here to see you, Coll,' Annie told him, striving to sound cheerful.

Coll slumped into the bed and closed his eyes, ignoring them both.

'Sit up, Coll and make an effort. Rab has been a good friend to us. The least you can do is be civil to him,' she hissed.

'It's a braw morning,' Rab greeted him, his eyes compassionate in a face still hidden by a thick, dark beard.

Coll stayed implacably silent. Rab raised an eyebrow and looked at Annie who lifted her shoulder in the minutest of shrugs.

'How about coming outside with me for a smoke, Coll?'

Coll shifted his weight across the bed, further away from his oldest friend.

'It's a braw morning. Makes you feel grand,' Rab went on, starting to pull the covers from his friend's motionless form.

'Leave me alone!' Coll spat suddenly, struggling into an upright position and shoving Rab violently away from him.

'Coll!' Annie rushed to the bedside in an effort to calm him down. 'Rab is trying to help you.'

'Why? Why?' he demanded, reaching up and grabbing a handful of the fine blonde hair he had once admired. Twisting it spitefully he forced her face close to his. 'Why are you two so anxious to get me out of this bed? Is it so you can get in it with him? Do you think I'm blind, or stupid? Do you think I haven't seen what's going on between you two? Do you think I don't know he comes here to see you, not me?' He spat his poison at her, then released her with a gesture of disgust.

She backed away, appalled. 'No!'

'Yes! Rab Bannerman has always been jealous. He's always wanted you. And I've seen the way you look at him.'

There was enough truth in that to make Annie look away in shame. Useless to explain that she had always loved Coll more, had always been faithful, had never, even in the privacy of her own imagination, allowed herself to stray beyond the bounds of friendship with Rab, even if, on occasion, that had been a deliberate and difficult act of self-denial.

'Think what you are saying, Coll,' Rab whispered, his voice cold and hard.

Coll laughed, a deranged, maniacal cackle. 'I know what I'm saying Rab Bannerman. You have slept with my wife. I've heard you, when you think I'm asleep, pumping yourself into her. Doing what I can't do.'

'NO!' Annie screamed it, sickened by the accusations. 'That is not true.'

'Don't lie to me! You were with him just now, outside. I heard you. I can see it on your face. I can smell him on you. Well, he can have you. I don't want you. Go on, go with him.'

Annie felt her stomach contract, felt vomit scorch the back of her throat and rushed to lean over the sink.

Behind her the door opened then closed again.

'That's right, walk away Rab Bannerman. You never did have any guts,' Coll called after him.

Annie straightened then rinsed her face in the cold water before turning to face her husband. 'He was the best friend you ever had,' she said, her voice devoid of all emotion now. 'He saved your life . . .'

'Aye and crippled me while he was doing it! Well he's gone now and good riddance.' He laughed again. 'He wouldn't have you. I gave you to him and he wouldn't have you. So now you're stuck with me.'

THREE

It was two years since Coll's vitriolic outburst. In all that time Rab had never again come near the cottage. If he and Annie met in the village their manner was restrained and embarrassed, their relationship defiled by Coll's venomous words.

Not that Annie often had the opportunity to venture into the village. Coll, who had finally dragged himself out of bed to hop and lurch around the house and garden, watched her every move. He complained if she was more than five minutes in the privie and timed her absences when she did have to leave him. If she was a minute longer than he thought she should be he greeted her return with a tirade of accusation.

Coll's pride refused to accept charity. Very soon after his accident he had insisted that Davy, the oldest of the three boys, should leave school and look for work. Dod Arneil, feeling some sense of responsibility for the man crippled while tending his sheep, had offered Coll's son a job as a farm hand. In truth he and his son, Charlie, were glad to have another strong lad about the place and went so far as to give him a room in the farmhouse. He took his meals with the family and sent his wages back to his mother.

The money young Davy worked sixty hours a week for didn't go far. The painkilling medicine Coll demanded for his almost constant headaches accounted for more than half of it. In desperation Annie turned to taking in laundry which, because of Coll's constant demands, Morag washed and ironed. At first they found customers among the village women who were quite capable of doing their own wash but felt it their Christian duty to help the unfortunate family. In fact few could afford the luxury of sending their wash out and after three or four months only old Mrs McFadden continued to give Morag a weekly bundle. If it wasn't for the laundry from Pitochrie Castle they wouldn't have been able to pay the rent.

Morag loved her twice-weekly walks through the woods to collect and deliver the castle laundry. Set in a clearing in the trees, Pitochrie Castle was, in fact, nothing more than a typically high and narrow tower house – an architectural style peculiar to Scotland. Its grey stone walls rose vertically for twenty-five or thirty feet before sprouting rounded turret rooms at every corner. These small towers, of various sizes, were topped by slated, conical roofs which tapered to a pennant-topped point. From the largest of these flew the flag of Scotland, the cross of St Andrew, which was visible above the trees for miles around. It wasn't a large house but on a misty day it had a fairytale quality and Morag could see why some ambitious ancestor of the present Laird had felt compelled to christen his home a castle.

Glad to get out of the cottage and escape from the tension between her mother and father, Morag never hurried. At the castle there was always someone to chat to. While she waited for the dirty linen to be bundled into the old pram she used to transport the heavy loads, Morag was usually invited into the kitchen and given a cup of tea and a slice of fresh bread, a scone or even, if there had been company the previous day, a fancy cake.

It was a rather unorthodox household. Mrs McManus,

the cook, a rotund, middle-aged woman, was in charge. She was helped by Flo Morrison, a cheerful farmer's daughter from the village who was only a year or two older than Morag. Flo seemed to do all sorts of things round the house from helping in the kitchen to washing the stairs, feeding the chickens and waiting at table. She, in turn, was helped by a tiny, silent girl, known only as wee Chrissy, who seemed to Morag to spend all her time cleaning the grates or peeling potatoes. Finally there was Mysie Burns, whose age Morag could only guess at as somewhere between thirty and forty. Mysie looked after Mrs Fraser, though she too had been known to help out in the kitchen. Then there was the ancient gardener and two young men who did odd jobs about the house, kept the garden in order and looked after Sir Angus's motor car and horses. And, of course, there was Rab Bannerman, the estate manager. But Rab lived in the lodge house and was rarely seen in the domestic quarters of the house.

When she was in an expansive mood, Mrs McManus could be easily tempted to talk longingly of the old Laird's days, in Queen Victoria's reign, when there had been twice as many servants, and even a butler, and each member of staff had had his or her allotted place and set tasks. That grander style of living had all come to an end with the present Laird, Sir Angus. He preferred the clubs and eating houses of London and saw no point in paying for a large staff when his wife, Lady Katrina, was the sole occupant of the house. Apart from hunting parties in the shooting season he limited his visits home to no more than one a month, leaving Lady Katrina to pass most of her time alone.

One day, soon after her fifteenth birthday, Morag took a pile of freshly laundered and ironed sheets, towels and tablecloths back to the house. Cook welcomed her warmly enough but Morag was aware of a strange tension in everyone around her. The kitchen was generally a well-ordered place but today there were unwashed dishes in the sink and teacups still on the huge wooden table. On top of the long range two pans of water simmered away for no apparent reason. Cook, who seemed unusually restless, wandered from stove to sink to window and back again and even seemed to have forgotten to pay Morag. The young girl was wondering whether it would be proper to remind her, uncomfortably aware that her mother would be waiting anxiously for those few extra shillings, when Mysie bustled into the kitchen. She too was looking curiously harassed. Her dark hair, normally restrained neatly under a white cap, straggled damply across a flushed and sweat-beaded face. Her white apron, starched to crackling crispness by Morag, hung limply over a grubby, blue dress and her plain face was creased with either anxiety or bad temper. In her hands she carried an untidy bundle of bed linen.

'Morag!' she greeted the girl with relief. 'I'm glad I've caught you. I wouldn't want this lot hanging round here for very long. I'm sorry they're in such a mess.' With that she dropped the bundle at Morag's feet.

'Well,' demanded Mrs McManus impatiently. 'Is there any word yet?'

Mysie shook her head. 'No. Not yet. Poor soul, it doesn't look good. It's taking too long.'

Mrs McManus nodded her head in sad agreement. 'Aye. Two days it's been now. And Lady Katrina, she's not strong.'

'And it's too soon,' Mysie added, pouring hot water from one of the pans into a bowl, ready to take it up almost a hundred stairs to Lady Katrina's bedroom. 'If only she could have waited another month or so.'

'Aye. It's just the same as last time,' Cook asserted.

'Looks like it. Well, I've got to get back. She needs me,' Mysie said, disappearing into the depths of the house.

Intrigued Morag bent to fold the sheets so that there would be room for them in the pram. Unsuspecting she extricated one from the bundle then gasped, dropped it on to the stone flagged floor and recoiled in horror at what she saw. In the centre of the snowy white linen was a huge, damp blood stain. Feeling suddenly faint she grabbed for something to support her buckling legs.

'Here, lass. Sit yourself down.' Mrs McManus steered her into a chair. 'Mysie should have warned you. But she's all of a dither. And I didn't think either. Och, and you just a young lassie, you wouldn't know what to expect.' She chafed Morag's wrists. The girl's pallor shocked her, her skin alabaster white against the rich red of her hair, her eyes a sudden, brilliant green.

'What is it?' Morag managed to ask when her head had stopped floating. 'Is someone hurt?' All that blood had reminded her of her father's accident.

'No, lass. No one's hurt.' Cook seemed embarrassed. 'Flo,' she called the young maid who was watching it all quite calmly. 'Take the lassie into the fresh air. Try to explain. You know . . . And get they sheets out of my clean kitchen.'

'Yes, Mrs McManus,' Flo said, glad of the excuse to get into the sunshine for a few minutes. 'Come on, Morag. You'll feel better outside.'

She led the younger girl into the cobbled yard. 'How do you feel now?' she asked kindly when they were both settled on a wooden bench overlooking Mrs McManus's fragrant herb garden.

'I'm fine,' Morag smiled, feeling slightly foolish. 'It was just the blood. I didn't expect it.'

41

'It's Mrs Fraser,' Flo explained with the natural ease of a girl raised on a farm where birth was accepted as the natural event it was. 'She's having a bairn. There's always a lot of blood when a bairn's born.'

'A bairn?' Morag murmured, thinking how foolish she had been. In the spring time, up in the hills, as many as ten lambs could be born in one day. She had watched the births many times, and knew there was always blood involved.

'You're not to tell anyone yet, mind,' Flo warned. 'It's too soon. And things don't always go well for Lady Katrina.'

Morag understood. It wasn't unusual for lambs to be born dead so the same was probably true for humans. 'I won't say a word,' she promised then added, 'I'd better go. Mam'll be wondering where I am.' And waiting for the money without which there would be nothing more than dry bread for supper this evening. 'Do you think you could ask Cook for my money? I think she forgot about it.' She hated to ask but knew Mrs McManus would never deliberately avoid paying her.

Flo laughed. 'Everything's upside down the day. The bairn's not due for another couple of months so it took them all by surprise. Wait here and I'll get it for you.'

A couple of minutes later she was back with a handful of coins.

'What's this?' a deep, familiar voice asked. 'Is there nothing to be done in the house?'

Flo leapt to her feet quickly, in awe of the laird's most powerful employee. 'Morag McDonald took faint, Sir. Cook told me to take her outside for a breath of fresh air.'

'Morag?' Rab stared at the pretty young woman who had now flushed an attractive shade of pink. 'Well, I would hardly have recognised you,' he laughed. 'And are you recovered, lass?' Rab seldom saw Coll's children these days and Morag had certainly changed since he had last spoken with her. No longer a child she had matured into a strikingly beautiful young woman, combining the best points of both her parents. Coll's colouring was enhanced by Annie's clear skin, upturned mouth and firm chin. But Morag's most beautiful feature was her eyes which were very direct, wide and green, set off to perfection by long dark lashes. Nor could Rab ignore the fact that her body was shapely, with the lissom grace more sophisticated women never achieved. And she shared her mother's proud bearing too. If it wasn't for her poor clothes she could be mistaken for the lady of the castle. He wondered if Coll and Annie were aware of their daughter's beauty. With looks like this she would need to be protected if she wasn't to fall foul of some unscrupulous man.

Unaware of his thoughts she nodded, 'Yes thanks Uncle Rab.' She laughed at herself for using the childish title then corrected herself awkwardly. 'Mr Bannerman.'

Rab smiled then turned to Flo. 'Is there any news?'

'No, sir. Not yet,' she replied, in her best voice.

'Well, you go on inside, lass, and I'll make sure Miss McDonald is all right,' he said, the faintest accent on the Miss.

As soon as Flo was safely indoors he sank on to the bench beside Morag.

'Are you sure you're better now?' he asked kindly.

'Yes, thanks, Uncle . . . Mr Bannerman,' she said. 'It was just a funny feeling in my head. I thought I was going to faint, but I didn't.'

'Ah . . .' Rab didn't like to ask anything else in case the cause was some female matter which would embarrass them both. 'I suppose you think you're too old to be calling me Uncle Rab now then,' he teased. Morag, his goddaughter, had always been his favourite of Coll and Annie's children.

'I thought you'd prefer it if I called you Mr Bannerman,' she admitted.

'Why?' he asked, puzzled.

'Well, I don't see you very often. I know you and Dad had a big argument.'

'Yes,' he agreed sadly. 'I feel very badly about it, lass. Your father and I have been friends all our lives. We've been through a lot together. I miss his friendship.' He ran a hand through his beard, a characteristic gesture when he was disturbed. 'But that has nothing to do with you and me. I would like to be your friend still.'

She smiled. 'I'd like that too.'

'If you won't call me Uncle any more, then Rab is what most people call me,' he offered.

Morag considered it for a moment. 'No, I like Uncle Rab.'

Rab felt absurdly touched. For a moment he could say nothing.

'I think Dad doesn't know what he's saying sometimes,' Morag went on, feeling a need to defend her father. 'It's his head. It hurts him so much. The pain makes him angry.'

'Is it still bad, then?'

'Aye. Worse now than it was at first. Maybe, if you came to see him?'

'No, Morag. I can't do that.' The brilliant blue eyes were suddenly shadowed.

'Why not?' she persisted.

'Tell your mother, if she ever needs anything she knows where to come,' he said.

44

'She needs a friend, Uncle Rab,' Morag said with sudden insight. 'Dad never lets her out of his sight. She never sees anyone or goes anywhere. I know she's unhappy.'

'Just tell her what I said. Will you do that for me, lass?' he asked softly.

She stood, ready to go on her way. 'I'll tell her,' she assured him.

'Good.' He stooped and kissed her gently on the side of the face, a chaste, fatherly kiss, full of affection. 'Come and see me sometimes, Morag, and bring those brothers of yours — if your mother says you can,' he added as an afterthought. 'I miss seeing you all.'

'I will,' she promised, wheeling the pram down the driveway.

'Rab said that?' Annie said when Morag repeated Rab's words, well out of her father's hearing. 'Och, he was always a good man,' she sighed. 'It's sad to lose a friend like that.'

'You haven't lost a friend,' Morag insisted.

Annie's mouth was downturned and quivering with sadness. 'Maybe not but we've lost the friendship. Your father . . . well, he said things that can't be overlooked.'

'I don't think Uncle Rab . . .'

'You don't understand, Morag!' Annie was suddenly angry. 'Please, lass, let it go. I'd be happy for you to see Rab, and the boys too. He's a fine man. He'll be good for them. But, whatever you do, don't tell your father. And Morag . . .'

'Yes?'

'Tell Rab thank you. When you see him.'

'Annie!' Coll's angry voice shattered the peace, scaring the birds from their perches. 'Annie! Get in here.'

Both women filed into the dark house. Coll hopped over to them, his face scarlet with fury. 'Where the hell have you been?' he asked his daughter.

'At the castle. For the laundry.'

'You were away for two hours. It doesn't take you that long. What were you doing? Tell me, who do you talk to when you go up there?' he demanded.

'Just Mrs McManus and the other women,' she said, flushing.

'Then why were you so long today?' he screamed at her.

'The laundry wasn't ready. There's extra. I had to wait,' she cried, pulling away from him and fleeing to the washhouse.

'It's him. Bannerman! I know you're seeing him. He's always been jealous. Always wanted you,' he bawled after her, no longer able to distinguish between his wife and his daughter.

Annie uncorked the medicine bottle knowing he would finally collapse with a blinding headache and beg for the pain to be eased. Those were the best times. Two spoonfuls of that stuff and he slept for hours.

Luckily the bloodstains, being fresh, washed out fairly easily. Morag finished the wash and pegged everything on the long lines strung between the trees, thankful it was a good day for drying.

By late afternoon the smaller things were dry enough to iron and she took them inside where her mother was waiting to help. Her father, as expected, had succumbed to a violent headache and was fast asleep. The women worked in silent companionship, grateful for the brief respite, the time to think private thoughts.

Unusually there was a fancy blouse, the sort of thing

46

Mysie normally took care of herself, in among the washing. It was a beautiful, delicate thing of lace, frills and tucks. After her mother had admired it, Morag ironed it, enjoying the intricate task. But then she discovered a tear on the sleeve. Without thinking twice she fetched a needle and thread and settled to repair the damage. When it was done she ironed it again then folded it carefully with the rest of the laundry.

'Well done, lass. You've made a good job of these,' Mrs McManus praised her after inspecting the linen for lingering stains. 'Och, what's this doing here?' she asked, holding the repaired blouse aloft.

Morag blanched. 'It was already torn when I washed it, honestly. But I stitched the tear anyway. I think it hardly shows.' For the first time it occurred to her that she might have done the wrong thing. 'I'm sorry if I was wrong. It's just that I do lots of sewing at home.'

Mrs McManus examined the stitching closely then passed the garment across to Mysie.

'Well!' Mysie exclaimed. 'I couldn't fault these stitches if I tried. You've a delicate hand, lass. Lady Fraser will be pleased. She was going to throw this blouse out. It must have got mixed up with the laundry by mistake.'

'Throw it out?' Morag was horrified.

Mysie smiled. 'Lady Katrina couldn't possibly wear something with a tear in it.'

'But you could have repaired it.' The words were out before Morag could stop them.

'I could have tried,' Mysie admitted. 'But I couldn't have done a job like this. Och, I'm fine at making things. I sew a neat enough hem and I've a Singer sewing machine for the seams, but I was never much of a hand at fine sewing. In fact there's nobody in Pitochrie

47

can sew as neat a darn as this. That's why so many things have to go out. They're not able to be repaired decently. It would cost too much to send to Edinburgh to have them mended.'

'Mam sews better than I do. It was her who showed me,' Morag said proudly.

'I wish I'd known,' Mysie smiled.

'If there's anything else to be mended, I'd be pleased to take it to my mother for you,' Morag suggested, knowing she had to take the opportunity to increase their income while it was still there.

'We'll mind that, lass,' Cook said kindly. 'Now, let me find some money.'

'No,' Morag protested quickly. 'I'm not due to be paid until Friday.'

'You've had extra work this week, lass, and you'll be paid fairly for it,' Cook insisted, handing Morag a couple of coins.

'Thank you.' Morag was touched by their kindness. 'Och, I nearly forgot. What did Lady Katrina have? Was it a girl or a boy?'

'Wheesht!' Flo seemed upset and dragged Morag out of the kitchen quickly. 'You shouldn't have said anything,' she admonished. 'The bairn was born dead. Lady Fraser is very upset.'

'Oh no! I'm sorry.'

Flo relented and smiled at her young friend. 'Aye. We all are. It's gey sad. It keeps happening. Poor Lady Fraser, she doesn't seem able to carry past the seventh month. Three bairns she's lost now. Sir Angus will be right upset too.'

Morag walked back to the cottage feeling as if the warmth had gone from the day.

Lady Katrina Fraser was exhausted. The labour, like all

the others, had been long, too long for someone of even her robust constitution. It had been a full twenty-four hours since her body had given up its tragic burden but she still felt as if she had been pulled apart then cobbled together again. Now all she wanted to do was sleep; to close her eyes on the world for ever so that she could forget the awful vacuum, the chilling silence that followed every birth. Silence at a time when the air should have been full of a child's first, halting cries. The sight of that tiny, shrivelled body would haunt her for ever.

There was a firm knock on her door. She stirred, opened her eyes reluctantly and called, 'Enter,' in a toneless voice.

'Sir Angus is coming up to see you, my lady,' Mysie said, attacking the dishevelled bed purposefully. 'Pull yourself up a little and I'll see what I can do with your hair.'

The change in Katrina was immediate. Summoned from London by the news of this latest miscarriage, Gus would not be in the best of tempers and simply couldn't be allowed to see her in this unkempt condition. 'Help me out of bed,' she ordered. 'I want to sit at the mirror. Then ask my husband to wait fifteen minutes.'

'Yes, Mam.' Mysie rushed to do her bidding.

Katrina lowered herself gingerly on to the ornate chair, facing her dressing-table mirror. The discomfort was minimal, less than she had expected. Already there was a spot of colour returning to her pale cheeks. Luckily Mysie had helped her to wash, no more than an hour ago, so she felt reasonably fresh and knew the soapy fragrance of lillies still hung about her. But she was aware of the bloody pad between her legs, conscious of the faint musty smell. The smell of failure.

Katrina settled herself at her mirror and, while Mysie

started to patiently untangle the fluffy, golden hair, applied rouge, powder and a lick of mascara, but with such a light touch that the effect was absolutely natural. Gus had married her for her beauty. It wouldn't do to let him think it was fading.

Mysie moved away to straighten the bed. Katrina put the finishing touches to her appearance and examined herself critically in the mirror, trying to see herself as Gus would. Her eyes, deep grey and widely spaced, looked dull today, drained of energy and there were bluish shadows under them which the powder couldn't quite hide. On the plus side her cheekbones seemed higher, more defined, and her skin had a translucent quality. Considering what she had gone through Katrina didn't think she looked too bad at all and perhaps the misleading fragile appearance would stir Gus to sympathy.

'Thank you, Mysie,' she smiled as the older woman settled her back in bed and arranged the pillows attractively behind her head.

'Stop fussing, woman, and get out. I want to speak to my wife in private.' Sir Angus Fraser spoke from the doorway, making both women jump. His rich voice already held the edge of impatience which invariably marred it when he addressed his wife.

'Yes, sir.' Mysie hurriedly left the room.

'Katrina. I hope you are recovering.' Angus dropped a perfunctory kiss on his wife's forehead then looked down at her without any particular pleasure.

Among his cronies Angus was considered to be an amiable, good-tempered fellow. When he descended on Pitochrie Castle in late summer, bringing with him a band of pleasure-seeking friends, all intent on massacring the local wildlife, he was a perfect, genial host. Few people realised that he successfully disguised a rather pedestrian intelligence, a distinct lack of humour and utter selfishness behind polished manners, admirable social skills and a ruthless ability to lie and cheat in almost any situation. Dark hair and eyes gave a rather misleading impression of intensity, a pencil-thin moustache added style while a slim frame gave an illusion of added height. A finicky insistence on the perfection of his wardrobe only added to the superficial charms of a man who could win a certain type of woman's heart with one flashing, white-toothed smile.

He had worked this charm on Katrina once. But these days he seemed to reserve a special kind of disdain for her. When he came to Strathannan it was with a reluctant regularity calculated to dispel any possible rumours about the state of his marriage; that and the need to impregnate his wife. They both knew he resented the time he was forced to spend here. And that resentment, underlined by carefully controlled anger, was all too apparent in his face now.

Katrina's heart sank. If only she could make him love her again. He had loved her once, of that she was quite certain. Loved her enough to choose her from the hundreds of young women who were flocking to share his name and fortune – what was left of it. She had set her mind on him from their very first meeting.

Their first year of marriage had been heaven, an empyreal time which had come to a sudden end with the traumatic loss of their first child. This was her third attempt to bear Gus the heir he needed. Without a son to inherit, the estate would eventually pass to the cousin he despised. After that first failure, which he had cruelly blamed on her love of dancing and socialising, Gus had made it perfectly clear that, until she delivered a healthy son, she would remain in Strathannan.

According to the doctor she should not risk another pregnancy but to admit that to Gus would be to end their marriage. She had fought long and hard to win Angus Fraser and nothing would make her give him up. She would bear him the son he craved. Then, duty done, and a suitable nanny engaged, she would be free to travel with her husband, to go to Edinburgh, to London, even to Paris and Rome and enjoy the life she had married him for. Under her submissive breast Lady Katrina Fraser had a heart of steel.

'I asked you when you expect to be out of bed, Katrina. Please do me the honour of paying attention when I speak to you.'

Katrina jumped. 'I am sorry, Gus.'

'Yes,' he agreed with heavy emphasis, his meaning unmistakable. 'I expect you are. What has the doctor said to you? Has he been able to explain why this should be happening?'

'He feels I am just unlucky,' she lied.

'Or careless.'

'Gus!' How could he be so unfeeling? 'Do you think I have not taken every possible precaution? I have confined myself to this house from the day I knew I was pregnant again. For the last three months I have barely left this room. I have avoided all exertion. I have eaten well and slept for ten hours every night. I have done everything to bear you a healthy child, Gus. Everything.' Tears overwhelmed her eyes. She turned her face away, knowing all too well how loss of self-control irritated him.

Angus Fraser allowed the silence to run while his wife composed herself, determined to say what he had come here to say, even if it did upset her.

'I am sorry, Gus. I am still very upset. I had hoped that, this time, I would be successful '

'But you weren't, were you?' It was so coldly said that Katrina shivered with apprehension.

'No.' How she longed for him to take her in his arms, to comfort and console her, to tell her there would be other opportunities. Instead he towered over her, radiating disapproval.

'I am disappointed in you, Katrina. Had I known, when we married . . .'

'Please,' she begged. 'It will be all right. I will have a child.'

'I need a son, Katrina,' he said passionately. 'I must have a son.' For a moment there was real pain, genuine emotion on his face. But it vanished as quickly as it had come, replaced by the hard, calculating expression she had seen there far too frequently. 'I have done my best for you, Katrina. You live in luxury in this house while I am obliged to secure our financial future in London. You are waited on, cosseted, given the best medical attention and denied nothing, and yet . . .'

'And I have done my best for you, Gus,' she interrupted him.

'Then your best is not good enough.'

'It is not my fault! I want a child as much as you do!' she protested.

'I think the time has come when we have to face facts, Katrina,' he went on ruthlessly. 'You are apparently unable to bear a healthy child. I have never made any secret of the fact that I need a son. The two things are incompatible, my dear.'

'What are you trying to say?' she asked, white faced.

'I am suggesting that we part. These things can be arranged. Naturally I will ensure that you suffer the minimum embarrassment.'

'You mean to divorce me?' she asked, appalled.

'Perhaps an annulment.'

'NO! No, Gus. Please,' she begged.

'We had an agreement, Katrina.'

It was true. But why should she, a twenty-one-year-old bride, have ever doubted her ability to bear a child? Gus, who had lost his first wife when she miscarried for the third time, had said he wanted a son, first, before anything else and she had promised. 'Gus, please.' The room was spinning.

'Here, drink this.'

Katrina felt the touch of cool water on her lips and opened her eyes to find herself cradled in Gus's arms. 'Thank you,' she whispered.

'I am sorry. I spoke too soon. You have had a difficult time. We'll talk about this later,' he said, setting her gently back among her pillows.

'No, Gus. We'll talk about it now. I can't stand to have this threat hanging over me.' By a miracle of self-control she contrived to keep her voice steady.

'I have been as honest as I can, Katrina. I don't believe there is anything else to discuss.' But he was looking at her with regret in his dark eyes now.

She seized her opportunity and took his hand. 'Gus, do you feel anything at all for me?' she asked boldly.

'You know I do.' He was surprised to realise it was true. She was a beautiful woman and beautiful women always attracted him. She more than most.

'Then give me one more chance,' she begged. He pulled his hand from hers and got up, putting his back to her. A terrible thought occurred to her. 'Is there someone else, Gus?'

'No,' he answered quickly. No one special, no one that she need concern herself about.

'Then let me try one more time. Please. I did so much

better this time. Three weeks longer than ever before. Another week or two and the child would have lived. Please, Gus. One more time.'

He turned and faced her again, knowing that a divorce would be a very messy solution, would be likely to do his burgeoning political career considerable harm. And he was hardly likely to find another woman who combined good breeding, physical allure and compliance as successfully as Katrina did. He sighed. 'Once more,' he agreed. 'We will try once more.'

The bed began to spin again. She closed her eyes and steadied herself before daring to answer. 'Thank you,' she breathed.

FOUR

Annie slipped out of bed. As quietly as she could she pumped water into the sink and washed herself thoroughly, praying that she would not find herself pregnant as a result of the night's activities. Coping with her husband strained her to her limits, a new baby would be more than she could face.

It was only in the last six months that Coll had begun to want sex again. It would be wrong to dignify what they did by saying they made love. They didn't. Coll merely used her body for his own needs. In her most bitter moments, Annie doubted he would have known the difference if she had substituted a sheep in their bed. There was no tenderness, no respect for her feelings or her needs, just an urgent, selfish, compulsion towards physical release. He didn't even care that she might become pregnant but pinned her down until he had emptied himself inside her, a thing he had always been so careful to avoid before his accident. Perhaps he simply no longer appreciated the risks. Annie, who had ached with desire, had yearned to have her strong, virile husband back, was disgusted by the whole business. There were times when she despised herself for allowing him to use her like this, but she knew that, if thwarted, Coll was quite capable of violence. In any case, he was still her husband and this was his right, as he liked to remind her.

On nights like this Coll's demands could be voracious.

It wasn't unusual for him to wake her a second or even a third time before finally falling into sated sleep, leaving her angry and tearful. Often she slipped into bed beside Morag in an attempt to avoid him. Tonight she hesitated, knowing that however careful she was, she disturbed the girl who worked hard and needed her rest. Undecided, Annie stood for a moment, screwing her eyes against the throbbing pain in her head. The fury and resentment she always felt when Coll used her this way invariably resulted in this painful band of pressure round her skull. From the cupboard by the sink she retrieved Coll's medicine bottle. Occasionally in the past she had taken a small dose and had found it to help. Tonight she measured herself a generous spoonful, knowing it would both kill the pain and allow her to sleep. She had done her duty for Coll once tonight, that was enough. She would sleep with Morag for the rest of the night.

Feigning sleep Coll watched his wife move round the shadowy room. She was a beautiful woman still, despite the odd strand of grey in her hair and the faint lines which had started to appear round her mouth. He smiled to himself grimly. If Annie's looks faded perhaps Rab Bannerman would lose interest. He turned his head slightly, so he could get a better view. The moonlight falling through the window lit Annie's naked skin as she splashed cold water on her full breasts, breasts he had sucked and kissed not ten minutes ago. He felt warmth building in him again.

Unaware of his covert enjoyment of her body, Annie pulled her nightdress on then stood at the sink, her back to him for a minute before slipping out of the room. Coll grunted his frustration. Annie had slipped off to the other room once too often. He would go and get her, make her come back. But he was tired. Even as he thought about it his eyes closed and he drifted into sleep.

His dream was an uncomfortable one. He woke only fifteen minutes later with heat burning through his body and knew he would get no more rest until he had satisfied the burning urgency in his crotch. He turned, expecting to roll against Annie's soft skin but found only cold sheets. Where was she? His mind was still fuddled, hazy. Bannerman! If Annie wasn't here she was with Bannerman, that was why she went to the castle so often. Or was that Morag . . . ? But then he remembered. Annie was in Morag's room. He had seen her go there himself. Well, he would teach her to keep herself from him. Grunting with the effort Coll hauled himself out of bed. Not bothering to cover his manhood, which was in a state of rigid arousal, he hopped across the room to his daughter's bedroom door.

The small room was dark, the bed just shadowy lumps. But Annie was there, sleeping like a child on her stomach, one shapely leg outside the blankets. Coll's groin was burning, ready to explode. In one quick movement he hauled the cover down. Then he stood, admiring her firm flesh as she stirred restlessly, the heat in his groin increasing until he could stand it no longer. Panting, he leant over her, ready to enter her from behind. 'Wake up, Annie,' he whispered hoarsely.

On the far side of the bed Annie stirred. The medicine was taking effect and she felt heavy headed and sluggish, on the very edge of sleep. With an effort she turned her head and tried to focus her eyes. What she saw shocked her to her core. Coll was poised over their daughter, his intention plain, steadying himself with one hand while the other moved to open Morag's legs. If it hadn't been for the fact that he was having trouble balancing on his one leg, she would have been too late.

'NO COLL!' she screamed, launching herself at him. She was aware of his baffled expression as her weight cannoned into him, taking him to the ground beneath her.

'Mam?' Morag was awake now. Slowly she turned over and sat up, dragging the sheet over her. 'What's going on?' she asked, blearily, staring at her parents who were tangled on the floor.

'Nothing,' Annie snapped. Aware of Coll's nudity, she clawed at the topmost blanket and threw it round him while he was still on the ground, only getting to her feet when she was sure he was decent. Coll himself stared from his wife to his daughter then hugged the blanket round him, shivering.

'Mam,' Morag was out of bed herself now. 'What happened?'

Annie was already helping Coll out of the room. 'Your father has a sore head again. That's all,' she lied. 'He came looking for me to give him some medicine. He lost his balance and fell . . . Get back to bed, Morag. I'll see to him.'

Morag crawled back into bed and was asleep again within minutes. Her father disturbing the whole household was nothing new.

Coll allowed himself to be led back to bed like a child. He said not a word but he was strangely subdued.

'I think you were sleepwalking, Coll,' Annie said, deeply shocked but too horrified to put it into words.

'I was looking for you,' he whispered as she lifted his leg and eased him under the covers. For a moment he looked into her eyes and she saw a shadow of the man she had married. 'Sweet Jesus,' he whispered in anguish.

'Help me.' In an increasingly rare moment of total clarity he had complete recollection of the past few minutes. Coll McDonald covered his face with his hands and wept.

'I'm right here beside you, Coll,' Annie answered, slipping in beside him. And that, she vowed, was where she would stay. Coll could never be trusted again.

Annie hurried down the muddy track. Water dripped off the trees, soaking through her shawl and right down to her underclothing. She glanced up. The hills, usually visible above the tree tops, were obscured by thick, grey mist. The trees themselves were dark and drooping under the weight of rain pouring through them. And it was so cold. She shivered, knowing that the summer was truly past now and this grim September morning was a warning that winter was on its way. The woodland was particularly depressing on days like this. The sound of raindrops seemed exaggeratedly loud. The sense of isolation, the uneasy feeling she had never been able to overcome, of something evil hidden in the trees, pressed in on her. How much better to have been on the open hillsides, even in a swirling mist. Given a choice she wouldn't have ventured out at all on a day such as this, but Annie's mission was urgent.

The junction in the track was nothing more than a vast, muddy puddle. Annie skirted it by forcing her way through the undergrowth which soaked her feet and deposited gallons of extra water over her shoulders. Shivering she took the path towards the castle, following the route Morag had taken with the laundry, less than fifteen minutes earlier.

Soaked, chilled to the bone, she stood outside the lodge and dripped a puddle on to Rab's doorstep, suddenly nervous about seeing him after so long. But there was no one else she could possibly turn to.

Rab answered her knock with a bad-tempered order to 'hold your horses'. It was another two or three minutes before he opened the door to her. The surprise on his face was comical. Buried in his luxuriant beard his mouth gaped and his vivid blue eyes opened wide in shock. 'Annie!'

'Well, Rab Bannerman. Am I to stand here in the pouring rain or will I get to warm myself at your fire?' she demanded.

'Come in, lass. Come in.' He stood back and ushered her inside.

Annie had never before been in Rab's home. A man who had never married, she had expected it to be masculine, without the comforts of a family home. Looking round now she saw she was mistaken. This room was warm and inviting. Rugs added colour to the polished floor, thick curtains kept draughts at bay and the chairs, spaced round a wooden table, looked solid and well cared for.

'I'm sorry to bother you, Rab.'

'You're not bothering me, Annie. Come on, the range is warm. I'll open the door and let more heat out. You look frozen.' He put his arm round her, ignoring the dampness and drew her into the room. 'Here. Take your coat off.'

'I'll not be staying, Rab. I just need to talk.'

'You'll at least let the warm air get to you while you tell me what's on your mind,' he insisted, taking her shawl and coat from her. 'But you're soaked to the skin! You cannot sit in those things. You'll get a fever.'

'I'll get another soaking on the way home so I might as well stay as I am.'

61

'Why on earth did you not ask Morag to give me a message? Isn't it her day for the castle laundry? I would have come to see you rather than have you walk all down here.'

'I know you would, Rab. But Coll wouldn't like it.' She smiled at him now, touched by his concern. 'And it's Morag I want to talk to you about.'

'Then sit yourself down near the heat. I'll mask us some tea, while you tell me what's on your mind.'

Now that she was here she found it difficult to say what needed to be said. 'I don't know if you can do anything, Rab. I'm just wasting your time.'

'Well, lass, you'll not know until you try me,' he laughed. When she said nothing more he added, 'Morag's a sensible young lassie. You must be gey proud of her. The boys too. I am grateful to you for letting them come here.' The hours the boys spent with him, learning skills more usually passed on by a father, were relished by them all.

'Aye. I am. Any mother would be proud of them. And it does the boys good to learn from you, Rab. With Coll the way he is there are many things they would not know about if it wasn't for you.'

'Aye,' he agreed wryly. 'Like snaring a rabbit.' He laughed at the irony of it then said more seriously, 'You wanted to talk about Morag?'

She nodded sadly. 'Och, Rab, I need your help. I want to find Morag a place. Maybe on one of the farms, or in one of the houses. So long as it's a decent place, with good people. You know more folk than I do. If you hear of anything suitable? She's a good lassie. She can bake and wash and sew. She's not afraid of hard work.'

'You want her to go into service?' Rab asked, in astonishment. 'But why? She'll not bring in as much

62

money as a maid in some house as she does now with her laundry.'

'I will do the laundry,' she said in a voice that made it plain her mind was already set. 'It's not right that a young lassie should be doing it.'

Rab brought tea and sat beside her, watching her closely. 'You've not answered my question, Annie. Why are you sending her away?'

Annie couldn't meet his eyes when she spoke. 'It's o'er lonely where we are. It's not good for a young lassie to be on her own. She needs to meet folk of her own age.'

He considered this for a moment then leant forward and grasped her chilled hands. 'I take it the lassie doesn't know what you're planning?'

She shook her head.

'Will she want to leave? She's very fond of you, you must know that.' When Morag came to see him, which she did about once a month, she always spoke of her mother with great affection.

Annie nodded again. 'I know that fine. Don't think that this is an easy thing for me to do, Rab.'

'Then tell me why you're doing it, Annie. What has Coll done to drive you to this?'

She looked up at him then, her eyes bright with unshed tears. 'I cannot speak about it, Rab.'

Then he was on his knees in front of her. 'Has he hurt her? Has he?' His heart was beating furiously at the thought that Coll might harm the girl he had grown so very fond of.

'No! No, not yet.' Her face flushed to think about it. Never, not even with her own husband in the days when they had enjoyed a pure and unsullied sexual relationship, had she been able to talk about the things which had given them both so much pleasure. To describe what

63

had happened in the dark hours of last night was an agony of humiliation. For Morag's sake she knew she had to make Rab understand.

'Not yet? What do you mean, Annie? Tell me what's happened.' That something traumatic had occurred was perfectly obvious. Only desperation could bring Annie here.

She took a huge breath, steadying herself for what had to be said. 'It's Coll. He's . . . he's confused. I don't think he realised it was Morag. He thought it was me.' Rab knew she had to be allowed to say this in her own time but already he had a grim foreboding of what was to come. 'Rab, Coll got out of his bed and came looking for me, in the night. He came into Morag's room because I sometimes go there to sleep after . . .' she swallowed.

'Go on,' he said gently, never letting go of her hands.

'She was asleep. I didn't hear him at first. He was standing over her.' She put her hands over her face. Rab stroked her hair softly. 'He was . . . He was ready. Oh God. If I hadn't woken up he would have used his own daughter. She wouldn't have been able to stop him. When he's . . . When he's excited he's . . . He's like an animal.'

Gently Rab pulled her into his arms. 'The bastard,' he whispered, anger clenching his fists, tightening his jaw.

'No!' Annie pulled away and looked him in the eye, pleading for him to understand. 'It wasn't like that! Coll would never knowingly harm her, or any of us. He didn't know what he was doing. He thought she was me. He gets so confused. That is why I have to let Morag go. It is not safe for her. In her own home, with her own father she is not safe.'

'And you? Would he have used you the same way? Forced himself on you?' he asked, anguish in his voice.

She looked away from those piercing eyes. 'That is different. Coll McDonald is still my husband. It is my duty,' she mumbled.

'Annie. Annie,' he muttered, gathering her close again. He had loved her deeply back in the days when he and Coll had each wanted her for his wife. When she had chosen to marry Coll he had accepted that he had lost her. Time had eased the pain until he could think of her and Coll as a pair without jealousy or resentment, though he had never ceased to love her. But now?

Here, in the strength of Rab's arms, the strain of the last three years was suddenly too much. Annie, who had watched the man she truly loved change into a bitter, unbalanced tyrant, riven by jealousy, broke down and sobbed for everything she had lost. When it was over she huddled against Rab and shivered, believing she would never be warm again.

'You cannot keep these clothes on,' he said, drawing her closer to the fire. 'You will be ill.'

'I must go home.'

'Is Coll waiting for you? Does he know you're here?' Rab asked, rummaging in a cupboard.

'No,' she admitted through chattering teeth. 'He was very upset last night – after he realised what had happened. This morning he said his head hurt. I gave him some of his medicine. More than usual. He is asleep.'

Rab turned round, horrified. 'He knew what he had done?'

'Only later. Not at the time. He cried, Rab. I have never seen Coll cry before.'

Rab couldn't trust himself to speak but busied himself finding something she could wear. 'Here,' he said eventually. 'This shirt will do, and these trousers. I've

65

turned them up at the bottom. They will do until you get home.'

Still she shivered in front of his fire, making no attempt to take her wet things off.

'Please, Annie. You will make yourself ill,' he begged, gently pulling her to her feet and undoing just the top button of her long dress. For such a big man he was very gentle.

'You are very kind,' she whispered.

'I am your friend, Annie. I always have been,' he answered.

Annie had always seemed a strong, fiercely independent woman, one who was well able to look after herself and her family. Seeing her now, broken and lost, he wanted nothing more than to draw her into his arms, to protect her from the hardships of life, to find some way to give her the happiness she deserved. And then she smiled up into his eyes. Rab bent his head and did what seemed natural and right, brushing her lips very, very gently with his.

Annie felt a fluttering in her stomach, a tightening of the muscles in her abdomen. When he lowered his face again she lifted hers to meet him, instinctively holding her pelvis against his, feeling him harden and grow.

Their kiss was long and deep. For Rab years of unfulfilled longing found release while Annie rediscovered the tenderness she had lost on the day of Coll's accident. Both vulnerable they clung together, heedless of what they were doing.

Annie, driven by a need too deep to deny, pressed herself to the pulsing heat of his body. Rab found the buttons on her dress and undid them, pulling the dress away from her shoulders. With her own hands she loosened her bodice and pushed the dress to the floor.

Together they eased off her underwear then stripped off Rab's shirt and trousers. When they were both naked he carried her to his bed.

Not since the early days of her marriage had it been like this. Never had her response been so intense. Somewhere in her consciousness she was shocked, not by her behaviour but by the urgency of her body. It was she who held Rab close, w. .pping her legs around him, pulling him deeply into her, clawing her nails into his back. It was she who guided him to satisfy her until, crying out, arching in an ecstasy she had never achieved before, her muscles gripped him, holding him as he gasped and trembled, releasing his seed deep inside her.

Exhausted, stunned, they lay unmoving and silent. It was Rab who moved first, rolling off the bed and pulling his clothes on hurriedly. Silently he gathered the clothes he had found for her and offered them to her, only then realising that she was sobbing silently.

'Annie,' he sat beside her, stroking her hair. 'Annie, don't cry. Please don't cry.'

Rubbing at her eyes she accepted the bundle of clothes and, holding them against her, to cover herself, she sat up. 'I'm sorry,' she whispered. Unable to look at him she slid off the bed and dressed quickly, keeping her back to him. 'I must go,' she rasped as soon as she was decent.

'I will do what I can for Morag,' he said softly, not knowing how to bridge the gulf that had opened before them in their moment of deepest intimacy.

'Thank you.' It was almost formal. Then she walked out of his house and back into the rain. They both knew she would never come back.

Morag brushed her long, auburn hair and stared at her

own reflection, seeing nothing, her eyes shadowed and dull. The events of the last few days had left her feeling confused, elated, rejected, excited and sad, in roughly the same proportion. Now the time had come to take her bag and walk the two miles to Pitochrie Castle, she would have sold her soul to stay at home.

'Are you ready, lass?' Annie called.

'Aye.' Morag slipped her brush into her canvas bag and carried it through to the main room where her mother was waiting.

'Do I really have to go?' she asked, sounding much younger than her nearly seventeen years.

Annie smiled, determined not to let her own emotions show. 'Aye. You do have to go. Och, Morag, I know you'll be happy there, else I wouldn't let you go. You'll meet people, see things. It's a different world, a big house like that. And you already know most of them. It's not like you're going to strangers. And you know the extra bit of money will help.'

'I suppose so,' Morag admitted reluctantly. 'But I still don't see why I couldn't have lived here and gone there to work every day.'

Annie pointed through the window to the thin covering of snow. 'That's why. It's only just November and already there's snow on the ground. It's maybe only two miles but it's a long walk in the winter. Anyway, that's the way things are done in big houses. The staff live in.'

'I'll be home on my half day,' Morag promised.

'Aye, lass, you do that. It'll give me something to look forward to.' Only she knew just how much she would miss Morag, especially now that the twins had both left home and gone off to Glasgow to seek work in the shipyards there. Davy, still working at Arneil's farm but with a cottage of his own now and a mind to marry a local girl, could no longer afford to make a contribution to his parents' household. Annie was happy for him, pleased to see him settling down. With Morag's wages and the bit she would make from the laundry, she and Coll would just about manage. As long as the rent was paid and Coll had his medicine they wouldn't need much to keep them. Annie shook herself out of her reverie to watch Morag bid her father farewell.

'I'll come home as soon as I can, Dad,' she promised, leaning forward to kiss his head.

'Aye. Make sure you do, and mind what you're doing up there. Keep away from Rab Bannerman,' he warned.

'Dad, Uncle Rab got me the job. He's the estate manager. If I see him I'll have to talk to him. Anyway,' she added defiantly, tired of his constant accusations against a man who had shown her nothing but kindness, 'he is my godfather and I like him.'

'Morag . . . ,' Annie warned, coming to stand beside her daughter.

'Is that why you're so keen to go up to the castle? So you can see Bannerman? So you can sneak down to his cottage after dark?' He struggled to stand, supporting himself on his crutches. 'Don't think I don't know about him and you,' he spluttered, looking straight at his wife now.

'I'd better be on my way,' Morag said, turning away with tears brimming in her eyes. She loved her father, knew he wasn't responsible for the hurtful things he said, but how she wished they could have parted with more affection, that she could have taken a more pleasant memory to the castle with her.

'Off you go now. They'll be expecting you.' Annie kissed her daughter, felt the desperate strength of Morag's hug then gently detached herself and stood at her front door, waving until she could see her no more. When she went back inside the house, tears were pouring down her face. Already the place felt colder, emptier.

'You shouldn't have let her go,' Coll said from the chair by the fire.

'It's time,' she said. 'We can't keep her here forever. She's her own life to lead.'

'Aye,' he said in one of the bewildering shifts between lucidity and the world of chaotic unreality he inhabited for longer and longer periods these days. 'Don't think I don't know why you had to send her away. It's for the best. I would kill myself if I harmed her.'

'Oh, Coll.' When he was like this her heart bled for him. But, even in his sane moments he no longer bore any resemblance to the Coll McDonald she had married. Physically he seemed to have shrunk. His once huge frame was nothing more than a ruined skeleton, held together by loose skin. His face was gaunt, with huge hollows under his cheekbones, the once warm eyes lost in deep shadows. Even his red hair was faded, gone wiry and sparse, like leaves on a dying tree. He was never at peace. In the four years since the accident he had seldom been free of pain. The stump of leg ached in the damp, and this house was always damp; the terrible headaches which had started with the accident had grown more frequent, more intense. When he was clear of physical pain he was tormented by mental demons. His only ease came in a bottle of medicine. A day never passed when he didn't spend several hours in a drug-induced sleep. Annie knew she gave him too much of the stuff but without it both their lives would be unbearable.

'My head is hurting me,' he complained now.

70

'It's too soon, Coll. You had some in the night. Try to do without. I'll read you Iain and Billy's letter if you like. They seem to have settled down all right. The woman they have lodgings with sounds a motherly soul.' But how would her boys, born to a life in the countryside, settle down to life in a two-roomed tenement?

'I'm not wanting you to read to me. What's it to me what they're doing? Ungrateful little bastards. They should have stayed here, where they're needed, not gone off to some heathen place like Glasgow.'

'There's no work for them here, Coll.'

'Then why didn't you ask Bannerman to fix them up? He seems to have taken care of everything else for you,' he bellowed. 'You think you've been so clever. But I know what goes on between you. Is he better than me? Is he harder? Is his prick bigger?' he raged, suddenly crimson faced with rage. Four weeks ago she could have ignored it, secure in her own innocence. Now her face burned as she remembered that stolen morning. Coll couldn't possibly know about that, this was nothing more than his usual raving, but the memory still seared her with shame. How could she have taken her pleasure so wantonly, so brazenly?

She jumped when Coll touched her, backed away when he grasped her breast with his hand. She should have known this would happen. These sudden bouts of anger often aroused him but she had been spared in the past by Morag's presence in the house. Now she could not avoid him.

'I'll teach you,' he panted, shoving himself into her, not even bothering to undress her properly first. 'I'll teach you. You're mine. Mine.' Abruptly he shuddered then rolled off her and shoved her on to the floor. Annie heaved herself to her feet and only just got to the sink in time to heave her breakfast into it, retching again and again.

Ten minutes later Coll was clutching his head, his body rigid with pain. Annie gave him two spoonfuls of medicine then lay down on Morag's bed and sobbed herself to sleep.

FIVE

'This is Morag McDonald, Lady Fraser.' Cook nodded at Morag who stepped forward nervously.

Katrina Fraser watched her with interest. 'Welcome to Pitochrie Castle, Morag,' she smiled graciously.

'Thank you, ma'am.'

'What lovely hair,' Katrina commented, raising a finely drawn eyebrow at Mrs McManus. Morag, who had had great difficulty in confining her thick, curling mane under the starched white cap the castle's female staff were expected to wear, flushed with pleasure at what she mistakenly took to be a kind-hearted compliment.

'I'm told you are a fine needlewoman. If that is so you will be truly appreciated here and there will be plenty for you to do. When Mysie leaves me I shall expect you to be able to take over from her. I hope you will find me to be a fair employer, Morag. You and I will get along nicely if you always attend to your duties efficiently.'

'Yes, Lady Fraser, ma'am,' Morag stammered.

Katrina smiled again, nodded at cook and turned back to the book she was reading.

'There, that wasn't too bad, was it?' Cook asked as they hurried down eighty-something stone stairs to the kitchen. 'You can help me today. Tomorrow you can go with Mysie, start to learn the job. And mind you learn it well. Lady Katrina likes things done just so. She'll not

73

accept sloppy work. When she rings for you she expects you to go to her immediately. And she can't abide untidiness about a person so you'd best be sure that hair's always back under your cap. She'll not have you attending her with it straggling loose as it is now.' Cook lifted a loose strand to make her point. 'You'll need to pull it back tighter than this, lass. Remember, if she's not satisfied with you she won't think twice about getting rid of you. Get on her wrong side, or mine, and you'll find yourself taking the laundry back from your mother.'

'Yes, Mrs McManus.'

That night, in the room she was temporarily sharing with Mysie, Morag's head was too full of her new experiences to allow her to sleep easily.

She had been offered this job because Mysie Burns had finally accepted Charlie Arneil's offer of marriage. Charlie had fallen in love with her and proposed two years ago. But, Mysie had asked herself and anyone else who cared to listen, what future could she have with a man who could not walk more than a hundred yards without being overcome by breathlessness? So she turned him down and waited, hoping for the better offer which never came. When he asked her again, just after the harvest festival, she accepted. At the age of forty-two she knew she wasn't going to get another chance. And at least Charlie wouldn't leave her destitute. Anyway, she told Morag, he had survived this long when everyone had thought he'd be six foot under before his thirtieth birthday. The way she felt some days he'd probably outlive her.

Morag smiled. Mysie was the sort of person who revelled in her own and other people's ailments. Anyone who was foolish enough to ask how she was stood every chance of getting a long list of all her imagined maladies with gruesomely detailed descriptions of her bodily functions. Despite that she was a kind-hearted person and Morag hoped that Mysie and Charlie Arneil would be happy.

The wedding was set for the first Saturday in the New Year, more than two months away yet. By that time, Morag would be expected to be capable of looking after Lady Fraser's clothes, to be able to keep the room as her new mistress liked it, to know Lady Fraser's routine and to have grasped the elements of hairdressing. It was a good position, one she would be proud to hold but, that first night, Morag could only remember Cook's hint that failure would result in her being sent home in disgrace. Then what would her mother do? Small though her wages were, Morag knew they were essential to her mother and father.

Beside her Mysie had slipped into a gently snoring sleep. Morag snuggled up to her warm back and closed her eyes. She would have to be up before first light tomorrow and if she was to be alert and ready to learn she had better get some rest.

On the floor below, Angus Fraser sat up in bed and watched his wife brush out her finely curling hair. 'Does the new girl suit you?' he asked.

'Yes. I think so. She has a lot to learn but she seems decent enough.' Katrina was mildly surprised. Angus's interest in his household was absolutely minimal.

'Will you put that bloody brush down and come to bed?' he demanded before she had time to pursue the thought.

She bridled at his imperious manner and narrowly resisted the temptation to crash the brush on to the highly polished surface of her dressing table. Forcing herself to smile she rustled over to the bed and slipped delicately in beside her husband. Desperate as she was to conceive a child, the actual act leading to conception brought her no pleasure at all, but there was no avoiding it.

'Why do you have to come to bed wearing enough clothes to give a dinner party in?' he asked, hauling away at the delicate lacing on the front of her nightgown. 'Or are you hoping I'll lose patience and go to sleep like a good boy?' It was nastily said.

'Of course not,' she lied, struggling out of the garment she had just spent the best part of ten minutes getting into.

'It's been over a year, Katrina,' Angus mused, admiring the perfection of her creamy body. 'I would have thought you'd have started another child by now. I trust you are remembering our agreement.' He smiled deceptively as he said it.

'You know I had to wait a little, to make sure I was fully recovered.' She ran a hand over his smooth chest, hoping to distract him. The fact that she had, as yet, failed to become pregnant again was starting to be a cause of deep concern for her.

'You have always conceived easily before. Perhaps you should see a doctor?' he suggested.

'No!' she panicked. If, as might be the case, this difficulty in conceiving was the result of her repeated miscarriages, then that was something she had to deny for as long as possible. But, in her own mind she was certain that this time the fault was not hers.

'No?' he repeated in his most patronising voice. 'Surely, if you are serious about keeping your side of our bargain, you should be only too keen to get expert advice.'

'Yes, I suppose so,' she prevaricated. 'But really, Gus, I have been poked and prodded quite enough. You are a man. You cannot possibly understand how humiliating these things are for a lady. I am certain everything will be all right. And the doctor did say, after the last time, that it would be better for me to be completely recovered. You know I don't want to let you down again,' she added, ingenuously. 'I think that might have been the problem in the past. I conceived again much too quickly, before I was ready for another pregnancy.'

'Rubbish!' he dismissed the idea contemptuously. 'Women are built for breeding.'

'You are hardly giving me a fair chance,' she retorted. 'Two nights every four or five weeks. Perhaps if you were to come home more often . . .' She got no further.

'Are you insinuating that this is my fault?' he asked, coldly angry.

'Of course not.' She denied it, conscious of her precarious position.

'I'll have you know that my family line goes back hundreds of years. What I put into you on two nights is better than most men give their wives in a lifetime. If you cannot function properly on what I am giving you then the fault is yours, not mine.'

Katrina sensed the arrogance, the absurdity of his words but her own understanding of her bodily functions was too limited to allow her to argue with any conviction. And in any case the last thing she wanted was for him to fling out of bed in a huff and waste yet another night. Deliberately she shoved aside her hurt and anger, and put her mind to the task ahead. After all, her future depended on her success.

Morag soon got into the rhythm of her job. By Mysie's

last week at the castle she could attend to Lady Katrina's needs as efficiently as Mysie had ever done. The only time she had any difficulty was on the two or three days of each month when Sir Angus was home, and for the few days beforehand. Morag wasn't the only one who lived in dread of his monthly visits. In the week leading up to his arrival the whole household was irritable. Lady Katrina herself became progressively more short-tempered, snapping at Morag, complaining about her meals and pacing restlessly until her husband finally made his appearance. Nor did her good humour return until he left again. Only when the wheels of his departing carriage could no longer be heard on the driveway did the house heave a collective sigh of relief and resume its well-ordered but relaxed air.

Morag had little to do with Angus Fraser, but what she had seen of him she had not liked. There was something about the way he looked at her that made her feel ashamed.

On one occasion when she was called upon to help Flo serve at table for a particularly lively dinner party, she was uncomfortably aware of the way his narrow eyes assessed her and shocked to see Sir Angus's hand resting on Flo's shapely behind every time she served him. She was careful to keep as far away from him as possible.

'I wouldn't let him do that to me!' she asserted later.

Flo laughed, a strange, brittle sound. 'You wouldn't be able to stop him. He's the laird. He can do what he likes.'

Morag stared at her, her mouth agape, wondering if that could possibly mean what she thought it did. 'Not with me he can't,' she said quietly.

Flo flushed and turned away. 'Aye, well, you'd better

just make sure he never gets you on your own then,' she muttered.

The wedding of Charlie Arneil and Mysie Burns was to be the biggest one the village of Pitochrie had known for years. Coming, as it did, hard on the Hogmanay celebrations, it was seen by many of the villagers as an extension of the festive season and they prolonged the holiday spirit to include the extra weekend.

Morag knew of no one who hadn't been invited. She, like the rest of the household, had been given the after-noon and early evening off. As Sir Angus and Lady Katrina were also attending the wedding they wouldn't be inconvenienced by the absence of their servants.

Much to her delight, Annie McDonald had been asked to make Mysie's wedding dress and had spent the last five weeks stitching industriously in every spare moment. Mysie, who had had more years than most brides in which to save for her big day, had not stinted in her choice of dress. She had chosen an ornate design with many tiny tucks, scores of beads and yards of lace trim-ming. To be sure of finishing the garment in time Annie had been forced to ask for her daughter's help. Morag had spent several evenings locked into her room, over-sewing seams and stitching on beads. Now, with only two days to go, she was going to spend her precious half day off help-ing her mother put the finishing touches to the gown.

Fortunately the last of the Christmas house guests had left the previous day, still barely sober after the New Year celebrations. Sir Angus had taken himself off to Edinburgh and would not return until Saturday, so the household was enjoying a brief respite. As soon as she had served Lady Katrina with her lunch Morag would be free to help her mother.

'Has your mother finished Mysie's dress?' Lady Katrina enquired as Morag served her with a fluffy omelette.

'There's just the trimming for the train to be stitched on, ma'am. We had to leave it until after the final fitting, to make sure it stayed clean and didn't get torn. It's very delicate. I'm going to help my mother with it this afternoon.'

'It is your half day off?' Katrina asked, casually. 'Thursday is not normally your free afternoon.' She would be very angry if the girl was taking time which wasn't due to her.

'Oh yes, Lady Katrina! I haven't been home at all over the Christmas and New Year time, what with us being so busy here. This is my first half day for five weeks. Mrs McManus said I was to take this afternoon.'

Katrina smiled thinly. 'I see. Perhaps Cook forgot that you will have most of Saturday free for the wedding.'

'Am I not to go, Lady Fraser?' Morag asked.

'If Cook has told you you may go then I suppose you must.'

'Yes, ma'am. Thank you.' Morag escaped from the room gratefully. Sometimes Lady Katrina's moods were as baffling as her father's.

The path through the woods was still white with frost where the weak winter sun didn't reach. The trees rose above her like ghosts, swathed in rime and, above them, dramatically silhouetted against the grey sky, loomed the hilltops, the snow lending them extra mystique. Morag shivered. She hated the hills in snow. It was weather like this which had caused her father's injuries, had changed him from the loving, even-tempered man who was already blurred in her memory, to the dictatorial tyrant who, at times, seemed barely sane.

Morag found her father dozing in front of a blazing log fire. The air was warm, heavy with the smell of burning pine and, under that, the lingering aroma of freshly baked bread.

As Morag closed the door behind her, shutting out the biting chill, Coll opened his eyes and gazed at her. It was many seconds before the look of disorientation cleared. Morag recognised the heavy, drug-induced stupor at once and wondered, not for the first time, why her mother seemed to encourage his addiction, making no effort to wean him from the narcotic.

'Morag, hen! Happy New Year!' Coll beamed and struggled to get upright. Morag knew better than to rush to his assistance and waited until he had his balance before kissing his cheek and returning the greeting, relieved to see he was as near normal as he ever was these days.

'Happy New Year, Dad. I thought we were going to have a mild winter but there's a good covering of snow on the hills the day,' she said.

'Is there?' he exclaimed, hobbling to the window and peering out. 'Aye. So there is. Still, old Teg will have the sheep off the braes.' Very often his thoughts took him back to those days of freedom on the hillfoots. 'Look, you can just see the rowan and there's our old cottage. Och, what I wouldn't give to be able to get back out on the hills.'

'Well, I'd rather be indoors by a good fire,' Morag declared, holding her hands out to the blazing logs. 'Where's Mam?'

Coll's brow creased. 'I don't rightly know. I've been sleeping.' Something stirred vaguely in the back of his mind then retreated again. 'She should be here!' he growled in one of his disconcerting mood changes. 'Annie! Annie, get in here. Where are you woman?'

Annie hurried into the room, huddled into her shawl.

'Mam! Happy New Year,' Morag rushed to embrace her mother.

'Happy New Year, hen.' Annie kissed her daughter but winced slightly at her enthusiastic embrace. 'I was in the privie,' she explained. 'I'll just put the kettle on. We'll have a wee cup of tea afore we start to work.'

Morag watched as her mother went through the ritual of warming the pot and brewing the tea before handing Coll the first cup. He took it without a word of thanks, appearing suddenly preoccupied and withdrawn.

'Are you all right, Mam?' Morag asked, shocked by her mother's pallor. Annie's skin seemed almost grey, her eyes deeply shadowed and dull.

'Och, it's nothing. Just a wee stomach upset, that's all,' Annie mumbled, avoiding her daughter's steady gaze.

'Aye,' Coll added loudly. 'A wee bit too much of the golden dew over the New Year. Your mother's not used to it, that's all.'

It seemed to Morag that he shot a warning glance at her mother but it was so fast that she couldn't be sure. She sipped her tea in silence then set her cup aside and rose purposefully. 'We'd best set to work if this dress is to be finished tonight. The light'll be fading in a hour or so and I'll need to know what I'm doing before we have to work by lamp light.'

'Wash your hands, lass, and I'll set out the dress.' Annie covered the big table with a clean white cloth then brought the bulky dress, swathed in a sheet, through from the bedroom and laid it out carefully. 'We'll need to be sure and keep it off the floor,' she said, drawing yards of lace edging from a paper bag. 'See. There's just a wee bit to be sewn round the hem then the whole of the veil has to be edged. I'll finish off here and you can start on the veil.'

Morag nodded, threaded her needle and set to work. After swapping accounts of the festivities the two women worked in near silence. By seven o'clock the dress was finished.

'Well, if I say so myself, it's a braw dress. Mysie's a bonny-looking woman. You'd never guess she was over forty and she'll make a bride to put many a younger woman in the shade,' Annie said with satisfaction, raising the top half of the dress off the table for Morag to admire.

'It's beautiful,' Morag agreed. Like Annie she could sew a neat, almost invisible stitch and make simple garments with complete competence, but something as complicated as this was beyond her skill. 'When people see this you'll have them queuing at the door asking you to make things for them. Even the Edinburgh dressmakers couldn't have made a better job of this dress.'

Annie laughed, 'Och, and how many customers would I get in Pitochrie? The women round here don't have the money, or the need, for fancy dresses. Most of them are quite capable of stitching their own skirts without paying someone else to do it for them.' And, she added to herself, she would be last person the local women would come to. After ten years in the village they still thought of her as a newcomer. Pitochrie was an insular little community, everyone seeming to have kinship with everyone else. She and Coll had found it hard to be accepted, especially by the women. Och, they all knew their Christian duty, would offer help if it was really needed, but would then retreat to their own firesides to congratulate themselves on their generosity. Real friendship was something they were loath to offer to an outsider. Living halfway up a mountain, so far from the village itself, hadn't helped Annie's cause and this cottage, tucked away in the woods, was no better. In any case Coll had never given her the chance to make friends.

'Still it wouldn't hurt, if anyone does ask,' Morag insisted. 'And it would be a lot easier than taking in laundry.'

'Anything's easier than taking in laundry, especially in this weather,' Annie said wryly. 'Just look at my hands. I've been rubbing them with goose fat, wrapping them in wool, straight off the sheep's back, and they're still cracked and bleeding.'

'I'll ask Mrs McManus if she knows of anything. I'm sure she rubs something into her hands at night.' Morag helped her mother to repack the dress then said, 'I'd best be getting back. I'll see you at the wedding.' She held Annie's upper arms as she kissed her and couldn't miss the grimace of pain which contorted her face.

'It's nothing,' Annie said quickly, giving her daughter no chance to ask. 'I slipped on the path, on the ice, gave my arm a bang, that's all.'

'Let me see.' Morag reached out to slip the shawl off her mother's shoulders. Annie tried to twist away but wasn't quick enough.

'Good God!' Morag was appalled. Running diagonally across Annie's upper arm, disappearing under the sleeve of her dress and just visible at the neck was a massive, swollen bruise. Right down the centre of it was a raised, white weal. Morag, who had seen similar, though less vicious marks on her brothers' legs, knew exactly what it was, and who had inflicted it.

She looked at her mother, saw the agonised plea in the pale eyes and felt the pressure of her mother's hands. 'Please,' Annie whispered. 'You'll only make things worse.'

Fury brought the blood rushing to Morag's face. She had to resist the urge to fling herself at her father, to attack him with the crutch he had so obviously used against her mother. When she looked at him she saw, with a blood-stopping shock, that he was watching her, had seen it all, that he knew she knew.

'NO. This is nothing to do with you.' It was whispered but desperate. Annie's hands tightened on her daughter's, restraining her.

Morag stopped, closed her eyes, took several deep breaths in the way her mother had taught her to control her fiery temper. 'I'll see you at the wedding,' she repeated, kissing her mother again.

Ignoring her father she walked out of the house and ran nearly all the way back to the castle.

Seated with the other castle staff, towards the back of Pitochrie's small kirk, Morag had a good view of the other guests. She was relieved to see that her mother was looking better today, the natural colour back in her cheeks. It even seemed that she had put on a little weight from the way her good coat, her only coat, was straining at its buttons. She ignored her father, but he seemed to be only half awake anyway. Her mother must have dosed him with medicine. Considering the unpredictability of his moods that was probably a wise thing to do.

Four rows in front of her daughter, Annie was uncomfortably aware of how tight her coat had become. Under her shawl her expanding girth was not so noticeable but she could hardly wear a shawl to a wedding. Luckily the dress she wore underneath had always been roomy. She had not wanted to come to this wedding, to expose herself and Coll to the curiosity of the whole community, but knew that to stay at home on such an occasion would be taken as an unforgivable slight by the entire village. If she stayed seated there was no reason why anyone should guess her condition but God only knew what Coll might be provoked into saying if anyone was tactless enough to comment. She had known for months, since early October, that her luck had run out, that she was pregnant. For weeks she had tried to close her mind to it, hoping against hope that she was mistaken, even – God forgive her – that she might miscarry. But it was not to be. Instead she had struggled against constant sickness, feeling that, at thirty-five, her family already grown-up, she was too old to birth another child. In her heart she knew this sickness was in her soul, knew that the child in her womb was not her husband's.

It had taken her until Christmas to tell Coll. She had chosen her moment with care, making sure he was relaxed, free from pain and as lucid as he ever was before telling him of her condition. His reaction had been instant, terrifying anger, a rage more violent, more destructive than anything she had seen before. Never, not even for a fleeting second, had he accepted the child was his, even when she insisted, reminding him of the times he had emptied his lust into her. Screaming his fury Coll accused her of sleeping with Rab on every possible occasion, of meeting him every time she left the house, of making love to Rab when Coll slept, even of deliberately drugging him to give her time alone with her lover. Beaten by her own shame she had not even tried to move when he lashed out at her with his crutch.

Her eyes seemed to have a will of their own, time and time again she found herself staring at Rab Bannerman's broad back. She had watched as he took his seat, his kilt swaying in perfect, pleated rhythm as he strode down the aisle, his back broad in the tweed jacket, his strong leg muscles clearly defined by his beige stockings. Flushed she lowered her eyes.

Twice he turned towards her. The first time, finding himself staring into the implacable hatred of Coll's face, he turned away. The second time Coll seemed to have drifted into a doze, his head tilted on to his chest. Rab caught Annie's eye and smiled. Annie felt her pulse rate soar, knew she was almost panting aloud, felt her clothes were choking her. Her face coloured again as her mind went doggedly back to that wet September morning, remembering the intensity of the pleasure he had given her. She looked away just as Coll jerked his head up and glared at her, almost as if he knew. But he couldn't possibly know of her shame, that the filthy suspicions which had poisoned his mind for the past five years now had a basis in truth; that the things he taunted her with, the accusations he flung at her, were now true; that she had betrayed him in the basest way. That the child was Rab Bannerman's.

Rab saw the colour which flooded Annie's face and turned away quickly, having no wish to draw attention to either of them in a community which noted the slightest nuance in any relationship. How he regretted that morning. Not the act itself, that would remain with him forever, a treasured memory. What Rab regretted was not having taken the chance to speak his mind, to offer Annie something more than his intangible support, to make her understand how much she really meant to him, to make her see that she was entitled to some joy in her life, to some relief from the tyranny of her husband. To tell her he loved her.

It was too late now. He had known Annie for almost as long as he had known Coll, loved her for all of that time too; had even loved her enough to watch her marry his best friend and be glad that she had found happiness. She wasn't the sort of woman to give herself lightly, so he knew she must feel something for him. But he also understood the shame she would be feeling, it had been clear in her face when she looked at him. It was obvious that she despised him for taking advantage of her when her defences were low. The memory of that morning would stay with her, like a wall between them, for the rest of her life.

After a few warning notes the pianist, the groom's second cousin, thumped out the traditional tune, jarring them all back to the real business of the day. The congregation rose, all turning, eager to get a glimpse of the bride, then subsided into stunned silence as Mysie, absolutely radiant, on the arm of her proud father, walked serenely down the aisle to meet her future husband.

After the wedding the guests were invited to celebrate with Mysie's parents. Following the local tradition every woman had cooked or baked something to help ease the burden on the bride's family. The result was a wide, if eclectic, choice of dishes from which the guests helped themselves freely, pausing only to comment that Mrs McFaddyen's sponge cake had not as many eggs as it should have done or that Mrs Morrison's scones were made with fresh milk, not sour, as should have been the case. There was tongue-clicking disapproval too for the quality of the potted hough which was Mrs Arneil's contribution, though her smoked ham was pronounced adequate. But no one could find any fault with the succulent roasted beef and chickens provided by Lady Fraser and cooked by Mrs McManus. Nor could anyone find anything to criticise in the oat cakes and bannocks, along with a couple of pots of home-made jam which Annie

McDonald had provided. The menfolk, naturally, supplied the whisky.

The Burns' house, like most of the others in the village, was small. In order to accommodate their guests most of the furniture had been taken above stairs and people took their refreshment standing up, even Sir Angus and Lady Fraser, though the choice which faced them was rather bewildering. Lady Fraser could not recall being obliged to eat and drink from mismatched china before and her carefully refined tastes left her ill-prepared for the tarry texture of the tea on offer. She looked in vain for milk with which to dilute it, realised that everyone else was relishing it straight from the pot and delicately abandoned her cup, wishing heartily that she could escape from this press of jostling, smelly bodies. Alas, she knew she would have to stay until the dancing started, as she and Angus were duty bound to partner the bride and groom for the second dance. Unusually, she and Angus found themselves in perfect accord. His cup soon joined hers, hidden behind the curtain, while he waited impatiently for the chance to take something a little stronger.

For once in her life Annie found herself being grateful for Coll's crippled state. It was obviously impossible for him to stand for any length of time and he was rapidly provided with a chair. It was only polite to supply one for his wife too so Annie found herself able to take off her tight coat and sit beside him, confident that her condition was hardly noticeable this way.

The company was eager for the serious business of the day so the meal was rapidly disposed of. The remaining food was cleared away, the dishes piled in, under and round the sinks and the table hauled into the garden to make way for the dancing.

Teg Robertson, who had been lured away from his sheep by the promise of free whisky in return for his services on the fiddle, took up his place by the fireside and was joined by Dod Arneil who was nimble fingered on his accordion. Mysie, suddenly shy, was led out by her new husband to accept the toast from the best man. Glasses, at last filled with whisky, emptied quickly as thirst overcame good manners and were speedily recharged. As they were drained for the second time the music began. To much clapping and stamping Charlie executed a sedate waltz with his wife, then, panting wheezily, invited his guests to join in.

To Katrina's fury, Angus had obviously made huge inroads into his hip-flask and was already slightly unsteady on his expensively shod feet.

'Angus!' she hissed furiously.

He looked at her like a surprised terrier. 'Yes, my dear?'

'For goodness' sake. Do you want to make a complete fool of yourself in front of these . . . these people? If you must drink yourself to a standstill then at least wait until we are home.' Even as she said it she was aware of a slightly muzzy sensation in her own head, no doubt due to the two generous glasses of whisky she had found herself obliged to drink.

He looked at the silver flask, seemed about to take another swig then obviously thought better of it, capped the bottle and returned it to his inside pocket. 'Let's go,' he muttered. 'We've been here too long already.'

'You have got to dance with the bride,' Katrina reminded him. 'And I must partner Mr Arneil.'

At the first pause in the music the Laird and his Lady advanced on their prospective partners. The other guests drew back to enjoy the spectacle. With rather set smiles

Angus and Katrina did their duty with as much dignity as they could wring out of the occasion. To Katrina's dismay, Angus was then immediately swallowed up by several men, all anxious to curry favour with their Laird. Angus, who believed that these people were too lowly to be of any importance, nevertheless saw no reason to decline their hospitality and accepted a large glass of whisky with relish. Not daring to make a scene in such company, Katrina merely made her well-bred excuses and fled, only belatedly realising that the coachman, like the rest of her staff, had been given the night off and she would have to walk the mile and a half back to the castle on her own.

She set off, a little erratically, down the forest track in such a fine fury that she forgot to be wary of the dark, hurrying carelessly over the rutted, slippery path. Inevitably she lost her footing and tumbled in an unladylike heap, ruining her dress. The shock stilled her, killing her temper, and for a minute or two she sprawled there, frightened she might even have done some serious damage. Cautiously she gathered herself into a half sitting position, slightly reassured to feel nothing more than a grazed knee.

'Lady Fraser!'

Katrina recognised Rab Bannerman's gravelly voice instantly. Humiliation overcoming fear, she started to struggle to her feet and found herself being assisted by a strong hand on her arm.

'Thank you, Mr Bannerman,' she said, mustering an admirable degree of dignity while giving thanks that it was too dark for him to see the embarrassed flush which was burning her face. 'I think I caught my foot in a hole.'

'It is very dark tonight, Lady Fraser,' Rab answered, taking off his jacket and flinging it round her shoulders. 'Take this. It's far too cold to be walking.'

'My husband Sir Angus thought he should stay for a little while,' Katrina explained unnecessarily to Rab who had last seen his employer take drunkenly to the dance floor with the suspiciously willing Flo Morrison.

'I was just on my way home too, Lady Fraser. If you will take my arm you will find the track easier.'

'Thank you.' Katrina slipped her hand through Rab's arm, feeling a disconcerting tingle of excitement to find herself alone with a man whose physical attraction had always been a source of discomfort to her.

Rab, though, his mind full of Annie McDonald, was immune to Katrina's rather delicate beauty. His single state seldom bothered him. He had long ago accepted that having lost the one woman he felt able to love he would remain alone and had come to appreciate the freedom his married friends had lost. Until one morning last September. Since then he had been overcome by a creeping dissatisfaction with his life, had found his sleep disturbed, his mind in turmoil. To be expected to celebrate another man's wedded happiness in the same room as the woman he loved while not able to do more than snatch covert glances of her had been more than he could bear. Lingering only long enough to drink the health of the newly married couple he had left the revelry as soon as he politely could. He escorted Lady Katrina home in near silence.

'Are you sure you are not hurt, Lady Katrina?' he asked as she fumbled with the door.

'No,' she started to reassure him them changed her mind. 'Well, my ankle is a little tender. Perhaps you could help me up the stairs?'

Rab obliged willingly enough and half way up the long stairway Katrina was very glad he was with her. Never before had she found herself alone in the house.

Its very stillness unnerved her. Even in her cosy sitting room with the lights burning the eerie feeling persisted.

'Would you mind staying with me for a little while?' she asked sweetly. 'This house feels very lonely tonight.' She gave a tiny theatrical shudder, designed to bring out his protective spirit.

'If you wish, Lady Katrina.' Rab had hoped to get home and drown his sorrows in private but even he could feel the coldness which seemed to have invaded the castle. And he could hardly refuse a direct request from his employer's wife.

'Would you care for a drink?' Katrina asked, walking across the room without the faintest sign of a limp and opening a cabinet.

'No. No, thank you.' Rab was suddenly uncomfortable.

'Oh, please do. I feel in need of something myself but I can hardly have a drink if you won't join me,' she smiled teasingly.

'A very small whisky then, Lady Katrina,' Rab capitulated.

Katrina poured a sparing amount for herself and topped it up with water then half filled a tumbler for Rab. With a glass in each hand she walked slowly across the room, stopping only when she was inches from him. The wicked seed of an idea which had slipped into her mind when Rab had helped her to her feet on the muddy path had rooted in the alcohol in her mind. Perhaps, just perhaps, this man could give her what her husband so wanted. It was an idea born of desperation. But who would be able to prove that any child she conceived wasn't Angus's?

'Your very good health,' she toasted Rab, so close now that he could feel the warmth of her breath on his face.

'My lady.' He downed half the whisky and still she stood, trapping him. By now he had realised that she was less than sober. 'I should be going. It wouldn't do for the others to return and find me here.'

She laughed, stepped closer still, her body just brushing his. 'I don't think we need to worry about anyone else quite yet.' As she spoke she leaned into him. He felt the soft roundness of her breasts as she lifted her mouth to his.

'No.' Rab didn't raise his voice but held her firmly on the upper arms and pushed her away from him.

'It's all right. No one will ever know,' she whispered, truly wanting him now, lusting for this rough country man more than she had ever desired her husband. 'Please . . .' she begged, her face flushed with need.

But Rab was already at the door.

She heard the neutral, 'Goodnight, Lady Katrina,' before the door closed behind him.

'I'll never forgive you for this,' she screamed after him, meeting nothing but the sound of his rapid footsteps on the stairs.

Katrina threw herself on a chair and wept.

Back in the village Annie was enjoying the music. Relaxed by the two glasses of whisky she had permitted herself to enjoy she envied the folk who were dancing, wished she too could join in but knew Coll would never permit it.

Morag thought she understood why her mother sat out the dancing. She could imagine precisely what her father would say if his wife accepted another man's invitation to dance. But there was no reason why she and her mother should not enjoy a couple of reels together, especially when the only offer she had had in the last hour had been from a very drunk, very insistent Angus Fraser. Uncomfortably aware of the fact that he was her employer and in a position of power over her, Morag had allowed him to take her on to the floor. The suggestions he had slurred into her ear while making clumsy attempts to touch her breasts had ignited her hot temper. Acting on instinct she had shoved him back against a wall and fled to the relative safety of her mother's side. Morag scanned the floor and was relieved to see that the Laird, like his wife, had apparently vanished. Now the majority of dancers were women. The men, having done their duty, were nearly all addressing the more urgent need to empty every single bottle of whisky in the house and were gathered on the stairs, by the sinks and in the garden. Those few stalwarts who were still partnering a woman on the dance floor looked, without exception, as if they would rather be anywhere else.

Minister Crombie, still in clerical garb, clomped round the floor as if he had just officiated at a burial; the two church elders George Finlay and Will Keir, both stern teetotallers and uncompromisingly dour men, glared at their more sociable neighbours, grudging them every minute of enjoyment. Tammy McHarg, the farrier, was so drunk he no longer knew where he was and was being dragged limply round the room by his enormous wife. The only other males on the floor were all under twelve.

'Come on, Mam. Nobody will take me up to dance. Come up with me, please?' She held out her hand to her mother who shook her head vehemently.

'No, lass. I'm happy enough watching.'

'Och, don't be so miserable. Away and enjoy yourself,' was Coll's unexpected comment. 'Go on, dance with the lass.'

'No.' Still Annie resisted.

'Will you bloody well get up, woman,' Coll roared, attracting several interested glances.

Annie was on her feet before he had stopped yelling, unwilling to draw any more attention to herself or her husband whose strange behaviour was already the talk of the village.

The dancers broke into two sets for a cramped eight-some reel and Annie found herself drawn into five minutes of chaotic enjoyment, unaware that her daughter's sharp eyes, and those of several village women, had found the real reason for her previous inactivity.

'Och, I've not danced like that for years,' she gasped, flushed and panting as the reel finished.

'Come away outside, Mam. It's too hot in here,' Morag said, leading the way into the small patch of garden, fighting a path through the men amid much ribald comment and finally sitting herself on the damp wall. But before she had the chance to speak to her mother Finty Chisholm, Flo Morrison's aunt and a notorious gossip monger, came up to them.

'I see you are to be congratulated, Mrs McDonald,' she said, casting a meaningful eye over Annie's blossoming figure.

Even in the darkness Morag could see the colour on her mother's face.

'So, when's the wean due? You'll need to take care, it being such a while since your last. Still, it's good to know Mr McDonald's still fit for his wee bit of fun.'

'Mrs Chisholm!' Annie's sense of propriety was affronted, adding to the perpetual shame she felt.

'You'll need to let me know when it's due, hen. You'll be wanting me as your midwife,' Finty added.

Annie had been so wrapped in misery that she had not yet even considered the practical arrangements. The knowledge that this loose-tongued woman was likely to attend the birth horrified her but, as she was probably the only woman available for birthings, it wouldn't do to offend her. She bit back the sharp retort which was burning her tongue and said, 'Late May, early June. And I would be very grateful to have you attend me Mrs Chisholm.'

Finty patted Annie's knee with easy familiarity. 'Well, be sure and call in to see me when you're in the village. It's best we get to know each other before that bairn's born.' And she was off, shouldering her way through the men who parted to let her through with none of their usual banter.

Well, she thought, as she searched out her closest friends, this was a piece of news to take the village by the ears. Annie McDonald was a mystery. When she and her husband, closely followed by Rab Bannerman, had come to the village from some remote highland place, ten years ago, Pitochrie had fairly hummed with rumour about them all. Some said Coll had been in trouble with the law, others that Bannerman was Annie's jilted lover. Certainly the two men had had a bond of experience between them which ran deeper than simple friendship. They were educated men too, well informed on politics and matters of law. Then there was the fact that all Annie's children were able to read, write and do arithmetic to a far higher standard than their classmates, suggesting that Annie herself had an education far superior to most women's. Even her manner, slightly detached, causing some to say she thought she was better than she was, had led to speculation about her background. But the wildest rumours had flown round

Pitochrie after Coll McDonald's accident. Why, many people had asked, when Rab Bannerman had saved his life, did Coll now refuse to even acknowledge the man? Finty rubbed her hands in glee, anticipating the satisfaction of unearthing the truth over the coming months, a feat which would increase her standing in the village to an all-time high.

'Why didn't you tell me, Mam?' Morag asked as soon as Finty was out of earshot.

'Och,' Annie shrugged. 'At first I wasn't sure. Then, well, I didn't keep so well to start with. I feared I might lose it.'

'And now? Are you all right now?' There was real concern in Morag's voice.

'Aye, lass. I'm fine now. The worst is over.' She tried to sound happy and excited about the prospect of another child. Finty Chisholm had taught her a sharp lesson. There was no reason on earth for anyone to think that this child was not Coll's, that this was anything more than a late addition to their family. No reason for anyone to think otherwise unless, by her manner, she gave cause for gossip. Well, she had betrayed Coll once but there was no reason to bring her shame to the whole village. As far as anyone else was concerned this was a much wanted child. Annie felt better for that thought, more positive than she had felt for months. She turned to her daughter with a smile. 'I was going to tell you on your next visit home. I didn't think it was so obvious.'

Morag smiled back. 'That's all right. But you'll have to take care. And what about the laundry? You can't do heavy work like that now.'

'Och, away and don't fuss, Morag. When I was carrying the twins I had you and Davy round my skirts and a croft to look after!'

'Annie! Annie! Where the hell are you, woman?'

Both women jumped off the wall at the sound of Coll's voice. Annie hesitated long enough to kiss her daughter. 'Away and enjoy yourself, lass. I'll get that father of yours home to his bed.'

Morag watched her mother hurry to placate her belligerent father with the first rumblings of unease in her stomach.

Pitochrie was a very subdued village the next morning. The number of people able to get to the Kirk was less than half what it normally was. Minister Crombie thoroughly enjoyed delivering a sermon on the evils of over-indulgence to a congregation who were already, if temporarily, converted.

Annie, preoccupied with her own worries, hardly heard a word the minister said. She had left Coll in bed, still sleeping off the effects of the previous day, glad to get this hour away from him and knowing full well that he was likely to be in a foul mood when she got home. And life wasn't likely to get any easier. A nagging pain in her lower back, accompanied at times by gripping pains in her abdomen, warned her that to continue to take in laundry was endangering her own life and that of the child in her womb. But how would they manage without the money she earned?

Rab Bannerman had decided to forego being subjected to Minister Crombie's predictable tirade. His head was throbbing with pain, the direct result of the half bottle of whisky he had consumed when he finally reached his own hearth side last night. Intense though the pain was it still couldn't keep his mind from wandering over the unpleasant incident with Lady Fraser. God knows how he would ever be able to face her again. It was possible that his position in the household might no longer be tenable. If there was any justice in the world Lady Katrina, who had obviously been feeling the effects of too much whisky, would have no memory of what had taken place. But Rab Bannerman had lost his faith in justice many years ago.

In the bed she shared with her husband on the few nights he felt able to spare her, Katrina Fraser awoke with a foul taste in her mouth and the memory of the previous evening burning into her mind. Even now she could still recall the way Bannerman had looked at her, as if she was something that had crawled out of a ditch. She would never, ever be able to face the man again. But it was unthinkable that she should ask Angus to dismiss him. That would only invite questions which Bannerman might, with his job at stake, be obliged to answer honestly. It was a shock to realise that she didn't trust her husband enough to rely on him believing her version of events, at least not until she had given him the son he wanted.

She eased herself gingerly out of bed and went to stand at the window, letting a draught of fresh air cool her throbbing head. During the night she had woken to the dull abdominal ache which presaged yet another wasted month. She dreaded admitting her continued infertility to her husband and knew that his patience was almost exhausted.

A choked snorting sound from the bed made her turn to look at her husband who was snoring like a sow in labour. Not for the first time she wondered why it was so important to please someone who pleased her not at all. In her heart she knew that Angus himself didn't

100

matter to her one bit. It was the lifestyle, the kudos of a title that had always been his attraction. After she had done her duty and delivered a healthy son perhaps they could come to some arrangement, one which would give them both discreet freedom. *When* she gave him a son.

SIX

Rab Bannerman frowned
at the pages of the ledger he was completing in readi-
ness for the Laird's three-monthly inspection. In the rent
column, for the first time in his term as estate manager,
there was an obvious deficit. An understanding man who
had every sympathy for the difficulties faced by some of
his hard-pressed neighbours, Rab was content to accept
payments as and when the estate's tenants were able to
make them and had seldom found his trust abused. But
the large sum now owed by the McDonalds was far
beyond the usual amount and made even more worrying
by the fact that they had made no attempt to speak to
him about it.

Rab sighed and rubbed his hand through his dark
beard, wondering how best to deal with this. With any
other tenant there would have been no problem, explanations would have been offered and arrangements to
pay made when he called to collect the rent. But, largely
because of his unhappy relationship with Coll, Annie
had not wanted him to call at the cottage and had got
into the habit of leaving the rent money with Mrs
McManus when she went to the castle for the washing.
He had heard, some weeks ago, that Annie was no
longer taking in the castle laundry which was now
going to the commercial laundry at Glenarg. Did she
dread meeting him so much that she could no longer
even bring herself to come near the castle? He sighed

again and slammed the book shut. Something would have to be done, and quickly, before he presented the quarterly accounts to Sir Angus who was notoriously unsympathetic to the difficulties of the villagers.

'Uncle Rab!' Morag's smile was one of simple delight. 'I haven't seen you for ages,' she laughed.

'You're looking even bonnier than ever, lass. I shall have to tell Mrs McManus to keep you indoors else all the village lads will be breaking their hearts over you,' he teased gently, well aware that more than one local lad had attempted, without success, to win her.

She blushed prettily, her green eyes sparkling with pleasure. 'Are you waiting for someone?' Rab had been sitting on a felled tree trunk, halfway along the woodland footpath, an uncomfortable place to wait on a damp, misty day such as this.

'Aye. You,' he admitted. 'I want you to give a message to your mother for me, lass.' Rab had taken pains to discover Morag's next half day off, correctly assuming she would spend it with her parents.

'A message?' she asked, intrigued.

'How are they?' he asked, anxious to forestall any questions, after all there was no point in worrying the girl unnecessarily.

'Dad's just the same as ever,' she said, perching beside him on the canvas bag he had set down to keep her skirt clean. 'He has his good days.'

'And your mother?'

'I think she's finding it hard. She seems so tired all the time.'

Rab stared at her. 'She's not ill?'

Now it was Morag's turn to look at Rab. Surely he knew? 'She's having a bairn,' she blushed faintly, suddenly embarrassed to be talking about her mother's delicate condition. 'I thought you knew.'

'No, no I didn't know.' He was filled with dismay. 'Is that why she stopped doing the laundry?'

'Aye. The work was too heavy. She needs to rest.'

And that probably explained why the rent hadn't been paid. But why, he asked himself, hadn't Annie explained her situation before the arrears had reached their current proportions? 'When's the bairn due?' he asked, conscious of Morag's keen scrutiny.

'In another three months.' Morag watched as Rab made a rapid mental calculation, saw the sweat bead on his forehead. 'Uncle Rab, is something the matter?'

'Matter? No, lass,' he answered quickly then, seeing she didn't believe him, he grunted and added, 'Maybe I shouldn't tell you this, but your mother and father are behind with their rent. That's what I want to see your mother about. I didn't realise she was . . . That'll explain why they can't pay, they'll be missing the wee bit she made from the laundry.' It was almost as if he was talking to himself.

'Behind with the rent!' Morag was horrified. Her mother was a proud woman who had impressed a healthy fear of debt into all her family. 'She never said anything to me. Is it very much?' Not that there was anything she could do. Her entire wages already went into the family budget.

'Och, it's nothing we can't put to rights. Don't you go fretting about it, lass. Ask your mother to meet me here the morn at this time. I'll sort it out with her then.'

Morag nodded. 'I'll do that.' She stood up and brushed her skirt off. 'I'd best be getting home. Mam'll be wondering where I am and I promised to help her with the baking.'

'Aye, off you go then,' he gave her a fatherly peck on the cheek.

'Uncle Rab,' she turned back after a few paces.

'Aye?' he asked, tearing his mind away from the turmoil which was engulfing it.

'You won't . . . I mean Sir Angus won't turn them out, will he? It's hard for them and they've nowhere else to go.'

'Nay, lass. Don't worry your pretty head about that. It'll be all right, I promise you that.' He smiled, the light catching the vivid blue of his eyes, crinkling them at the corners, giving the impression of strength and reliability that Morag loved. It never occurred to her not to believe him.

Morag found her mother up to her elbows in flour, the small house full of fragrant heat.

'I thought you were going to wait for me to help you with that?' she scolded, dropping a kiss on her mother's flushed cheeks.

Annie pushed a strand of hair back, leaving floury marks on her brow. 'Och, it's hardly fair for you to work here in your free time. Anyway, your father's asleep so I thought I'd better make the most of it.'

'You'd have been better to put your feet up and have a rest yourself,' Morag insisted, worried by the too rosy glow on her mother's face. 'Let me wash my hands then I'll finish off here. You make yourself a cup of tea and sit down a while.' As she spoke she sluiced her hands in the sink and wrapped her mother's spare apron round her.

'You're a good lass, Morag,' Annie smiled and surrendered her place without too much fuss.

Morag busied herself with the dough and set it to rise

near the range before finally joining her mother by the fireside.

Behind them Coll snored gently, and never moved despite the clattering of bread tins, the noisy swoosh of the water pump, or the clang of the oven door when Morag removed the scones her mother had already baked.

'He had a terrible head when he woke,' Annie explained. 'He had some of his medicine so he'll sleep for a couple of hours yet.'

'He has too much of that stuff,' Morag said quietly.

Annie glared at her daughter, not needing to have the truth pointed out to her. 'Don't you dare to criticise me, Morag McDonald. You're not the one who has to cope with him!' She blinked hard to contain the tears which sprung to her pale eyes.

Morag flushed, startled by the emotional response from her mother who was normally so controlled. 'I'm sorry,' she offered then went on doggedly. 'It's just that stuff's so expensive.'

'And that, Morag, is my concern, not yours.' Annie was too proud to admit, even to her daughter, just how desperate their plight was.

'And the Laird's concern too,' Morag went on. She might have inherited her father's vibrant colouring but her determination was her mother's and every bit as strong.

Annie paled, losing her high colour with alarming speed. Morag waited a second before pressing on, resolved to say what had to be said while she still had the opportunity. 'Rab Bannerman stopped me on my way here today. He told me about the rent. He wants to see you tomorrow. He'll meet you at the bend in the track, just after noon,' she blurted it out before Annie could interrupt and added, 'Why didn't you tell me, Mam?'

'And what good would that have done?' Annie demanded derisively, her pride stung. 'What could *you* do about it?'

Morag knew there was no way in which she could ease her mother's burden and looked away. 'I'm sorry.'

'You're a good lass,' Annie said, though it was obvious she was still very angry. 'But Rab Bannerman had no right to discuss our private business with you.'

'He wouldn't have needed to if you'd spoken to him yourself. He's worried, Mam. He wants to help, that's all.'

'I don't need help from anyone,' Annie retorted. 'Least of all Rab Bannerman.'

Morag was stunned by the bitterness in her mother's voice. 'I thought he was your friend?'

'You have said more than enough, Morag,' Annie warned coldly. 'In future I'll thank you not to gossip about me with Rab Bannerman, or anyone else. Now, I've things to see to before your father wakes and you'd best get back before it starts to get dark.'

Never before had Annie sent Morag away without offering her a meal. Hurt, Morag slung her shawl over her shoulders but turned as she reached the door. 'Tomorrow, Mam. See Rab tomorrow and sort it out.'

Annie was so nervous that she could eat nothing. To make matters worse Coll was alert and, for once, free from pain, not needing the medicine which would have conveniently sent him to sleep while she went to keep her appointment.

'And where do you think you're going?' he demanded, lurching around the room after her, his crutch thumping unevenly on the flagged floor.

'To the village,' she lied.

'Why? We've bread, there's bacon in the press, plenty tea, tatties and carrots. There's no need to go out the day.'

'I have to go out, Coll,' she insisted.

'Not until you tell me why,' he growled, barring her way.

'It's a woman's thing,' she dissembled desperately.

'What is?' he persisted, still refusing to move.

'Och, Coll, will you leave me some dignity?' she asked, forcing a smile to her face. 'If you must know I'm having trouble moving myself. It's common enough in pregnancy. I'm going to ask Finty Chisholm for something to ease me, that's all.' And would now have to trudge all the way into the village for the proof, when she was already bone tired.

Coll had the grace to look ashamed. 'Och, right you are then,' he conceded, moving aside.

'And don't go fretting if I'm a wee while,' she said, tightening her shawl against the gusty wind which was bending the tree tops. 'I've to find Finty first and then I daresay she'll have to make something up for me.'

'Take your time, hen,' he said, hobbling back to his chair. 'Take your time.'

The wind was bitter, working its way through the loose wool of her knitted shawl and creeping down her neck and across her shoulders with icy fingers. The hand which clutched her shawl close round her throat was soon numb with cold. Annie shivered. She had never become accustomed to the claustrophobic atmosphere in the woods, still longed for the open spaces of the hills. Above her the trees cracked and whined as the wind whipped through them, increasing her unease. She walked on, head bent against the blast.

'Annie. Over here.'

108

She jumped, span round and only then did she see Rab emerging from the undergrowth, his gun slung casually over one shoulder. 'What a fright you gave me,' she said, sounding sharp and angry.

Rab's smile never faltered. 'It's more sheltered among the trees,' he said. 'Unless you'd rather come home with me while we talk.'

'No!' she almost shouted.

'Come over here then, it's dry enough under the trees.' He led her to the shelter of a huge oak and delved into his canvas bag. 'Take this home with you, Annie. The rabbits are unwary at this time of year. I've too many for my own use.' He offered a fair-sized animal which would make a good meal for her and Coll for the next two days.

'No,' pride made her shake her head.

'Och, and what's the harm in a bit of fresh meat for the pot? If you won't take it it'll likely turn before I have the chance to eat it myself. You wouldn't have the poor animal die for nothing would you?'

In spite of herself she smiled and took the animal by its hind legs then placed it in the angle of a low branch. 'Thank you,' she muttered.

They stood uncomfortably, neither knowing quite what to say, until Rab finally broke the silence. 'Why didn't you tell me about the bairn?' he asked, watching her closely.

Annie turned away from him, looked blindly into the rustling undergrowth.

'Annie?'

'And why should I have to tell you anything, Rab Bannerman?' she retorted at last, spinning round to face him, her pregnancy now obvious under the ill-fitting coat.

'Because the child is mine,' he said, so quietly that his voice mingled with the soughing wind.

'No,' she whispered.

'Yes. Och, Annie, do you think I've no ability to count months?' He reached out to her, longing to take her into the shelter of his arms, to still the shivering of her body. She moved away so sharply she almost fell then shrugged off his steadying hand angrily.

'And what would you know about such things?' she hissed.

'Enough to know the child is mine,' he insisted, a spark of anger in his own eyes now.

'Then you should know enough to understand that I am still Coll McDonald's wife. In all ways.' She saw him flinch.

'Annie . . .'

Annie bit back the groan of pain which so nearly escaped her and, taking a deep breath, turned to him. 'There is nothing I want to say to you about this child. To Coll, to everyone else, and even to me, this is Coll's bairn. Nothing you can say will ever make me admit otherwise.'

'I could help you, Annie, if you'd let me. I'll not turn away from my responsibilities,' he offered gently.

'You have no responsibility for me, Rab Bannerman,' she yelled at him. 'What happened between us was . . . was a terrible mistake. It shames me to think of it and it will never, ever happen again. I am married to Coll, and this child is his responsibility, not yours.' Pulling her shawl close over her face she started to walk away from him, leaving the rabbit on the branch.

'Annie! Wait!' he roared. Grabbing the rabbit, his canvas bag and his gun he hurried after her, catching her as she stepped back on to the still deserted track.

'I have to go to the village,' she said, trying to push past him.

'We still have some business to discuss.'

'There is nothing I want to talk to you about.'

'Not even the rent you owe?' he asked.

Annie stopped, abruptly. She had been so upset she had forgotten exactly why he had asked to see her. 'I have no money to pay you now,' she told him.

'You should have come to me before. I could have helped you. I can see how hard it must be for you,' he said.

'I will take care of it,' she insisted, not meeting his eyes, shame at her debt almost as great as the shame of her remembered passion. Even now, in the midst of all her troubles, she knew, if she let him touch her again, if she allowed herself to meet those clear, blue eyes, to see the genuine compassion she knew was there, she would be lost, that she would not be able to help herself, that her body would betray her again.

'How?' he demanded. 'How do you hope to pay three months' rent by Friday?'

'Friday?' she echoed, horrified.

'Sir Angus has asked me to take the ledgers to him on Friday morning. He will see for himself.'

'Sweet Lord,' she breathed. 'I cannot pay you before then.'

'Then let me help,' he repeated.

'No,' she was adamant. 'I do not need your help.'

'But you do, Annie. Sir Angus will not tolerate arrears. If he takes it into his mind to evict you, you will find yourself put out before the next week is over.' He saw the panic flash across her face, saw her control it and admired her all the more. 'Let me pay it for you. No one need know. It can be between the two of us. Pay me

111

back as and when you can.' For a moment he thought he had managed to talk sense into her. She seemed to hesitate, as if she knew there was nothing else she could do. 'I'll take care of it today, lass.'

'You will do nothing of the sort, Rab Bannerman. Coll McDonald will not accept charity. And neither will I.'

'Help from a friend is not charity,' he retorted.

'I have written to the twins. Iain and Billy have good jobs in the shipyards in Glasgow. They will be able to help us. And that's as it should be – the family helping one another. We don't need anything from you. And don't think to pay it for me without telling me. You can tell Sir Angus that I'll be bringing the money to him myself.'

'You are a stubborn, stupid woman, Annie McDonald.' Rab's temper finally exploded. He flung the rabbit carcass at her feet and stomped away into the trees. Annie stared after him, pain stark on her proud face. Then, swallowing some of her pride, she slowly bent to retrieve the muddied animal.

Morag was tired, aching in every limb and knew she would have to be up at six the next morning. Despite that, worry about the unpaid rent was keeping her awake. Perhaps she would get off more easily if she read for a while.

Lady Katrina ordered books in their dozens which arrived in crates from Edinburgh every three or four months. When she had finished with them she allowed her staff to have their pick. Morag had been amused to discover that, on wet days, old Dram, the morose gardener, was often to be found in one of the outhouses, puffing contentedly on his smelly pipe and engrossed in

112

a romantic novel. Her current book was an unlikely but enjoyable tale of a farm girl who fell in love with the son of a rich family. Morag had reached the point where the young man's mother had contrived to end the romance and was intrigued to discover how they would overcome the obstacles placed in the way of their happiness. It would be the ideal thing to take her mind off her parents' problems. She glanced at the small table beside her bed and was annoyed to see the novel wasn't there. Then she remembered. She had taken it downstairs with her to read in her free half hour after dinner last night. She hesitated a moment, knowing she shouldn't really go back downstairs, that she would be in serious trouble with Mrs McManus if she was discovered. She opened her door carefully and crept to the top of the stairs, listening intently. Any noise from below always echoed loudly up the stone stairwell but tonight there was the total silence that said everyone was safe in bed. Taking the candle from her room she made her way carefully to the kitchen.

The book was where she had left it, on the seat in the inglenook. The fire had burned low but the area was still cosily warm, much warmer than her attic bedroom. What harm would she be doing if she sat here and read for half an hour? She could even light one of the oil lamps and save her candle for another night. Drawing her feet up beside her on the cushioned seat Morag was soon immersed in her story. She read on, right to the end, then relit her candle and extinguished the oil lamp guiltily, realising she had stayed on for much too long. It must be at least one o'clock, probably later. She would never manage to get up in the morning. The fire was still glowing but dully now. Morag leaned forward to give her hands a last heat then stepped backwards out of the ingle, checking the cushion was straight, the lamp in its original place.

As she stepped down on to the stone flags of the kitchen floor she was grabbed from behind. Her heart leapt so violently that it actually hurt. Her candle and its holder clattered to the floor. Instinctively she started to scream but no sooner had she opened her mouth than a hand clamped over it, stifling her. Another one found its way to her soft breasts. Anger overcoming fear she thrashed and twisted to no avail then bit down into the bony hand which covered her mouth.

'Bitch! You bloody little bitch!'

Morag recognised the voice immediately and turned round in horror. The room was in darkness, the faint glow from the fire the only source of light. Even so she knew the shadowed figure in front of her was Angus Fraser. She glanced at the corridor leading to the stairway, wondering if she could get away from him but it was too late, he was already moving back to her.

'What are you doing here?' he asked angrily.

'I was just going to bed,' she answered, backing away.

'Stand still when I'm talking to you.' He reached into the gloom and grabbed her arm.

'Let go. You're hurting me,' she protested, trying to dislodge his fingers. To her amazement he laughed.

'Is that the way to speak to your employer?' he asked, coming very close to her. Too close. 'Stay still,' he ordered, when she tried to squirm away. 'I'm not going to hurt you.'

Morag knew she would never win a struggle with him. Tall and lean though he was, Sir Angus was no weakling. She stayed perfectly still, wishing she could see him more clearly, make out the expression on his face.

'That's better,' he laughed again. 'Now, suppose you tell me what you are doing here at this time of the night?' He sounded quite reasonable now and Morag knew she was in the wrong.

'I came to fetch my book, sir. I couldn't sleep.'

'Reading! But it's after one o'clock.'

'I meant to go back to my room, sir. But it was warmer here. I didn't mean to stay so long and I was only reading.' She was terrified he might think she was trying to help herself to extra food, or candles, or worse.

'You know I should tell Mrs McManus?'

'Yes, sir.'

'Do you think I should?' he asked, his voice almost a whisper now. She shivered.

'I don't know, sir.'

'I could have you dismissed.'

'No . . .' Morag had a sickening feeling in her stomach.

Sir Angus stepped closer and pulled her to him, shoving his face hard against hers, thrusting his whisky tainted tongue between her lips while his hand massaged the soft flesh under her dress. Morag drummed her hands into his shoulders and wrenched her face away in disgust, thinking she might actually vomit.

Incredibly he laughed again. 'No, oh no, that won't do.' He held her, pinning her arms at her side, forcing her into stillness. 'Is a little kiss such a terrible thing to a beautiful girl like you? Is it such a high price to pay? A kiss or two in return for keeping your position in the house?' Now that her eyes were used to the darkness she could see he was grinning as he spoke.

'Please, let me go,' she begged, keenly aware of his reputation, knowing this would not stop with a mere kiss.

115

He pressed his hand back over her mouth. 'Quiet. Unless you want to raise the whole house. Then what would they think?'

She shook her head violently, her eyes flashing fear and fury.

'That's better. Come on, Morag.' He moved his hand from her mouth and slipped it down on to her breasts where her nipples were taut with fear against the fabric of her nightdress. 'All you have to do is keep me company for a minute or two and then you can go back to your room as if nothing has happened.'

'Don't do that!' she pleaded, her voice a whisper of fear.

He ignored her, pushed her backwards towards the long kitchen table then shoved her back on to it. 'I know you don't mean that,' he rasped, his hands hot on her body.

'Angus? Angus? Is that you?' Katrina's unexpected voice, echoing down the stairwell, made Angus leap away. Seizing her chance, Morag slipped off the table and straightened her clothes.

'Yes, my dear,' Angus walked swiftly along the short corridor to the bottom of the stairs and called up to his wife.

'What was that noise?' she asked, her voice sounding hollow from so far away.

'Nothing. I knocked into something in the dark, that's all. Go back to bed. I'll be with you shortly.' He waited until he heard the sound of their bedroom door closing then turned back to Morag. Seeming completely unruffled he smiled at her. 'Well, it seems I am to be denied the pleasure of your company tonight. Never mind. I am sure there will be other opportunities. Why don't you just go on up to bed? Quietly now. We don't want to disturb anyone else, do we?' He stood aside and allowed her to pass.

116

Desperate to get away from him, Morag ran from the kitchen, and up the stairs, not stopping until she reached the safety of her own room.

Katrina Fraser watched the girl's frantic flight from the shelter of her darkened landing then crept back to her own room, taking care that no whisper of sound carried downstairs to her husband. By the time Angus joined her, murmuring about having gone downstairs for fresh water to ease his thirst, she was already feigning sleep.

Angus Fraser had spent almost the entire morning going over estate matters with his manager, Rab Bannerman. It was something he loathed but felt duty bound to do on a regular basis. Only interested in the estate as a source of income, Fraser knew enough to admit, but only to himself, that Bannerman ran it more efficiently that he ever could and rarely had cause to argue with the other man's judgement.

It was customary to offer his manager a suitably modest luncheon on the four occasions each year when they went over the books together but, for some reason, Bannerman declined the offer and hurried off with almost indecent haste, not even lingering to make his excuses to Katrina, which would have been the polite thing to do. Fraser shrugged, glad to be rid of the man who, by the sheer breadth of his knowledge and the quickness of his mind, always managed to make him feel inadequate. Lighting a cigar he opened the ledger again and ran his eye over the rents column until he came to the entry for the McDonalds. Then, a grim smile on his lips, he moved to his study window and stood there for a few minutes, enjoying the splendid view of the hills before tugging the bell rope. To his disappointment it was Flo who answered.

117

'Tell Mrs McManus to send the McDonald girl to me at once.'

'Yes, sir.' Flo ran back to the kitchen so fast that she almost fell headlong down the stairs.

She delivered her message to an audience who fell immediately into awed silence. Sir Angus rarely took any interest in the staff, preferring to leave domestic matters to his wife. Anything which required his personal intervention was assumed to be very serious indeed.

Morag received her summons in panic-stricken stillness and had to be led to the stairs by Mrs McManus.

'If you're in any sort of trouble, Morag, you'd best tell me now, quickly.' Her own job could be at risk if the incident which had attracted Sir Angus's wrath was her responsibility.

Morag hesitated then gabbled. 'He caught me in the kitchen last night, after everyone was in bed. I was reading a book. That's all. Honestly.' She couldn't bring herself to add the horrific details.

'Good Lord! You know better than that. Haven't I told you not to come back down here? Well, you've only yourself to blame.' She gave the girl an unsympathetic shove up the stairs then sat down to await her return in nervous silence, fully expecting to be summoned next.

The climb upstairs seemed never ending. Morag reached Sir Angus's study with her heart beating furiously, her breath coming in rasping pants. Resting a minute to try and calm herself, she then rapped on his door and, hearing his loud 'Enter', forced herself to face him calmly.

'Ah, Miss McDonald,' Sir Angus turned and smiled, his eyes raking her body.

'Sir?' The memory of last night still raw in her mind, Morag kept her chin up, but refused to look into his hooded eyes.

'Don't be afraid. I only want to talk to you,' he said, walking round her. When she didn't respond he went on. 'You know I could ask Mrs McManus to have you dismissed?' As he spoke he ran a finger along the nape of her neck where the glorious auburn hair escaped in wispy strands from under her cap.

'Yes, sir,' she said again, wincing at his touch, wondering whether the disgrace of being dismissed would be worse than the shame of allowing him to touch her again. She had decided she would rather face her mother and father with the truth, knowing her mother at least would believe her, when she realised exactly what her dismissal, the loss of her wages, would mean to them.

'But it need not come to that,' he was back in front of her now, smiling.

She stayed silent.

'I am sure you and I could come to some . . . some arrangement,' he drawled, running a finger over the front of her starched apron.

'No!' she stepped back. 'Please, I can't.'

He fingered his moustache and looked at her speculatively. 'Before you make any hasty decisions there is something you should see. Come here.'

Reluctantly she crossed the room and stood beside him, keeping as far away as she could.

'Do you know what you are looking at?' he asked, his voice cool and controlled.

'No, sir,' she admitted, making nothing of the columns of figures in dense, black ink.

'Well, concentrate. Read the title at the top of this page,' he ordered.

'Rents, sir.'

'Well done. Now, down this side are listed the names of everyone who rents property from me. See, there is your family. McDonald.'

'Yes, sir.'

'Yes, sir,' he mocked. 'In this column, under the date, are the amounts paid. Put your finger here, by the dates for November. You can see, can you not, that your parents have paid their rent when it was due?'

'Yes, sir.'

'Good. Now move on across the pages.' He watched as she turned the page into the new year, smiled when he saw the shaky finger stop.

'And what are you seeing now, Miss McDonald?' he asked.

'Nothing, sir.'

'Nothing. And that is precisely what your parents have been paying me. Nothing. If you look to the right-hand column you will see the amount they now owe me.'

Morag looked and blanched at the amount. 'Sir.'

'Why do you think this should have happened, Miss McDonald?'

'My father is a cripple, sir. He lost a leg in an accident when he was shepherd at Arneil's farm.'

'So he did. I do seem to remember something about that. But that was before your family lived in their present house so it has nothing to do with the rent being unpaid.'

'It's my mother, sir,' Morag ventured desperately. 'She's not well. She can't work just now. But she will be better soon.'

'And what is wrong with her?' he asked, already knowing the answer from what Bannerman had told him but anxious to put the girl at the greatest disadvantage.

'She is expecting a baby, sir,' Morag muttered, lowering her eyes.

'So, it would be very hard for them to be without a home, would it not?'

Morag gasped. 'You can't do that, sir. They will pay you, as soon as my mother is fit again.'

'I can do whatever I like, Morag,' he smiled. 'So, unless you can suggest a way of settling the account, I am afraid I will have no choice but to evict your family.'

'I haven't any money, sir,' she cried, her voice a strangled sob.

'I wasn't necessarily thinking about money,' he said, his eyes resting on the swell behind her apron bodice, his message unmistakable.

'I can't,' she whispered it, tears of terror filling her eyes.

Angus slammed the book shut, making her jump, then sat in his chair, turning his attention to other papers on his desk. Confused Morag didn't know what she was supposed to do.

'Am I dismissed, sir? Have I to pack my bags?' she asked.

He looked up at her and smiled. 'Well, that is up to you. If you want your mother and father to stay on in their cottage then I suggest you do not lock your bedroom door tonight. If I do find it locked then I will expect to find you gone by tomorrow night and your parents out of their house by the end of the week.'

'Sir!' she protested, then turned and walked to the door. He rose from his desk and put his hand over hers as she turned the knob.

'Morag,' he whispered gently. 'Be sensible. I am showing

121

you a very pleasant way out of a difficult situation. You are a very desirable young woman. Do this for me and you will not find me ungenerous.' With that he opened the door for her and she found herself back on the stairs with nowhere to go but back to the kitchen.

'Morag, lass, come and sit down. You look terrible,' Cook was on her feet the minute she saw her. 'Is everything all right? What did he say? Does he want to see me?'

Morag took a deep breath. 'It's all right, he doesn't want to see anyone else.'

'Thank the Lord for that,' Cook breathed. 'And what about you, lass? Did he not dismiss you?' That was what they had all been expecting.

Morag shook her head and sipped gratefully at the cup of strong tea Flo pressed into her hands. 'He told me off. That's all.'

'Aye, he can be a stern man, Sir Angus,' Cook said, her fear receding. 'You did a stupid thing, Morag. You know fine that no one's allowed back downstairs after I lock up. You're lucky to still have your job. If it happens again I'll be the one who sends you packing.'

'Yes, Mrs McManus.'

'Right. Well, we've wasted enough time. Tidy yourself up and wash your face, Morag. Lady Fraser's been ringing for you for the last ten minutes.'

Even before she left Sir Angus's study Morag knew what she would have to do. There was simply no choice. There was no point in discussing it with her mother. She would be appalled, would insist that Morag returned home and what good would that do any of them? What would happen to her mother, her father, her unborn brother or sister, if they were thrown out of their home? It was not as if there was anyone they could turn to. Davy, her elder brother, had married Isabel McLaren, a local girl, rather more hurriedly than was proper. Within six months they had become the parents of a bonny bouncing ten-and-a-half-pound son who not even the most generous-souled villager could believe was premature. Their tied cottage was shared with Isabel's parents and two sisters who had lost their own home when Isabel's father's chest complaint had finally forced him to stop working. They were in no position to help. Iain and Billy, both working in the Clyde shipyards, still lodged with an elderly widow-woman in a two-roomed tenement. They were no more able to shelter their parents than their elder brother. In any case, Morag knew her father would refuse to even consider moving to the city. He made little secret of his contempt for the twins, regarding them as traitors to their kind for so readily abandoning the country in favour of the different standards of Glasgow. On the rare occasions when they had come home they had been treated to a series of bitter diatribes in which Coll accused them of turning their backs on their responsibilities to their parents, of spending their money on loose women and drink. Small wonder they no longer bothered to visit.

There was no one else who could possibly help them, or her. Except Rab Bannerman. Morag hated the idea of confessing to her godfather any part of what had happened but, desperately needing support, eventually asked Mrs McManus's permission to go and see him after dinner, saying she had a message for him from her mother.

'You'll not find him home the night, lass. He's gone with Charlie Arneil and Ewart Morrison to sell sheep at the Perth market. They won't be back till the morn at the earliest.'

Hope destroyed, Morag locked herself in her bedroom and waited, her stomach churning with fear. One by one she heard the others come to bed. Mrs McManus's firm-footed tread along the landing to her room on the far corner, then young Chrissy who occupied the tiniest room, next to Cook's, where the older woman's snoring made her feel less alone during the dark nights. Finally Flo ran lightly up the stairs, humming to herself as she walked past Morag's door to her own room, two doors along. She called out a cheerful goodnight as she passed but Morag couldn't bring herself to answer. At least her own room, with a large storeroom between her and Flo, was reasonably private. If Sir Angus did venture up here tonight no one else was likely to hear him. It was a very small consolation.

As soon as she was sure they were all safely in their rooms, Morag unlocked the door. Leaving the room in darkness she slipped into bed and huddled miserably under the sheets.

The old house seemed to creak more violently. The wind, nothing more than a gentle breeze, seemed to tear at the window frames while even her breath seemed loud enough to drown out the sound of an approaching footstep. With every nerve tensed to warn her of his arrival, Morag lay and waited for the Laird.

She must have fallen into a light sleep. She opened her eyes, instantly alert, and knew that the noise which had disturbed her was the sound of her doorhandle turning. Peering into the darkness she saw a shadowy figure enter her room, saw it move towards her and jerked away from the hand he put out to touch her.

'So, you decided to be sensible?' Angus Fraser asked,

his voice softer than she had ever heard it, almost as if he was drunk, but there was no smell of spirit on his breath that she could detect.

He sat on the edge of her bed and, to her absolute horror, started to strip off his clothes. She averted her eyes but looked round when he got to his feet and quickly pulled back her curtains, letting enough moon-light into the room to see by. Almost as quickly he was back at her side, gently drawing the covers back. Then he laughed, a huge guffaw, terrifying in its loudness.

'Ssushhh.' It was out before she could stop it.

'Ah, so you are not sleeping,' he said, reaching for her shoulder and pulling her into a sitting position.

'How could I be?' she retorted bravely.

'Indeed, how could you be?' he agreed. 'It would be almost impossible to sleep fully dressed, boots and all,' he laughed again, his hands already working at her clothes.

Instinctively she tried to stop him but found herself restrained by strong, sinewy arms. 'We have a bargain, Morag McDonald,' he whispered into her ear. 'You may struggle if you wish but it will be easier if you do not.' And still his hands worked away at her clothes until she was wearing nothing but her drawers, her hands clenched over her breasts, the tears running freely down her face.

She no longer resisted but obeyed him dully, standing so that he could remove the final shield to her decency. But then, when she was naked, he pushed her away. 'It is not too late. You may still change your mind,' he said, his voice hard. 'You have only to say and I will creep out of here, and not come back. And you will leave before tomorrow night to help your parents move out of their cottage.'

'No,' she whispered.

'No what?' he insisted. 'You don't want me here? Is that what you mean?'

'No,' she repeated.

He turned away. 'Then pack your things.'

'No!' she said it louder now. 'Don't go.' Her humiliation was complete.

'Are you quite sure, Morag McDonald? I would not have you say that I took you by force.' His smile was one of victory, had no tenderness in it.

'I am sure.' Her head came up defiantly, wanting him to see she was not beaten.

'Good,' he nodded his approval, he liked spirit in his women, had had enough of dead unresponsiveness from Katrina. 'You have a body to match your face. Quite beautiful.'

Instantly her hands flew to cover her nakedness but he pulled them away again. His body was already throbbing. He had wanted this exquisite girl in his bed from the very first day he had seen her, had expected her to be more willing, as the housemaids usually were, as young Flo had been. Surely she understood that this was almost part of her duties, that if she co-operated, she would be well rewarded with enough money to buy herself a decent trousseau. Accustomed to having women eager for his attention, Angus's pride was shaken by Morag's obvious lack of interest but his determination was sharpened. He advanced on her purposefully. Morag backed towards the bed until she could go no further. Then she felt his arms go round her, felt herself pushed on to the softness of her sheets, felt his mouth on hers, his tongue between her lips. She froze, terrified of what was to happen next.

Although she had been brought up in a household

with four males, Morag had none the less never seen a man naked. Despite the sometimes ribald chat in the kitchen, her knowledge of what happened between animals, Morag was totally unprepared for the sight of Angus Fraser's manhood as he positioned himself over her. Her body tensed and she lay stiff and rigid as he tried to prise her legs apart, his desire growing more urgent with every passing moment.

'Damn you,' he hissed, 'this will hurt you more than it has to if you are going to lie there like a plank of wood.'

She deliberately turned her face away, avoiding his attempts to kiss her, then screwed her eyes shut as he rutted over her, making no movement, no sound. He might have forced her to agree to this but she would make sure he had as little pleasure from it as possible.

The pain seemed to burn right to her chest, she felt sure she was fatally split but clenched her fists and stayed absolutely still.

Suddenly it was over and Angus, damp with sweat, collapsed on top of her, panting heavily. Finally he hauled himself off her and moved away, pulling his clothes on in silence.

At last he was fully dressed. 'If you want me to keep to my side of the bargain you will have to learn to be more welcoming in future.'

'In future? You will come here again?' The words rasped in her throat.

'Of course. I shall expect your door to always be unlocked when I am at home, Morag,' he warned her.

As the door closed quietly behind him, Morag turned her face into her pillow and sobbed.

On the floor below, Katrina Fraser lingered at her door long enough to hear her husband's soft footsteps returning down the stairs before slipping back into bed.

The knowledge that Gus had enticed her maid to share her bed with him did not disturb Katrina unduly. Gus became very rapidly bored with these unsophisticated girls and they certainly weren't a threat to her own position. The McDonald girl would be no different and she would distract his attention from her, reducing his demands to a quick, dutiful performance in the quest for an heir. Perhaps she would be wise to turn a blind eye, in the hope that it would encourage him to stay in Strathannan, away from the more serious temptations of the capital.

Katrina was not naive enough to suppose her husband, a notorious womaniser before their marriage, would remain faithful while he was away from the estate. From time to time rumours reached even her relatively remote corner and Katrina knew his name had been associated with more than one society lady. And those were the alliances which really frightened her because, if she failed to give him what he wanted – and the signs were not encouraging – one of those women could ultimately replace her. If that happened she could find herself reduced to nothing, her ambitions in ruins. No, she decided, frowning at the half-written letter to her mother, a little harmless fun with an inconsequential housemaid, someone under her own eye, was infinitely preferable to a liaison with another wealthy socialite.

Morag was so preoccupied that she hardly noticed the first real day of spring as she followed the familiar path to the cottage. Last night Sir Angus had again come to her room, as he had done every night for the past week.

128

Now her body ached with fatigue and her eyes were still gritty with the tears which had kept her awake long after he had gone back to the warmth and comfort of his own bed. Above her the skies were blue, streaked with light white clouds, the hills sharp and clear in mottled green and brown and the trees were budding with promise. The air was warm, the breeze gentle and filled with the bright sound of birds, released at last from the chill starvation of winter. Plodding on, her head bowed by shame and anger, her heart filled with hatred, she saw nothing of the emerging season.

As she rounded the corner in the track and saw the little house, in its dank, shadowed corner, she was aware, for the first time, of the place as her mother saw it. Dark, chill and untouched by the new season. Sighing she walked on, knowing her mother would already have seen her approaching, wondering if her welcome would be a warm one. Since her last visit, when they had parted on bad terms, she had heard nothing from her mother and, despite her resolution not to blame her mother for what had happened to her since, she could not banish the feelings of anger and bitterness from her mind.

'Morag!' Annie stepped from the door and waved cheerfully and Morag relaxed a fraction, quickening her step.

'How are you, Mam?' she asked, kissing her mother's cheek as they went inside.

'Och, I'm fine. Uncomfortable, but that's only natural,' Annie admitted.

'And Dad?' Morag looked at her father who was sleeping in his chair.

Annie sighed. 'He's not been so good this month. The pain in his head gets worse and there are days when he doesn't know where he is, thinks he's back on the hills.'

129

'Maybe you should ask the doctor to look at him,' Morag suggested.

'And where would I get the money to pay him? In any case there's nothing to be done. I always knew he would get worse.' She sounded resigned as she handed Morag a cup of steaming tea. 'It'll be easier when I'm back to normal.'

Morag smiled and let her mother chat on, unwilling to destroy the easy atmosphere before she had to. It was another hour before she finally broached the subject which had brought her here.

'Mam, did you go and see Uncle Rab?' she asked, trying to sound casual.

Annie bridled at once. 'Morag, I thought I had made it clear to you. Mind your own business.'

'It is my business, Mam,' Morag said, so angrily that Annie looked startled. 'Sir Angus called me in to see him and asked about the rent money.'

'Sir Angus?' Annie repeated. 'But why?'

'To ask what you were going to do about it,' Morag prevaricated, unable to tell the complete truth.

'When was this?'

'Two weeks ago. On the Friday after I came to see you last time.'

'Och, that's all right then,' Annie sighed.

'All right?' Morag was astounded. 'All right for me to be told about it, to have him threaten you with eviction? He means it, Mam. He will put you out if we don't pay the arrears. We have got to do something,' Morag pleaded desperately. The thought of the debt remaining unpaid, of having to continue to allow Sir Angus Fraser to take his payment in that other way, made her feel sick.

'Mind your tone when you talk to me!' Annie snapped. 'If you had given me half a chance I would

130

have told you it's taken care of. The rent is paid.'

'Thank God.' Morag breathed a long sigh of relief and fell back against her chair. 'Thank God. But how? Where did the money come from? Was it Uncle Rab?'

'No, it was not Rab Bannerman,' Annie answered slowly. 'Though, to give him his due, he did offer. No, it was your brothers. I wrote to them as soon as you left. Iain and Billy came here on Friday with the cash. They gave it to Sir Angus themselves on Friday night, along with the rent for the next two months. They're sending us a wee bit every week, just until I'm fit to work again. They're good lads,' she added softly.

'Sir Angus had his money on Friday night?' Before he had come to her room for the first time. Morag knew she was going to be sick, rushed wildly for the closet.

'Morag, are you all right?' Annie was waiting for her outside the rickety, timber door and put her arm round her daughter as they walked back up the garden to the house.

'Yes, yes, I'm all right,' Morag sobbed through streaming tears.

'Och, lass, I'd no idea you were so worried. Surely you knew your brothers would help?'

'I never even thought about them,' Morag admitted miserably.

'Come on, lass. Stop that crying. Didn't I tell you to mind your own business? Did you think I would do nothing?'

'I'm sorry,' Morag sobbed, managing to smile. 'I wish you'd told me, that's all.'

'Well, it's all sorted now and that's the main thing. And next time, Morag, leave me to deal with my own problems.'

SEVEN

T he expression on Sir Angus's face as he drove up Pitochrie Castle's drive was one of extreme petulance. He would have much preferred to stay in London where a certain beautiful lady had made the recent past such a pleasure, but it was six weeks since he had been in Strathannan and he was duty bound to return.

It was already May and still Katrina showed no sign of producing the heir he so badly needed. He had given her every opportunity to do her duty, so she had only herself to blame now that he had decided to carry out his threat and instigate divorce proceedings. Telling her was not something he looked forward to so he would leave it until Monday morning and then beat a hasty retreat back to London. In the meantime, if Katrina decided to be difficult he could always console himself with the little McDonald girl. Not that that was likely to be very rewarding. Morag McDonald had been a tremendous disappointment. He had expected her temperament to match her flaming hair, expected passion and excitement, but in bed she had lain as woodenly as Katrina. In fact, in the dark, it would be hard to know which woman was beneath him. No, he decided, he couldn't expect much fun here this weekend. The sooner he got back to London, and to the warmer, more welcoming arms of Annabella Crichton, the better.

Katrina heard the car crunch on the gravel and knew

it was Gus without even having to look. Waving away Morag's anxious offer of help, she hurried to look herself over in the mirror, tweaked her finely curling hair and hurried downstairs to give him an enthusiastic welcome.

Angus, who was used to his wife greeting him with cool dignity after he had puffed his way up a hundred stairs to her sitting room, was astounded.

'You look lovely, my dear,' he complimented her, realising that she did indeed look absolutely ravishing. Perhaps it was simply because she was smiling, when the best he was normally offered was a cool nod and a faintly irritated frown.

'It must be the weather,' she laughed. 'Isn't it wonderful? I'm just going to have tea on the lawn. Why don't you freshen up and then join me?'

'Yes. I'll do that. Thank you, my dear.' Aware of the watching servants who all seemed as bemused by the change in their mistress as he was, he pecked her on the cheek, though she looked lovely enough to take straight upstairs to bed, and took himself indoors.

He handed his cane and hat to Morag who was waiting with lowered, hate-filled eyes. If her identity registered with him he gave no sign of it but went bounding up the stairs to his room.

Half an hour later, Angus and Katrina were comfortably ensconced in wicker chairs set up on the lush lawns at the back of the house enjoying cucumber sandwiches, delicate cakes and Darjeeling tea poured into delicate porcelain from a silver teapot. Sheltered from the sun by the dappled shade of a venerable oak, they could have been in the south of England. But the unique architecture of their rather forbidding house and the magnificent backdrop of blue and green hills behind it

133

were undeniably Scottish. Angus and Katrina however seemed impervious to the beauty and talked almost exclusively about the delights of London. Encouraged by Katrina, Angus told her of the latest gossip, the scandals, the fashions. She listened with unfeigned fascination, longing for the day when she might, at last, join him there and have her share of pleasure. The conviviality lasted throughout the evening and by the time they retired to bed, Angus was in a very mellow mood.

Katrina waited until Angus clambered enthusiastically into bed beside her. Encouraged by her happy disposition he did not foresee the need to visit Morag that night and turned to his wife, reaching for her soft breasts.

Katrina placed a smooth hand over his questing fingers and stilled them. 'I don't think that would be very wise, Gus.'

He drew his hand away as if stung. 'Damn it, Katrina,' he muttered angrily. 'You could have warned me that you are indisposed.' He assumed her reluctance was due to the usual monthly incapacitation.

She laughed, a high, gleeful chuckle. 'No, it's not that, Angus. In fact it's quite the opposite.'

He stared at her for a full minute as understanding dawned. 'Do you mean that you are pregnant?' he asked at last.

'Yes!' She confirmed it triumphantly.

'Why didn't you tell me before?' he asked.

'I wanted to choose the best time, Gus, to tell you in private, without the servants watching.'

'Well,' he blustered, 'that's marvellous.' But she had given him similar news on other occasions. 'Are you sure? Have you seen the doctor?'

'I spoke with him this morning. All being well your son will be born some time in November.'

Angus felt a sense of profound relief, tempered by the knowledge that her previous pregnancies had ended in disaster. If only she could produce an heir this time, how much easier it would be. After all, Katrina and he suited one another. She allowed him sufficient freedom to enjoy himself without finding it necessary to make ridiculous scenes about unimportant things. He would be very fortunate to find another woman who was prepared to be quite so understanding.

'You will have to take great care of yourself,' he warned her.

'Yes, Gus, I am well aware of that. Which is why you must be patient with me. You do understand, don't you, that I cannot share my bed with you until after the child is born? The doctor did say it would be foolish to take any risks.'

He grunted. 'I suppose so.'

'Don't look like that,' she teased, too excited by her own condition to be offended by his manner. 'You will have your little boy before Christmas, Gus, I promise you that much. And then it will all seem worthwhile.'

'Yes, and if it is a boy, then you will find me very grateful, my dear,' he promised. 'Now. I will sleep in my own room so that you can get your proper rest.'

'All right. Goodnight, Gus.' She offered a smooth cheek which he duly kissed.

Five minutes later Angus was creeping up the stairs. His body, teased into hot anticipation by his wife, was burning for relief. Glancing furtively along the corridor to make sure he wasn't going to be seen, he hurried to Morag's door and tried the handle. It was locked. Angus knocked as loudly as he could and was rewarded by nothing more than total silence. Again he knocked then, giving in to a fit of frustrated temper, lashed out with his finely shod feet, bruising his toes, all to no avail. Eventually he was forced to admit defeat and creep all the way back down the stairs to his cold and slightly damp bed.

In the bed she shared with Coll, Annie McDonald eased her swollen body into a different position, searching vainly for comfort. It made no difference. Whatever way she lay the child seemed like a leaden weight, dragging at her back. She sighed and got up, hoping a drink might ease her and allow her some sleep.

Padding softly to the door, trying desperately not to disturb Coll, she slipped out into the moonlight. For the time of year, mid-May, it was unseasonably warm and she felt a desperate need for some fresh air. The moon was high and bright, illuminating the hill tops with eerie light. Looking up at them from her front door, Annie longed to be up there, where there were no huge trees to hem her in, where the view stretched for mile after mile, back into the highlands she loved. But even the forest seemed more benign tonight with the silvery light opening up the dark shadows which made night-time trips to the privie a frightening experience. As she stood on her doorstep, looking down the long track, a fox darted out of the undergrowth and crossed to the other side, the light glancing off its coat. It stopped, ears erect, then hurried on. Above her something flew low then settled on a tree, hooting softly. On any other night the noise would have scared her but tonight she felt an unusual calm. Even the child in her womb had stilled.

Annie finished her drink then crossed the garden to the closet, feeling a sudden need to empty her bladder. The rush of liquid that erupted from her, accompanied by the first tightening of her womb, was so unexpected that for several minutes she simply sat where she was. Then, moving cautiously, she made her way back to the cottage and crept into bed.

Minutes later another contraction gripped her, bringing a hint of pain with it. Annie tensed then relaxed as it passed off. The old clock on the dresser had shown a few minutes after two. All six previous labours had been long, well over sixteen hours, so there was plenty of time yet.

Three hours later the pain was so fierce that she was beaded with sweat. Coll turned but, thanks to the medicine he now took as a matter of routine every night, did not wake. In between pains Annie was getting anxious. Finty Chisholm had promised to attend her and, well aware of Coll's inability to fetch help should it be needed, had arranged for one or other of her own seven children to call at the cottage every day after school to see that everything was all right, though no one expected anything to happen for at least another three weeks yet. Annie already knew that by four o'clock this afternoon she would no longer need the midwife's help. That left Morag. The girl had arranged to give up her half days for the past month so that she could take an hour off each morning to check on her mother. But it had been after eleven before she had appeared yesterday and Annie feared that even that might be too late. Another pain gripped her, tearing viciously into her abdomen. Well, she told herself when it was over, she had birthed four live and three dead children already and whatever happened this time it couldn't possibly be any worse than bringing the twins into the world. They had both greeted life with the soles of their feet, causing Annie an agony she would never forget. Surely this child would be easier and it wasn't as if she didn't know what to expect. So, if the child wouldn't wait, she would just have to deliver it herself.

Cook came into the kitchen wearing a wide smile. 'Well, here's some braw news,' she announced. 'Lady Katrina's expecting a bairn. Now,' she said over the hubbub of chatter from young Chrissy, Flo and Morag, 'we all know what happened before and she's very anxious to take good care of herself this time. Sir Angus doesn't want her doing anything too taxing and the doctor has told her to rest up.' She turned to Morag. 'It'll mean more work for you, lass. She'll want her breakfast in bed and she doesn't like being on her own for too long so you'll likely have to sit with her from time to time.'

'Yes, Mrs McManus.' Morag was pleased for her mistress but dismayed at the thought of running up and down all those stairs, fetching and carrying. Lady Katrina, though usually fair, could be very demanding. Enforced idleness was likely to bring out the worst in her.

'Oh, and I'm sorry lass but I don't think I can let you home to see your mother every morning now. If Lady Katrina rings for you and you're not here there'll be real trouble. I daren't risk it.'

'Can I just go this morning, Mrs McManus, please? Then I can tell her to make some other arrangement.'

Cook was well aware of Annie McDonald's predicament but her first responsibility was the smooth running of this household. 'No, lass. I can't let you do that. You'll have to make do with your usual half day from now on. I'll let you have Thursday afternoon. You can tell her then.' Seeing Morag's worried face she added, 'Och, look, I've to go into the village myself this morning. If you like, I'll give Finty Chisholm a message and ask her to call in to see her.'

'Thank you, Mrs McManus.' And Morag had to be satisfied with that.

Mrs McManus was longer in the village than she had expected to be. By the time she had called into the fleshers to berate him for daring to send inferior beef to the house and had then lingered to chat with Mysie Arneil, she was well behind time. Instead of the leisurely stroll she usually enjoyed, Mrs McManus found herself bustling back along the path with flurried haste. Only when she got to the fork on the track did she remember her promise to Morag. There was no question of going back to give Finty her message now. If she did that she would never have lunch ready on time. But her conscience stabbed her. She could see the McDonald cottage at the bottom of the other track. If she hurried she would just have time to call in on Annie McDonald in person. And it would be interesting to see Coll. Rumour had it that he was little better than a madman these days.

Five minutes later she was rapping loudly on the door, then when she got no reply, she banged again. Impatience getting the better of her, Mrs McManus shoved the door open and stepped inside, her eyes taking a few seconds to adjust to the gloom after the bright sunshine.

When she could see clearly her heart contracted in fear.

Annie lay back on her pillows, her sweat-drenched face pallid and contorted in pain. When the contraction passed she looked up and gasped with shock. 'Mrs McManus!'

'I came to tell you Morag can't come the day,' the older woman gabbled. 'It's Lady Katrina. She's pregnant and needs looking after.' While she spoke she fidgeted nervously. The title of Mrs went with her position in the household but in fact she had never been married. She certainly had no first-hand experience of birth and had not the faintest idea of what to do. The sight of Coll, slumped in a chair, clasping his head in his hands and moaning like an animal, added to her panic.

'Mrs McManus I'm right glad to see you. Could you please get a message to Finty Chisholm for me?' Annie got her plea out between shafts of pain, seemingly unaware that she was half naked, the sheet slipping from her straining body, her legs drawn up in agony, very nearly exposing areas which, in Mrs McManus's opinion, no one else should ever see.

'Yes. Yes. I'll see to it.' Cook was already on her way out, glad to escape, terrified of her inability to cope with the situation, embarrassed by what little she had seen. Slamming the door she fled.

The last time Cook had moved so swiftly she had been plain Peggy McManus, running errands as a kitchen maid. She practically flew up the track and arrived at the Lodge gates in a lather of sweat and confusion.

'Whoa there,' Rab called, having seen her frantic approach. 'What on earth's wrong with you, woman?'

Suddenly aware of the picture she must present, Mrs McManus made a valiant effort to collect herself. Gasping for breath, sweat trickling down the sides of her scarlet face, she blabbed. 'I'm needing to send for Finty Chisholm. I'll send one of the gardener's lads.'

'You've just come from the village. Is she not there?' Rab asked. 'And if it's for Lady Katrina surely it's the doctor you're needing?'

'No. It has to be Finty. She specially asked for Finty. Och, out of my way, Mr Bannerman. That woman's about to drop her wean and no one there to help her.'

In a horrible flash of understanding Rab knew who she was talking about. 'Annie McDonald? Is it Annie McDonald you're meaning?'

'Aye. And who else did you think was about to give birth?' she retorted impatiently, forgetting the respect his position merited.

'But the bairn's not due for three or four weeks yet.'

'Tell that to Mrs McDonald!' Cook was too flustered to wonder how Rab Bannerman came to know so much about Annie's dates.

'You go back and stay with her. I'll go for help,' Rab ordered.

'I can't do that. What would Sir Angus say?' She was terrified by the very idea, knew she would never cope. 'I've to get back. I'm late as it is.'

'Go on then,' he dismissed her angrily. 'I'll deal with it.'

In a froth of relief Mrs McManus scurried up the drive, eager to deliver her news. To her intense disappointment Morag was busy with Lady Katrina and, out of fairness, Cook knew she could say nothing until she had spoken with the girl. If she was to get any work out of her today it was probably best to leave telling her until there was some positive news. She could hardly admit what sort of confusion she had left at the cottage.

Rab hurried up to the house, searching in vain for the gardener's lads only to discover they were both over at Ewart Morrison's farm, collecting seed potatoes.

Judging by Cook's agitated state there was no time to lose so he helped himself to Sir Angus's best horse, saddled him quickly and set off at a gallop for the village. As luck would have it Finty Chisholm had been called to aid Teg Robertson's wife, who had just miscarried her twelfth child, and wasn't expected back in the village for

141

some time. Rab could do nothing more than leave an urgent message for her. That done he got back on the horse and rode to the McDonald cottage.

He knocked but, getting no reply, let himself in. His only concern was for Annie whose distress was evident.

'Rab!' she cried through the pain which now seemed to assault her without stop.

'It's all right,' he said, feeling some of Mrs McManus's helplessness. 'Finty will be here soon.'

'I need her now!' Annie grunted, trying to resist the terrible urge to bear down. Too late he realised his mistake, knew he should have brought some other woman here with him. 'Hold on, Annie. She won't be long.'

'Coll,' she gasped. 'See to Coll.' Abruptly she flopped back against the pillows, glad of a brief respite from the pain. 'Give him some medicine. It's the brown bottle, under the sink. Two spoonfuls.'

For the first time Rab thought about Coll and looked round, trying to find him. He was huddled in a chair, shoved into the furthermost corner, his hands clasped round his head which was bent almost to his thighs.

The bottle was where Annie said it would be. Rab took it to Coll and gently tried to ease the man's head up. To his surprise Coll had tears in his eyes and seemed to be perfectly clear headed, though in pain and extremely distressed.

'I never thought I'd see the day when I'd welcome you into my house again, Rab Bannerman,' Coll said with an echo of his old humour. 'But I'm right glad to see you now.'

Rab's hand shook as he poured the medicine. The sight of his old friend had driven even thoughts of Annie from his mind. Coll was thin, gaunt faced and hollow eyed, almost unrecognisable. His hair was thin, faded to a dull sandy colour and his eyes were huge, dark orbs.

'Here, take this.' Rab offered the spoon then went to pour a second dose.

'No,' Coll stopped him. 'I don't want to sleep, not today. I'll just have enough to ease the pain. I can't think when it's this bad. I'm no use to her, no bloody use at all.'

'Just sit still, Coll, give it a chance to take effect. I'll sit with Annie until you're ready.'

Coll closed his eyes and nodded, wincing at the pain the motion caused, but then caught Rab's arm with a burning hand. 'Look after her, Rab.'

Rab nodded.

'Is he all right?' Annie asked, her voice tense and clipped.

'Aye. I've given him some medicine.' Rab felt useless, didn't know what to do, where to look. When Annie groaned, her face contorting, turning scarlet with effort, he shuffled around uncomfortably.

As she relaxed Annie found the energy to laugh. 'Well, that's the first time I've seen you stumped, Rab Bannerman. Och, it's only nature taking her course and nothing to be afraid of,' she said, gritting her teeth in preparation for the next contraction. 'Hold my hand, Rab. That's all you need to do. Hold my hand and don't let go.'

Sometime in the next half hour as Annie's child battled its way free, Coll came to stand beside her. 'You're doing well, lass,' he said, propping himself up and stroking her face gently.

'Aye, too well,' she answered. 'This bairn has no intention of waiting for Finty Chisholm. It's coming now!'

Rab had carefully positioned himself so that he was

looking back, over her head, hoping to spare them all some embarrassment. Despite the note of desperation in Annie's voice he stayed precisely where he was.

'Oh God . . .' Annie groaned, pushing until her veins bulged. 'For goodness sake, will one of you help me!' she cried, past caring which one of them it was.

Coll hobbled to Rab's side. 'Rab, please, I can't do this. You have to help her.'

'No,' Rab still didn't turn round. 'It's your place, Coll.'

'And how the bloody hell can I help?' Coll roared. 'I need both hands on these crutches just to keep myself upright. Get off that bloody chair and help her! I'll stand right behind you, but you've got to help her.'

But it was Annie's agonised scream that finally got Rab to his feet. Like Coll he had seen enough animals making their bloodied entrance into the world to have some idea of what to expect and he placed himself between Annie's legs, rolling his sleeves above his elbows and looking a great deal calmer than he felt.

'There. Look. There's its head! One more shove Annie. One more.' Coll wobbled dangerously on his crutches and strained forward to watch as his friend's huge hands cradled the emerging head.

'That's it, lass. And again.' Coll called encouragement to his scarlet-faced wife as the child slithered into Rab's arms.

'It's a lassie,' he called jubilantly, jerking forward so violently that he finally lost his balance and clattered to the floor. 'I'm all right. I'm all right,' he groaned.

Annie was already sitting forward, anxious for a first glimpse of the child and caught Rab's eyes as he looked up at her.

Rab struggled to contain his emotion, managed to stop tears actually rolling down his cheeks as he turned the infant and placed her gently on her mother's stomach. 'It's a wee girl,' he choked. 'The bonniest wee girl.'

The child stirred, opened her eyes briefly, giving a flash of brilliant blue, and flailed her tiny fists.

'What the devil's going on here?' Finty Chisholm burst into the room, tossed her coat on to the floor and elbowed Rab aside, her sense of decency outraged. 'For goodness sake, let's get you covered up and sorted out, lass. You men ... out! Outside. Now.'

His eyes still swimming with tears Rab made his way to the sink, sloshed water over his arms then joined Coll at the door. He helped him hop over the high step into the garden then sat on the low wall beside him. In his mind he carried a picture of those little eyes, that brilliant blue, a blue that belonged to neither Coll nor Annie. But what about the fine cap of sandy hair? In that second Rab understood he would never know who had really fathered the child, knew too that it no longer mattered.

Beside him Coll smiled gently. 'I owe you my thanks, Rab,' he said. 'I don't know what would have happened if you hadn't been there.'

Rab grunted, embarrassed. 'I think Annie would have coped.'

'Aye. Maybe so. She's a fine woman. But just the same.' He held out his hand and Rab grasped it firmly.

'I've missed our friendship,' Rab said eventually. 'It's not been the same.'

'Nor will it be,' Coll answered, making Rab glance sharply at him. 'Och, that doesn't mean what you think it does. It did something to me, that fall, the bang on the head. Sweet Lord I can't tell you about the pain, what it does to me. Sometimes it's that bad I'd do anything to be rid of it. That medicine's the only thing that gives me

145

any peace. And Annie too. It's better I take it than not. Sometimes the pain, it makes me do things, say things, terrible things. Like the real me is somewhere else, watching and listening, but not able to stop it. That's when I take the medicine and it's like everything gets muffled. I got to like the stuff. Like it too much. I can't manage without it now. Spend half my bloody life in pain and the other half in a daze.'

'It's all right, Coll. You don't have to explain.'

'Aye. Aye, I do. You don't understand. I never really blamed you. It was just an excuse. I hated you because you had everything. I was just a cripple, a mad cripple at that. I was afraid she'd leave me, scared she'd end up with you after all. After what you did for me, I didn't trust you with her. My best friend since we were just wee lads and I didn't trust you with my wife.' Coll rubbed his brow, trying to keep the pain at bay.

Rab swallowed hard, was unable to stop his mind going back nine months in time. He swallowed the painful lump in his throat and rasped, 'Forget it, Coll. It's over and done with. I'm still your friend, no matter what. And proud to have you call me your friend too.'

'That's good to know, Rab.' Coll winced and rubbed his forehead again. 'It's this bloody pain, it'll do for me in the end. I know it. She knows it too. Och, you never think you'll come to this.' He groaned and stood up, hitching himself onto his crutches. 'I'm not meaning to embarrass you, Rab, but you don't know what it's like. I'm more often off my head than anything else these days. God knows when I'll be able to talk honestly to you again.'

'It's just the medicine, Coll. Maybe if you cut down?'

'No, it's not that. I used to kid myself it was, but it's me, and it's getting worse.' He hobbled a few yards down the garden then swung round awkwardly. 'Just promise me one thing?'

'Name it.'

'Annie and the bairn. And young Morag. Look out for them, Rab. If anything happens to me, keep an eye on them for me.'

'Nothing's going to happen to you. You're better today. Maybe this bairn's what you needed.'

'Just promise me, Rab,' Coll insisted.

'I promise. I never did stop watching out for them, Coll.'

'Right then. If you two have finished with your blethering there's a young lady in there waiting for her daddy to give her a name,' Finty's strident voice broke the spell holding the two men.

'Right, lad, help me through this door then,' Coll said, waiting for Rab.

'No, I'll away home.'

'And start Annie thinking I've fallen out with you again?' Coll asked, leaving his friend no choice but to follow him into the house.

'There you are! And I was starting to think you'd gone off to celebrate without first having a look at her now she's all clean and sweet,' Annie greeted them. 'Come and have a good look at your daughter, Coll.'

Rab watched as Coll duly examined his perfectly formed daughter. When his turn came she seemed too small, too delicate for his large hands and he contented himself by running a finger through the downy crown of hair.

'And what are we to call her, Coll?' Annie asked, sitting upright in her bed and looking happy but tired.

Coll shrugged. 'I can't say I know much about lassies' names,' he said sinking into his chair and looking suddenly exhausted.

'What about Ayleen?' Annie asked. 'I've always liked it. It was your mother's name, Rab, wasn't it?'

'Aye, that's right. Ayleen Finlay McCracken Torrence. And then she stuck Bannerman on the end of it all when she married my father. When anyone asked her name she gave them the whole lot,' he chuckled.

'She was a kind-hearted woman. I was fond of her too. I never met anyone who could find a bad word to say about her. I'd like to think my daughter could be like her.'

For the third time that afternoon Rab found himself choked with emotion. He stood and kissed Annie lightly on the forehead. 'Well, with parents like you, the lassie's got a good start. Now, I'd better away home and give the good news to that other daughter of yours.'

Katrina Fraser was determined to make the most of her pregnancy. Even in the warmest days of summer, when the sun streamed into her bedroom, making it unbearably stuffy, she never woke before eleven. She then expected breakfast to be served to her, in bed, the minute she rang for it. Cook was obliged to abandon whatever she was doing and rush to prepare her mistress's tray which Morag then carried upstairs. Minutes later the bell would ring again. Time and again Morag toiled all the way upstairs to find Katrina picking at her food, complaining that it was too cold, too hot, overcooked or not what she had ordered. Morag had no choice but to return the tray to the kitchen and ask for something else, often finding herself the target of Mrs McManus's wrath as a result. Some mornings the bell rang six times inside an hour. Morag would arrive hot and breathless merely to be asked to straighten the covers or even to pass a paper from the bedside table. But at least she didn't have to worry about Sir Angus who had gone to India in some sort of diplomatic role and wasn't expected back until the early winter, the announcement of which had sent Lady Katrina into such a fit of furious temper that the doctor had had to be sent for.

'I'm not surprised you're always so tired,' Cook chided Morag one morning as she sat bleary eyed over breakfast. 'You don't eat enough to keep a sparrow alive. Get that inside you, lass. If you take ill you'll be no help to anyone, least of all that poor mother of yours.'

Sighing, Morag applied herself to clearing the bowl of creamy porridge which had been set in front of her. Though, as for cook's claim that she was losing weight, Morag knew the opposite was true if the size of her stomach was anything to go by. She had a bulge under her apron, luckily hidden by the full skirted dress, which was almost a big as the one flaunted by Lady Katrina.

Cook jumped and looked up in irritation when Morag dropped her spoon, sending it clattering to the floor. 'For goodness sake, Morag. Wake yourself up. If you've finished there I'm sure you should be starting to do Lady Katrina's sitting room.'

Morag, white faced and panic stricken, escaped, running up the stairs to her room and shut herself in with her fear. Trembling, she counted back to those nights when Sir Angus had visited her room. It had been early March and since then she had not seen her monthly flow, had been so concerned with other things that until now she hadn't even noticed. But she had never needed to keep track of it before.

Shivering despite the summer warmth she stripped off her clothes and ran her hands over the firm roundness of her stomach, pressing gently. And her breasts were bigger too, the nipples larger, browner.

149

Still shaking she dressed again. It couldn't be true. This couldn't be happening, not to her. Surely this sort of thing only happened to married people. But her own sister-in-law, Davy's wife, had found herself pregnant before marriage. God, how little she really knew about things which mattered. Slumping down on the bed, Morag knew it was true, knew that just as ewes produced lambs after the rams had mounted them – something it had been hard to avoid seeing on the hillsides – it was perfectly possible for her to produce a child after allowing Sir Angus to do something very similar with her.

Somehow she got through the day, fighting feelings of rising dread, wondering what she could do. She certainly couldn't turn to her mother for help. Annie was a strict, church-going woman and would be shocked to the core to think that her own daughter could do such a thing. And if her father found out the shock could kill him. Nor could she possibly face her uncle Rab with something like this. She couldn't bear for him to know about her shame. And she had to keep it from Mrs McManus. A disgrace such as this would bring instant dismissal. The one person she could conceivably approach, Sir Angus, wasn't even in the country. But surely, when she told him what had happened, he would help her. After all, this would be his child and she had heard them say how much he wanted a son. She would just need to wait and, if this horrible thing was true, speak to him about it when he got back. Morag counted. Nine months from March took her into early December, very close to the time Lady Katrina expected her child to be born. Dear God, she prayed. Let him come back in time.

That night she locked herself in her room and painstakingly unpicked her spare uniform, letting it out to

150

hide her rounded belly. In her closet she had one pair of stays, passed down to her by her sister-in-law but, until now, never worn. As soon as her increasing girth started to become noticeable she would lace herself into them and no one would ever know.

While Katrina's pregnancy proceeded without alarms, Morag hid her own gently expanding figure under the stays. But as early as August they were biting into her and she knew she couldn't hope to conceal her condition indefinitely. Unable to face the thought of what might happen to her in the future she worked on doggedly, pinning all her hopes on the return of Sir Angus.

Then, just before midday on a late September day which was full of the burnished colours of autumn, when the hills were at their magnificent best, clothed in misty, purple softness, Morag heard a carriage in the drive. Katrina's doctor, who came from over the county border, in Perthshire, wasn't due to make a call here today, and none of Katrina's few friends were likely to make an unannounced visit at this time of the day. The only other person likely to arrive unexpectedly was Sir Angus himself. But surely it was too soon for him to be coming home? Her heart thumping with hope Morag flew to the window of Katrina's bedroom and peered out.

'Who is it?' Katrina called from the dressing table.

'I don't know.' Morag stood as close to the glass as she could but the house was so tall that any vehicle coming to a stop close to the lower walls could not be seen from up here.

'Quickly, girl. Come and finish my hair.' Katrina, who was heartily fed up with her own company, knew it couldn't possibly be Gus but she was so bored that any visitor was welcome.

Morag secured Katrina's wispy blonde hair with trembling fingers which suddenly lacked their usual skill. Katrina was too excited to notice and span round eagerly when there was a loud knock at her door. 'Who is it?' she demanded, not giving Flo time to speak.

'Two gentlemen, Ma'am. A Mr Menzies and a Mr Lawrie, his assistant.' She held a gold edged card out to Katrina.

Katrina turned it over in her fingers, a puzzled frown on her face. Menzies was a colleague of Angus's. If this meant, as she was beginning to suspect it might, that Angus was going to be delayed she would be very angry indeed. 'Show them into the drawing room. I'll be down as soon as I can.'

'Yes, ma'am.'

Katrina took her time, already composing, in her mind, the biting letter she would despatch to Gus if her supposition proved correct. This was his son and heir she was carrying, ruining her figure, keeping her penned up in this dreary backwater, and now it looked very much as if he wouldn't even be home in time for the birth. She had been absolutely enraged when he had told her about the trip in the first place and had only been placated when he had vowed to be home before the birth. And now this.

In the dining room, where she was now setting the table for luncheon, Morag was conscious of hurrying foot-steps and an unusual babble of urgent voices. Laying the knife in place and pausing briefly to check that the table was correctly set out, she made her way back to the kitchen, anxious to know the cause of the disturbance.

'There you are, Morag! I want you to telephone and

get Doctor Drummond here at once. Hurry now. I would have done it myself but you know how I hate that contraption.' Cook flapped her hands, obviously in a state of near panic. 'Och, it's awful, terrible. What on earth will the poor woman do now,' she wailed.

'What's wrong?' Morag directed her question at Flo because Cook was clearly beyond a sensible answer.

'It's Sir Angus,' Flo whispered. 'He's dead.'

'Dead?' Morag repeated, conscious of a strange rushing noise in her ears.

'Aye. Cholera. In India. He's been dead for weeks.'

But Morag heard no more. The rushing noise had filled her head with whirling blackness and she crumpled to the floor without a sound.

When she opened her eyes again Cook was waving something under her nose, making her eyes water.

'For goodness sake, Morag. Lady Katrina needs you up there with her. Pull yourself together, lass.' She jerked round as Flo came back into the room. 'Did you get through to the doctor?' she asked.

Flo nodded. 'Aye. He'll be here as soon as he can. And Mrs McFarlane sends her respects.'

'It'll be all round Strathannan by now then,' Cook commented, knowing full well that the telephone operator at Glenelg could rival Finty Chisholm as a source of gossip.

From the sink, where young Chrissy, the maid of all work, was up to her elbows in greasy water, came the sound of howling.

'Och, in the name . . . !' Cook hissed. 'Stop that awful noise and get on with what you're doing.' Cook knew the girl 'wasn't all there' but had little time to spare for her now. 'Flo, come and see to Morag. As soon as she's able send her up to Lady Katrina.'

With that she puffed her own flustered way upstairs to tend to her mistress.

'Come on, I'll help you up on to a chair.' Flo eased her arms round Morag and dragged her into a seat at the table. Morag groaned and looked as if she was about to pass out again.

'No, I'm all right,' she coughed when Flo waved the smelling salts under her nose again.

They sat on for a few minutes, the silence broken only by young Chrissy's continuous sniffing. Finally Morag struggled to her feet.

'I'd best go upstairs,' she said.

Flo nodded but as Morag made her way slowly across the kitchen Flo's eyes followed her very closely indeed.

When the doctor eventually arrived he gave Katrina something to make her sleep and left a small bottle of liquid to be taken, if it was needed, in the night.

'You will have to take great care of her,' he warned Morag. 'A shock like this could cause untold harm to the baby.'

Katrina, watched over by Morag who made up a bed on the floor of her room, slept fitfully, waking in the night and sobbing quietly until Morag persuaded her to take another draught of medicine.

In the morning she woke heavy eyed, complaining of a headache, but refused another dose of medicine. To Morag's surprise she insisted on getting out of bed at her usual time.

'The doctor will be back soon. I think you should stay in your bed until he comes. You have to think of the baby,' she chided gently.

'I am only going to sit by the window,' Katrina promised, her face looking drawn, her eyes swollen.

And there she sat, not moving, all day, watching the steady stream of callers, who came to offer condolences. The doctor, when he arrived, announced that Katrina was better than he had expected her to be and saw no reason to come back for anything other than his regular call, unless he was asked to do so.

By the end of the week it was clear that Katrina, still pale, and swathed in black, which made her look fragile and vulnerable, had weathered the worst of the shock.

The servants, wearing black armbands, went about their duties as quietly as possible and Morag, no longer needed at Lady Katrina's side at night, went back to her own room.

Since that awful announcement in the kitchen she had lived in a state of numbed shock, performing her duties automatically, her brain mired in despair. Until then she had almost blocked the reality of her situation from her mind, telling herself that when Sir Angus came home, he would know what to do. His death had destroyed her last hope.

It was another two weeks before the memorial service was held in the village kirk and a stone erected to Sir Angus's memory in the corner of the churchyard reserved for the Frasers. When most of the mourners had gone, Katrina finally turned to face the two men and one woman who had remained. Her expression was stony.

'Well, Edward, I believe you wanted to speak with me? Now is as good a time as any,' she said, dislike plain in her voice.

'First, let me say again how very sorry I am. You have our greatest sympathy, my dear. Angus was a wonderful man. He will be greatly missed.' Edward Fraser, Angus's cousin, smiled unctuously and pulled at the points of his straining waistcoat. He was short, fat and bumptious with a bullying manner and a loud voice. Even more offensive was the smell of camphor and stale sweat he carried with him. Katrina knew it would linger on for hours after he had left.

'Yes. We are very, very sorry,' Emily, his wife, a small, deceptively mousy-looking woman added, barely able to contain her excitement, her avaricious eyes flitting round the room in constant assessment.

'Hmmm.' The other man, older, greyer, cleared his throat obviously.

'Mr Dalrymple,' Edward ushered him forward and he stood, his back to the fire, and shuffled some papers in his hands.

'I feel it would be easier if I tell you, in layman's terms, the essence of your husband's will, Lady Fraser,' Dalrymple said, his pale eyes gentle.

'Thank you, Mr Dalrymple,' Katrina nodded.

'Fortunately Sir Angus had the forethought to make a new will before he set out on his . . . er . . . tragic journey.'

'New will!' Edward exclaimed loudly.

'Yes. Of course it makes little difference in the end but it does clarify matters. It will make things a little easier, you understand.'

'Please go on, Mr Dalrymple,' Katrina said softly, feeling her confidence soar as she caught the uneasy glance between Angus's objectionable cousin and his grasping wife.

'Well, as you know, it was Sir Angus's wish for the Pitochrie estate to remain in the Fraser family, to be under the control of someone of that name. Like most men he arranged for it to pass to the next male heir. I am sure you are all aware of that.'

He waited while they all nodded their assent, Katrina with calm dignity, Edward and Emily with almost indecent enthusiasm.

'In that case I am sure you will be relieved to know that Sir Angus made special provision for this very sad circumstance. I shall read you his very words, added two days before he left the country for India and witnessed by myself.' He cleared his throat again and took two steps forward. ' "If my wife is delivered of a female child, I name my cousin, Edward, or his male descendents, as my heir. If, as is my dearest wish, the child is male, the estate, in its entirety, will pass to him, to be administered on his behalf until he reaches the age of twenty-five, by his mother, my wife, Lady Katrina Fraser." ' The lawyer looked up and addressed Katrina directly. 'Of course, Lady Fraser, provision has been made for you and the child, should it be female. Would you like me to read the relevant passages?'

'No, not now.' Katrina waved her hands, well aware that if she failed to produce a son she would be reduced to a tiny house somewhere with nowhere near enough money to sustain the lifestyle to which she felt entitled. The pleasure she had expected to feel at Edward's discomfiture had evaporated with the sudden realisation that it was by no means certain that she would produce a live child at all, let alone a son.

The lawyer was speaking again. 'Of course, until we know the outcome of . . . of Lady Katrina's . . . er . . . condition the matter cannot be settled. Provision has been made for you to continue as you are until such time . . .'

'Yes, yes, thank you Mr Dalrymple,' she put him out of his embarrassment abruptly. 'Well,' she said, turning to the dumbstruck Edward. 'I don't think there's anything any of us can do for the moment.'

157

'Why wasn't I told?' he blurted out suddenly. 'This is preposterous!'

Katrina rose to her feet, allowing her abdomen to push forward, making her condition obvious to them for the first time. 'And why should I have discussed such a delicate matter with you, Edward?' she demanded furiously.

He glared at her then rounded on the unfortunate lawyer. '*I* am Sir Angus's heir. At the time of his death I was the next in line.'

'I am afraid it is not as simple as that, Mr Fraser,' the lawyer said, his voice carefully neutral. 'It is an unusual situation but not an unknown one. And, of course, Sir Angus's estate is not in any way entailed. It was his right to dispose of his property in any manner he thought fit.'

'Come, Emily. I will not sit here and listen to this.' Edward, fiery faced and blustering with shock, stormed across the room to face Katrina who was tugging the bell rope. 'Don't think you've heard the last of this. I will challenge this in the courts if necessary.'

'If I might advise you, Mr Fraser,' the lawyer spoke up. 'Anything like that is a little premature at this stage'

'Mind your own bloody business,' Edward rounded on him, causing the smaller man to take a rapid step backwards. Fury stoked even higher, Edward stalked back to Katrina. 'If that child is a girl I will have you, your staff, and everything that might remind me of you, out of here within the month.'

Katrina blanched but kept her pale grey eyes on his face. 'Good afternoon, Edward,' she said icily when Flo came into the room in answer to her summons. 'Show Mr and Mrs Fraser out will you please,' she added, turning her back on them. 'Is there anything else I should know, Mr Dalrymple?' she asked the lawyer.

'I have written the terms of your husband's will down for you, Lady Katrina. These occasions are very upsetting and I feel you would be better to study them in your own time. I doubt there is anything there that you are unaware of but, for the time being, let me assure you that, whatever happens, you will be provided for.'

'But, if the child is a girl, I will have to leave Pitochrie. The London house and the vast bulk of Angus's interests will pass to Edward?'

'I am afraid that is correct, Lady Fraser.'

Katrina did her best to be polite to the man who had discharged an unpleasant duty to the limit of his ability. 'Then I do not think I need to detain you any longer, Mr Dalrymple.' She softened his dismissal by adding, 'You are quite right. It has been a very upsetting day for me and I have the child to think about. I really should get some rest.' She jerked the bell rope again and this time it was Morag who appeared to see the lawyer out.

'Did he really say that?' Cook asked, her eyes wide.

Flo nodded. 'He says he'd get rid of us all. I heard him. Right angry he was,' she shuddered. 'Let's pray Lady Katrina has a wee laddie. If he puts us all out I don't know what I'd do. I can't move back home, there's no room now and my sister won't have me there with her. And there's nowhere else round here, nowhere like this.'

Cook shook her head. 'The Lord only knows where a woman of my age would find another post.'

While the conversation in the kitchen proceeded along its gloomy lines, Katrina Fraser paced her drawing-room floor in growing agitation. Her whole future depended on her giving birth to a live son, something she had consistently failed to do in the past. On three previous occasions she had suffered months of pregnancy only to lose everything in a few hours of bloodied agony. 'Oh God,' she prayed. 'Please give me a son, a healthy son.'

EIGHT

Katrina's pregnancy entered its final two months with no sign of the problems which had doomed all her previous attempts to bear Angus a son. As each week passed the more hopeful she became that she carried the healthy heir she so desperately needed. Determined to produce the son who would be her passport to a secure future she made herself a virtual prisoner inside Pitochrie Castle, keeping to her own rooms, not even venturing into the gardens for fear that the long climb back up the stairs would trigger the premature labour she lived in dread of.

Meanwhile, Morag laced her own swollen figure ever tighter into her vicious stays, gasped when the child within her kicked out in protest, and struggled to close the line of straining buttons which ran down the front of her dress. No matter how straight she held herself, nor how desperately she held her breath, the buttons simply refused to meet over her stomach. To make matters worse the ties on her white apron were barely long enough to make even the skimpiest bow at the back and the apron itself seemed to be resting on a sudden ledge above the thrust of her pregnancy. She did her best to disguise her condition by making sure she always held something in front of her, a pile of clothes, a pot, anything to keep Mrs McManus's eyes from her waistline but, with a feeling of leaden desperation, she understood that she couldn't hope to hide her condition for much longer. The moment she had been dreading ever since learning of Sir Angus's death had finally arrived.

The following afternoon, her half day off, Morag sat beside the fire in her parents' house, watching as her baby sister suckled contentedly. Looking at the soft smile which lit her mother's face Morag doubted that she would ever be able to feel such pleasure in the child she was carrying.

Ayleen's eyes closed and she stopped sucking, her tiny, milk-speckled chin dipping sleepily under her mother's breast. Annie made herself decent, settled her baby daughter in her wooden crib then sat down opposite Morag.

'Well, she should sleep for a wee while now,' she sighed. 'Och, I'd forgotten what hard work bairns are.' She looked at Morag and frowned. 'For goodness sake, lass, take that shawl off. You're as red as a beetroot.'

'It's cold in here,' Morag shoved her chair back from the roaring fire but stayed huddled in her rough shawl, knowing that to remove it would make her condition obvious. She had been here for almost an hour and still hadn't found the courage to say what had to be said.

'Cold? With a blaze halfway up the chimney,' Annie scoffed, looking at Morag more closely. 'Are you not well? Have you a temperature?'

'No!' Morag twisted away from the hand which would have tested the heat of her forehead.

Annie shrugged, tired of Morag's moodiness. 'Honestly Morag, I don't know what's got into you these days. If you stay all wrapped up like that you'll feel the cold all the more when you step outside again. Now, make yourself useful and infuse some tea. A hot drink will do you more good than sitting there all wrapped up like an old wifie. And mind you're quiet about it. I don't want you waking the bairn or your father just yet.'

162

Coll was asleep, looking frail and old beyond his years. Since the birth of Ayleen his condition had worsened. He still had his lucid moments but even a double dose of medicine no longer eased the pain as it once had. There were times when the agony, made worse by Ayleen's cries, was so intense that he prayed for death to come quickly. On better days, such as today, the pain would subside for long enough for him to escape into an hour or two of restless sleep.

Morag rose soundlessly, and turned to the range before slipping her shawl from her shoulders, a set, determined look on her pale face. She brewed the tea in silence, unable to speak for the fear which was making her feel sick and causing her hands to shake, rattling the china. Eventually she turned and, stepping carefully over her father's outstretched leg and his discarded crutch, bent to hand her mother a cup. When she straightened again she dropped her hands to her sides, making no attempt to hide the bulge under her uniform dress, and stood, as if offering herself for inspection.

'Morag!' Annie's voice was an appalled whisper. Morag felt instant tears flood her eyes, tears of shame and relief that her mother finally knew.

'I tried to tell you, Mam.'

Annie's face was grey with shock, her eyes wide, her mouth hanging open. Slowly she set her cup on the floor and rose to her feet. 'A bairn! You're going to have a bairn,' she stammered at last.

Morag nodded miserably.

'Sweet Lord!' Annie stared at Morag as if she was still unable to believe the evidence of her own eyes. 'When?'

'I'm not sure. At the beginning of December I think.'

'You think?' Annie repeated, loudly, angry now. 'You went with a man so often that you can't even be sure when the bairn's due? Who was it? Who have you been with?' She grasped her daughter's shoulders and shook her so hard that Morag bit her tongue.

'No. It wasn't like that,' the girl protested weakly.

Coll stirred, groaning in his sleep. Abruptly, Annie shoved Morag away from her and thumped down into her chair. 'You little slut,' she hissed.

Morag dragged a hand over her eyes. She was long past the stage where tears might help her. 'Mum, I don't know what to do,' she begged. 'Please, can I come home?'

'You want to come home?' Annie asked, outraged. 'NO! No, I will not have you parading your shame for everyone to see. My God, Morag, it's taken years for these people to accept me, now you want to disgrace us all in front of them?'

'I've got nowhere else to go, Mam. I can't stay at the castle for much longer. When they find out they'll put me out. Please, Mam. Help me.' Behind them the baby wailed. Annie hurried to pick her up, to comfort her before she woke Coll. Looking at Ayleen's blue eyes, eyes which were the image of Rab Bannerman's, she felt herself softening then shoved away the unwanted emotion. That had been different, she loved Rab, had always loved him.

'Who is it?' she hissed viciously. 'Who is the father? Is it one of the lads at the castle?'

Morag shook her head dumbly.

Annie swallowed her temper. Maybe it was not too late to save the situation. 'Look, Morag, it's better that you tell me. If it's one of the lads then maybe we can talk to him, to his folks. It's not too late to arrange a wedding.'

'NO!'

164

'NO?' Annie screamed back, her fragile restraint gone. 'No? You come here, brazen as you like, asking me to help you but you won't even say who you've been with? Or have you been with so many you don't even know which one it was?' One look at her daughter's face was enough to tell her that wasn't the case but she was too angry to stop now. Drawing her hand back she slapped Morag hard across the face. Ayleen, jolted by the force of the blow, opened her tiny mouth and roared in fright.

'What the hell's going on here?' Coll asked, pulling himself upright, wincing with the pain which always held his head in its grip.

'You tell him,' Annie yelled, dragging Morag over to face her father. 'Go on. You tell him.'

'Mam . . .' Morag choked, sobbing now.

'Tell me what?' Coll asked, getting himself up on to his crutch.

'Look at her! Open your eyes, Coll McDonald, and look at your daughter's shame.'

Morag stood with her head lowered as her father's eyes raked over her swollen body. 'Bloody hell,' he whispered.

'Do you see?' screeched Annie. 'She's having a wean. Do you see?' After all she had been through, with a tiny infant and a dying husband to tend to, now this. Forgetting her own fall from decency Annie could only look at her daughter and feel disgust. 'She's been with a man. Look at her,' she yelled.

'BE QUIET WOMAN!' Coll bellowed, silencing his wife and stemming his tiny daughter's tears. 'Right. Now, we'll not get anywhere by screaming and yelling at one another. Sit down, both of you.'

Annie soothed her young daughter and laid her back

in her cot before mustering her dignity and sitting in her seat, near the fire.

'And you, lass,' Coll said, the calm kindness in his voice giving Morag some hope.

Coll eased himself back into his chair, bracing himself against the pain any movement caused in his head. There were times when he thought his skull would burst open, times when he wished it would. Now he ignored it and turned to Morag.

'It it true, lass?'

'Aye,' she nodded.

'Then you'd best tell us the name of the lad responsible.'

'Aye,' Annie added bitterly. 'Who is it?'

Morag shook her head and mumbled, 'I can't.'

Annie started to say something but Coll silenced her with a snapped 'Quiet' and turned back to his daughter. 'Och, lass, how can we help if you won't tell us? You're not the first lassie to have jumped the gun. I dare say it's natural enough. Look what happened with Davy. It turned out all right with them. I dare say your lad will do right by you when we've had a word with his folks.'

'It's too late,' Morag said dully.

'Is he one of the castle laddies?' Coll asked.

Morag shook her head again. 'No.'

'If he's trying to wriggle out of it, I'll soon get some sense talked into him,' Coll promised. 'I'll speak to his folks, and to Lady Katrina too if I have to, but don't you worry yourself, he'll do what's right in the end.'

'You don't understand,' Morag looked at her father with tears flooding her green eyes again. 'It's too late. He's dead.'

There was a long, dreadful silence.

166

'Sir Angus,' Annie breathed, a note of disbelief in her voice. 'Are you trying to say you let Sir Angus . . . ?'

Morag nodded.

'I don't believe you! What would he want with a girl like you?' Annie was on her feet again, jerking Morag round to face her. Ayleen whimpered again then broke into an angry yell.

'See to the wean, Annie,' Coll ordered. 'Take her away outside and leave me to deal with this.'

Annie gave her elder daughter a look of searing contempt then gathered the baby to her, wrapping it in her shawl before going out into the garden, slamming the door behind her. Coll waited until she was gone then said sternly, 'Now, look at me when I'm talking to you, Morag, and tell me who fathered this bairn.'

'It was Sir Angus,' she mumbled, looking away quickly.

'And did he force you, lass?' Even before his accident Coll had heard tales of Sir Angus's behaviour.

'No. He didn't force me. Not the way you mean.'

Coll couldn't bring himself to believe that his beautiful, innocent daughter had willingly lain with Angus Fraser.

'Not the way I mean?' Coll repeated Morag's words. 'Well, lass, you were either willing or you weren't. Which was it?'

'Och, Daddy,' she sobbed. 'He made me. He said if I didn't he would put you and Mammy out of the house. It was before Ayleen was born and Mammy couldn't work and the rent money was owing. I didn't want to. And he never even told me that the money had been paid. I had to do it. I never even thought I could have a bairn. I didn't know . . .'

'The bastard!' Coll thumped his fist on to the wooden arm of the chair, then sank his head into his hands as pain overwhelmed him.

'Daddy. Daddy, are you all right?' Morag asked, rushing to his side.

'Aye. Aye.' He brushed her aside impatiently. 'Do they know?' he asked abruptly. 'At the castle. Do they know?'

'No. I've told no one. But they'll know soon enough. I can't hide this for much longer. What am I going to do, Daddy?' Suddenly it was as if the years rolled away and she was a five year old again, broken-heartedly pleading with her father to mend her favourite doll. Somehow he had always managed to make things right then and she trusted him to do the same now.

'Och, my poor lass.' Coll put out a hand and rumpled the soft, auburn hair. 'Don't you worry, we'll think of something. I'll look after you.'

She felt his arm go round her, let her head fell to his chest, let him comfort her as he had so often done when she was a child.

Coll sat with his eyes closed, feeling the rage burn inside his head, feeling the pressure build, the pain sear through him, worse than it ever had, until he thought he would black out. But gradually it receded to a pounding, sickening ache, leaving him feeling weak and making it impossible to think, to concentrate.

'I'm sorry, Daddy,' Morag whispered.

'Ask your mother to come in again, lass, we need to talk this through,' Coll mumbled, feeling that the words weren't coming out as they should.

Morag stared at him, trying to make sense of the jumble of noise he was making.

'Get your mother, lass,' he repeated frantically, struggling to get on to his one good leg, tottering wildly as the room swung round him.

Morag hesitated, still trying to make something of the

awful noises her father was making. Only when he crashed to the ground at her feet did she finally turn and run screaming for her mother.

They buried him five days later, laying him to rest in a plot in Pitochrie kirk yard, not far from the memorial to Angus Fraser.

Pale, but with her hair faultlessly arranged in a neat coil, her coat freshly sponged and pressed, her shoes polished, Annie stood through the ceremony with a dignity which was so restrained it seemed almost uncaring. Morag resented it, knowing that even in the depths of grief her mother was being careful of the impression she was making. Supported by her sons and refusing even to look at her older daughter, Annie accepted the condolences of the villagers with a solemn formality which even Lady Katrina had failed to achieve. Relegated to the edge of the family group, Morag shivered, glad of Rab Bannerman's supporting arm. When it was over she lingered, saying a private, tearful farewell to her father, then looked up to see her mother watching her from the gate. Assuming she was waiting to walk home with her Morag hurried to her side. To her horror, now that there were no witnesses to carry tales back to the village, Annie's face contorted with hatred.

'Mam . . .' Morag started.

'Don't you dare speak to me,' Annie hissed. 'No matter what the doctors say, Morag, your father was getting better. I know it. It wasn't any tumour that killed him. You killed your father, Morag, as surely as if you'd taken a gun to his head yourself.'

Morag merely stared at her, too stunned to move, and Annie walked away to join her sons who all turned to glare resentfully at their sister before forming an impenetrable wall around their mother. Rab, who had watched from the other side of the road, looked first at Annie, then at Morag. The girl looked desolated, destroyed and absolutely alone. His heart went out to her.

'Come on, lass,' he said, putting a strong arm round her trembling shoulders. 'Your mother's overwrought. It's natural enough under the circumstances. Give her a day or two and she'll regret what she said.'

'No, she's right. It was my fault,' she choked.

'Och, you know that's not true, Morag! You heard what the doctor said. Your father had a tumour. That bang on the head caused it, he was never right after that. And that's what killed him.'

'But he wouldn't have died just yet. It was me that did that to him, upsetting him like that.'

'Morag, lass,' Rab sighed, wondering how best to deal with the girl, feeling out of his depth, 'be sensible. I'm right sorry if you fell out with your Daddy, but a wee argument didn't kill him.'

'Aye it did!' she retorted angrily. 'You don't understand.' She was crying now, her tears mingling with the cold winter rain which was starting to fall. 'Mam's right. I killed him.'

Rab frowned, sensing there was more to this than grief. 'Look, it's pouring down. Let's away back into the kirk until it stops.' He drew her into the now empty building and shoved her into a back pew. 'Right,' he said. 'Now tell me what's going on, Morag.'

Morag took a deep, shuddering breath and started haltingly on her story. Rab heard her out mutely, unable to trust his voice to say anything for a long while after she had subsided into unhappy silence.

'My God,' he said at last. If Angus Fraser had still been

alive, Rab believed he would have killed him then, with
his bare hands if necessary. But that would be of no help
to Morag now. She sat beside him like a wraith, her eyes
huge and shadowed, her lips trembling with the effort of
control. Even her personality seemed faded and he understood just how innocent, how vulnerable she was,
and how alone. Reaching out he pulled her to him,
cradling her protectively.

Morag felt the springy texture of his beard resting on
the top of her head. 'My daddy was holding me like this
just before he died,' she choked.

'He loved you, lass. He would have helped you any
way he could.'

'I know.'

He held her in silence until she was ready to move
away from him then said, 'None of this is your fault,
Morag. You can't blame yourself for any of it.'

'He would still be alive if I hadn't said anything,' she
insisted.

'Maybe,' he nodded and she looked at him, shocked to
know he agreed with her mother. 'But it wasn't you that
killed him. It was the fall that did that, nearly six years
ago. Your father was dying, Morag. This would have happened anyway. It could have been young Ayleen crying, it
might have been your mother. They were always arguing
weren't they?' he asked, gently. 'It might even have been
me. Anything could have done it. All it needed was for
him to get angry, or excited. I'm sorry it had to be when
you were there, lass, but it wasn't your fault.' He waited
but she merely shook her head. 'Look at me, Morag.'

Slowly she lifted her head and gazed at him with
limpid, pain-filled eyes.

'You know I always tell you the truth, don't you,
Morag?'

'Aye.' But she still didn't sound convinced.

'And I'm telling you, as God is my witness, that this was not your fault. Now, lass,' he went on, 'you've got other problems to put your mind to. Have you thought about what you are going to do? Is there anyone you could go to for a wee while?' It was clear that she couldn't go to Annie, not yet anyway.

'No, there's no one.'

He sighed. 'Aye, I think you're right. Your father has no relatives left in the highlands and your mother has nothing more than a cousin there these days. And a hard-hearted woman she is too if I mind rightly,' he laughed, bringing a weak smile to Morag's face.

'I can't stay at the castle. They're bound to realise soon.'

'And I've no solution to give you now. If I were you I'd stay where you are for as long as you can. I'm sure your mother will come round before long. She's not a bad woman but she's had a terrible shock. She loved your father and it will take her a wee while to adjust. By the time you have to leave the castle she'll likely be glad to have you back home.'

'And if not?' she asked.

'If not . . . Well, I suppose you'll have to come to me. Though God knows what Finty Chisholm will make of that. It'd fuel that gossiping tongue of hers for the next ten years.'

At last he got a true smile. 'Thank you, Uncle Rab.'

'But I doubt it'll come to that. Your mother'll be happy to have you once she's had time to come to terms with losing Coll.' He rose to his feet. 'Now, mop your face off lass and I'll walk you back to the castle. You'll need to try and keep that wee secret of yours to yourself for a wee while yet.'

Though still mourning her father and deeply unhappy about the rift with her mother, Morag returned to the castle and the sympathy of the staff there feeling that she had at least found a way to get through this. Lacing herself firmly into the stays which were now leaving deep red sores on her body she did her best to be patient.

The weeks wore on, dragging slowly by, each day bringing fresh discomfort and the ever present fear of discovery. To her continuing distress, although she made a point of trailing through the early winter frosts at least once a week, her mother remained intractable and the cottage door stayed closed to her.

'I don't think she'll ever forgive me,' she confessed her fear to Rab as they stood in the castle drive, talking, after one of her abortive visits home.

'It's early days yet,' Rab reassured her, but he was increasingly worried for her. To him her pregnancy was obvious and he couldn't understand why no one else at the castle had guessed her condition. 'It takes time to get over something like that. Even if she won't see you now, once she sees her grandwean, everything will be all right, you'll see.'

Katrina Fraser glanced out of her high window with idle interest, longing for her body to release her from its uncomfortable burden. Perversely she found herself resenting each passing day and looked towards the time when she would finally give birth with increasing dread, fearing that the child she carried would be a girl. Katrina knew Edward Fraser well enough to understand that if that was the case she, and her new daughter, would find themselves without a home in which case she might even have to fall back on her own mother's reluctant hospitality.

Preoccupied with her thoughts, she looked on with scant interest as her maid stood in close conversation with Rab Bannerman. She had seen them together quite often recently, a natural consequence of Coll McDonald's death, she supposed. A funny business that, she mused, idly wondering what, exactly, had been the cause of the rift between Morag and her mother. The McDonalds seemed to attract speculation. According to Cook, who kept her very well informed of what went on, both within the high walls of the house and outside, they were newcomers, in village terms, and their arrival from some remote highland glen had been shrouded in mystery. Made all the more interesting because Rab Bannerman, who had turned up within weeks of the McDonalds, was so obviously close to both Coll and his wife. There were even those who were suggesting that the latest addition to the McDonald family was not a McDonald at all.

Katrina watched as Rab bent and kissed his god-daughter's cheek and had the kiss returned by Morag who had to stretch to reach a patch of bare flesh above his beard. She stiffened and watched much more intently as the girl, wrapped closely in a coarse, woollen shawl, picked her way carefully up the frosty drive.

When Katrina finally turned away from the window her face was twisted into a hard smile. She had a long memory and the humiliation of Rab Bannerman's rejection on the night of Mysie's wedding still smarted. If the tender little scene she had just witnessed meant what she thought it did, she had finally found a way of hurting him without endangering her own position.

Katrina wasn't foolish enough to think that, even if she did have a boy, she would be able to run the estate on her own, especially when she would be held accountable for her son's future interests. It was obvious that Bannerman was a very capable and trustworthy estate manager – too good to be easily replaced. There was no point at all in getting her revenge in a way which was likely to have an adverse effect on the running of the estate, but he had just handed her the perfect way to even the score. By the time the village gossips got hold of this he would hardly be able to hold his head up in public.

'Tell Morag McDonald I want to see her, in my sitting room, in ten minutes' time,' Katrina instructed a curious Flo when she came in answer to the bell.

Morag received her summons with a thudding heart. Every call to Lady Katrina filled her with dread. Each passing day brought the prospect of discovery nearer. She hauled off her cap and repinned it more securely then smoothed the front of her apron surreptitiously, holding her breath in and straightening her back. But nothing she did seemed to make her condition less obvious. She walked out of the kitchen and up the stairs wondering if tonight was the night she would find herself at Rab's door begging for shelter.

Behind her Cook and Flo exchanged loaded glances.

'Well,' Cook whispered, 'I don't know how much longer she can hope to keep Lady Katrina from seeing the obvious. If she doesn't tell her soon, I will. She's an affront to all decent women.'

'Is Morag having a bairn too, Cook?' wee Chrissy piped up from the sink where she was scrubbing at a pile of dishes.

'Mind your mouth!' Cook snapped. 'And get on with your work. Never mind listening in on other people's conversations.'

'Ah, Morag.' Katrina looked up with a deceptively friendly

smile which managed to take in the full length of Morag's body. The girl was carrying it well, she decided. But really her condition was obvious, the wonder was that she hadn't noticed it before now. 'I think, Morag, that you have not been quite honest with me,' she said.

'Ma'am?' For a moment Morag had hoped this wasn't what she had thought it must be.

'Do you really think I am so stupid that I would not see your condition?' she demanded. 'I have waited, hoping that you would tell me yourself, but it is clear that you are trying to keep it from me for as long as possible.'

Katrina had expected some sort of denial and was surprised when Morag simply said, 'Yes, ma'am.'

'Is that all you can say?'

'Yes, ma'am.'

'You know, of course, that you cannot possibly stay here?'

'Yes, ma'am.' Morag kept her head high.

'I suppose your mother knows?' Suddenly she understood the cause of the rift between Morag and her mother.

'Yes, ma'am.'

The impassive, unchanging answer was beginning to irritate her. 'And are you planning to marry the father?' she asked, gratified to see the colour rise on the girl's face at last.

'No, ma'am.'

'No?' Katrina was horrified to see tears flood the girl's eyes. She quite liked Morag, had found her a willing and pleasant maid and would be sorry to lose her services. Almost against her will she found herself sympathising with her. After all, Rab Bannerman was a fine-looking

176

man and it was easy to see how she might be attracted to him. 'Why not? Surely there's no reason for him not to marry you?'

'He can't, ma'am,' Morag whispered.

In three strides Katrina was across the room and tugging vigorously at the bell rope. Gus, she was sure, would have dealt with this efficiently and there was absolutely no reason why she should not do the same, and do her young maid a service at the same time. She would also get a great deal of pleasure from seeing Bannerman forced to marry a girl who was obviously far too young for him, all under the curious eyes of the whole village. The thought almost made her laugh and it would certainly liven up the dreary last weeks of her pregnancy. The girl didn't look much above five months gone. She would make sure the wedding was postponed until after her own confinement so that she could witness Bannerman's downfall at first hand. When Cook puffed into the room she said, 'Mrs McManus. Please have Chrissy or Flo take this message to Mr Bannerman for me.' She sat at her desk and scribbled a note as she spoke. 'I do think I should speak to Mr Bannerman, Morag, don't you?,' she asked. 'Perhaps I can persuade him to face his responsibilities.'

Morag's face flared with colour. 'No!' she shouted, panicking.

'No?' Katrina was at her haughty coldest. 'You are in my service, Morag, and therefore, to a certain extent, my responsibility. Especially when the father of your unborn child is also in my employment. Despite the fact that you have behaved in a most immoral manner, as a Christian woman I am obligated to try and help you. I certainly do not expect you to challenge my decisions!' She rose and held out a folded paper to Cook. 'Have this delivered at once. Miss McDonald will wait here with me until Mr Bannerman arrives.'

Cook, cheeks flushed with excitement, took the paper and headed for the door.

'No,' Morag begged. 'Please . . . please wait.'

Cook hesitated then looked to Lady Katrina for guidance.

'One more word girl and I will send you home to your mother tonight,' Katrina stormed.

'It wasn't Mr Bannerman,' Morag whispered.

Katrina closed her mouth and beckoned Cook back into the room.

'How dare you lie to me when I am doing my best to help you,' she said icily. 'I don't know why you are trying to protect him. I saw you with him, only this afternoon. You can't deny that?'

'No, ma'am. But Mr Bannerman is my godfather, nothing else.'

'Are you telling me he is not the father of your child?' Katrina asked, disbelief loud in her voice.

'Yes, ma'am.'

'Then you had better tell me who is responsible,' Katrina persisted.

'I can't, ma'am,' Morag whispered, looking fixedly ahead.

Sure the girl was trying to protect Bannerman, for some reason best known to herself, Katrina, reluctant to lose her chance of getting even with him, resorted to threats. 'It seems to me, that since your father is no longer alive, your mother is not entitled to a house on the estate. Normally, of course, I would not think about putting a woman and baby out of their home, but, if you feel unable to be honest with me, Morag, after all I have done for you, then I do not see why I should show any consideration to your family. Especially when there are others who would be glad of such a comfortable home.'

Morag was visibly shaken. The blood drained from her face and she felt the anger well inside her. The Frasers had threatened her once before, and this situation was a direct result of that threat. Well, she decided, it wouldn't work a second time. The spark which had deserted her since she had discovered the truth of her pregnancy suddenly returned, lighting a fire in her green eyes, setting her chin in a determined jut, so like her father's, and adding steel to her voice. If they were going to turn her away then they would know the truth.

'The child is Sir Angus's.'

Cook's eyes nearly popped from her head. Lady Katrina opened her mouth to speak, found the words would not come then resorted to walking round the room, vainly striving to find some composure. Her mind seethed. It had been on the tip of her tongue to call the girl a liar but, now that it had been pointed out to her so bluntly, she recognised the truth. Had she not seen Angus sneaking to the girl's room with her own eyes? And at the time she had been glad to have him otherwise occupied. But, even so, there was something not quite right about it. The girl's pregnancy was obviously less advanced than her own. And at the crucial time surely Angus had already left for India.

Morag, who had expected a furious dismissal, was astonished to be asked, 'And when is this supposed to have happened? When is the child due?'

'March, ma'am. I think the child will be born in three or four weeks from now, in early December.'

'My God!' Katrina whirled round, paced furiously round the room again. 'But that is when my own child will be born,' she accused.

179

'Yes, ma'am.'

'You little hussy,' she spat, narrowly restraining herself from slapping out at the girl who was still standing with that defiant look in her eyes. She could not bear it if this rough country girl gave birth to Angus's son while she herself was delivered only of a daughter. 'You will have to go. I cannot have you under my roof for one more minute,' she screeched, almost in hysterics.

'Yes, ma'am.' Morag turned away, her face betraying nothing. She had had months to steel herself for this inevitability. She was following Cook into the cold passageway before Katrina's voice halted them.

'Stop! Come back in here. Both of you.' There was still a desperate note to Katrina's voice but the wild fever had gone from her eyes and she seemed calmer.

'Mrs McManus, fetch me my Bible,' she ordered, her eyes never leaving Morag's face. The girl's eyes met hers steadily and it was Katrina who looked away.

Five minutes passed in tense silence before Cook reappeared with a black, leather-bound Bible.

'Come here,' Katrina ordered Morag, clasping it with both hands.

Katrina's sitting room suddenly seemed a mile wide. Morag crossed it slowly, marvelling at her ability to set one steady foot in front of the other, to maintain this façade of calmness when all she wanted to do was run away, to hide her shame forever, to drown it in the fast rushing waters of the Annan, to be done with it all.

'Now, put your hand on my Bible.' Katrina knew that Morag would never be able to bring herself to tell a lie while her hand rested on the sacred book. She covered the girl's hand with her own, keeping it firmly in contact with the book and was surprised to feel it tremble slightly. 'You will swear, on this Holy Bible, that my husband, Angus Fraser, is the father of the child you carry. That there is no possibility of any other man being responsible.'

Morag reached out with her other hand, clasped the book firmly, looked Katrina squarely in the eyes and said, 'I swear Angus Fraser is the father of my child, that he is the only man I have ever been with.' Her voice shook a little but the words were clear.

Katrina retrieved her Bible and wandered over to her window, looking out over the darkened grounds, lost in thought. Perhaps, just perhaps, if she failed to produce the son who would make her future safe, perhaps Morag . . . ? But no, it was too dangerous and in any case her own child was going to be a boy, she knew it, felt it in the way he kicked, the way he moved, more restlessly surely than any girl ever would. But, maybe, just in case, she should keep the McDonald girl here, with her.

'How many people know you are pregnant?' Katrina asked.

'My family, Uncle Rab. And you, ma'am,' Morag answered, confused now.

'And Mrs McManus,' Katrina added.

'I'm afraid Flo and Chrissy know too, ma'am,' Cook added.

Katrina rounded on her furiously. 'And why was I not told?' she demanded.

'We've only just realised, ma'am. She's kept it well hidden,' the older woman lied.

'Yes.' The glance Katrina bestowed on Morag was filled with contempt. 'By rights I should insist on you leaving here this very moment.' But perhaps, she mused, that wouldn't be wisest thing to do. The unsuspecting Morag was offering her a second chance. God knows she'd earned it over the years of suffering unproductive pregnancies. Even if the worst did happen and her own child was a girl, even if Morag then gave birth to a boy, the problems were insurmountable. There was the girl herself who was unlikely to want to part with her child. Or would she, Katrina wondered. To give birth to an illegitimate child was the worst possible disgrace. It would ruin the girl's chances of marriage and make her unemployable. If what she said was true and no one outside her family and the staff here knew of her condition then she might be only too glad of the chance to pretend it had never happened. But it would never work. The doctor in charge of her own case was a reputable man and if a girl was delivered then his records would show just that. And Morag herself would need help when the time came and no midwife could be trusted with something as momentous as this. No, the whole thing was impossible. Nevertheless Katrina already knew she would allow the girl to stay on.

She turned back to the waiting women and said, almost graciously, 'Morag, I am prepared to be generous to you. You have been a good maid and it would be most inconvenient for me to have a stranger tending to me at this time. You may stay here until my own situation is settled.'

Morag grasped at the reprieve. 'Thank you, ma'am.'

'There are certain conditions.'

'Yes, ma'am.'

'You will continue with your duties. You are young and strong and the work is not onerous. You will tell no one, absolutely no one, about your condition and you will not set foot outside the castle, not even into the grounds. Is that understood? By both of you?'

'Yes, ma'am,' Morag whispered. 'But what will I do when the baby starts to come?' She asked the question for which Katrina had no answer, so much depended on the outcome of her own delivery.

'We will make some arrangement,' she replied, deliberately vaguely, her voice shaking slightly at the audacity of her half formed plans. 'I will hold you responsible, Mrs McManus. If any word of this leaks out you will both find yourselves without employment. I will not have this household the subject of gossip. If all goes well I may allow you to continue here in the position of nursemaid to my son.'

Cook nodded, as mystified as Morag was by Lady Fraser's attitude.

When it became clear that Katrina had nothing more to add, Morag managed to say, 'Thank you, Lady Fraser.' But the confusion was so plain on her face that Katrina felt obliged to justify her decision.

'I know you are puzzled, Morag. But you are carrying my dear, dead husband's child. To be honest, however reprehensible your behaviour has been, I have a duty towards it, for his sake.' She contrived to allow a few drops of moisture to escape from her pale eyes as she spoke.

'Yes, ma'am.' Morag shuffled uncomfortably, desperate to escape to the privacy of her own room and deal with this alone, aware of a huge feeling of relief which was threatening to reduce her to tears.

'Right.' Katrina rose to her feet, brisk and businesslike again. 'You will inform the rest of the staff, Mrs McManus. I suggest you keep the outside workers out of the house as much as possible. And I repeat, no word of this is to go beyond these walls.'

'Yes, ma'am.'

Katrina turned her back and stared out of the window so they couldn't see the smile of victory which was spreading over her face. Bemused, the two other woman left her to mull over her actions. Morag fled to her room while Cook returned to the kitchen to warn Flo and Chrissy about the dire consequences of any careless gossip.

NINE

'Come on, hen, let's get you tidied up.' Annie leant over Ayleen's cot and gathered her daughter into her arms, nuzzling her face playfully into the child's tummy. She was rewarded by bubbles of delicious laughter. Humming contentedly she laid the squirming bundle on the floor and whipped the damp cloth off of the infant's bottom. Freshly wrapped and sweet smelling, Ayleen was then deposited on the mat in front of the fire where she settled down to play contentedly with her toys. Old tins, filled with dried beans which made a satisfying noise when shaken; a wooden cart, a relic of the boys' childhood, could be loaded and dragged along the floor; wooden blocks in bright colours could be piled until they fell with an exciting clatter; a robust doll – one of the many gifts which Rab showered on her – allowed itself to be dismembered and even thrown down without ever losing its painted smile.

Annie settled into her chair, content to watch. And to think she hadn't really wanted this child, had done everything she could to dislodge the pregnancy, never dreaming that she would find so much pleasure in this late addition to her family. She wondered what Coll would have made of this active scrap of mischief and knew, had Coll still been alive, the child would have been quieter, her natural ebullience curbed by the constant need for quiet, that her own joy in her daughter would have been marred. Her stomach twitched with a spasm of guilt when the thought that Coll's death had been a blessing insisted on surfacing yet again.

She missed him, of course she missed him. After more than twenty years in the company of one man, raising four lively youngsters together, this sudden plunge into widowed motherhood had left her feeling adrift, lost, with too much time simply to sit and think. But always she came to the same conclusion. Things were better this way. Not that she wouldn't have given years of her own life to have kept Coll as he was, before the accident, but nothing could ever be the same after that. Despite his moods, his cruelty, his jealous rages, there had been enough of the original Coll left to make seeing him fade, inch by pain-racked inch, a dreadful ordeal. One guilt-ridden part of her had felt relief when he died, relief both for herself and for him; the other half had felt a sense of failure. Perhaps if she had been more understanding, had given him less of the medicine, he might have recovered. She had known he was dying, even without the doctor she would have known that, but even so the end had come so suddenly that it had been shock. If only Morag hadn't upset him . . . Annie tried to drive that line of thought out of her head. She recognised her own ambivalence towards Coll's death and knew Morag wasn't responsible for what had happened to Coll. But it made no difference. She still hadn't been able to forgive her daughter.

A familiar rhythm of light taps on her door banished her painful thoughts and brought a fresh smile to her lips. Automatically her hand went to her hair, patting it needlessly into place. 'Come in, it's open,' she called and turned to greet Rab with a warm smile.

Dressed in his working clothes of coarse green, corded

trousers tucked into thick woollen socks, and a heavy green jacket, over a flannel shirt and thick jumper, his gun slung casually under one arm, Rab stepped inside and closed the door quickly behind him. He propped his gun in the closet by the door, well out of the child's way, then shrugged himself out of his jacket in the manner of a man at ease with his surroundings. He was smiling as he crossed the room, the warmth shining from his brilliantly blue eyes which, these days, gazed out from a deeper web of lines when he laughed. Above his thick beard his cheeks were pink. 'My, and it's cold out there. I think we're going to have a gey hard winter this year. We'll have snow early,' he predicted, kissing Annie's cheek.

Ayleen scrambled across the floor in her own unique way, hands and feet pattering over the mat, her knees straight and her little bottom stuck up into the air. Reaching her objective she plumped into a sitting position and reached her hands up in a beautiful appeal.

'Och, and what are you up to my wee lassie?' Rab picked her up, tossed her into the air and caught her amid squeals of delight which reached a frantic crescendo when he rubbed his beard into her bare neck.

Annie, hearing the familiar words again, said nothing. Still she refused to admit that Ayleen was his daughter. In all truth she could never be sure, but Rab had made it clear that whatever the truth of her conception, he thought of her as his child. That he loved the little girl dearly was plain in the way he looked at her. That Ayleen adored him just as much was equally obvious. Leaving them to amuse each other, as they did every night, Annie turned her attention to their evening meal.

It was wonderful, the three of them here together, the only disappointment came when he left for his own home late in the evening, as he always did. How glad she had been of his company in the awful weeks after Coll's death. How natural it had been to have him with her and how easily they had come together, this time without guilt. It was strange, but neither of them had felt they were being disloyal to Coll in any way, even though he had been less than three weeks in his grave when Rab had first taken her to bed. But it was something they had to keep a secret, at least for the time being. Such a relationship would be frowned upon so soon after Coll's death.

'Right then. Come to the table, Rab,' she called, laughing as he scooped the child up and slid her deftly into the highchair he had spent weeks making for her.

Rab felt a deep contentment, something he had almost lost hope of experiencing at first hand. Like Annie he mourned Coll. The friendship they had shared had been something beyond price and he would never have wished to win Annie this way. But Rab was a pragmatic man, tempered by hard experience to accept what life threw at him and make the very best of it. He had loved Annie for as long as he could remember, even resigning himself to the role of loyal friend when she and Coll had married. Now he felt no sense of betrayal to have taken Coll's place quite so quickly. His happiness would be complete when they married but, whereas he would have gone ahead and seen the minister at once, Annie, who was more concerned than he about what others might say, had insisted they wait for a year. If that was what she wanted he wouldn't argue, so long as she didn't expect him to stay out of her bed until then.

'I was thinking,' he said to her as they lay together later, still damp from energetic love making.

'What?' She twisted in his arms.

'About Morag,' he said, feeling her tense as he spoke the girl's name.

'I don't want to talk about her,' Annie retorted, pulling the covers more closely round her shoulders, putting just that little bit of distance between herself and her lover. 'Och, why did you have to go and spoil the evening?' she asked.

'Because she is the one thing that stands between us,' he insisted, refusing to be put off.

'I'll not see her, Rab. Not yet.'

'Annie, you can't go on blaming the lass for something that was not her fault.'

She sighed. 'Och, Rab, I know that and deep down I know she wasn't responsible, but I can't help the way I feel. The baby and everything . . .'

'The lassie needs her mother's support,' he persisted gently.

'She's managing very well without me!' she retorted. 'You told me yourself that she's getting to stay on at the castle. I know fine that she's hiding herself away up there but after the wean's born everyone in the village will know about it. Think of what they'll all say.'

'Think of what they'd say about us,' he commented wryly.

'They don't know about us,' Annie slid out of bed and dragged her dress over her head.

'Annie . . .' he sighed, knowing whatever he said now would result in bad feeling. 'I promised Coll that I would look after you, all of you. To my mind Morag's . . .'

'I see!' she interrupted him angrily. 'That's why you're here, is it Rab Bannerman? Just doing your duty. Is that it?'

'No!' He bit back the furious words which strangled his tongue and hauled himself back into his trousers, feeling he needed the dignity of clothes for this conversation. Then he sat on the edge of the bed watching Annie tidy her hair wondering how a woman so warm and sensual, so generous, so basically good, could turn her own daughter away in her time of greatest need. It was true what the other men said – women were beyond male understanding. He ran his hand through the thick, dark bristles of his beard, a gesture Annie knew and understood.

'Then why are you here?' She would make him say it, suddenly needed that reassurance.

'Because I love you,' he said, almost angrily. 'But can't you understand I love Morag too? Och, I've known her since she was a day old. I've watched her grow from a wee bairn to a beautiful young woman. The daughter of my two oldest friends, of the woman I love. How can I stand by and do nothing to help her?'

Annie felt her stomach tighten. 'I'll not have her back here, Rab.'

'Why not? She needs you, Annie.'

'She didn't need me when she went with Angus Fraser,' she retorted. 'This is her own doing, Rab. Anyway,' she added, disconcerted by the accusation she saw in those clear eyes, 'she's well taken care of. She'll be better off with Lady Katrina than she would be here.' It was the argument she always resorted to, the one thing that salved her conscience.

'I'm not so sure,' he countered, rubbing his beard again.

'I'll not have her back here, not with an illegitimate bairn and the whole village tattling behind our backs. Can't you see it's better this way? No one knows. If this got out in the village she'd be shunned. No decent lass would be seen with her. Everyone would talk.'

'I know that well enough!' he exploded. 'All those fine, church-going folk who love nothing better than watching someone else's shame. But they'll find out in the end.'

'Not if she stays where she is,' Annie insisted stubbornly.

'Talk sense woman! The lassie can't stay walled up in the castle forever. Gossip has a way of getting out.'

'I'll not have her back here,' she repeated, coldly.

'You'll maybe have no choice. What happens if Lady Katrina's bairn is a lassie?'

'It'll be a boy.'

'And just as likely not! If Edward Fraser takes over the estate there'll be no place for any of us. Lady Katrina will have enough problems of her own without Morag too. I've heard that if it's a lassie Katrina will go back to her mother's house.'

'She'll still need a nursemaid,' Annie insisted stubbornly.

'But not one with a bastard child!'

Annie winced at the harshness of the word but all she said was, 'Keep your voice down. Do you want to wake the bairn?'

Rab took half a minute to curb his rising temper, understanding Annie well enough to know that the more he argued with her the more obstinate she was likely to become. He walked over to the cot where Ayleen slumbered on innocently, feeling the familiar surge of love as he gazed at her pink-skinned perfection. He looked up, found Annie watching him and smiled. 'Come and sit down, woman. It's no good us arguing. If you won't have the girl back here then something's got to be done for her and we'd best talk about it.'

As always Annie's love for this man overcame her

anger and she allowed him to steer her to a fireside chair.

'It's no good you trying to talk me into having her here,' she warned him.

'All right,' he admitted defeat with a shrug of his shoulders. 'But it's true enough, what I said. She's all right until Lady Katrina has her own wean. But even if it is a boy and Lady Katrina stays at the castle, maybe it's not the best place for Morag.'

'Why not?'

'You said it yourself. People will talk. She won't be able to keep a secret like that for very long. And the folk round here will make her life a misery. Whether she lives at the castle or here with you, she'll be an outcast. No local lad will look at her, she'll have no friends.'

'She should have thought of that before.'

He ignored her. 'Maybe she'd be better to go away. To start again somewhere else.'

'Where?' Annie demanded. 'And no matter where she went she'd still have a bairn. And no man to make it decent.'

'She'd not be the first to claim she was a widow.'

Annie snorted her derision. 'At not yet nineteen! And how is a girl of her age supposed to go where she's not known? Where would she live? How would she feed herself?'

'She's handy with her needle. Maybe she could make something out of that?'

'And what is she to live on meantime?' Annie demanded. 'No, Rab. I know you're trying to help, but it won't work.' Though the idea of having her daughter's disgrace removed from Pitochrie where it was certain to come to light and reflect on herself was an attractive one.

'Do you remember my sister?' Rab asked suddenly.

'Beth? Aye, of course I do! She was a fine woman.' And dead, three years past.

'Aye, she was that. Two bonny weans she had. The wee one, Maureen, she's just over three years old now. The lad's a year or so older. Quite a handful for a working man with no wife to help him.'

'Aye. It's a shame for him. He's a good man, your brother-in-law. Donny, isn't it?' Annie asked, wondering what this was leading to.

'Aye, Donald Archibold. He's a baker to trade. He's a fine house in Kilweem but it's not easy for him, running a business with the bairns always at his back.'

'What are you getting at Rab Bannerman?' she demanded impatiently.

'Well, I was wondering . . .' he rubbed at his beard again. 'Och, maybe he wouldn't like the idea, but I know he's set against marrying again.'

'Oh.' She had wondered if he was trying to marry Morag off to his brother-in-law.

'But he does need some help. Can't afford to pay a housekeeper or anything like that. He's just an ordinary working man. But he might not mind the idea of a lassie like Morag helping out in return for her keep. She'd be safe with him. He's a decent man,' he added.

'If he's that decent he'll not want a young lass and her fatherless brat living with him,' Annie objected.

'Maybe not,' Rab conceded. 'But we'll not know that until I've asked him. I thought I might pay him a visit. It'll need to be soon though. I'd like to have this settled before the bad weather sets in. And before that child's born.'

Annie appeared to think about it then asked, 'Kilweem? Where is Kilweem?'

Rab smiled and leaned over to kiss her. 'See, you don't like the thought of losing her, do you?' he teased. 'You'll come round in time, you'll see, and this way she won't be so far away.'

She had the grace to smile back at him. 'I hope so, Rab. I know what you must think of me, but I can't help the way I feel. Perhaps this would be the best solution.'

'Aye, I think so too. And Kilweem is a braw wee place.'

'Where is it?' she asked again. Since coming to Pitochrie from the highlands Annie had seldom needed to leave the village, had little knowledge of Strathannan outside her immediate area.

'It's a tiny fishing village, on the coast, about fifteen miles from here. It has a marvellous beach. Just the place for growing weans.'

Annie nodded. 'When will you go?'

'As soon as I've asked Lady Katrina for a day or two off. She's owes me some time so I don't think there'll be a problem. But I'll not say anything to Morag yet. It wouldn't do to raise her hopes for nothing.' He got to his feet, pulled her into his arms and kissed her, winding his tongue round hers until she thought she would melt from the surge of desire he roused in her. 'I'd best be getting off home,' he chuckled, slipping a hand inside her dress.

'Aye,' she smiled back, running her hands over his broad back, pressing her pelvis into him until she felt him stiffen against her. 'But not just yet.'

'I'd just like a wee word with Morag, Mrs McManus. In private.' Rab said, striding into the castle's warm kitchen and surprising Mrs McManus over a cup of tea.

'Well, I hope you won't be long,' she sniffed. 'We've a lot of work to get through the day and Morag's gey slow these days.'

He eyed her cup pointedly. 'It seems to me that you're not so overworked that a few minutes of Morag's time will bring the household to a stop, Mrs McManus.'

She flushed guiltily. 'I suppose I could send Chrissy away to the village for messages and I've got to see Lady Katrina with the household accounts. Flo's busy upstairs so I can let you have ten minutes with her,' she conceded. 'But no longer if you please, Mr Bannerman.'

It was three weeks since Rab had last seen Morag. Her pregnancy was now obvious but, in contrast to the wan, colourless creature who had cried brokenheartedly through her father's funeral, now that her immediate worries were resolved, she was positively blooming. Her hair, inadequately restrained under the stiff, white cap shone with coppery highlights, picked up by the healthy colour in her cheeks and the sparkle in her clear green eyes. Gone was the plodding step which had so mirrored her depression and now, even with the unbalancing weight of her pregnancy, she walked lightly, the lift of natural pride back in her chin.

'Morag, lass,' Rab rose to greet her with unfeigned affection. 'You're looking well.'

She laughed as she sat opposite him at the table. 'I feel wonderful. I think it's because I don't have to pretend any more. How's mother, and Ayleen?' Despite her mother's rejection she never failed to ask after her family.

Rab smiled, his fondness plain for the infant who could so easily be his daughter. 'Aye, your wee sister's a right wee tyke. Your mother can't take her eyes off her for a minute without her getting her wee fingers into something she shouldn't. Always into mischief.'

'I wish I could see her,' Morag said wistfully.

'Aye, lass,' he caught her hands across the table. 'I know you do. Be patient. I'm sure everything will work itself out in the end.'

'Maybe,' she said, doubtfully.

Rab let a minute pass in silence then said, 'Morag, lass, there's something I need to talk to you about.'

'What?' She had heard the rare note of uncertainty in his voice and looked at him curiously.

'It's about your mother and me. Something I wouldn't like you to hear from anyone else.' For all their caution Rab knew his relationship with Annie would not long escape the attention of the village gossips. Only yesterday evening he had bumped into Finty Chisholm as she walked up the path to Annie's cottage. It wouldn't take her long to draw the obvious conclusion, if she hadn't already done so. Instinctively he knew that Morag would be badly hurt to hear of it from someone else.

'Aye?' she encouraged him.

'Well,' Rab was embarrassed. 'I've been seeing a lot of your mother. Och, you know fine that I was always fond of her.'

'I know,' she nodded. In the happy days, before her father's accident, it had been no secret that Rab had once walked out with Annie but had lost her to Coll, all long before they left the highlands.

'The truth is,' he stumbled on, 'your mother and I . . . Well, lass, I've asked her to marry me. And she has said yes.'

Morag's mouth drooped open. 'So soon?' The words were out before she could stop them.

'We'll wait, of course. Your mother thinks it wouldn't be right to get married for a year or so.'

Morag was torn between happiness for Rab and the

196

feeling that they were being disloyal to her father. 'I'm pleased for you,' she muttered.

'Och, lass, don't take it so hard and try not to think badly of me,' he said, squeezing her hands. 'I've always loved your mother, since I was just a lad. But she liked your father better and it was the right choice. They were happy together. But now Coll's gone . . . well,' he shrugged, unable to explain the explosive attraction they felt for one another, the protectiveness he felt for Annie, the pleasure they gave one another. 'I'll be able to look after her, and Ayleen,' he ended lamely.

Morag nodded, and looked away, not wanting him to see the tears which had suddenly flooded her eyes.

'I thought it better that you know, Morag. I wouldn't want you to think we're carrying on behind your back. We're neither of us ashamed and if we don't want the whole village to know then that's out of respect for your father.' He watched her, desperately seeking some sign that she understood, that she was truly glad for them, but her face was closed, her eyes like deep winter pools, cold and unfathomable.

She stood up. 'Thank you for telling me.' It was horribly polite, almost formal.

'I'm sorry if you're upset, Morag. I'm very fond of you and I don't want to lose your friendship,' he said softly, watching her closely and moving round beside her.

At last she looked up, into the dark blue of his eyes. 'I'm surprised, that's all,' she said, softly, her eyes filling with tears again. 'I still miss Dad. So much seems to have happened so quickly.' She drew a huge, sobbing breath. 'I'm sorry, Uncle Rab. Please, we're still friends, aren't we?' Suddenly she realised what it would mean to her if he was no longer there for her.

He almost choked on his own emotion, his relief was so great. 'Aye, lass. We're still friends. We'll always be that. And,' he added when he had himself under control, 'don't think I want to replace your father. I could never do that.'

'You're still my Uncle Rab?' she laughed softly.

'Still your Uncle Rab,' he agreed, holding her to him, wondering how such an innocent girl, still little more than a child, would ever cope alone with a bairn of her own to bring up.

Echoing down the staircase came the sound of Cook's heavy footsteps. 'I'd best be off, lass, or Mrs McManus will be complaining that I'm keeping you from your work. Och, before I go . . .' He turned back from the door. 'I'm away down to the coast for a couple of days, to see my brother-in-law. You'll be all right until I get back?' There should be no need for her to have to come to him now but he didn't like to go without telling her.

She laughed. 'I'm fine. But I think you'll get a proper battering from the weather if you mean to go today.' She pointed to the sky which was almost slate grey. 'It looks as if it's going to snow.'

He squinted up to where the hilltops were lost in threatening clouds. 'Aye, it doesn't look too good does it? Mind you, they never have the bad weather on the coast like we do up here. I'll see you next week, lass.'

He was wrong. Even in Kilweem the snow swirled down in an ever shifting, dense white curtain. The boats, bobbing in the tiny harbour on a swell deadened by the snow, lost their definition and appeared through the gloom as misshapen white monsters. The village itself disappeared under a carpet of snow as deep as anyone could remember while the steep little wynds which

198

twisted down to the sea became blocked with snow which thundered off the roofs.

Rab, thawing out in the warmth of his brother-in-law's bakehouse, knew the narrow country lanes he had travelled to get here would be impassable by now and counted himself lucky not to have become stuck in one of them. Even when it started to thaw here there would be no guaranteeing he could get back to Pitochrie, at least not for a day or so. The sea breeze might bring relief to the coastal villages but up in the hillfoots the snow would lie in drifts for days to come. Well, it would be pleasant to spend a day or two with his brother-in-law who was a good-humoured man who enjoyed company. And he need have no worries about those he had left behind in Pitochrie. The farmers, suspecting an early and hard winter had long ago made their arrangements; the castle had laid in its winter stores weeks ago and Annie too was well provisioned and had enough peat and wood to last until Easter if necessary. Rab stretched out his feet to the blazing fire and happily resigned himself to an unscheduled holiday.

TEN

Katrina watched the countryside disappear under a shroud of snow and shivered in the draughts which whistled under heavy doors and sturdy windows. With her view obliterated by dense, swirling flakes she felt trapped. All day she paced restlessly, unable to settle to anything. If she sat for any length of time she got cramp in her legs and heartburn under her ribs. When she stood her back ached.

For the fourth or fifth time she returned to her sofa, picked up her book then dropped it after reading less than a paragraph, the unlikely romance seeming contrived and laborious. Idly she flicked through the pages of a magazine then tossed it aside too and went back to the window. Still the snow fell, more thickly than ever. Briefly she wondered whether she would have been better to accept her mother's advice to go home to Stirling for her confinement. She had resisted the invitation, anxious both to have the doctor she knew attend her and to bear her son in the home he would inherit. In the end they had reached a compromise by agreeing that her mother should come to Pitochrie next week, in time for the birth. At the time Katrina hadn't spared a thought for the weather, had never even considered the possibility that her mother would be unable to reach her. But surely, by the time her son was born the snow would have melted.

Huge flakes drifted against the glass, covering the

leaded panes until there was only a small circle of transparency left in the shimmering whiteness. Hating it she forced the window open against the wind feeling the chill cut into her warm face. Then she brushed off the snow piled high on the ledge and leant out to watch it disappear, engulfed by the powdery whiteness below. As she stretched over the sill she felt a sudden pain in her groin and jerked upright, startled by the sharpness of it. She froze, relaxing only when it did not return after two or three minutes, then shut the window carefully and returned to her sofa. That would teach her a lesson, she thought, picking up her book again. From now on she would sit as still and quiet as possible. The last thing she wanted was to find herself in labour two weeks too soon, especially in these conditions.

When Morag went to bed she was bone tired. The sudden cold snap and Lady Katrina's bad temper had resulted in twice as much work for her. She had lost count of the buckets of coal she had hauled up the stairs in order to keep the fires blazing.

She rolled into bed and huddled under the blankets, shivering. Her room, like those of the other servants, was under the roof. There was no fireplace and it was so cold that the window had been frozen into its frame for at least two weeks. In the mornings the water in her jug was solid and even her chamber pot – preferable to the frigid bathroom in this weather – was iced over. If the weather stayed like this she would be glad to take up her place in Lady Katrina's warm dressing room next week, where it had been agreed she would sleep, in case Katrina had sudden need of her in the night. And surely, she thought as she finally drifted into sleep, her own time could not be long delayed.

It felt as if she had barely closed her eyes when she was shaken awake by an unsympathetic hand. She struggled to sit up and stared at Cook, shivering in her nightdress with a blanket thrown round her shoulders. Morag could hear the older woman's teeth chattering with cold and the candle she held flickered dangerously with the shaking of her hand.

'Wake up, lass. Wake up,' Cook yelled frantically. Behind her the door opened again and Flo, also shivering, appeared in the gloom.

'What's going on?' she hissed. 'You woke me up and if you're not careful you'll wake Lady Katrina too and then we'll end up fetching coal and pots of tea up and down the stairs all night.'

'It's Lady Katrina who woke me up!' Cook bellowed above Flo's complaints. 'And I can't understand why neither of youse heard her too, the noise she was making.'

'Oh God!' Morag was out of bed with surprising speed considering her bulk. 'It can't be the baby. It's not due yet.'

'I'd better get dressed.' Flo hurried to the door.

'No. Telephone to the doctor first. Ask him to come at once,' Cook said. 'I'd have done it myself but I can never hear what's being said to me through that funnel thing.'

'What about the snow?' Flo asked. 'He'll never get here if it's like it was earlier.'

The women stared at each other in horror until Morag rushed to the window and rubbed the frost with her hand. 'I can't see,' she cried in frustration.

'Telephone for the doctor, Flo. Maybe it isn't as bad up by Perth way.' But Mrs McManus sounded anything but confident.

'If I can't get Doctor Drummond I'll try to get Doctor Simpson from Glenelg. That's less than six miles away so he should be able to get here all right.' And Flo was gone, pattering down the stone stairs in her bare feet.

'Right, Morag. You go and stay with Lady Katrina. I'll get some water boiling and lay out fresh linen.'

Morag hurried to her mistress's room and, to her relief, found Katrina sitting up in bed, looking calm and only slightly apprehensive.

'Is Doctor Drummond on his way?' Katrina asked.

'Flo's telephoning to him now, ma'am,' Morag told her. 'Are you sure the baby's coming?' To her unseasoned eyes Lady Katrina did not look as if she was in labour.

'Of course I'm sure,' Katrina snapped.

'Och, no need to worry yet a while,' soothed Flo who had just come into the room. 'It can take hours.'

'And what do you know about such things?' Katrina demanded, shifting uneasily in her bed and gritting her teeth against a new pain.

'I've been with two of my sisters and my sister-in-law when they had their weans, ma'am,' Flo told her with a satisfied air. 'And unless the pains are regular there's no need to worry.'

'You stupid girl!' Katrina screeched. 'I've been having regular pains for three hours.'

'Oh, ma'am!' Flo was dismayed. 'Why did you not call us before?'

'I tried, but no one heard!' Katrina retorted. 'Is Doctor Drummond on his way?'

Flo shuffled nervously. 'He doesn't think he'll be able to get here. The snow's right thick in Perthshire too.'

'Oh God,' Katrina groaned.

'I tried the doctor in Glenelg as well, Doctor Simpson, but he says it's too bad to come out too. He'll try and get here as soon as the weather clears.'

203

'What about Pitochrie?' Morag suggested. 'There's no doctor there since old Doctor McEwan died, but Finty Chisholm acts as midwife.'

'NO!' Katrina shuddered. 'I will not have that dreadful woman up here.'

'Anyway,' Flo added helpfully, 'Finty lives a good way outside the village and she doesn't have a telephone.'

Now Cook joined the gathering round the bed, her stout arms laden with fresh linen and towels. 'Surely Finty would be better than no one,' she suggested.

'And who are you going to send out in this weather to fetch her?' Katrina demanded acidly. 'Just look out of the window. It's snowing harder than ever, you'll never get through.'

The three other woman regarded each other dubiously. 'Well,' Cook said. 'I'd go if I could but I'm too old to be ploughing three miles through the snow. Morag's in no condition to go anywhere and we can't trust Chrissy in these conditions. Anyway, she'd forget where she was going before she was half way to the village.'

'And Flo can't go. She's the only one of you with any experience of this sort of thing,' Katrina said wearily now.

'It's a pity none of the lads live in,' Cook offered unhelpfully. The gardener and all the outdoor staff had their own homes, mostly in the village.

'What about Mr Bannerman?' Flo asked. 'He'd be able to fetch Finty back.'

'He's gone to Kilweem to see his brother-in-law,' Morag explained, extinguishing their last hope.

'Aaaahhh,' Katrina groaned as pain fired through her abdomen, succeeding in bringing their attention back to her.

'Don't worry, Lady Katrina,' Flo said. 'As long as

everything's normal I know what to do. And Doctor Drummond did say everything was fine when he was last here and that was only the day before yesterday.'

Katrina, realising she needed her staff to stay calm, managed to smile. 'Yes. He did say that.'

'Anyway,' Flo went on, encouraged by the positive response, 'I expect one of the doctors will manage to get here before the bairn's born. It always takes ages with a first one.'

'This isn't my first though, is it?' Katrina exploded, tensing for yet another wave of pain.

'Oh no, neither it is,' Flo mumbled, looking worried again.

'Och, away out of the way, Flo. Morag will stay with Lady Katrina,' Cook decided, overcoming her panic at last. 'And if the worst comes to the worst I'm sure we'll manage.'

Katrina sighed and sank back among her pillows. 'Will someone fetch some coal up here,' she complained weakly, 'I'm cold.'

Dawn was hailed by misty light filtering through the snow-dressed glass. Morag slumped exhaustedly in the chair by Katrina's bed, doing her best to encourage her labouring mistress. With pains coming every five minutes and getting more ferocious every time, Katrina was uncomfortable and fractious.

'Is it still snowing?' she asked between pains.

'It's hard to tell, ma'am,' Morag answered, glad to be roused from unpleasant contemplation of her own imminent confinement.

'Don't just sit there, Morag,' Katrina said petulantly. 'Open the window and have a proper look. If it's stopped the doctor might get here in time yet.'

Morag wrestled the window open and stared out. The wind had dropped but the snow was still falling in steady, silent flakes. The hills were lost in the general whiteness but the trees were just visible, their laden branches drooping under their burden. The ground was nothing but undulating softness and everything was absolutely still and silent. She shivered and slammed the window shut.

'It's still snowing, ma'am,' she said quietly. 'I don't think anyone will be able to get through for a day or two.'

Katrina slammed her hand into her pillow. 'It simply isn't good enough! I am sure Doctor Drummond could get here if he really wanted to. If something goes wrong I shall hold him responsible.'

'Nothing will go wrong, ma'am,' Morag soothed. 'Just try to stay calm.'

'Go and do something useful, Morag. You're making me more nervous than ever, hovering around me with that scared face. Look, you've let the fire get low. Put some coal on it. Whatever happens we've got to keep the room warm. The baby can't be allowed to get cold. When you've done that go downstairs and help Cook. Flo can sit with me now.'

Morag was doing Lady Katrina's ironing when Mrs McManus rushed in, clearly agitated.

'Morag, come on. It's starting and Flo needs our help.'

Morag put the hot flat-irons on to the flagged floor to cool and winced at the pain in her lower back when she straightened up.

'Hurry up, Morag.' Mrs McManus was almost dancing with nervousness.

Morag hurried up the stairs as fast as she could, feeling the weight of her own pregnancy drag at her, and arrived red faced and panting.

Katrina was now flat in bed, writhing in agony and grunting with effort. Flo was mopping her face with a cool cloth.

'What do you want me to do?' Morag asked, pressing a hand to the hot stitch in her side.

'We need more coal. The fire's going down and there's none left. Then I want fresh water, more clean sheets and towels. Oh, and the cradle. We should have it in here.' Flo, feeling herself to be in charge, barely looked up.

Leaving Cook to wring her hands and mutter anxiously to herself at the bottom of the bed, Morag dragged the intricate, white-painted crib through from the dressing room then fetched the linen from a corridor cupboard. Next she carried a jug of fresh water up from the kitchen and finally turned her attention to the fire. It was low and the brass scuttle was empty.

The five spare scuttles were normally filled by one of the lads and left in the kitchen. This morning they were all empty. Morag knew she would have to fill at least two of them.

Throwing a shawl round her shoulders she forced the door open, stepping back quickly when snow spilled into the kitchen. Gritting her teeth against the cold she plunged outside, sinking almost to her knees in icy softness.

The coal store was on the back wall of the stable block, a few feet from the kitchen door but the snow had drifted high, burying it and the shovels which were usually stacked next to it. Sighing, Morag kicked into the soft snow until her feet met something solid. Using her hands she scraped away the snow until she found the door which covered the opening through which the coal could be shovelled. Then she had to plunge her arms, up to the elbows, in fresh snow until she found a shovel. By the time she started to dig the coal out her fingers were so numb that she could hardly keep her grip on the handle.

She worked as quickly as she could, filling first one scuttle and dragging it into the kitchen then starting work on the second. It was half full when a sudden cramp in her abdomen caused her to buckle on to her knees. She stayed there, sweat breaking out on her forehead, until the pain eased off, then very slowly and still on her knees, she used her bare hands to gather the rest of the coal. When she finally got it indoors she was dizzy and slightly nauseous but she only allowed herself a couple of minutes' rest before dragging the scuttle up to Lady Katrina's bedroom.

She could see at once that the child was about to be born. Katrina screamed and strained until the cords on her delicate neck stood proud and white. Flo, sweat beading her own brow, was poised to guide the baby out.

'Quick, Morag. Get that fire built up,' Cook shouted urgently. 'You've been far too long. The room's getting cold.'

Morag bent to fling the coals on the dying fire, felt the cramp shoot through her body again and gasped with the pain of it. Behind her Katrina gave a strangled cry and Morag turned just in time to see a tiny, red, blood-stained body slither from between her legs. Her own groan of agony was lost in the general exclamations of relief as the child made its way safely into the world. Only when she fell to the floor, toppling against the waiting crib, did anyone turn to look at her.

Katrina found herself alone with her baby and just

young Chrissy for company. Everyone else had rushed off to attend to Morag who was obviously about to give birth to her own child.

She sneaked another look at her new-born daughter who had been placed snugly in the crook of her arm. She felt not even the slightest stirring of affection. What she did feel when she gazed at the innocent child was deep, resentful anger. 'Here,' she said loudly, waking Chrissy who had fallen asleep, despite being the only member of the household to have slept through the previous night. 'Take it. Put it in its cot then leave me alone. I want to sleep.'

'Yes, ma'am.' The young girl extricated the baby awkwardly from its mother's arms and tucked it into its cradle before tiptoeing out of the room.

Alone at last Katrina turned her head into her pillow and wept.

Morag emerged from a sea of never ending pain to face a weakness so great that she had hardly the strength to open her eyes. Somewhere between her legs her insides were spilling out but she was past caring, hadn't even the strength to keep her eyes open for long enough to see the child.

Flo gathered the bloodied sheets and tied them into a bundle, brushing back the hair from her sweat-drenched face. She was almost as pale as Morag and, now that the immediate crisis was over, found she was shaking uncontrollably. With a small gasp she collapsed on to a chair. 'I didn't know,' she admitted. 'I didn't realise it could be so bad. All that blood. . .'

'You did your best, Flo,' Cook assured her. 'It must have been all that running up and down the stairs that set her off. The lassie wasn't fit for such heavy work. I don't know why Lady Katrina didn't just send her home to her mother weeks ago! Still, at least the wean's safe, though what sort of life it'll have, I don't know.' She tutted over the tiny babe then wrapped it securely in a cut down blanket and placed it in the drawer which had been hurriedly emptied for it.

'Poor wee thing,' Flo said, coming to look at the infant. She looked back at her patient who was so pale her skin was almost transparent. 'She's still bleeding. If it doesn't stop soon she'll die.' Her voice cracked, on the edge of tears. 'What will happen to the bairn if that happens?'

'Maybe she should have thought of that before she got herself expecting,' was Cook's cold comment. 'You've done your best for her, Flo. All we can do now is wait for the doctor to arrive. Now, you away and tidy yourself up. I'll go and tell Lady Katrina what's happened. We shouldn't have left her for so long. Chrissy can come and sit with Morag.'

Cook puffed off to deliver the sombre news to Katrina who was now sitting up in bed, looking puffy eyed and miserable.

'Well?' she demanded as soon as Mrs McManus entered her room. 'What did she have?'

Aware of Lady Katrina's disappointment and the consequences the birth of a girl would have, Cook tried to divert her. 'Flo's gey worried about Morag. The lassie's lost a lot of blood.'

But, rested now and alert, Katrina's only interest was in the sex of the child. 'What is it?' she demanded impatiently. 'A girl or a boy?'

'A boy, ma'am,' Mrs McManus mumbled.

Colour flared in Katrina's face then faded again. 'I see. And did you say Morag has had a difficult time?'

'Yes, ma'am. It doesn't look good for her at all. She's hardly breathing and still bleeding. It's the afterbirth. It didn't all come away.' They both knew that, untreated, it was a death sentence.

'Has she seen the child?'

'No, ma'am. I don't think she knew what was happening to her.'

'Bring the baby to me,' Katrina ordered suddenly.

'Ma'am?' Mrs McManus was sure she had misheard.

'Bring Morag's child here. I want to see it,' Katrina snapped.

'Yes, ma'am.' Cook scurried away.

'Is it healthy?' Katrina asked, when Cook came back with the sleeping child in her arms.

'Aye, he's a fine wee thing. About eight pounds or so I should think.'

Katrina turned her face away and looked out of the window, hiding her tears. 'It's stopped snowing,' she whispered after a long silence.

'Och, so it has!' Cook, the child still in her arms, raced to look out. 'It's turned to rain and the snow's already turning to slush. Surely the doctor will be here soon.'

'When he does get here ask him to look in on Morag first,' Katrina said with a sudden beaming smile. 'Now, give that poor little scrap to me. He'll be warmer here.' She held her arms out, ignoring her own daughter who was slumbering peacefully at the side of the bed.

Cook was back in her kitchen, musing over her mistress's strange behaviour, leaving Chrissy to her vigil at Morag's side and Flo to attend to the neglected household chores, when the bell jangled wildly. Thinking there was some emergency she dashed upstairs with as much speed as her ageing legs would allow.

To her astonishment Katrina was sitting on the edge of the bed with the little boy sucking lustily at her breast.

'He's a beautiful child,' Katrina said, smiling dreamily as Cook rushed in.

'Aye, he is that, poor little soul,' Cook agreed.

'Sit down, Mrs McManus, I want to talk with you before the doctor arrives.'

'Shall I fetch you some tea first, Lady Katrina?'

'No! Sit down.'

Cook obeyed and waited silently.

'Mrs McManus, what I am about to say must remain between us. I am going to trust you to keep this to yourself.'

'Yes, ma'am.'

'I am very sorry for Morag. If you are right, she may die and this poor little boy will have no mother or father.'

'It's gey sad, ma'am,' Cook muttered, the edge of disapproval clear in her voice.

'I feel I have a responsibility for this child, Mrs McManus. He has Angus's blood in his veins.'

'Yes, ma'am,' Cook whispered, flushing with embarrassment. 'But there are places . . . homes for weans like that.'

'I am well aware of that, Mrs McManus. Please do not interrupt.'

'Yes, ma'am.'

'How long have you been here, Mrs McManus?'

'Och, nigh on forty-five years, ma'am. I started as a kitchen maid when I was just a lass of thirteen.'

'So, this is your home?' Katrina asked, finally taking her eyes from the child to watch Cook closely.

'Aye.'

'If Edward Fraser takes over this estate, Mrs McManus, where would you go?'

'I don't rightly know, ma'am. I'm likely too old to get another post. I suppose I'll have to ask one of my sisters to take me in.'

'How very unpleasant for you,' Katrina purred.

'Yes, ma'am.'

'Now, Mrs McManus. I want you to understand that although what I am going to suggest might shock you, it is for the best. You would benefit as much as anyone else.'

Cook nodded, blowing her nose noisily.

'I propose that this shall be my child.'

Cook's head jerked up. 'The wee boy, ma'am?'

'Yes. He will be my son.'

'But you have a bonny wee lassie, Lady Katrina!' Cook's shock was obvious.

'Yes. And as a result I will have no home of my own, and neither will she. The settlement made by my husband will give me no option but to return to my mother's home. I will have to leave Pitochrie. And so will all of you. If that happens what will become of this little boy?'

Cook might be slow in her movements but her mind was still agile. She understood completely. 'I know what you're meaning, ma'am. But what about the wee girl?'

'I shall take the boy as mine and keep the girl here with me too and allow her to be brought up with my son. It will be seen as an act of charity but I will love her just the same. This way will be so much better for everyone. For the boy, for my daughter, for me. And for you too, Mrs McManus. Think about it.'

'I understand, Lady Katrina,' Mrs McManus said. And indeed it did seem the best possible solution. Each child would have a secure, loving home and, perhaps the most important thing of all, her own future would be settled; the evil day when she would have to beg a home with one of her sisters delayed for the foreseeable future.

Katrina saw the small smile which twitched at the corners of Cook's mouth and knew she had won. 'Well?' she demanded. 'Do you agree? Can you persuade Flo to see it our way?'

'Yes, ma'am, I am sure she will be sensible. But what about Morag? I mean, the lassie's ill but she may recover.'

'We both know how unlikely that is,' Katrina sighed. 'I wouldn't have had this happen for the world and,' she flushed slightly then knew she had to go on now or risk losing everything, 'I hope, with all my heart that the girl recovers, but there is no time to lose. The doctor, when he arrives, must believe the boy is mine! If Morag gets better, well, I think a woman on her own would rather her child was a girl, don't you? It would be company for her later.' She paused a moment then asked, 'You are sure she doesn't know she gave birth to a son?'

'Quite sure, ma'am. The poor lassie was out cold. Too weak to care.'

'Well, there's no problem then, is there? If Morag gets better I will allow her to remain here. Her daughter will be brought up with my son. Naturally I would want her to have the very best. And, Mrs McManus . . .'

'Yes, ma'am?'

'You would find me very generous in my appreciation. I think I could find you a house on the estate for your retirement and . . . and some sort of gratuity to make your old age more comfortable. And of course there would be something for Flo too, just to let her see how much I value loyalty.'

'Yes, ma'am. Thank you, ma'am. Leave it to me to explain things to Flo.'

'Good,' Katrina smiled and stroked the little boy's downy head. 'And you will make sure Chrissy knows I had a son?'

Cook snorted. 'Don't worry about Chrissy, ma'am. The lassie's away with the fairies half the time. She won't know any better.'

'You can't do that!' Flo was horrified.

'Don't be so stupid,' Cook retorted. 'If you think about it for a minute you'll see it's for the best. Both the weans will be provided for this way. What on earth would happen to that wee laddie without a mother or father to care for him? Lady Katrina would be within her rights to send Morag and the wean away. And what would happen to them then? We all know Annie McDonald doesn't want anything to do with it.'

'I suppose so,' Flo agreed reluctantly. 'But what will we tell Morag?'

'That she has a bonny wee lassie,' Cook told her sternly, looking at the still figure on the bed. 'But I don't think the poor girl will ever know.'

'No,' Flo whispered. 'She's hardly alive. I don't think it'll be long now. Still,' she added, 'it's not right. We shouldn't do anything until after . . . until we know if she's going to recover.'

'That'll be too late! The doctor will be here soon and we have to let him think Lady Katrina had a boy.'

'No, I can't do it,' Flo shook her head vehemently.

'Well, you might as well start packing your bags. As soon as it's known that Lady Katrina had a lassie, Mr Edward Fraser will be over here with his own staff and we'll be out on the street! Och, Flo, use your head will

215

you! Lady Katrina is just trying to do her best for all of us. And,' she added slyly, 'she did say something about showing her appreciation. Money,' she said starkly, 'for your loyalty.'

'What?' Flo turned wide eyes on her.

'You'll need it if you get married. It's gey hard setting up a home these days.' Cook was well aware that Flo had marriage with one of the lads from the village in mind.

'Well . . . in that case,' Flo stammered, 'and it doesn't look good for Morag, does it?'

'No, it doesn't. Here, put the wee lass in the drawer there, in case the doctor comes. I'll away and call Chrissy back to sit with Morag and then we'll tell Lady Katrina she doesn't have to worry.'

Chrissy sat with the unmoving Morag while Cook whistled busily in the kitchen. Flo, her mind occupied with the prospects for her own wedding if Lady Katrina did give her some money, busied herself tidying Katrina's room.

'Oh dear,' Katrina sighed, 'I do wish the doctor would hurry up.' Her concern wasn't for herself but for Morag, especially now that the question of the child had been so happily resolved. It would be so much simpler if Morag could recover to take charge of the girl. A charitable gesture was one thing but to allow the illegitimate child of a servant to remain in the castle after its mother's death would cause intense speculation. 'Have a look out of the window, Flo. I'm sure I heard something then.'

Flo crossed to the window and gazed out over a dreary scene. The snow was already melting under the combination of rain and sun which had alternated throughout the day. The trees dripped and drooped,

216

while the emerging hilltops had darker streaks in the crevasses where the melting snow swelled the mountain steams to violent torrents. And, plodding through the slush on the drive, came two old horses, drawing a dilapidated cart. Two men huddled wetly on the driving board.

'It's Jim Kineil, Lady Katrina. And I'm almost sure that's Doctor Drummond with him.' Flo beamed.

'Off you go then and make sure he sees that poor girl first,' Katrina instructed. 'And Flo . . .'

'Yes, ma'am.'

'What Cook spoke to you about earlier . . . Make certain wee Chrissy doesn't say anything stupid.'

'Yes, Lady Katrina.'

By the time Flo had hurried downstairs, Cook had already admitted the doctor and was leading him, huffing and puffing, up the long staircase. Flo intercepted them.

'Excuse me, Mrs McManus. Lady Katrina says the doctor's to see to Morag first.'

The elderly man's eyebrows shot up. 'Morag? Who is this Morag? I understood I was called to attend Lady Katrina's confinement.' It was only the thought of the nice fat fee his attendance here would merit that had enticed him out into the snow today.

'Lady Katrina had a wee boy this morning and they're both fine,' Cook explained, raising her voice over his attempt to interrupt. 'But one of the lassies who work here has had a bairn too. She wasn't due for a week or two. I think it was all the running around after Lady Katrina that started her off. The bairn was born a wee while ago and she's right as rain but the lassie is very poorly.'

'It's only right I see Lady Katrina first,' he insisted,

ministering to servants was something he left to less eminent physicians.

'No.' Flo led him on past Katrina's door to the room which sheltered Morag. 'Morag is very ill, doctor. She's Lady Katrina's personal maid and Lady Katrina is very fond of her. You've got to help her.' Resolutely she opened the door and guided the protesting man in. His objections died as soon as he saw the condition of the girl on the bed. Rolling his sleeves up he was at once practical and efficient.

'Is the child well?' he asked as he checked Morag's pulse.

'Yes, doctor. A fine wee lassie. Sleeping soundly.' Flo indicated the drawer.

'It was a boy!' Chrissy rose from the chair where she had been watching over Morag, puzzlement plain in her face.

The doctor looked at her sharply.

'No, Chrissy. It was Lady Katrina who had the boy. Go and see for yourself and tell Lady Katrina the doctor is with Morag.' Flo hustled the youngster from the room and Chrissy went with a frown of confusion on her brow.

'She gets awful mixed up sometimes,' Cook explained smoothly. 'She's a wee bit simple headed.'

'I know the family,' Flo added. 'They're all a bit slow.'

Doctor Drummond nodded absently then instantly forgot young Chrissy as he bent to attend to his patient.

For more than half an hour he massaged Morag's soft abdomen, pushing so hard that Flo was frightened he was inflicting even more damage. But, when she was sure it had all been for nothing, something dark and bloody slipped from his patient and, almost immediately, the flow of blood from between her legs slowed to almost nothing.

He washed his hands and arms in the warm water Flo had brought for him and sighed. 'That's all I can do. It was the afterbirth, it had separated. She was bleeding to death. She may be too far gone already. There's no way of knowing. Keep her warm and if she wakes get plenty of liquid into her. Don't let her move around under any circumstances. There's nothing more I can do for her. Get the local doctor to take a look at her if she doesn't improve.' He closed his case and strode to the door. 'Now, take me to Lady Katrina.'

Katrina was sitting up looking radiantly happy as she nursed her son.

'I'm afraid you're too late, doctor,' she smiled. 'I managed perfectly well without you.'

'So I see. So I see,' he boomed jovially. 'And a splendid little fellow he is too. I'll just have a quick look at him.' Expertly unwrapping the child he examined its navel then handed the baby over to Flo to be dressed again. 'It appears you were in very good hands, Lady Katrina,' he smiled. 'But perhaps I should examine you, just to make sure everything is in order.'

'NO!' The thought filled her with horror. 'I can assure you that everything is fine, doctor. I feel wonderful.'

He nodded, well used to this attitude from his patients. 'If you are sure.'

'I am as well as I possibly could be,' Katrina assured him with absolute honesty. 'I am much more concerned about Morag.'

'I have done all I can for her, Lady Katrina. All we can do now is wait.'

While both babies thrived on the attentions of a nurse from the village who fed the little girl on fresh goats' milk from Morrison's farm leaving Katrina to derive immense pleasure from nursing her son, Morag hovered colourlessly between life and death. It wasn't until the third day that her eyelids fluttered open. Flo who was stationed at her bedside sprang to her feet and put a cup of water to the girl's pallid lips.

'Just take a wee sip, Morag.' She tipped the cup and was moved to tears to see her friend gulp desperately at the tepid liquid. Exhausted, Morag's head slumped to the pillow, her eyes closed, and she drifted back into the shadowy world which seemed to have trapped her. After that Flo woke her hourly by gently pinching her cheeks, flicking at her cold fingers and even dripping icy water on her face so that she could dribble warm broth and water between her lips. The next day, though Morag stayed in a deep sleep, a gentle hint of colour was replacing the dreadful grey which had tinged her skin.

It was a full week before she finally opened her eyes properly. 'Can you hear me, Morag?' Flo asked gently.

Morag nodded but her eyes had a look of fear in them as she stared round the room. 'This is Sir Angus's room,' she croaked, her voice low and harsh.

'Aye,' Flo said, smiling broadly. 'We've been taking care of you in comfort.'

Morag closed her eyes as the memories flooded back. She had been in Katrina's room and the baby was being born but after that she could recall nothing at all. 'Did . . . did Lady Katrina have her bairn?' she whispered eventually.

'Aye. A fine, healthy boy.' The lie came easily. Lady Katrina was so often to be found nursing the little boy that it seemed that he was indeed her son. 'And you've a bonny little daughter.'

Morag stared at her, as if she hadn't understood then, hardly able to find the strength to move, slid her hands down to her stomach. Where there had been an uncomfortable lump there was now a soft flatness. 'A wee girl?' she echoed.

'Aye. She's right bonny.'

'Can I see her?' Morag struggled to sit up but Flo pushed her back gently. 'Lay still. You had a hard time having her and you've been in this bed a week now, scaring us all half to death. Just rest there a while and I'll fetch her to you.'

Morag was so weak that she had no choice but to lie back. Flo hurried away to tell everyone the good news. Then she and Cook followed the nurse into the room and watched as Morag met her daughter for the first time.

'Here, lass. You know me don't you? I'm Mary Murchie from the village and I'm looking after the weans until you're strong enough to do it for yourself.' Flo propped Morag up on her pillows and the nurse placed the child in Morag's arms.

'Och, she's beautiful,' Morag whispered, beaming with happiness as the little girl opened her pale, grey eyes and looked right at her. 'I really hoped I would have a wee lassie,' she admitted when she felt able to speak. Over her head Cook and Flo exchanged quick, relieved glances.

Her daughter cradled protectively in her arms, Morag fell into a deep, healing sleep.

ELEVEN

Morag was enchanted with her tiny daughter. She spent hours simply watching her, marvelling at her infant perfection, grateful for the unexpected kindness of Lady Katrina who was allowing her to remain at the castle while she convalesced.

'What are you going to name her?' Annie, sitting stiffly by Morag's bed, asked.

'Emmelina,' Morag answered firmly.

'Emmelina!' Annie spluttered. 'What sort of name is that for . . .' She bit off the rest.

Morag had hoped that this visit would be a reconciliation but Annie had barely looked at the little girl sleeping innocently in the lined drawer which was doing duty as a crib. Her cold, disapproving manner hurt Morag deeply. Now, sensitive to the slur the child would carry because of the circumstances of her birth, she reacted bitterly to her mother's words. 'Say it, Mam. A wee bastard. Is that what you meant?'

'Well, isn't that exactly what she is?' Annie retorted. 'You'll never live this down, Morag. You've ruined yourself, brought disgrace on the whole family. You'll never get a husband now. No decent man would want to know you. And as for this child. What hope will she have?' Annie sighed then moderated her tone and broached the subject which had led her to swallow some of her pride and come here today. 'Och Morag, it's not too late. There's a place in Edinburgh takes in children like this.

Give her to me and let me take her there. It'll be for the best. Maybe some good family would take her, bring her up as their own. Then we can put all this behind us. You could even come home . . .'

'No! She's mine, Mam, and she's staying with me. Maybe I won't be able to buy her new clothes and fancy playthings but she'll grow up knowing she's loved.'

Annie's mouth set into a rigid line. 'It's your life. I've offered you a way out but if you won't take my advice then don't think you can come running to me when things get hard. This is your shame, Morag and I want none of it.' She glanced briefly at the child and snorted her derision. 'Emmelina! A fancy name won't change what she is.'

Morag kept her head down to hide the tears which had filled her eyes and whispered, 'She deserves a beautiful name. I won't hide her away, Mam. The fault was mine, not hers. Anyway,' she added, 'Emily was Grandma McDonald's name.' Her father's mother had been an infrequent visitor to the McDonald household but her kindness and good humour had made a lasting impression on the young Morag.

'Your grandma was a God-fearing woman! She'd be affronted.' Annie surged to her feet and rebuttoned her coat, pulling her shawl close against the winter weather. 'I don't think there's much point in me staying any longer, Morag. I've given you the best advice I can. If you won't take it . . .' she turned and walked stiff-backed to the door then turned back. 'There's a pram in the yard for you. I don't suppose you've even thought about things like that.'

Morag's heart lifted a fraction. 'Thank you.'

'Och, don't bother to thank me. It's Rab you should be grateful to for that. Got it from some family over

223

Glenelg way. And he's making a cot for the wean too, though why he should bother is beyond me.' With that she slipped through the door and hurried out of the castle, careful to avoid having to talk to anyone who might know of her daughter's disgrace.

Anxious not to impose on Lady Katrina's generosity, as soon as her strength started to return, Morag began to take over her new duties as nursemaid to little Angus, releasing Mary Murchie to return to her own family. In fact most of Morag's time was spent with her own daughter. Katrina, who was enraptured with her son, kept him with her constantly, expecting Morag only to attend to his small items of laundry and his night-time feeds.

Morag couldn't help comparing the little lad with her own daughter. He was a fine, healthy boy with plump limbs, a thick cap of hair, which had an auburn tint to it, and a lusty wail. Fortunately for the peace of the household he was a contented child and seldom cried without reason, allowing himself to be easily comforted by a warm cuddle or a few soft words. Morag's generous heart soon found it had enough love to spare for both children. Emmelina – or Ina as everyone insisted on calling her, apparently sharing her mother's opinion on the child's full name – would always hold first place in her affections but little Angus Fraser had captivated her too, almost, she thought, as if he was also her child.

Compared to Angus her tiny daughter seemed fragile with her fluffy blonde hair and long, thin limbs but, like her sturdy half brother, she was perfectly healthy. Unlike little Angus, Ina already showed signs of a determined personality, refusing to sleep until she decided she was ready and complaining vigorously if her bottle of warmed goats' milk did not appear the second she was hungry for it.

Looking down at her daughter's busy face as she sucked away at her bottle, all the bitterness and anger Morag had felt during her pregnancy vanished. She was under no illusion, life would be hard for her with an illegitimate daughter, but here, under Lady Katrina's protective wing, she was sheltered and secure. Or so she thought.

Every time Katrina saw Morag with her son she experienced a gut-twisting spasm of guilt and jealousy, though seeing the little girl she had carried inside her own body for nine long months brought no emotional response at all. Increasingly she regretted her commitment to Morag and wished only to be rid of what she saw as a threat to her son's future, a threat which, in her mind, increased daily as the child's hair darkened to a shade which so very nearly matched Morag's own. There were times too when she thought she saw similarities around his mouth and eyes. By the time he was three months old Katrina knew that, one way or another, Morag and the baby girl had to leave. But it had to be done carefully. Simply to turn the girl and child out might very well lose her the support of Cook and Flo who both knew far too much about the truth of little Angus's birth. No, she decided, she could not fire the girl without good reason. But there were ways . . .

Morag suddenly found herself overwhelmed with work, expected to run the nursery and take her share of chores round the house. And no matter how hard she worked it seemed she could never please her mistress who frequently found reason to complain. Luckily for Morag, Angus spent most of his time with his doting mother – almost as if Katrina didn't trust her with her son – and Ina still slept most of the day away in the warmth of the kitchen.

Then, just as the spring of 1908 was making its first tentative challenge to winter, Ina caught a cold. Her little nose turned bright red and she sniffled and coughed miserably, demanding her mother's constant attention. Lady Katrina had left the sleeping Angus in Morag's care while she paid a social call and Morag watched over him in the warmth of the nursery while cuddling her daughter anxiously. Ina had just fallen into a restless sleep when Katrina surged angrily into the room.

'Cook tells me that that child has a cold,' she said in such an accusing tone that Morag sprang to her feet, wondering what on earth she had done to annoy her mistress.

'Aye, she's a wee bit restless but she's a lot better than she was yesterday.'

'Whatever are you thinking of! I will not have her in here with Angus, spreading her germs about. Take her upstairs to your own room at once.'

'It's awful cold up there, Lady Katrina,' Morag spoke out bravely in defence of her child.

'Do not argue with me!' Katrina snapped. 'In fact, Morag, I have been meaning to talk to you for some time. I have decided to employ a nursemaid for Angus. My mother has recommended a young woman called Clara Ingham and she will be arriving here on Sunday. Please have your things out of the nursery by then.'

'Ma'am?' Morag gasped. 'I thought I was to be the nursemaid? Have I done something wrong?'

'It is obvious to me that you are taking advantage of my kindness, Morag. Today, for instance, here you are nursing your daughter when you should be attending to

226

my needs, and those of my son. And I have heard that you are frequently late in the mornings. Twice recently there has been no fire in my sitting room after breakfast.'

'Angus is still waking in the night, ma'am. I have to feed and change him. And Ina.'

'That is no excuse. I have been more than generous with you, Morag, allowing you, and your child, to remain here because I was misguided enough to think I owed it to my husband to ensure that his child had a decent home. You should be grateful to have a roof over your heads and I certainly expected you to be making more of an effort to please.'

'The little ones take up so much of my time, ma'am.'

'I realise that in trying to help you I made a mistake, Morag. You are only just nineteen and too young for such responsibility. But even you should have known that you could not possibly allow that child to be in the same room as Angus while she is unwell. I simply cannot allow you to put my child at risk.'

'Yes, ma'am.' Morag was too aware of how much she depended on Lady Katrina's goodwill to argue and she was probably right about the cold.

'From Monday you will resume your old duties. The care of your own child is your concern. I will allow her to stay here so long as she does not disrupt the smooth running of the household. For now, do as I say and put her to sleep in your room then go and help Mrs McManus. And, Morag.'

'Yes, ma'am?'

'I hope you will not give me any further cause for complaint.' With that Katrina strode from the room, leaving Morag to trail her daughter upstairs to the chill of the attic.

'Morag! Will you please stop that wean from wailing. She's giving me a headache,' Cook, up to her elbows in flour, complained.

'She's hungry. She should have had her lunch an hour ago,' Morag retorted angrily.

'If you had finished your chores on time she would have been fed!' was the waspish reply.

Morag sighed and hurried to replace the rags she had been using to polish the silver. 'Come on my wee Ina,' she said, lifting the child from the makeshift playpen where she spent most of her waking hours, protected from the hard flags of the kitchen floor by nothing more than an old blanket.

'God knows what you're going to do when she's too big for that thing,' Mrs McManus went on. 'I can't have her running round under my feet all day. She shouldn't be in here. It's dangerous with all the pots and the open fire.'

'I know. But what else can I do? Lady Katrina won't let her into the nursery and I can't leave her on her own in my room all day.'

'You'll have to ask your mother to help you out, Morag. I can't have this child in my kitchen.'

Morag shook her head, causing a damp tendril of coppery hair to escape from her cap. 'Mam won't help. She's only seen her a couple of times. She's shamed by her.'

'Aye, I can see she would be,' Cook agreed nastily. 'But you'll have to do something, Morag. Lady Katrina was complaining again yesterday about the noise she makes and she's says her good dress has been waiting for you to mend that tear in it for nearly two weeks now. If you're not careful you'll find yourself without a job.' And a very good thing that would be too, she thought. Having Morag and her bastard child in the house was an insult to all decent women – and a nasty thorn in her own conscience.

'I do the best I can, Mrs McManus,' Morag pleaded.

'Maybe, but it's not good enough.'

On her next half day, Morag tied seven-month-old Ina in her old pram, laughing as the child rocked wildly on the creaking springs, chortling with delight at this rare treat. Stifled by the restrictions and hostility of the house, where only wee Chrissy still treated her with any kindness, Morag was determined to escape for a few hours and give her baby daughter a taste of clean, fresh air. Above them the hills stood out in shades of muted brown and green against the clear blue sky and Morag felt a rush of nostalgia for the freedom she had found there in her own childhood. For a moment she even played with the idea of walking up the long mountain path to dangle her feet again in the clear stream as it tumbled in frothing bubbles over the rocks of the hillside, yearning to let her own child taste the simple pleasures of the hillfoots. But it would be impossible to push the heavy pram up the steep, rocky path.

Reluctantly she followed the track through the woods towards the cottage, knowing that she owed it to Ina to try and find some way of making Annie accept the child. As she walked, the warm summer air brought an attractive flush of colour to her pale cheeks. Her hair, unbound, rippled round her shoulders in deep, auburn waves. Her stride, unimpeded by the rutted track, was free and loose, so that anyone seeing mother and child on this glorious summer day would have imagined them to be enjoying a carefree afternoon walk. The furrow of worry between Morag's troubled eyes would have dispelled that impression immediately.

She made a point of visiting her mother at least once a month, always hoping for some sign of forgiveness. But Annie remained stubbornly hostile, seeming to grudge her daughter even an hour of her time and steadfastly ignoring Ina who, sensing her mother's unhappiness, was always at her irascible worst. Morag had little hope that today would be any different.

Her fears were well founded. A little more than an hour later Morag trudged back up the woodland path. Ina, exhausted by her own tearful reaction to her mother's distress, had finally slumped against her pillow and was fast asleep. Looking at her Morag felt a surge of choking anger. With tears still clinging to her dark lashes, her little pointed chin still quivering and her fine, fair curls tousled, Ina looked angelically beautiful. How, Morag asked herself again, could her mother's heart be so hardened against her own grandchild? This latest visit had been just as she had expected it to be. Annie had been cold and distant, taking minimal interest in her grandchild and, most hurtful of all, actively discouraging Ayleen from playing with her. Ayleen, a pretty, mischievous toddler, had been first confused and then openly rebellious, earning herself a sharp slap across the back of her dimpled legs when she returned again and again to Ina, offering to share one toy after another with the open friendship of childhood. Morag had almost cried for the injustice of it but had held her tongue, knowing she couldn't afford to antagonise her mother any further. In the end, to save Ayleen from further undeserved punishment, she had exiled Ina to her pram in the garden.

It had taken Morag the best part of forty-five minutes to gather her courage and beg Annie for help in caring for Ina.

'Mam, if I don't do something soon, I'll lose my job.

230

Lady Katrina is always complaining about Ina and Mrs McManus says she gets in the way. It's not good for her, Mam, cooped up like that all day. She needs to be outside, in the fresh air. I don't know how much longer she will be able to stay in the playpen. In another four or five months she'll be walking and won't want to be caged up all day. She gets bad tempered enough now because there's not enough room for her to roll about.'

'I told you no, Morag, so there's no point in talking about it.'

'She's your grandchild, Mam. And Ayleen needs someone to play with, stuck away down here with no one else for miles.'

'I can barely hold my head up in the village as it is. I'll not have that child here, starting their tongues wagging all over again.'

'Those miserable busy-bodies in the village are more important to you than your own family, are they?' Morag demanded furiously.

'Up in the hills I never had the chance to make friends with the other women. Even after we came down here, what with your father the way he was, they all avoided us. It's only in the last couple of years that I've had friends, people to go and chat to, folk who would help me if I needed it. Good, church-going folk who are black affronted by lassies like you. So, aye, their opinion is important to me,' Annie said, a slight quaver in her voice betraying her emotion.

'It's a good job they don't know about you and Uncle Rab then, isn't it?' Morag hit back furiously.

Annie's reaction was instantaneous. She lashed out, slapping Morag hard across the cheek. 'Don't you ever speak to me like that again,' she hissed, barely able to control her voice. 'Now get out and don't come back until you can apologise.'

Morag made her way slowly back up the track, but, unable to face the continuing reprobation at the castle, she made her way into the village. It was months since she had been there, forced into hiding by her pregnancy. But, with her mother's words still biting into her, she was determined to be seen, to make everyone understand that the shame was theirs, not hers, was in their narrow, unforgiving minds.

Pitochrie was a small village, an uneven road lined, for about two hundred yards on either side, by houses. With few exceptions they were all of the same kind, high-roofed, single-storey, grey stone cottages in blocks of four or five, fronting directly on to the road, their inhabitants being judged by the curtains at the windows and the cleanliness of their front steps.

The village had been built in the more prosperous time of the late Angus Fraser's grandfather to house the estate workers and most were still occupied by their descendants. Some of the men still worked for the estate, like the gardener and the two outside men who did oddjobs around the grounds, or Watty Mathieson who as game-keeper, responsible to Rab, kept one eye on the grouse moors and another on the river, making sure no one helped themselves to more than a modest amount of the castle's livestock. Still others were employed as labourers on the two farms. There were few families who didn't have relatives in the village and newcomers were regarded with universal suspicion which made it hard for them to win acceptance in much under twenty years.

A flesher, a general store and a post office were lined up on one side of the street with the public house and the kirk as unlikely neighbours on the other. Slightly

232

apart from the common housing, at the Glenelg end of the village, were a dozen or so slightly larger houses, with the school and the farriers forming a tangible barrier between the two halves. This end of the village boasted the minister himself and the schoolteacher among their locally illustrious residents. Those who were rich enough to have their own detached properties lived even further along the road, their houses set back in long gardens, their privacy further protected by muslin curtains. The two or three families with real money luxuriated at the end of long drives in choice spots beside the Annan or under the hills, advertising their social standing by the number of servants they employed and by the length of time they could delay before settling their accounts with the local tradesmen.

The most influential man in the village was the minister. Few dared miss kirk on Sundays without a solid excuse. Those who were rash enough to stay abed while their neighbours nodded to the tedious drone from the pulpit could expect to be brought to task publicly, either by the minister in person or one of his equally unforgiving elders. Week after week the congregation had the sins of lust, greed and sloth drummed into them, to the point where the more susceptible women felt it was a sin to enjoy their husband's attentions and blushed at the thought of buying their own knickers. There were many more, like Finty Chisholm, who went through life grabbing any chance for a good time with both hands while putting on a suitably pious face for Sundays. And there was nothing any of them enjoyed more than the spectacle of someone else's disgrace.

Morag emerged from the track on to the main street just as Ina woke up and struggled to pull herself into a sitting position. Stopping, Morag lifted the little girl and

233

tied her firmly to the sides of the pram, talking to her all the time, her love obvious in the way she handled the child. Opposite, the curtains of a house twitched then settled again.

Further down the street, Mysie Arneil gossiped with two other women. Seeing Morag approaching they nudged each other and watched with tight-lipped disapproval as she steered the pram towards the shops.

'Hello, Mysie,' Morag smiled, delighted to have found someone to talk to.

Mysie nodded coldly then turned her back and resumed her conversation, pointedly excluding Morag.

Morag hesitated for a moment then stuck her chin in the air and marched past them, feeling their unfriendly eyes boring into her back.

At the small general store she parked the pram and went inside looking for thread with which to repair a skirt. The shop was seldom empty. Even when the women had bought their messages they lingered to chat, sitting on the wooden chairs at the side of the counter until they had caught up on all the local gossip. Morag wasn't surprised to find three women nodding and clucking their tongues over some piece of scandal.

'Good afternoon,' she said, but warily now and wasn't surprised when they ignored her.

The grocer, Bernie Burns, looked up briefly then continued to cut slab after slab of cheese. In the end Morag asked, 'Have you any white thread please, Mr Burns?' in her most pleasant voice.

Bernie looked up slowly then raked her body with a look of absolute contempt before turning to his shelves. He came towards her with the reel of thread in his hand and thumped it on the counter in front of her, not saying a word.

234

'It's a beautiful day, isn't it?' Morag included the three women in her smile, saw them frown their disapproval and added, 'I've been taking Ina for a walk. The fresh air is doing her good,' refusing to let them cow her.

They all looked away, staring at the shelves, examining their fingers or rummaging through their handbags. Morag smiled grimly and looked back at Bernie Burns.

She waited for him to tell her the price but he stayed resolutely silent, his mouth welded in disdain. Finally losing patience she asked, 'What do I owe you, Mr Burns?'

'Penny ha'penny,' he growled, taking her money and turning his back on her.

'Wonder she's got the cheek to show her face in decent company,' one of the women muttered, just loud enough for Morag to hear.

'Little slut,' another one said, gaining confidence.

Morag's composure deserted her. Flaming colour filled her face and she hurried from the shop, coming face to face with Mysie and her cronies who had been staring at Ina as if she was an exhibit in a freak show. Someone had turned the pram so that the child, who was sobbing with fear, was facing the blank wall.

'Get away from that pram,' Morag screamed. 'Leave my baby alone.'

'Mind your mouth, Morag McDonald,' Mysie retorted. 'That's no way to speak to your betters. You would be better on your knees in the kirk, asking God for his forgiveness, than parading your sin round where it offends decent folks.' Too late Morag remembered that Charlie Arneil was now a church elder.

'It's you that's in the wrong, Mysie Arneil,' Morag rounded on her. 'Taking out your spite on an innocent child because you're too old and dried up to have one of your own. And as for being my better . . . you were a maid at the castle just the same as me and I heard Sir Angus had his way with you whenever he wanted.'

She knew that had been unforgivable, even if it was based on the truth, but couldn't help a small smirk of satisfaction when Mysie gave a thin shriek, covered her burning cheeks with her hands and looked desperately from one agog friend to the other. Seeing nothing but speculation in their expressions she turned and fled.

Morag took advantage of the distraction to wheel Ina quickly along the street, feeling that unfriendly eyes were watching her from behind every window. She was walking so fast that she almost knocked Willie Chisholm over before she saw him.

'Whoa . . .' he laughed jumping aside nimbly.

'Sorry,' she muttered, trying to walk past him.

He stopped her by grabbing the handle of the pram. 'What's the hurry, Morag? Have you no time these days to say hello to an old friend?'

Morag had no option but to stop. Willie wasn't very bright but had been friendly with all three of her brothers and had been a frequent visitor to the shepherd's cottage where he had teased Morag mercilessly. She had loathed him. But that had been years ago and, physically at least, he had changed. She remembered a tall, gangling lad with wild black hair and a swarthy complexion, made darker by the pre-beard fuzz which had decorated his upper lip. Like all of Finty's unruly family he was never clean. Morag could remember her mother ordering him to wash in the stream before she would allow him to spend the night with the boys in the loft – and Willie's angry pride as he marched off down the brae, mortally offended. The next day Finty herself had puffed her way up the hill to defend her family's honour amid much shouting and cursing which had reduced Coll and the boys to the loud, helpless laughter which had completed her defeat. The young man facing Morag now was still recognisably the same person but he had broadened into manhood and the fuzz was now a dark shadow in need of a shave. The slightly vacant smile which seemed a permanent fixture on his face exposed teeth which were filmed with yellow slime and his hands were ingrained with dirt.

'I see the old witches are giving you a hard time,' he commented.

She shrugged as if she didn't care. 'I've better things to do than worry about them.'

'Where are you going?' he asked.

'Home. Ina will be needing her tea soon,' she answered, starting to turn into the lane by the side of the school which led to the forest track.

'I'll walk a wee way with you then,' he offered, falling into step beside her.

'There's no need.'

'You're looking braw, Morag,' he cut across her objection. 'Aye, you always were a bonny lass, even when you were a bairn. I've always liked you, Morag.'

Oh no, she thought and said, 'Goodbye, Willie, I'll need to get a move on.' She shoved the pram hurriedly on to the track.

'You're not in that much of a rush.' He grabbed the pram handle again. 'And I was only being nice to you. They say you've no friends, what with the wean and all. But I could be your friend, Morag.' As he spoke he clamped an arm round her and attempted to kiss her.

Morag saw the dirty teeth coming at her and scrambled out of the way, putting the pram between them. 'Don't,' she hissed.

'Och, don't be like that. Come on, Morag. You could do it with me if you like. Then we'll be friends won't we?' He was still smiling and Morag knew he had no real comprehension of what he was saying. 'I'll pay you. We'll do it here, in the trees, no one will know.' As he spoke he put his hand in his pocket, drew out a handful of coins and rattled them at her. Morag found her legs wouldn't work, the shock of his last words had fixed her to the ground. 'You don't need to be shy with me, Morag. I know about you because my mam said you were a whore. Look, I'll give you a tanner, but don't let on to my mam, mind.'

To his horror she burst into tears and raced off up the track, the child bouncing wildly in the pram in front of her. Willie stood and stared after her for a few minutes then stuck his hands back in his pockets and sauntered back to the village. So much for his mother, he thought, and he'd be sure and tell the other lads that Morag McDonald wasn't a whore at all. Unless a tanner hadn't been enough . . .

Ina's screams of delight as she lurched from side to side finally got through to Morag who looked back to make sure Willie wasn't following then slowed her pace. Her tears had dried, burned away by anger but now depression was growing deeper with every step. It had been a mistake coming here, thinking all she had to do was show her own pride in Ina and everyone would forgive her. Now they would never accept her and worse, would never accept Ina either.

She took her time going back to the castle which even in the bright sunshine looked cold and forbidding. There was no warm welcome there for her either. Between them Cook and Lady Katrina seemed to find fault with everything she did. The strain of constantly chiding

Ina for making a noise and trying to curb her naturally boisterous nature was making Morag tense and miserable.

'Morag. Why so glum, lass?' Rab emerged on to the track.

'I've been to see mother.'

'Ah . . . I see.'

'And then I went into the village and they called me names.'

'Och, lass.' Rab's heart ached for her. 'Come home with me for a wee while. Let me see how this wee madam's coming along.' With practised ease he extricated Ina from the big pram and carried her easily along the track to the lodge house.

'Right wee lass. Off you go. Let's see what mischief you can get into here,' he chuckled, setting the little girl on her bottom on his sitting-room floor.

'Ina, leave that alone,' Morag hurried to move the child from where she was pulling herself to her feet, ready to explore the exciting contents of Rab's open-fronted cabinet.

'Morag, sit yourself down and leave the wean in peace. This isn't Pitochrie Castle and there's nothing here that she can damage. I long ago removed everything that is valuable or fragile away from the fingers of wee Ayleen.'

Morag smiled and sat back in the big, old chair. 'I'm just so used to having to keep her out of things,' she explained ruefully.

'Aye, they can be a handful, right enough,' he agreed, laughing at the child who was now round his feet. 'Here's your tea, lass. And there's a wee bit of stew here for the wean. She can have her tea here then you won't have to hurry back.' He busied himself at the stove with the air of a man well used to fending for himself then perched Ina on his knee and shovelled the heated mess into her eager mouth. 'This is your mother's stew, meant to be for my midday meal but somehow I ended up in the pub instead.'

'Oh.' Morag grimaced.

Rab guffawed. 'By the look on your face you'd think it was poison but the bairn seems to like it well enough. I take it you and your mother didn't enjoy your visit then?'

Morag couldn't help telling him the whole story, only managing with great difficulty to contain her tears when she came to the bit about Willie Chisholm.

Rab looked grave. 'Och, lass, you know as well as I do that poor Willie's only fifteen ounces to the pound.'

'I know that well enough, but he said his mother called me a whore. And Mysie, and the other women, even Mr Burns, they were all horrible to me. And to Ina too. What am I going to do, Uncle Rab? It's awful at the castle. Lady Katrina complains about me all the time, no matter how hard I work and Mrs McManus moans about Ina being in the kitchen. I know I can't stay there much longer.'

'Don't go letting evil old windbags like Mysie Arneil and Finty Chisholm upset you, lass. And Mrs McManus has aye had a face sour enough to turn milk.' He attempted a laugh. 'I dare say they've a few secrets in their own closets. They'll be on to your mother and me next but at least that would take their minds off you, eh lass?'

Morag smiled at last. 'I said that to Mam this afternoon,' she admitted. 'She slapped my face for it.'

'Well, I dare say you were out of order.'

'Aye,' she admitted. 'I lost my temper.'

'Just like your father,' he smiled, rubbing at his beard. 'Your mother didn't tell you then?'

'Tell me what?'

'We've been to see the minister. We'll be wed in August.'

'I'm glad,' Morag smiled back. And she was.

'I was a bit worried about what you might say to it, lass,' he admitted, scooping the last of the stew into Ina's mouth then cuddling her into him. To Morag's amazement her active little daughter snuggled in as if she wanted to sleep. 'I know you weren't best pleased to start with.'

'Och, it wasn't that I wasn't pleased. It just seemed so soon . . . after Dad. I am happy for you, and for Mam too, honestly.'

'Good. Now then, what are we going to do about you?'

'Maybe, once you're married, you could persuade Mam to have Ina?'

'I'd like that fine, lass. But, you know, I don't think that's the best idea. Maybe you should go somewhere else. Get a new start.'

'Leave Pitochrie?' she gasped.

'Aye. Why not? What's here for you now? You've seen for yourself what the villagers are like. They've got long memories and they'll not let you, or the wee lassie, forget. You'll not find many friends and the laddies'll not want to know you.' It sounded harsh but Rab understood these people well enough to know he was speaking the truth. 'And though I love your mother dearly I know there's too much Kirk in her to forgive you easily, Morag.'

'But it's so unfair,' she cried angrily. 'I mean, look at you two.'

Rab grinned wryly. 'Ah, but it's not what you do, it's not being caught doing it that counts. Even if you came to live with us you'd never get another job round here, you'd never be able to make a life of your own. You're a beautiful young woman, Morag, you deserve another chance. But you won't get it in Pitochrie.'

'I don't see I have much choice. I've no money. I don't even know anyone outside the village.'

'But I do.'

She stared at him. 'You do? What do you mean? Do you know of another job somewhere?'

'You could say that. Here, put the wee lassie in her pram and I'll tell you what I've got in mind.'

She did as she was told then came back and waited impatiently for him to go on.

'Do you remember that I was away when wee Ina was born?'

'You went to see your brother-in-law.'

'Aye.' Rab settled back in his chair and lit his pipe. 'He's a fine man. His wife, Beth – my sister – she died four years ago now and left him with two bairns to raise. Well, he's a baker, has his own bakery with a house attached. It's hard work, especially with the children. He's no mind to take another wife but he does need help.'

'And you think I could go there?'

'Aye. I do.'

'But what about Ina? He'll not want me there when he finds out about her.'

'He knows about her.'

'You've already spoken to him?'

'Well, I thought it was better that way. No point in raising your hopes if he was going to say no.'

'And he says I can go there?' she asked, barely containing her excitement.

242

'He'd be right glad of the help. You'd be working for him. It won't be easy with three children and a house to run and I dare say you'd have to help in the bakery from time to time but he's a fair man. And a decent one, if you know what I mean. He'd not . . . not bother you.'

'Where does he live? Is it far from here?'

'Not far. It's still in Strathannan. A wee place on the coast. A fishing village it is and right bonny with a wee harbour and a braw long sandy beach. Och, it would be a wonderful place for the wee lassie and it's not so far away that you couldn't get home.'

'What's his name?' she asked.

'Donny. Donald Archibold,' he answered, watching her closely. 'Think about it, Morag. There's no hurry. Maybe after the wedding.'

'Yes, yes, I'll think about it. It might be the best thing, though I've never been away from the village before now.' She frowned across at Rab. 'What happens if we don't get on, if he decides I won't do?'

'I think you and Donny will suit one another fine. Don't go looking for complications, lass.'

Morag saw such kindness in those clear blue eyes that she was very close to tears again. 'Thank you, Uncle Rab,' she said, hugging him.

'Och, I just want to see you smiling again, lass, that's all,' he laughed away his embarrassment. 'Now, you'd best be getting that wee soul off to her bed. Think about what I've said and let me know what you decide.'

The more Morag thought about Rab's suggestion, the more attractive it seemed. But, though she knew Rab was right — there was no future for her in Pitochrie — she was nervous about leaving everything she knew and apprehensive about her ability to provide for Ina. She had no money of her own and could hardly expect a man she had never met to take responsibility for a growing child, however kind he might be. A week and then two passed as she wavered in indecision. And then it was taken out of her hands.

Clara Ingham, the nursemaid engaged by Lady Katrina, was a shy, obviously well-bred girl who had had difficulty settling into her new post, so far away from her newly widowed mother and three sisters. Brought up to believe she would never have to work but would find herself a moderately wealthy husband, she had watched her younger sisters all make good marriages while her own age crept up to twenty-five without a single offer. Even so, with the generous dowry her father had planned to provide she had hopes of finally netting a staid but reliable banker. Then her father's business had collapsed, leaving debts so huge that he had shot himself messily in his study. His wife had no choice but to go and live with her sister and his eldest daughter was left to take her own chances in life. Clara had accepted her fate stoically but spent many nights alone in the nursery, crying herself to sleep, even eating there on her own, until Mrs McManus, alarmed by the dark circles under the girl's eyes, persuaded her at least to take her meals with the others in the kitchen. Gradually Clara made friends of them all and very often brought young Angus with her to play with Ina while they ate. To their mutual delight Morag and Clara had formed a friendship which allowed them to perform small favours for each other. Clara, who obviously loved children, occasionally looked after Ina when Morag was attending to Lady Katrina while, in return, Morag gladly sewed blouses and skirts for Clara.

That particular day Lady Katrina was expecting week-end guests and had ordered an elaborate dinner. The kitchen was in uproar and Ina, cooped in her pen, complained shrilly, until Mrs McManus's patience was finally exhausted.

'Morag, take that bairn up to Clara, for pity's sake,' she yelled in exasperation.

Morag gathered the child up, relieved to get her out of the kitchen where she could so easily be hurt, and hurried up to the nursery. Clara accepted her extra charge with a smile and before Morag left the two children were playing happily side by side.

With an easy mind she returned to the kitchen. When, an hour later, Lady Katrina's bell jangled frantically she wiped her hands and dashed upstairs, not suspecting what lay in store for her. As soon as she entered Lady Katrina's sitting room she knew something was badly wrong.

'Ma'am?' she asked.

'This time you have tried my patience too far, Morag. I won't stand for any more of your lazy ways.'

Morag, her heart hammering, watched as Katrina paced the room, obviously in a furious temper.

'Well, what have you got to say for yourself this time?' Katrina demanded.

'I'm sorry, ma'am. I don't know what I've done,' Morag stammered, searching her mind frantically for some task left undone.

'You know very well what I'm talking about,' Katrina screeched. 'You have left that child of yours with the nursemaid. In the nursery with my son. I will not have it!'

Morag rushed to defend herself, 'Mrs McManus told me to take her there. We're so busy in the kitchen ...'

'This is an outrage! How can you dare to think I would allow you to take advantage of me like this? After all I have done for you!' Katrina failed to keep the note of triumph out of her voice. 'I warned you. Well, this time you have gone too far. You will leave at the end of the month. And don't think you will have a recommendation from me.'

'Yes, ma'am.' All Morag felt was a enormous wave of relief. The decision had been made for her. She would go to Kilweem and leave her unhappiness behind.

Katrina glared at her, disappointed that she had been unable to wrench a more satisfying reaction from the girl. 'Get out,' she snarled. But when the door closed behind Morag, Katrina allowed herself to smile.

The last few months had been a terrible strain. Katrina had watched helplessly as her beloved son grew to resemble his real mother more and more with each passing day. The constant fear of discovery, the possibility that Morag herself would see what was surely so obvious, was making her ill. Night after night she woke, drenched in the cold sweat of terror, terrified of losing him. The truth was that even the matter of the inheritance no longer seemed important. It was little Angus himself who had claimed her heart. She wrapped him in fierce, protective love, love which was denied any other outlet, and knew that without him she would be nothing. Now, at last, with Morag gone, she and her son would be safe.

TWELVE

Morag held her lively daughter tightly as the old horse plodded steadily along. Everything she owned in the world was piled into the cart which trundled along behind them. Beside her Rab held the reins loosely in one hand and the stem of his old pipe in the other and whistled contentedly to himself. That, and the excitement of the journey down to Kilweem, through countryside she had never seen, was helping to ease her nervousness at the thought of what lay ahead.

Already the hills were falling away and the Strath was opening up in front of them. Morag swivelled and looked behind her. In the distance, the lonely rowan tree drew her eye towards the hillside cottage where they had all been so happy. Beneath that, through the trees, she could still see the flag on top of Pitochrie Castle, poignant reminders that she was leaving everything she knew.

Rab, who had experienced very similar emotions when he left the highlands, years ago, glanced quickly at her. 'It's a beautiful county, Strathannan,' he said, casually. 'There's no more hills as high as those but you'll find the coast just as braw.'

'I've never even seen the sea,' she admitted, making an effort for his sake. 'Glenelg is the furthest I've ever been.'

Rab laughed. 'Aye, that's the way in the villages. I doubt many folk from Pitochrie have been to the coast.'

'Which way do we go?' she asked. 'Will we go through Inverannan?'

'No, lass. That's away to the west. It's a braw place too. The county town of Strathannan. It sits on the river, just before it runs into the Forth, away along the coast.'

'This river?' Morag nodded to the gently flowing Annan which meandered through the Strath.

'Aye. We'll follow it for an hour or so but it goes away that way. We need to go straight on, over there.' He used the stem of his pipe to indicate the rolling hills in front of them.

'It looks braw,' she said, looking at the patchwork of fertile fields ahead.

'It's different from Pitochrie already, isn't it?' he smiled. 'Better land here than in the hillfoots. That's wheat in those fields, and cows. Not so many sheep down here.'

They went on in silence. It had all happened so fast. It was less than two weeks since Katrina had dismissed her and now, before she had had time to think, she was on her way to Kilweem.

In truth she was glad to be going, it was only fear of the unknown that was unnerving her. Annie and Rab were due to be married this coming Saturday, five days from now. The service would be in Pitochrie kirk, to be followed by a party in Annie's home. The whole village would be there and Morag had looked forward to joining in the celebrations, thinking it would be a happy note on which to leave the village. But . . .

'This is my day, Morag, and I'll not have you there with that wean to spoil it for me. I'll not have them gloating over your disgrace on my wedding day.' Annie's face had been set and cold and Morag knew nothing she could say would make her mother change her mind.

Nor had she appealed to Rab to mediate on her behalf. He had done so much for her already and she had no wish to be the cause of arguments between him and her mother so close to the day of their marriage.

Annie had said her farewells at the cottage gate, allowing her daughter to kiss her briefly on the cheek before retreating to the shadow of her doorway to watch the cart make its way up the track. Morag had waved at the tall, stiff-backed figure who kept her hands implacably folded over her white apron.

They trotted on through ever changing countryside and eventually started climbing as the gentle fields gave way to low, tussocked hills. Rab reined in the horse, unhitched him and let him wander to a stream to drink. Morag jumped down and spread a blanket on the rough grass and took bread, cheese, apples and a flask of cold tea from a basket.

'We'll give the old horse an hour before we go on,' Rab said, settling back and closing his eyes.

'How much further?' Morag asked before he could fall asleep.

'Och, an hour and a half, maybe two. See,' he sat up again. 'Take yourself to the top of that hill, it's not far. You should be able to see the sea from there.'

Morag picked up Ina and scrambled up the slope with her, laughing as her feet slipped on the grass. A few minutes later she arrived panting at the top and discovered a view she would remember for the rest of her life.

Spread before her was the intricate coastline of Strathannan, glorious in bright sunshine. A panorama of undulating fields stretched away to the east and west, falling gently towards the sea. Just visible, where the fields seemed to meet sparkling blue water, were the red roofs and church towers of a village. Further along the

249

coast, in both directions, she could see other villages, half hidden, nestling prettily in sheltered bays. All along the coast were ribbons of golden sand. The water itself was the colour of the sky and there were several boats, smoke drifting from their funnels in puffy clouds as they made their way towards the open sea. Across the water, slightly to the west, sheathed in gentle, misty blues and greens, was the opposite shore, too far away for the details to be clear. Straight in front of her, for as far as her eye could see, was the North Sea. Morag gazed, transfixed by the absolute beauty of the view until, rapidly becoming bored, Ina wailed loudly.

Morag looked down the hill at Rab who was asleep, his back resting against a grassy tuft, then sat down and rocked her daughter until she too closed her eyes. Then she sat for an hour in perfect silence, simply drinking in the details of all she could see.

When Rab shouted to her she went back to the cart with a heart more peaceful than it had been for many months. If that beautiful coast was where she was to live her new life she was already sure she would be happy.

'Morag McDonald meet Donald Archibold.' Rab winked at her and Morag found her free hand engulfed in a huge, red paw. She smiled timidly and looked up at the biggest man she had ever seen.

He towered over them all, making even Rab look insignificant, and his girth was in proportion to his height. His receding hair was sandy coloured and his gentle, blue-grey eyes were lit by a kind smile which made shining moons of his freckled cheeks. Morag, who had been expecting a man of about Rab's age, was surprised to realise he was much younger than that, not more than ten years older than herself.

'Welcome, lass. Now don't look so scared, I'll not eat you,' he boomed.

'This is my daughter, Emmelina, though everyone calls her Ina,' Morag said, half expecting him, even now, to ignore the child or show his disapproval in some other way.

'Well, and you're a bonny wee thing,' Donny laughed and the child stretched a tiny hand towards his face. 'And this here is Maurice. He's six years old and almost a man, eh son?'

Morag turned her smile to the sturdy lad who was standing stiffly at his father's side. The boy said, 'Hello,' but didn't smile.

'And this wee lass is our Maureen. She's four.' He fastened his big hand gently on the girl's shoulders and steered her out from where she had been hiding between his legs.

Morag found herself looking at a tiny, delicate child with a mass of dark curls and huge brown eyes. She crouched down to the little girl's level and said, 'Hello, Maureen. I'm Morag.' The child's face broke into a shy smile before she scurried quickly back to her father.

'Right then. Let's get your stuff off the cart. Come on, lad, you can help,' Donny ordered. 'Maureen, you take Morag and Ina and show them their room.'

In less than an hour Morag was standing outside the bakery, waving goodbye to Rab, gamely choking back tears. Only when the sound of his horse's shoes on the setted streets had finally faded did she turn to inspect her new home properly.

From what she had seen, Kilweem was a bigger, more prosperous village than Pitochrie. They had come down an unpromisingly narrow street which had suddenly broadened out into a sort of square with shops dotted

251

between the houses on both sides. In the middle was a tall, rectangular structure, with a clock set into it which, according to Rab, was the tollbooth. The bakery itself was an old, rambling, three-storey building with a pantiled roof, facing out over the setted square.

With a final desperate glance in the direction of Rab's departure she made her way back inside and found Donny waiting for her. 'Do you want me to start making the supper?' she asked.

He laughed. 'Plenty of time for that tomorrow. Come and have a cup of tea with us then you can take the rest of the day to unpack your things.'

They sat, rather formally, round a huge wooden table in the kitchen. Ina, secure in her high chair, laughed at them all and Maureen, perched on a chair with her chin barely reaching the table top, soon forgot to be shy and played with the baby. Maurice stared sullenly at his plate, doing his best to ignore them all.

'It's strange for him too,' Donny explained. 'He'll get used to you in his own time. He's had a lot of freedom, too much, and he needs someone to keep a firm eye on him while I'm working. I'll be honest with you, Morag. He didn't want you to come and he'll maybe play you up for a while. You'll need to be strict with him but if he gives you any lip you let me know and I'll sort him out.'

The boy, a miniature version of his father, glared briefly at her then lowered his eyes back to his plate.

'I'm sure we'll be all right,' Morag said, feeling far less confident than she sounded.

'You'll have plenty to do, mind,' Donny went on, helping himself to his third bread roll and spreading it liberally with butter. 'I'm at work from three in the morning until one in the afternoon. That's when the

252

shop closes. I'm away to my bed by eight most nights, and the bairns too. Maurice here goes to the school but Maureen's too young yet so you'll have her with you all day. It's up to you how you organise your time. So long as you keep an eye on the weans and look after the house you'll get no complaints from me if you want to go for a walk or take the weans to the beach.'

Morag nodded then looked up and found him laughing at her. 'Och, lass, put a smile on that bonny face. I know fine that we're all right strange to you now but you'll soon feel at home and I'm right glad to have you and your wee lassie here.'

After supper Morag went to look at her room. It was on the top floor and looked out over a row of fishermen's cottages and a hotchpotch of roofs. Disappointingly there was no glimpse of the sea. The room itself was quite large with a fireplace, a good-sized brass bedstead, a wardrobe and a soft chair. The furniture, as in the other rooms, was old and heavy, as though it had been there for many years. Thick, but dusty, curtains hung at the window and the floor was covered with brightly coloured rag rugs. Ina's cot fitted neatly in the corner. The three gas wall-lamps would make the room snug and welcoming after dark.

Her first night in her new home was a strange one. Morag woke several times, disturbed by the unfamiliar noises of the old house and the regular hours struck out by the tollbooth clock. Just after three she heard the floorboards creaking followed by the sound of a muted cough and knew Donny was starting work in the bakery which took up the ground floor of the old building. She dozed a little then and woke with the dawn to the appetising smell of baking bread. Leaving Ina asleep in her cot she dressed quickly and made her way down to the bakery.

'Hello, lass,' Donny greeted her, red faced and running with perspiration as he scooped loaves from the depths of the huge oven with what looked like a flat-bladed spade. 'You're early out of your bed. The bairns won't want to rise for another couple of hours yet. It's only five o'clock.'

'I know. I'm used to getting up early at the castle,' she smiled at him. 'Can I help you here until it's time to get the breakfasts?'

He seemed to hesitate. 'Aye, if you like, though I'll not expect it of you every day. You'll be busy enough without this.'

'I don't mind.'

'You will,' he laughed, a deep, rumbling sound. 'But maybe we should have a wee chat, you and I, while the bairns can't hear us. If you want something to occupy your hands, these pies need to be filled and have their lids put on.' He dumped a huge pan of cooked meat on the table.

This was it, she thought, the inevitable lecture about behaving herself, keeping the child out of sight. Resignedly she rolled up her sleeves and set to work, glad to be able to keep her face turned away from him.

'She's a bonny wean, your Ina,' Donny said, mixing flour and fat together energetically. 'Maureen seems right taken with her. They'll be good for one another.'

'And Maureen's a lovely wee thing,' answered Morag, who had been enchanted by the little girl.

'She's like her mother. And Maurice is a good enough lad too.'

'Does he remember his mother?' Morag asked hesitantly. 'Maybe that's why he didn't want us here.'

'Beth died when Maureen was born,' Donny said quietly. 'Wee Maurice wasn't two years old at the time. He can't recall much about her. No, I think it's just that he liked things the way they were.' He flopped the pastry on to the table and started to roll it out. 'But it's you I want to talk about, Morag.'

'What do you want to know?' she asked nervously.

'Nothing personal. Rab's told me all I need to know about you and the baby and the rest of it's your business, not mine. You've come here to get away from the old gossips in Pitochrie and I don't want to be reminding you of them all the time. But, well, Kilweem is just a village too. The women will already know you're here. They'll have been watching you arrive from behind their curtains and they'll be exercising their tongues this very morning, you can be sure of that.'

'I was hoping . . . Och, I was stupid. I thought, maybe . . . Maybe they wouldn't need to know.'

Donny watched her carefully. 'Well, lass, I don't believe in telling untruths. I'd take my belt to the lad if I caught him out in a deliberate lie. But there are times when you have to do something that's against your conscience to protect the people you love. Do you see what I mean?'

'I think so,' Morag worked on diligently but her face was scarlet.

'Now, you've the wee girl to think about. The truth would hurt her. And I've my reputation to look after. It wouldn't do to have them all think I'd taken a young woman to live with me, flattering though that might be,' he guffawed, making Morag giggle suddenly. 'And my own two bairns would suffer if the villagers thought I was up to no good. So we have to think up something to tell them.'

'What?'

'Well, I'm pretty sure that no one round here knows anyone in Pitochrie. I think we'll just say you're a relation of my wife's. At least that will be true now that old Rab's marrying your mother. If anyone asks – and they will – we'll say your husband died, the influenza maybe, and you got put out of your house. How does that sound?'

'Pretty good for someone who doesn't tell lies,' she laughed.

'Aye, it does, doesn't it? You stick to that story, lass and no one will think anything of it. Especially if you put a ring on that finger of yours. We'll tell the bairns the same thing and then your secret will be safe.'

'Thank you,' she whispered, choked. 'You're being very kind.'

'No, lass. Not kind. Practical, that's all. Now, if you've finished with those pies, you away and start the porridge. I'll be up for my breakfast in an hour or so.'

Curiosity made the Kilweemers friendly. Wherever she went Morag was greeted by smiles and women who wanted to chat. Wearing the old, loose fitting ring Donny had found for her she repeated her story nervously, unwittingly giving an excellent impression of a grieving young widow. She found nothing but sympathy.

Ina, revelling in the new-found freedom both in the house and on Kilweem's beautiful, sandy beach, blossomed. Maureen, shy at first, soon lost her inhibitions and liked nothing better than to go to the beach with Morag and Ina, a treat her father seldom had time for. Only Maurice continued to be difficult. The little boy made no secret of his pique, speaking only when spoken to and, if his father wasn't around, resorting to open defiance. Clinging to the hope that, in time, he would learn to accept her, Morag was patient. She treated him in exactly the same way as the two girls, never forced herself on him and took care not to let him see her disappointment when he failed to respond. Somehow she never seemed able to break through his resentment.

'Shall we go to the harbour and watch the boats coming in?' she asked him one day, well aware that this was one of his favourite pastimes.

It was something she enjoyed too. Kilweem's harbour was tiny, protected by a thick wall which enclosed it on all four sides with only a narrow opening allowing passage for the fishing boats. She loved the hurly burly when the boats came in and often took the girls to watch with the other women as the men unloaded the catch and spread their nets to dry, marvelling at the dexterity of the fishwives who worked in the gutting sheds, splitting the fish and tossing them into wooden boxes or crates of salt. 'Well,' she asked Maurice. 'Shall we go?'

'No,' he retorted, sticking his bottom lip out stubbornly.

'I thought you liked it there?'

'I do,' he muttered. 'But not with you. I'll go on my own.'

'You will not,' she said firmly. 'Your father told you you weren't to go to the harbour on your own. It's dangerous. You could fall into the water and drown.' The gangs of small boys who played among the crates and ropes were the scourge of the quayside, often damaging the nets and always infuriating the fishermen. And the danger was very real. The women had told her about a young lad, just about Maurice's age who, last year, had slipped into the water between the harbour wall and a boat and was crushed to death when the boat drifted in on him.

'I'll do what I want,' the little lad roared his defiance. 'You can't tell me what to do.'

'What was that?' Donny, who had come from the bakery for his breakfast, thundered. 'You will do what Morag tells you, lad, or I'll take my belt to you.'

'It's not fair,' Maurice yelled. 'Before she came I used to go to the harbour. You never stopped me then. She's spoiling everything.'

'I didn't know you were going there,' Maurice bellowed, 'until I started getting folk coming to the door to complain about you. And you won't go there now unless Morag is with you.'

Maurice slipped down from the table and ran for the door. 'I wish you'd never come here,' he screamed at Morag before running off and clattering downstairs.

'Let him go,' Donny ordered as Morag started to go after him. 'I'll deal with him when he comes in.'

'I'm sorry, Donny,' Morag said, feeling she had failed them.

'Och, it's not your fault, lass.' He took her hand and squeezed it affectionately. 'The boy's had too much freedom. He'll come home when his belly starts to rumble. You take the lassies to the harbour. He'll likely be back when you come home.'

But when they got back, three hours later, Maureen clutching a slippery fish which had been dropped on to the pavement at least four times, there was no sign of Maurice. He still hadn't returned when Donny closed the shop at one o'clock.

'He wasn't at the harbour then?' he asked.

Morag shook her head. 'No. And I asked round the village but no one's seen him.'

'Little tyke,' Donny exploded. 'I'll leather him when he gets home. Let me drink my tea and I'll go and find him.'

It was two hours before he came back. 'No sign,' he said grimly. 'He'll be hiding out somewhere. Maybe he's down at the harbour now, watching the boats. They'll be getting them ready to go out when the tide turns in an hour or so. I wouldn't put it past him to be on one of them. Maybe I'll just have another wee look.'

Morag watched him set off down the steep wynd which led to the harbour then, leaving the children in the care of a willing neighbour, set off round the village again, hoping for some sign of him. By now several villagers had joined in the search for the little lad but no one had any news and the light was starting to fade.

Although Donny had already checked the beach, Morag wandered down to the Butts, a steeply sloping street of fishermens' cottages which led directly on to the sands alongside the rocky point which separated the harbour from the beach.

She walked along the tide line, calling Maurice's name loudly, anxiously scanning the dunes which were already retreating into shadows. She went on for more than three miles before finally giving up and retracing her steps. Desperately worried she sat for a minute on the rocks, just out of reach of the incoming tide, trying to imagine where a little boy might choose to hide. Then she recalled what had happened the last time she had brought the children to play here. Maurice and Maureen had ended up enjoying a noisy game of hide and seek among the dunes but, when it was Maureen's turn to find Maurice, she had hunted and hunted without success. Finally, she had stood on the sand and yelled that she gave up and Maurice had emerged triumphantly from a shallow, cave-like hollow in the rocks.

Morag clambered over the rocks, towards the side of the point which faced the harbour, until she could go no further without wading through the water which was making the submerged rocks dangerously slippery. 'Maurice,' she yelled, wondering where, precisely, his little hidey hole had been. Again she shouted his name and, just as she was going to give up and go back to the village, she heard something. It was a faint, quavering noise that might have been nothing more than the sound of the sea.

'Maurice,' she yelled again. 'Are you in there?'

'I'm here,' came a small frightened voice.

'Where? Shout again, Maurice,' she called, listening intently.

'Round here,' his voice came back, more strongly now. 'Round the corner.'

Morag plunged heedlessly into the cold water and made her way carefully round the slimy headland. 'Shout again, Maurice,' she called.

'Here! I'm here!' And this time he sounded very close.

Morag clung to the rocks and edged her way towards the voice. 'Where?' she called, peering into the darkness.

'I'm cold,' the child cried and just then she saw the pale shape of his face as he peered out at her from the darkness. She scrambled frantically towards him on her hands and knees, cutting her skin on the hidden rocks and there he was, hunched on the floor of a miniature cave, just deep enough to hide in, with the rising tide already covering his legs.

'Och, Maurice . . .' She held out her arms and he launched himself into them, sobbing and shivering. 'Hold tight,' she said, inching her way back towards the sand.

'There.' She set him down gently and collapsed beside

him. 'You're safe now.' Relief was making her voice tremble. 'Are you all right?'

He nodded. 'I hid there but I fell asleep and when I woke up the tide was up and I couldn't get back. I thought I was going to drown,' he wailed.

Morag put her arms round him and hugged him close. 'Och, Maurice, we were so worried about you.'

'Am I in a lot of trouble?' he asked, his eyes huge and round in the darkness.

'No. I'm just glad to have you back all safe and sound,' she reassured him, cuddling him close again. 'Come on, we'd best go and tell your dad you're safe.'

They walked up the Butts side by side. When they were almost at the top she felt his small, cold hand slip into hers and grasp it tightly.

THIRTEEN

The next year passed in a blur of contentment. The children settled down well and Morag found Donny a warm, humorous man to live with. He treated Ina with the exact same blend of patience and discipline which he used on his own children and she plainly adored him.

As in most families, many of the clothes which Maureen outgrew found their way on to Ina's shoulders though, by the time she had finished with them, they were fit for very little else. When Ina needed something which had to be bought it was often Donny who mentioned it first, before giving Morag money for whatever was necessary. After this had happened three or four times he said, 'That lass of yours is part of this family and I'll not have her going about looking like a ragamuffin. If she needs shoes and none of Maureen's fit her properly, you ask me for the money. Do you understand?'

Morag soon saw why Donny had needed help with his family. He worked very long hours and never seemed to take a day off. Even on Sundays he spent most of the day in the bakery, cleaning it, making small repairs and, reluctantly, keeping his books. The only time he relaxed was after the children were in bed when he sat down for a couple of hours with a glass or two, and sometimes more, of whisky. It was the only thing about Donny which made her uncomfortable. She hated to see him on the nights when over-indulgence made him querulous and unsteady on his feet, and it was even worse if the drink made him maudlin. But she told herself that a man who worked as hard as he did had to find some way to relax. In any case, she had no right to criticise an otherwise even-tempered and generous man.

Although she was settled in her new life, and fond of the children, Morag yearned for adult female companionship. So, as soon as Maureen started school and she had a little more time on her hands, she began to help Donny by serving in the shop whenever she could, enjoying the chance this gave her to chat with the local women. Even Ina was in her element here, giving the children who came in with their mothers the tiny rolls Donny always made from the left-over dough. When she tired of that she would spend an hour or more rolling and tugging bits of pastry into shapes which Donny then baked in the oven for her, just as he had done for Maureen. They were wonderful times with many moments of shared laughter and affection, almost, mused Donny, as if they were a real family.

On fine afternoons Morag got into the habit of taking Ina to the harbour or beach before going on to collect Maureen and Maurice from school. The harbour was the gathering place for the village women who liked to sit on the old crates which littered the area and watch their menfolk unload their catch while the children played, well away from the water's edge. A little further along the quayside the retired fishermen also gathered, smoking pipes and tying nets while shouting advice and criticism to the workers, all the time gossiping as eagerly as the women. The fishermen themselves were accustomed to working with an audience and took it all in good spirit, exchanging banter with the older men, and sometimes with the women.

It wasn't long before Morag got to know most of them, though not well enough to join in the light-hearted teasing which amused everyone so much. She soon learned that, like Pitochrie, many of the Kilweem families were related to one another, that most had lived in the village, fishing the North Sea, for generations. The Mcleans, the Moys, the Burns, the Camerons and the McArdles were all families who had a grandfather on the quayside, and sons – and even grandsons – working the boats.

Morag soon realised that it was the McArdles who were the largest family in Kilweem with a seemingly never ending stream of uncles, aunts and cousins to be found in every other house in the village. Between them they ran two boats, one belonging to each of two cousins, inherited in each case from their fathers, two elderly and gnarled brothers who were among their fiercest critics on the quayside. Each boat was crewed by McArdle sons and sons-in-law, men mostly well into their forties. The three or four younger men who could be seen cleaning the holds and scrubbing the decks were grandsons of the old men.

One of these young men in particular always seemed to find some excuse to come across and speak to the women and it was soon obvious to everyone that he had a special reason for doing so. Graham McArdle never took his eyes off Morag who responded by blushing until her face clashed with her hair, making her the butt of much good-natured teasing from the other women. Day after day he lingered on the quayside, trying to get her to chat with him and frequently earning a roared rebuke from his uncle on whose boat he worked, much to the amusement of everyone else.

Secretly Morag was delighted. Though the other young

women, those who hadn't been lucky enough to attract his attention, maintained that Gray was 'nothing special', she thought he was the best-looking young man she had ever seen. A year or two older than Morag, he, like all the McArdles, had light brown hair and sleepy lidded eyes. Unlike certain senior members of his family, he had a ready laugh, an open, cheerful face and skin which was still fresh and youthful, as if he didn't yet need to shave every day. He was smaller than the others too but compact and muscular, his arms tanned and sinewy. For the sake of her closely guarded veneer of respectability, Morag didn't dare encourage him, frightened of drawing attention to herself in a way which might encourage folk to re-examine her carefully fabricated past. But Gray McArdle was persistent and despite her good intentions she couldn't help being drawn to him.

The day came when he contrived to walk up the wynd from the harbour at the same time as she did. Morag had wondered why all the other women had found something to detain them; now she knew.

'I'll walk back with you,' he called, taking his time to catch up with her while he admired the natural swing of her hips and the glint of reflected light on her coppery hair.

'You're going in the wrong direction, Gray McArdle,' she laughed, her green eyes sparkling. 'Don't you live on the quayside?'

'Aye. But I thought I'd take a wee walk before my dinner. Get some good fresh air in my lungs,' he laughed, knowing she didn't believe him. 'You don't really mind, do you?' he asked, suddenly serious.

'No, I don't mind at all,' she answered him honestly.

After that she often found him at her side, sometimes on the way to the boats, other times on his way home.

On the days when the boats didn't put to sea it became his habit to wait to meet her in Marketgate when she went to collect the children from school. Sometimes he would stand talking to her outside the bakery for as long as five minutes.

Watching them one afternoon through the bakehouse door, Donny Archibold felt anger welling against the young man who was monopolising so much of Morag's time. Almost against his will he found himself standing in the doorway, glaring at them. Intimidated by the huge, angry man, Gray quickly said goodbye and took himself home.

'Is something wrong?' Morag asked Donny, upset by the thunderous expression on his face.

'Nothing,' he snapped, leaving her to take the children upstairs.

When his bad mood continued after dinner Morag put the children to bed and came downstairs, ready to confront him.

'I'm off to bed,' he said, draining his whisky glass and getting to his feet as soon as she went into the room, though normally he would have lingered in companionable silence for half an hour or so. He swayed slightly and Morag realised he was drunk.

'It's early yet,' she said.

'I'm tired.'

'You're not tired, Donny Archibold. You're just in a foul temper with me about something. You'd best get it off your chest for if you go on like this you'll upset the children.'

The fiery spirit loosening his tongue, Donny threw caution to the wind and exploded. 'It's you, letting young Gray McArdle hang around. You'll be getting yourself a bad name, young lady.'

266

It stung, like a slap on the face. She simply stared at him and said, 'Why?'

'Isn't it obvious?' he said coldly, fear of rejection making it impossible for him to tell her the truth, that he had fallen under her spell, that he loved her, that to see her with another man was destroying him.

'No! Not to me it isn't,' she retorted, devastated to know that her faith in him had been misplaced, that he did hold her past against her.

'Well it should be.' But now his fuddled brain was starting to see he had spoken out of turn.

'Gray McArdle is a respectable lad. He wants to walk out with me. What harm can there be in that?'

'You'll get yourself hurt, lass, if you're not very careful,' he warned her.

But Morag was too angry to pay him any heed.

She and Gray did what all the other courting couples did. They moved in gentle stages from holding hands on the quayside to kissing in the country lanes round the village and cuddling on the beach. Gray was a responsible lad, brought up in a huge but close family where the brothers protected their sisters fiercely. He knew that if he ever got a lassie into trouble he would face the unbridled wrath of four generations of McArdles. It was such a powerful deterrent that he even asked Morag's permission before kissing her for the first time; though once that permission was obtained he wasted no time in utilising it to the full.

For Morag, whose experience of men was limited to those emotionless nights with Angus Fraser, it was a revelation; she felt that her life had been transformed. Days when Morag saw Gray were brighter, happier and found her humming to herself as she went about her chores. If she didn't see him for a day or two she fretted impatiently, wishing time away until she could meet him again.

Donny, who was well aware of the reason for her mercurial moods, resorted to terse belligerence but Morag was too self-absorbed to notice.

She and Gray had been winching for two months or more, their relationship common knowledge throughout the village, when an autumn evening found them at the far end of the harbour wall, hidden in the darkness as they looked out over the swelling sea. His hand was round her waist, a liberty he would not dare to take in public, and she was standing close in to the warmth of his strong young body, her head resting on his shoulder. When he bent his head to kiss her she responded warmly, loving the feel of his tongue in her mouth, the strength of his arms around her. She turned to him, allowing him to draw her body against his and, for the first time, felt the stiff heat of his arousal. Gray groaned softly and moved a hand to her breasts. Feeling his body pulse he took her hand and placed it over his erection. For a moment Morag let her fingers linger there, feeling the urgent flash of need in her own body then, reluctantly, she drew away.

'No, Gray,' she whispered.

He sank his face to her shoulder while his pulse slowed then raised his face and kissed her gently. 'I love you, Morag McDonald,' he told her softly, cupping her face in his work-roughened hands.

Morag's heart juddered. 'I love you too, Gray,' she answered quietly.

Again he pulled her to him, again she pulled away. 'No,' she repeated.

He smiled. 'I know. I'm sorry. But it's only natural for

me to want you, isn't it? But it's all right. I won't force you.' He knew she was a decent girl who wouldn't allow him to take liberties. 'Come on, we'd best get home.' Smiling he took her hand and they walked up to the village together, not caring who saw them.

'Och, I nearly forgot,' he said as he kissed her good-night in the doorway of the bakery. 'Mum wants you to come and have dinner with us on Sunday. It's about time you met the rest of the family.'

Sunday found Morag wearing her best, dark green woollen dress which complemented her auburn-haired colouring perfectly. She brushed her hair till it crackled and gleamed then pinned it tidily away from her face to hang in luxurious waves over her shoulders. A combination of nerves and happiness brought a glow to her cheeks and her eyes were pools of excited green light.

After a couple had declared their love for one another, meeting the families was the accepted next step before a proposal. Assuming that everything went well this afternoon, Morag had every hope of her engagement to Gray McArdle being announced before the month was out.

Donny, not trusting his tongue, had taken all three children for a long walk along the beach leaving her to hover restlessly in the sitting room, waiting for Gray to come and collect her. When she heard his determined rap on the heavy knocker she flew downstairs.

Gray stood there in his Sunday best of dark corded trousers, white shirt and tie, a marginally outgrown jacket straining across his shoulders. His hair was newly trimmed and recently flattened by water, droplets of which hung about his ears, and his face glowed red from a scrupulous shave. Deprived of his comfortable, every-day clothes he looked incredibly young and awkward.

He opened his mouth to say hello, then stopped, unable to take his eyes off her. 'You . . . you look beautiful,' he stammered at last, wondering how, of all the young men in the village, he had been the one to win her.

She laughed, bubbling with pleasure. 'Thank you, sir.'

He grinned suddenly then bowed theatrically and offered his arm. 'Madam.'

The McArdle house was at the far end of the quay, its front door looking on to the harbour and its side wall on one of the many narrow wynds which straggled down from the village. Like most of the fishermen's homes it was well furnished, clean and warm, testimony to their prosperity. Morag saw none of it, was aware only of a sea of interested faces staring at her as Gray steered her up the forestair and through the front door, straight into the large room which was kitchen, sitting room and dining room all in one.

Remembering his manners, Gray led her round, making the necessary introductions. There was his great-grandmother, a wrinkled old woman who had pride of place in a stiff-backed chair by the fireplace and who looked at Morag from rheumy eyes, muttered something through toothless gums and looked away again; with their backs to the fire, two elderly men – who were often to be seen bickering on the quayside – were introduced as Gray's grandfathers; a smooth-skinned, white-haired lady occupied a lesser chair opposite that of her mother and was wife to one of the old men which, Morag assumed, made her Gray's grandmother. She smiled warmly and whispered to Morag to take no notice of the men who had given her nothing more than a cursory nod before returning to some minor disagreement. Gray's father Morag had seen on his boat many times and from what she knew of him he was a bad-tempered man whose voice could regularly be heard roaring above the general din and clamour of the harbour. Today he smiled, took her hand and bid her welcome. Gray's three sisters and four brothers, three of them with their spouses, Morag already knew. Judging by the racket issuing from the adjoining bedroom there were obviously younger children too. Lastly Gray took her by the hand and threaded his way through the throng of people to a small, grey-haired woman who, helped by her daughters, was battling to produce a meal for more than twenty people. She turned a flushed face towards them, wiped her hands on her apron and surveyed Morag severely. Morag knew she was face to face with the real power in the McArdle family.

Hetty McArdle was a woman who ruled her family with iron discipline. Morag had seen her about the village but, although Hetty always nodded politely, she never lingered to gossip. The other villagers held her in great respect and there was a steady stream of callers at her door, seeking advice.

After what seemed a very long time, a full minute during which Morag felt the woman was looking into her mind and finding all her secrets, Hetty said, 'Right, lass, get your sleeves rolled up and help us to set the table.'

Behind them, two of Gray's brothers were hauling a drop-leaf table into the centre of the room while everyone else flattened themselves against the walls to make room for it. Even when the leaves were opened, Morag couldn't see how they would all manage to sit round it.

While she put out plates and cutlery the men made benches from planks resting across stools. In the end they jammed three people at each short end and six along the longer sides, leaving the children to manage as

271

best they could on the floor with their plates balanced on their knees.

Huge bowls of potatoes, turnips, carrots and cabbage were placed in the centre of the table where they were instantly fallen upon by the men. Dishes of succulent cod, cooked in onions and milk, were emptied and replaced by others before the women finally took their places.

Morag squeezed herself between Gray and one of his sisters and ate in the silence which had fallen while everyone did justice to their food. When the first course was finished an enormous, steamed dumpling was unwrapped, filling the house with spicy steam before it was cut into generous slices and distributed.

As soon as that had disappeared the sisters rose, cleared the table with noisy efficiency and started to wash the dishes but when Morag got up to help she was told to sit still.

'Thank you for the meal, Mrs McArdle. It was wonderful,' Morag said politely, striving to make a good impression on her stern-faced hostess.

'Aye, well at least *you've* got manners, lass. I'll say that much for you.' Hetty McArdle looked pointedly at her family and was rewarded instantly by a chorus of belated appreciation. 'So,' she went on, 'you've taken up with our Gray?'

Morag coloured slightly under the clear grey eyes but held her back straight and answered, 'Yes, Mrs McArdle.'

'Now then,' Gray's mother went on. 'I believe in plain speaking and I won't change my ways for some slip of a lassie. Our Gray seems to think he's fallen in love.' The note of disparagement was clear, as was Gray's embarrassment.

'Mam!' he protested.

'Keep your mouth closed, lad, and listen to what your mother has to say,' his father warned.

'First off, you make sure you behave yourselves. I've raised three lassies and four lads and not one of them has got themselves into trouble. I'll not have you two letting the family down. You want to go courting, you do it where we know what you're up to. You can come here on Sundays and walk in the village during the day but I'll not have the two of you sneaking off to the beach.' She paused and waited.

Morag was aware of twenty pairs of eyes all watching her. She looked straight ahead and said, 'Yes, Mrs McArdle.'

'Good. I'm telling you this because you've no mother here to keep an eye on you. It's for your own good. I've brought my lads up to know right from wrong but nature has a way of throwing common sense out with the fish bones and there's no point in putting temptation your way.' It sounded kinder and Morag looked up and smiled hesitantly into those shrewd, grey eyes. There was no answering smile on Hetty McArdle's face.

'Right,' Hetty rounded on her family. 'Youse lot away outside. It's a braw day for a walk. Take the weans with you, they're making enough noise to crack the foundations. You've all heard me give these two the same talk as I've given you all, but what I've got to say to Morag McDonald now is not for your ears.'

Like magic, Gray's brothers and sisters rounded up their families and disappeared. The two old men wandered off, still squabbling, with Gray's father close behind.

'You too, Gray. There's no need for you to hang around here,' his mother ordered. To Morag's disappointment he obeyed meekly.

Now there was only the great grandmother, who appeared to be asleep, Gray's grandmother and his mother left, the two older women facing Morag across the table. Morag sat and looked at her hands, feeling uncomfortable and resentful. And angry with Gray for not warning her of what would happen.

Suddenly, after a long silence, Hetty reached over the table and took her left hand, twisting the ring Donny had given her round and round on the slim finger. 'This ring is far too big for you,' she said.

Morag flushed with guilt but thought it better to say nothing and firmly pulled her hand back.

'She's a bonny bairn, that wee girl of yours,' Hetty went on. 'How old is she now?'

'Nearly three.'

'Gray's fond of children but it's never easy, taking on someone else's wean.'

Morag's stomach tightened. She had told Gray the same story that she had told everyone else and he had accepted it easily even though, unwilling to lie to him, she had never elaborated beyond the basic details.

'It must be hard, without a father for her,' Hetty persisted.

'Donny's very kind,' Morag took refuge in the truth. 'He treats her just like his own children. I'm very grateful to him.'

'You have your own room there do you?'

So that was it! Hetty McArdle was worried about her relationship with Donny. For a minute or so she had been frightened that it was her past which was going to be examined. Morag relaxed fractionally.

'I know what you must think, Mrs McArdle,' she spoke out confidently now, wanting to make this woman see she wasn't intimidated. 'But Donny has been very

274

good to me. I keep house for him and look after the children and in return he has given me a room of my own, my keep and a good home for Ina. I would hate folk to think wrong of him for it. He's a very good man.'

'So it seems. How do you come to know him?' Hetty probed.

Morag did her best to smile and sound convincing. 'He's my stepfather's brother-in-law.'

'Rab Bannerman's your stepfather?' Hetty asked sharply.

'Yes,' Morag was beginning to see that this women missed very little. 'Do you know him?'

'I know of him. He comes to see Donny once or twice a year. He's Angus Fraser's man is he not?'

Morag swallowed hard. 'Angus Fraser died more than three years ago.'

'And what about your own man? You're gey young to be widowed.'

'He got the influenza and died.'

'Before the wee lassie was born?'

Morag had to think quickly, trying to remember if she had ever told anyone that her imaginary husband had died before Ina was born. She didn't think she had. 'No.'

'Must have been a terrible shock, losing your man like that.'

'Yes, it was.' Morag couldn't meet Hetty's eyes.

'He worked on the Fraser estate, did he?'

'Yes.'

'And losing your home too.' She was obviously well informed.

'Yes.'

'I suppose that's why you came to Donny Archibold. Nowhere else to go.'

'Aye. That's right.'

'I don't know what your mother was thinking of. I would have thought she could have taken you in, under the circumstances.' Hetty watched the young girl closely, knowing her suspicions had been right. 'Unless there was some reason . . . ?'

'I . . . I don't get on with my mother. She's just got married again. She didn't want us there.'

'Strange though.'

'What is?' Morag snapped.

'You getting put out of your house. What with Rab Bannerman being your stepfather and all, and in his position. I should have thought he could have persuaded them to let you stay,' she sighed then looked at Morag with a tight smile. 'I've a sister who lives in Glenelg – that's not far from Pitochrie is it? She gets to know most of what goes on in the villages up there. It's gey strange but she can't recall a young man dying of the influenza, though she did say something about a young lass from the castle having a wean, and her not married. I don't suppose you know who that was do you, hen?'

Morag was close to tears, understanding very well that Gray's mother had guessed the truth. 'I really have to go now, Mrs McArdle. Donny will be wanting his dinner and the children too.' She made for the door blindly.

'Right you are, lass. I don't suppose we'll be seeing you again. Och, and lass . . .'

'What now?' Morag swung round, holding her head high and jutting her chin out defiantly.

'I think we can keep this conversation between us, you understand what I mean. If you do the right thing . . .'

'Oh I understand all right, Mrs McArdle. I understand.'

She opened the door and rushed out, banging into Gray as she went.

'Hey,' he called after her. 'Morag! Wait a minute. What's wrong?'

'Graham, come in here, lad,' Hetty called.

'What's wrong with Morag?' he demanded, facing his mother angrily. 'What have you been saying to her?'

'Sit down, Gray. We need to talk,' Hetty McArdle smiled fondly at her favourite child. He would be hurt, there was no doubt about that, but better he heard the truth now than let himself be snared by some trollop and her bastard child.

Donny, who was just in from his walk, was settling down in front of the fire when he heard the outside door bang. 'Here's your mam, lass,' he told Ina who was allowing Maureen to take her coat and shoes off. The wee girl's face lit up and Maureen and Maurice both looked up with expectant smiles. Not for the first time that day Donny realised how much they would miss her if she married Gray McArdle. Him most of all.

After Beth's death, Donny had been sure that he would never remarry, that he could never love another woman as much as he had loved his first wife. And then Morag had come into his life, hurt and vulnerable, rousing him first to a strong protectiveness and then to affection which had deepened, almost without him realising it, to love. It had taken Gray McArdle to make him understand just how deeply he loved Morag but by then it was too late.

To their collective disappointment Morag's footsteps clattered on upstairs and then they heard the resounding bang of her bedroom door. They waited but after the loud creak of the bedstead as she threw herself on it there was silence.

'Want Mammy,' Ina said plaintively.

Donny frowned. 'Aye, I know you do, hen. Stay here a wee minute and I'll go and fetch her. I expect she thinks we're still out on our walk.' He ruffled the child's hair affectionately and hurried up the stairs.

Morag's door was firmly closed. Donny hesitated a minute before knocking. It was obvious to him from the uncharacteristic way Morag had crashed upstairs without even bothering to look in on the children that something was wrong. That was confirmed by the muffled sniffling coming from her room. He knocked gently.

'Morag. Are you all right?' he called softly.

'Go away,' was the waterlogged reply.

'Can I come in?' he persisted. She didn't answer. 'Morag, come on lass. Open the door.'

Eventually he heard the bed creak and soft footsteps. The door opened and he peered inside to see her staring out of the window with her back to him. Shutting the door behind him he crossed the room slowly and stood behind her. 'What's wrong, lass?'

She sniffed. 'Nothing.'

Gently he put his huge hands on her shoulders and drew her round to face him. 'What sort of nothing makes you cry like this?' he asked, brushing tears from her face.

She shook her head, dumbly, unable to find a voice to tell him of her humiliation, her pain.

'Och, lass . . .' he sighed, pulling her against his broad chest and letting her sob freely. When at last the tears stopped he detached her gently. 'Well, that's this shirt had a good wash,' he joked softly, brushing at the damp material.

She attempted a woeful smile. 'I'm sorry,' she croaked.

'Now, sit down and tell me what happened.' He led

her firmly to the bed and held her while she stammered out her story.

'Well, I should have expected that from Hetty McArdle. There's not much escapes her. But she's not a bad woman, Morag. She'll have been thinking about protecting her family, not hurting you. She'll not gossip about you. Your secret will be safe with her.' He tried to reassure her, knowing that he must not let her guess how glad he was that the affair was over.

'I don't care about that! I love Gray.' She was close to tears again.

Those last three words cut into Donny but his voice was gentle when he said, 'You should have told him the truth.'

'I meant to but it was so hard. I know he'd have been shocked. He thinks I'm a "nice" girl. Do you know, he hardly tried to touch me, he even asked if it was all right to kiss me.'

'That shows he respects you.' Donny wondered why he was speaking up for the lad.

'He won't respect me now though, will he?'

'Dad! Dad!' Maurice's voice came up the stairs.

'What is it?' Donny snapped.

'There's someone here to see Morag,' the boy yelled.

'Who is it?'

'It's Gray, Dad.'

Donny looked at Morag who was shaking her head violently. 'Right, lad,' Donny opened the door and spoke to his son. 'Ask him to wait in the sitting room for a minute. Morag will speak to him in a wee while.'

'No,' she whispered desperately. 'I can't.'

'You must. Do it now and get it over with. He's a good lad and he deserves that much from you.'

'He must hate me,' she wailed.

'How do you know? You don't know what he's come to say to you.'

'You think he might still want me?' she asked, hope flitting across her tear-stained face.

Donny knew Hetty well enough to know there was not the smallest chance of that but said, 'If he really loves you, lass, he'll still want you. If not, then you would have been making a mistake marrying him. But you'll not know unless you talk to him. Go and wash your face. I'll take the children into the kitchen and leave you two to sort this out in private.' He was gone before she could say thank you.

Gray sat uncomfortably in the living room, twisting and untwisting his hands. When Morag came hesitantly into the room he jumped to his feet and he saw, at once, that she had been crying.

'What do you want, Gray?' she asked, not knowing where to start.

'You've been crying,' he said, his own unhappiness making limpid pools of his eyes.

'I didn't think you'd want to see me again,' she mumbled.

He shrugged, struggled visibly to find the right words then blurted out, 'What my mam says about you, it's not true, is it? I told her she was wrong. I know you wouldn't lie to me.'

'It is true,' she whispered.

His mouth sagged open. 'No!'

'It is. I'm sorry, Gray. I meant to tell you but . . .'

'You lied!' he shouted angrily now. 'You lied to me. All this time and me thinking you were a widow, like you said. And all the time . . .'

'No! Sit down, Gray,' she begged, trying to take his

hands. 'Let me tell you what happened. It wasn't what you think.'

'Get your hands off me,' he yelled, knocking her arms away and making for the door. 'You're a slut, a cheap little slut. No wonder Donny Archibold doesn't like me hanging round here. I bet you warm his bed for him too, don't you?' He charged out of the room and banged down the stairs leaving her shaking in the middle of the room.

'He wouldn't listen,' she sobbed to Donny when he came in a minute or so later. 'He called me a slut.'

'Then he can't really care about you,' he responded firmly.

'I thought we would get married, that we'd have a home of our own.'

'One day you will,' he promised, his heart pounding.

'No, I won't! Who would have me?' she retorted, sounding angry now. 'My mam was right, I'm ruined. I'll never have a husband or a family. Before long everyone in Kilweem will know and it'll be just like Pitochrie, only worse because they'll all know I've been lying.' She stood up and started to walk agitatedly round the room. 'I'll have to go. I can't stay here. Everyone will think that we're carrying on together. That's what Gray thinks. I'll pack our things. Go back to Pitochrie. Rab will let us stay there for a while.'

'No! I won't let you,' he roared, making her stop and stare at him.

'You won't want us here when the village starts talking about us,' she cried.

'They won't start talking. Hetty will keep her word and make sure Gray does too. But I wouldn't care anyway. Och, Morag, I don't want you to go. I'd miss you. And what about the bairns? Maureen and Maurice are gey fond of you and I love Ina like she was my own bairn. You can't separate them now.'

'I would miss the children,' she admitted slowly.

'Then stay here and marry me,' he said.

'Marry you?' she asked, gaping at him.

'We've been sharing this house for over a year and getting along very well. And I don't want to seem cruel, lass, but it's true enough, what you said. No one else is likely to offer, not with young Ina.'

'I don't love you.'

'But I love you,' he said it at last. 'And the little lass too. Maybe that's enough to be going on with. I'll treat you well, you know that. And we'd be contented enough surely. Aye, and it would stop the tongues wagging too, wouldn't it?'

'I . . .' Morag didn't know what to say, her brain was spinning under the strain of the day. 'You're only saying that because you're sorry for me,' she accused him eventually.

'No, lass. I was going to ask you anyway, but I left it too late and young Gray got in before me.'

'Honestly?' she asked slowly.

'Aye,' he smiled. 'Honestly. We're a family already, aren't we? I'd like it to stay that way.' There was such warmth in his eyes that she believed him absolutely.

'I didn't know. I can't think,' she said, a note of panic in her voice as she rubbed at her aching temples.

'No, I know you can't. It's all too sudden. You away upstairs, lass, and pack your things.'

'What?' Confused as she was, she actually thought he was going to send her away now.

'Och, I'm only going to take you back to Pitochrie for a week. It's time your mother saw her grandwean again. And you need time to think. I'll come back for

282

you next Sunday, you'll have had time to make a decision by then.'

'And if I say no?'

'Then it's up to you. Me and the weans would like you to come home again and there's no reason why we can't go on as we are.'

'You're a kind man, Donny Archibold,' she said huskily, her throat raw from crying.

'And you are a beautiful, generous woman. Young Gray McArdle will live to regret today, and, if I'm lucky, I'll have reason to be grateful to Hetty McArdle for the rest of my life.'

'Well, lass, come home to see us at last, have you?' Rab greeted them cheerfully, lifting Ina down and shaking Donny by the hand. 'My, it's good to see you. Come along in.'

'I can't stay long,' Donny warned. 'I've left the weans with a neighbour so I don't want to be too late back.'

'You've time for a wee dram surely?' Rab insisted, his eyes twinkling merrily. 'I've a bottle of your favourite malt waiting for you.'

'In that case . . .' Donny, easily tempted, grinned and started to follow Rab into the house.

Suddenly shy, Ina lifted her arms to Donny who scooped her up and carried her inside, bending low to avoid cracking his head on the lintel.

'Gosh, you've grown,' Morag smiled at Ayleen who was watching her older sister from disturbingly familiar blue eyes. Like her mother she was immaculately neat — too neat for a child of her age, Morag thought — her dark blonde hair caught in two tight braids, her boots gleaming and her little face freshly scrubbed. Even the impractical white pinafore which covered her dress was smooth and uncreased. 'How do you stay so clean and tidy?' Morag asked. 'Ina always looks a proper mess.'

'You'll have to be firmer with her,' was Annie's cheerless remark.

Morag's heart sank. She had hoped that the passage of time would have taken the sting out of her mother's bitterness but it seemed that Annie's feelings hadn't mellowed.

'I hope you don't mind us being here, Mam?' she said to her mother's stiff back. 'I've missed you and I don't like to think you're still angry with me. Can't we try to be friends?'

Rab raised a warning eyebrow at his wife. Annie looked flustered for a second then turned to her daughter with a tight smile. 'Aye, well what's done is done. I dare say I was hard on you, Morag, and I'm sorry you had to go away. Still it all worked out for the best and I'm right glad to have you visit.'

They passed a rather strained hour, feeling more like strangers than family, before a slightly less than sober Donny insisted he had to leave.

'I'll be back on Sunday,' he assured Morag, lifting Ina to kiss her goodbye. 'Have a good time, lass. And think over what I said to you.'

'I will,' she promised, then stood at the door watching as the cart rattled away up the muddy track. On Sunday he would expect an answer. But would she be able to give him the one he wanted? 'Oh Gray,' she whispered, turning and going sadly back inside the house.

It was a strangely unsettling week. Though Rab made them very welcome and even Annie seemed to thaw a little, Morag was aware of an undercurrent of tension in her mother and was saddened to realise Annie would be glad when her visitors went back to Kilweem.

'If you won't let me do anything to help you I might as well take the lassies for a walk,' Morag said on the second day. She was irritated that Annie trusted her to do very little about the house and found trifling faults with the small chores she did do. Even more annoying was the way her mother constantly scolded Ina, expecting her, like Ayleen, to sit quietly with books and crayons for hours at a time, an impossibility for a high-spirited child. Morag felt very sorry for her young sister who seemed unnaturally restrained and reluctant to do anything which might crumple her clothes and attract her mother's wrath.

'That's a good idea,' Annie agreed with tactless enthusiasm. 'But you just take Ina. Ayleen can stay here.'

'Don't you want to come?' Morag turned to the girl who seemed torn between upsetting her mother and going off with this exciting older sister. 'We'll go into the woods and play hide and seek if you like.'

The little girl's face brightened.

'Let me take me her, Mam,' Morag pleaded.

'Och, all right then. But don't go letting them get themselves into a mess,' Annie warned.

'For goodness sake!' Morag cried in exasperation. 'If they get dirty, which they probably will, *I'll* wash the clothes. I'm quite good at that, or don't you remember that we used to take in washing?'

Annie flushed angrily. 'Just don't go into the village, that's all,' she snapped.

'I thought I'd buy some sweeties to take back for Maureen and Maurice,' Morag said wickedly, knowing her mother was worried that all the old gossip would be re-ignited.

Away from Annie's watchful eyes, Ayleen was a bright, lively child. She soon forgot her mother's instructions and was tumbling through the fallen leaves as wildly as Ina. Morag watched them fondly then waited for them at the end of the track, looking back at the little house.

How dreary it looked, with the damp leaves falling everywhere. There seemed to be no light, no beauty

286

about the cottage. The air carried the unpleasant smell of rotting vegetation and musty dampness that the sea breezes on the coast would have dispersed long before it had time to settle. And it was so still, the smoke from the chimney rose in a long column then hung heavily at the level of the trees tops, adding to the claustrophobic feel of the area. Morag shivered, suddenly wanting to get as far away from the place as she could.

'Come on,' she called the girls who arrived breathless and giggling. 'Let's take Ina and show her the castle, shall we, Ayleen?'

'Daddy at castle,' Ayleen pronounced solemnly.

'Daddy?' Ina said but Morag knew she was thinking of Donny. 'Soon, Daddy will come for us soon,' she said.

'Mrs McManus, are you there?' Morag poked her head round the back door of Pitochrie Castle and shouted.

'Who is it?' A voice called and a young girl in the house uniform appeared.

'I'm Morag McDonald,' Morag said smiling. 'I used to work here.'

'Morag? The one who had the baby?' the girl blurted, but Morag laughed and said, 'That's me.'

The girl stood aside and let Morag and the children into the kitchen.

Mrs McManus turned from the oven and stared at them, her heart pounding in guilty shock as she looked from Morag to the child who so resembled Lady Katrina. 'Morag McDonald! Well, and I didn't expect to see you back in these parts!' she gasped at last.

'I'm visiting my mam for a few days. I couldn't go away again without coming to say hello,' Morag said, sensing the older woman's lingering hostility.

'Well, it's not really convenient this morning, Morag.

I'm gey busy. But I suppose I could spare you five minutes.'

Morag sat at the huge table, perching Ina firmly on her knee where she would not be able to get into mischief. Ayleen clambered on to a chair and sat, a model of good behaviour.

'How is everyone?'

'You know Flo's married?' Mrs McManus said, relaxing a little when she realised this was nothing more than a social call. And what else could it be, she told herself. There was no way that Morag could ever discover the truth about Ina's birth.

'Aye, Uncle Rab writes and tells me most of the news.'

'We've two new lassies. That's Tina, Flo's youngest sister.'

Morag laughed. 'I didn't recognise you.'

'And the other lassie is Bessie Burns. She'll be younger than you too. Clara's still here, though Lady Katrina's talking about a governess for the boy next year so I don't know what'll happen to her then, poor thing.'

'What about wee Chrissy?' Morag asked.

'Och, she's still here. Still as daft as can be. She's away to the village the now and knowing her she'll take all morning.'

They chatted on until Lady Katrina's bell rang and Tina hurried off to see what she wanted.

'She's going out,' she announced when she returned a little later, 'I'd to pin her hat for her.'

'If Lady Katrina's going out do you think I could go up and see Clara?' Morag asked. 'I'd like her to see Ina.'

'Be quick then. Clara's not got time to waste chatting. Leave Ayleen here, I'll give her a piece of cake and some milk. Would you like that, hen?' Mrs McManus's manner was noticeably warmer towards the estate manager's adopted daughter.

Morag and Ina climbed the stairs to the nursery.

'Come in,' Clara called then clapped her hands and ran at her friend in delight. 'Morag!'

'I can't stay for long but Lady Katrina's gone out so she needn't know I've been. Och,' she added, staring at the child playing with toy soldiers on the floor. 'Isn't he a fine lad?'

Realising he was the subject of discussion, Angus Fraser scrambled to his feet and looked at Clara for reassurance. He was tall for his age and sturdy with it but seemed shy and rather unsure of himself.

'It's all right, Angus, this is Morag. Don't you remember her? She used to work here.'

He shook his head but smiled an attractive, freckle-faced grin which instantly reminded Morag of her brother, Davy.

'Come and say hello to Ina, Angus,' Morag said gently. 'You and she were born on the same day so you are exactly the same age.' She crouched down as she spoke and encouraged him to come to her. He did, bringing one of his soldiers and offering it silently to Ina. 'Thank you,' Morag laughed. 'He's very well behaved,' she said, looking at Clara. 'Clara? Are you all right?' The other woman was as white as a sheet as she stared at the happy scene.

'Yes . . . yes. Dear Lord,' she blurted out suddenly, 'That child is the absolute image of you.'

'Do you think so?' Morag asked innocently. 'Most people say we're not one bit alike. Where she gets that hair from I don't know. My mother's fair haired but nowhere near Ina's golden colour and as for those curls.'

'Not the girl! Angus! He's your absolute image.'

Morag turned and looked at the boy whose attention was all for Ina. Certainly his hair was the same glorious shade of auburn as hers but as for the rest, he looked more like Ayleen than anyone else. Except for his eyes. Ayleen's were blue – like Rab's, she realised suddenly – while Angus's were the same green as her father's, as hers. Suddenly there was a loud rushing noise in Morag's ears. Her head began to spin as shock overwhelmed her mind. She felt as if she was going to faint but closed her eyes for a moment and, with a great effort of will, controlled herself.

It was a coincidence, she told herself when her head had stopped reeling. Lots of people had red hair, though few had this exact, lustrous tint, and green eyes were common enough, especially with that hair colour. But maybe there was something in the shape of his mouth too, but no, that was simply letting her imagination run away with her.

'It's the hair,' she murmured weakly. 'How funny.' But time and time again her eyes were drawn back to the child.

Somehow she got through another ten minutes with the flustered Clara before taking Ina's hand and making her way downstairs, her mind still in turmoil. As they passed the floor which housed Katrina's bedroom she hesitated, remembering something she had seen there many times. Quickly checking to make sure no one else was coming up the staircase, she crept along to Katrina's door and listened. There was no sound from within so she slipped inside, pulling Ina with her. Once inside she went straight to the small corner table where a series of posed photographs were still arranged in heavy gilt frames, just as they had been when she worked there.

At the back there had been one of Katrina and her

parents. It was still there, a formal, sepia study of a woman, sitting stiffly on a chair, her unsmiling husband behind her, and a child of about seven or eight years old. Morag extricated it from the mass of other pictures and stared at the little girl, captured so unnaturally more than twenty years ago. It could have been Ina. There was the same heart-shaped face, the identical, tiny mouth and a similar cap of light curls. Deep inside her, Morag's stomach seemed to knot itself in agonising spasms. She could feel the agonised beating of her own heart while her skin prickled with fear. The picture slipped from her nerveless fingers and crashed to the floor, cracking the glass. The noise brought her back to her senses. Hurriedly she stooped and retrieved it. She almost stood it back in its place on the table but then wrapped the whole thing in her handkerchief and pushed it into her pocket. With any luck it would be weeks or even months before the loss was discovered and by then nobody would connect it with her visit.

She hardly noticed the girls' determination to play in the woods on the way home and allowed them to run freely, giving herself some time to think. Not that it took much effort to work out what had happened, she thought bitterly. Katrina Fraser had been desperate for a boy, they had all known that, but to need a boy so badly that she would swap her own child for someone else's? Could any woman really do that? And then to treat that child as badly as she had treated Ina? Morag's emotions struggled with the evidence, daunted by the enormity of it. The sweat of pure horror ran down her back and again she felt light-headed. Shaking, she collapsed on to a fallen tree trunk and waited until she had herself under control, knowing she couldn't face her mother in this overwrought state. But no matter how hard she thought about it, pure logic insisted that the child in the nursery, the one with her hair and, now she thought of it, the same cleft in his chin – the little boy who looked so much like her brother Davy had as a child – was her son, while Ina could only be Lady Katrina's natural daughter. She took out the picture and stared at it for a long time before finally putting it away again and calling the children.

'Sweet Jesus,' Rab breathed as he stared at the picture. 'I knew she was a ruthless woman, but this!' He rubbed his hand through his beard and for once, seemed at a loss. 'It could just be coincidence.'

'But it's not only Ina, it's Angus too. Clara was right, he really does look like me. Haven't you seen him recently, Uncle Rab?' Morag asked hunching further into her coat. She had asked him to walk with her, knowing her mother couldn't possibly hear this, and the night was sharp with approaching winter.

'No,' he admitted, 'not for a long time. He's not allowed to talk to the likes of me. He spends most of his time with his mother. She dotes on him from what I hear.'

'But he's not even her child!' She still couldn't understand how any woman could knowingly abandon her own child in favour of another.

'Look, lass, don't go upsetting yourself about this. You could be wrong. In any case you'd never prove anything and even if you did, where would that leave Ina ?'

'Ina's been with me from the day she was born. I love her more than anything in the whole world. But that doesn't make what Katrina Fraser did right! She's got my son.'

'You can't be sure of that, Morag.' Rab warned her.

'And before you do anything, think very carefully about what this could do to both children.'

'Clara told me that Angus loves Katrina very much. It would be cruel to take him away. I could never hope to give him half as much as she can. It's too late to change anything now,' she sighed. 'Anyway, what hope would I have? Like you say, I could never prove a thing like that.'

'I suppose someone else must know. Whoever delivered the babies ...'

'Aye, I hadn't thought! Flo and Mrs McManus were there. I could ask them.'

'Best leave well alone, lass. You've just said you wouldn't change anything and you don't want to risk losing Ina.'

'I won't lose her. She's mine,' she said, fiercely protective. 'But I want to know, Uncle Rab. I need to be sure.'

'If you start asking questions, who knows what might happen.'

She sighed. 'I suppose so.'

'So long as Katrina never decides she wants her daughter back,' Rab mused, half to himself.

'No, she needs a son. Without him the castle might still go to Sir Angus's cousin.'

'Not any more. He died. Even if Katrina had had a daughter, she would have inherited now. There is no one else.'

'Uncle Rab,' she said hesitantly, 'I was thinking. What if something happened to little Angus? God forbid it should, but children are such fragile things. She might remember Ina then.'

'Aye, maybe. But she couldn't do anything about it, lass. It's too late now. If you are right and the babies were swapped around, then the same people who were willing to say Angus was hers would be the only ones who could support her claim to Ina. They'd never do it. They'd all end up in the jail. Katrina too. Anyway, the lad's fine and healthy. You know . . .' he hesitated then went on. 'You'd have to go to court in a case like that. People like us can't afford lawyers and . . . well, as a woman on your own, with an illegitimate child, I don't think you'd stand much chance against the likes of Katrina Fraser.'

'Don't worry. I'll save a little corner of my heart for Angus but I won't risk ruining his life, or Ina's. Anyway,' she deliberately changed the subject, feeling unable to control her tightly reined emotions any longer, 'I'm not on my own. I'm going to be Mrs Archibold and Donny will adopt Ina and make it all legal.'

'You and Donny!' Rab exploded.

She nodded. 'He asked me last week.'

'Does your mother know?'

'No. I came home, to think it over. But I'll tell him yes when he comes for me on Sunday.'

'Congratulations, lass. Donny Archibold's a fine man and he'll take good care of both of you.'

'Aye,' she said, a tremor of doubt in her voice. 'He will, won't he.'

Rab drew her into his arms and hugged her. 'I hope you'll be very, very happy, lass. Of all the people I know you surely deserve happiness the most.'

'Thank you, Uncle Rab,' she whispered, thinking of Gray and how happy she might have been with him.

'And now to tell your mother,' he laughed. 'My, and won't she be relieved to have her daughter a respectable married woman at last.'

With her decision about Donny made, Morag would

have enjoyed basking in her mother's sudden approval but for the fact that she knew there was something she must do if she was ever to have peace of mind again.

After three consecutive sleepless nights, and days of being unable to eat or even carry on a sensible conversation, she decided to act. Taking only Ina with her this time she walked back to the castle and told Mrs McManus that she wanted to see Lady Katrina.

'I don't know, lass,' Cook hesitated. 'I'm not sure she'd want to see you.'

'I'm not going until she does,' Morag insisted, her face set and hard.

'Lady Katrina is indisposed,' Mrs McManus insisted after she'd delivered Morag's message to her mistress.

'Then I'll talk to you.' Morag dragged out a chair and sat down. 'For your sake it would be better if the other girls didn't hear this.'

'Now just a minute.' Cook was all outraged dignity. 'What's all this about and who do you think you are to come back here and start ordering my staff about?'

'I'm the girl who could get you into serious trouble, Mrs McManus,' Morag said coldly.

'Out,' Mrs McManus ordered the avid maids tersely and they disappeared up the stairs.

'You too,' she turned to wee Chrissy who was at the sink, looking just as Morag had remembered her.

'No. Chrissy can stay. Come here, hen. I want you to listen to this too.'

'I've not done anything wrong,' Cook insisted hotly.

'No? What about the night you gave my son to Lady Katrina and gave me her daughter instead?' she hissed.

'What?' The colour drained from Cook's face. 'I've never heard anything so ridiculous,' she blustered.

Morag stared at her but Mrs McManus met her gaze

so steadily that Morag started to wonder if facing Lady Katrina was the right thing to do.

'Och, Cook, you do so remember,' Chrissy said suddenly, beaming. 'Lady Katrina had a wee lassie. I remember cos she was crying about it. And Morag had a wee boy. And then they changed over and everything was all right again. Flo said everybody was happy and I wasn't to say anything to anyone.'

'Stupid girl!' Cook spat, raising her hand, ready to strike.

Morag stood up and caught her arm. 'You can't hit her for telling the truth. Now, take me to Lady Katrina or shall I go up myself?'

Sudden sweat beading her upper lip, Mrs McManus led the way upstairs.

'I said I didn't want to see you!' Katrina stormed when Morag walked into her sitting room, minutes later. Angus, who had been playing on the floor, fled to the shelter of his mother's skirts.

'Take Angus up to Clara,' Katrina ordered quickly.

'No. Leave him where he is,' Morag insisted.

'How dare you!' Katrina screeched.

'You're upsetting the wee lad, Lady Katrina,' Morag pointed out. 'Anyway I would like the chance to see my son again. And I've brought your daughter for you to see. She's a fine lass. She looks just like you did at her age.'

'My God . . .' Katrina turned so pale that Mrs McManus, thinking she was about to faint, helped her to a chair. 'What do you want?' she rasped.

'I just want you to know that I know you took my son.' Morag sat opposite Katrina and took the bemused Ina on her lap. 'And there's no point in denying it. Anyone can see the truth, just by looking at them. Angus is

296

like me, the image of my brother. And Ina, Lady Katrina, is exactly like you were as a child.' She took the broken picture from her bag and handed it to the other woman.

Katrina gazed at the photograph then at Ina. 'I won't let you have him,' she cried hysterically. Mrs McManus waved smelling salts under her nose and offered her a drink of brandy which Katrina gulped at. Colour gradually returned to her face. Morag waited with an outward show of complete calm. 'You'll never get him,' Katrina repeated, more calmly now.

'You are a wicked, evil woman, Lady Katrina, but Ina is my daughter now. I wouldn't part with her, not for all the money in the world.'

'Then what *do* you want?' Katrina demanded.

'Your word that you will never try to take her from me.'

'You have it,' Katrina agreed instantly.

'Do you think I would trust you after what you've done?' Morag sneered. 'I want it written down.'

'No.'

'Yes. Or I will see a solicitor. I have witnesses, people who were here when the babies were born.'

'Chrissy,' Cook snorted. 'That lassie's no right in the head. No one would believe her.'

'Maybe, maybe not. But do you want to risk it?' Morag persisted.

Katrina stared at her son, looked again at Ina then back at the old photograph. 'She is like me, isn't she?' she whispered at last.

'As Angus is like me,' Morag added. 'And anyone looking at us together would see it too.'

'All right,' Katrina decided sharply. 'Just wait a minute and I'll do it. But you'll have to sign something too. I won't risk you taking Angus from me either.'

'I'll never do that,' Morag said softly, smiling at her wide-eyed son, feeling a painful tug of emotion for this child she had lost.

Katrina rose and went to her desk where she scribbled furiously for a minute. 'There,' she said thrusting two sheets of paper to Morag. 'We will both sign them and keep a copy each.'

Morag signed her name carefully and handed one sheet back to Katrina. 'Thank you.'

'For goodness sake, keep that where no one will find it,' Katrina said desperately. 'If anyone finds out about this just remember that your signature is on it too. That makes you as guilty as I am.' She grabbed the paper and locked it in her bureau.

'All I'm guilty of is loving the child I have always believed was mine.' Morag's voice shook slightly. 'The child you turned your back on – your very own daughter. How could you do that?'

Katrina glared at her, her face bleached of all colour, but it was she who dropped her eyes from Morag's accusing stare.

'Get out,' she choked. 'I never want to see you, either of you, again.'

'I won't come back, Lady Katrina. And I'll never forgive you. Be sure and take good care of my son.' She looked at her child for the last time, dropped a soft kiss on his head then took her daughter by the hand and led her firmly from the room. Outside she dropped to her knees and caught the startled little girl in a fierce hug. 'Och, Ina,' she cried. 'I don't know what I would have done if I'd lost you.'

'Morag! Morag!' Maurice and Maureen were off the cart and running to Morag before Donny could hitch himself

298

off the high seat. Ina jumped up and down in excitement, raising her hands towards Donny who chuckled and picked her up.

'Congratulations, man,' Rab slapped him heartily on the back. Donny froze for an instant then turned quickly to Morag. 'Morag? Does this mean . . . ?' he asked.

'Aye,' she laughed, running to him. 'I'll be right glad to be your wife, Donny Archibold. That's if you still want me.'

'Of course I still want you,' he roared, plucking her off her feet and spinning her round as though she weighed nothing at all.

FIFTEEN

From below came the sound of the villagers celebrating, aided by the bread, pies, bridies, sausage rolls and cakes which Donny had spent all the previous day and most of this morning making, all washed down by copious amounts of whisky and beer.

Morag stood gazing out of the bedroom window, across the wet pantiles, grey slates and crow-stepped gables which characterised the Kilweem skyline, seeing none of it. A bare two hours ago she had stood in church and taken solemn vows she was incapable of keeping, knowing, even as she repeated the words, that she was committing blasphemy, a gross betrayal of a kind man who deserved better. How could she love Donny when her heart belonged to Gray McArdle?

Bracing herself to return to her guests she turned to the long mirror and smoothed the perfect fall of the ivory-coloured dress, a dress not quite white, in which she had walked down the aisle, on Rab's arm, to her new husband. Donny, his huge frame seeming to fill the entire space at the bottom of the aisle, had been proud and smiling, seemingly unaware of the disapproval radiating from Minister Porteous who had, of necessity, learned that Morag was not the tragic young widow the village believed her to be. It was only his abiding respect for Donny Archibold which had finally persuaded him to lock away his principles and marry the couple. He had stood before them, the expression on his face as black as his robe, his voice as starkly bleak as the white cross of material at his throat, and lectured them, not on the sanctity of the married state, as he had always done at previous weddings, but on the sins of deception, and lying, and fornication. Morag's face had flushed with mortification. The day was tainted by shame.

The colour in her face faded during the wedding breakfast but she knew the Minister's comments had caused speculation which had been further exacerbated by his stubborn absence from the celebrations. Gradually the redness paled, even the natural bloom of colour faded from her cheeks and the dull ache behind her eyes grew to an overpowering thump. The face which looked back from the mirror now bore signs of strain. The contrast between her thick, auburn hair and the bleached white of her skin was too marked. Her eyes looked heavy and dull, their colour indiscernible and her mouth, no matter what she did, seemed determined to return to that tight, unsmiling line in which she had set it when Minister Porteous had first glared at her that morning.

Was this sad-faced young woman really her, she wondered? Could she really be the girl whose wedding was being celebrated so loudly downstairs? What had happened to the wild, carefree lass who had tumbled through the Pitochrie woods with her brothers, the girl who had run barefoot across the hillsides without a worry in the world? Morag smiled wistfully. The past could never be recaptured and anyway, what about the cold, or the hunger, which even Annie's assiduous housekeeping had not always been able to prevent? Here in Kilweem, with solid, dependable Donny, her daughter would never know that sort of deprivation and she

301

would be safe from the shame of her birth. For Ina's sake Morag knew she had to put her love for Gray McArdle behind her and work to make a success of her marriage with Donny.

'Are you all right, lass?' Donny himself slipped into the room quietly and came to stand behind her, his reflection filling the mirror. She could smell the whisky on his breath, could see the tell-tale pinkness in his eyes.

'Just tired.' She forced a smile knowing he deserved to enjoy the day.

'Aye, it's hard work getting wed,' he chuckled, rubbing her arms gently, longing to feel the softness of her breasts under his hands, feeling his own body responding to the thought. He moved away quickly, knowing that now was not the time to make love to his wife for the first time. 'Still, folk're starting to leave now. Another hour and we'll be on our own.' He opened the door and waited for her.

'Aye,' she agreed, her dread filling her heart. 'Another hour.'

'Och, Morag, lass . . .' Donny groaned as her nightdress fell to the floor, leaving her naked in the soft light filtering through the window of the bedroom. He scrambled inelegantly out of his own clothes, the drink making him overeager and clumsy. Morag suppressed a gasp and forced herself to stay where she was. Without his clothes Donny seemed even more massive, so tall that she barely reached his chest. His beefy shoulders were as broad as a doorway, his legs like the boles of trees and, like the rest of his body, covered in a thick mat of wiry hair. And there, in the same gigantic proportions as the rest of him, already thrusting out at her from between his thighs, was the thing which frightened her most.

Donny gathered her in his arms and carried her effortlessly to the bed where he kissed her, starting with her mouth then moving down, ever lower, the heat of his body contrasting sharply with the iciness of her shivering flesh. She tried to respond to his kisses but, as he moved away from her mouth, she lay rigid and tense, her hands clenched at her sides, her breath coming in shallow, distressed gasps.

Donny, normally so gentle, so patient, writhed on top of her like another person, like some kind of primeval animal, driven only by instinct. When he thrust into her she tensed then lay perfectly still, her arms over her face while he rammed himself into her. Finally he shuddered, stiffened for a moment then collapsed over her, still murmuring her name. She shoved at him impatiently, wanting nothing more than to be able to turn away and close her eyes.

On their wedding night Donny and Morag Archibold lay back to back, each totally misunderstanding the other. Even through the alcohol-induced fug in his brain, Donny was confused, and hurt. He had expected Morag to welcome him, if not passionately then at least with enthusiasm. After all, it wasn't as if she was a virgin who knew nothing about her own body and less about the male. She was experienced, had a child to bear witness to that experience, so there should be no need for false modesty or shock. But, to his dismay, that was exactly how she had reacted, lying there with tears running down her face, making him feel guilty for doing what was only natural. Yet even now he wanted her again, could feel himself hardening with the desire to make her respond to him, to force her to wrap herself round him as his first wife had done, to make this something they could enjoy together. Carefully he eased on to his other side and pulled her gently back against him.

Morag allowed Donny to hold his hot body against her back and still felt nothing but revulsion. And hated herself for it. Donny was a kind and generous man and he deserved better from her than this. She made a conscious effort to relax, even let her buttocks worm back into him but tensed involuntarily as he stretched a hand round to her cool breasts. When he rolled her on to her back she came easily enough and put her arms up to bring his face on to hers, but when he entered her she stiffened so harshly that her delicate arms were like bands of iron round his bull-like neck. She kept her arms wrapped round him, tried to will her body to respond but all she felt was dry soreness and irritation. When he was finished she breathed a soft sigh of relief and quickly turned back on to her side, her disappointment in herself almost as great as his.

On the surface things went on much as before. Donny, who had to leave his bed at three o'clock in the morning, always enjoyed his customary couple of glasses of whisky in the evenings but then retired to his bed hours before Morag who crept silently between the covers, praying that her sleeping husband would not wake. Only on Saturday nights and Sunday mornings did their sleeping patterns coincide. Morag came to dread the day which should have been the most precious one of the week.

Weeks passed and still she was unable to give Donny what she knew he needed. She never refused him, she was too fond of him to inflict any more pain than she was already doing. Nor could she claim that Angus Fraser had left an indelible mark on her, because there were

304

times – too many times – when she closed her eyes and wished it was Gray McArdle who was sharing her bed and her body.

At first Donny was patient but gradually he understood that it would always be like this. In the end there was no love in what they did in bed at night, nor any affection, no desire to please the other. He took what his body demanded and she suffered him in silent resignation which gradually seeped into their everyday life, poisoning it.

With Ina at school Morag found she had more time on her hands. She helped Donny in the bakery, serving in the little shop in the mornings but escaping gladly in the afternoon to join the other women at the harbour to buy fresh fish and watch the boats. The talk was all of the war. The newspapers were full of it but Kilweem, at first, was barely affected, most of the men staying with the boats.

Gray McArdle still worked on his uncle's boat but as a fully fledged fisherman now, storing experience against the day when he would take over and captain his own boat. Morag could see that he had earned the respect of the other men, that the youngsters jumped to obey him. He had lost the boyish look, had broadened and darkened, but the flash of humour round his mouth was just the same. He never spoke to her but she knew, from the way Gray's dark eyes always sought her out, that the spark between them had never truly died. Often his wife, Mary, and their young son, William, joined the women and Morag felt a stab of jealousy which made it impossible for her to make a friend of an otherwise popular young woman.

In the winter, the women retreated to their own firesides, leaving the windswept harbour to the fishermen but Morag, wrapped in a heavy coat, thick stockings and sturdy shoes still found herself drawn to the quayside where she would stand shivering, to escape the even colder atmosphere in her own home, in the hope of seeing Gray.

'What are you doing here?' he asked her one day. 'You'll freeze to death standing there.'

'I like to watch the boats,' she said, hardly able to look at him. 'Anyway, I need some fish for the tea.'

He turned silently and took a huge haddock from the trays stacked on the quayside, awaiting the attention of the women in the gutting sheds. 'Here then. Now away home before Donny comes looking for you.'

'He'll not do that,' she whispered.

'Away home, Morag,' he repeated, turning back to his work.

'Fish again!' Donny complained that evening.

'It's good for you,' she retorted, refusing to look at him.

Sitting with her family in the kirk the next Sunday, Morag felt someone's eyes on her. She glanced up and found herself looking into Gray McArdle's weather-browned face. He smiled then quickly looked away. Morag felt her pulses race but dropped her own eyes and tried to concentrate on Minister Porteous's interminable sermon.

After the service, Donny and his friends walked home together, his head towering over the others, leaving her to follow with the women. She called the children and started to make her own way down the road but found her arm held lightly.

'Morag, wait,' Gray, whispered. 'Walk with me.'

She darted a startled look at the other women. 'I can't . . .'

'Och, no one'll think anything of it,' he assured her, falling into step beside her.

Like everyone else they talked about the war which was starting to claim so many lives but all the time she was aware of him beside her. Too soon they were at her door where Donny was waiting. 'I'll see you again,' Gray said innocuously, and loudly enough for the others to hear, then he grinned at Donny, took his own wife's arm, sat his son on his shoulders and strode off to his own home.

The next day he appeared in the bakery to buy himself a pie, something he had never done before, and lingered, making casual conversation until another customer disturbed them.

The boats were out for three days after that but when they returned Morag wandered down to the quayside and every time she looked at Gray he was looking at her. She left abruptly, almost running up the wynd to her own home, frightened of her own emotions, knowing she couldn't let this go any further.

For months, everywhere she went she saw him. The only time she felt safe from herself was when the boats were at sea. Otherwise he was there, in Marketgate when she did her shopping, and again in the kirk, but sitting in front of her this time so that she couldn't avoid looking at him. He came into the bakery, buying bread and pies which he surely couldn't need, confusing her so much that she dropped his change, sending it scattering over the floor. She bent down to gather it up and found him there too, his head inches from hers.

'Meet me tonight,' he whispered urgently. 'At the bottom of the Butts. Nine o'clock.'

307

'I can't,' she breathed, her heart pounding.

'I'll wait for you,' he said, taking his change and walking out of the shop before she could argue further.

Morag watched the hands of the clock move inexorably towards nine. With fifteen minutes to go she rose slowly and walked upstairs to join her husband in bed.

Donny, who had been on the edge of sleep, welcomed her warmly. She clung to him when he came to her, raising her body to meet his, closing her eyes as he entered her, feeling her body respond as it had never done before. But the face she saw above hers was Gray's. When Donny rolled away and sank into a contented sleep she turned her head into her pillow and wept bitterly.

A week passed and Gray stayed away. The boats put to sea and came back again and still she didn't see him. As each day passed the more restless she became, eaten with longing for something she knew she could never have. Guilt drove her to join Donny in bed every night, forcing herself to respond to him as she had done that previous night, acting a passion she was incapable of feeling for him. Not a man given to deep thought, Donny responded vigorously, sinking each night into greater contentment, grateful that, at last, his wife was behaving in the way he had longed for, that his marriage was mending.

'Morag!'

She was rushing along Marketgate with a basketful of messages, knowing Donny was waiting for her to help him in the bakery. When she heard the voice she stopped.

'I'm in here,' Gray's voice came to her from one of the dark, narrow side wynds. 'Hurry up, before someone sees you.'

Quickly looking round to make sure no one was

watching her she turned and hurried towards him. 'What do you want, Gray?' she asked, already knowing the answer.

He took her arm and led her round a corner so that they were sheltered from passers-by by the high walls of the neighbouring buildings. Almost roughly he pushed her against one of these walls and brought his mouth on to hers.

'No,' she broke away and shoved at him. 'No, Gray. I can't,' she cried.

'Yes, you can,' he insisted, making no attempt to keep her there by force but looking deeply into her troubled eyes.

'No,' she moaned, as if she was in pain, but not moving away.

'Morag,' he said, raising one hand to push the hair back off her face. 'I had to see you.'

She shook her head but her hand reached up to his and held it against her cheek. He was so close now that she could feel his breath on her face, could see herself reflected in his dark pupils. When he kissed her this time she knew she was lost. His tongue twined with hers greedily, exploring her mouth more passionately than he had ever done before. Through the barrier of their clothes she could feel him, hard with desire, and she pressed her pelvis into him desperately.

Minutes later she finally pulled away from him. 'I've got to go,' she mumbled. 'Donny'll be wondering where I've got to.'

'Meet me tonight,' he demanded. 'On the beach.'

'I can't.'

'You can,' he insisted. 'You must. Please, Morag.'

'Are you coming to bed, lass?' Donny asked at half past

eight, recapping his whisky bottle and putting it away in the fireside cupboard. Morag knew her hands were trembling when she answered. 'No, not yet. I've a wee bit of a headache. I think I'll go for a wee walk first.'

His concern was instant, compounding her guilt. 'Sit still. I'll make you a cup of tea, that'll help.'

'No!' She stood up suddenly. 'No,' she repeated, more softly. 'I could really do with some fresh air.'

He shrugged. 'All right. I'll go on up. Don't be long.'

She listened until she heard the bedroom door close then hurried down the stairs and out on to the street.

It was late March and pitch dark as she hurried along Marketgate then down the Butts and on to the beach. She stood for a moment at the place where the cobbles disappeared under the sand but there was no sign of Gray. Half relieved, half disappointed she decided to walk for a few yards along the beach before going home.

'Did you think I'd stood you up?' Gray asked, laughter in his voice.

She jumped and peered into the shadows of the dunes where a denser shape was emerging. 'You gave me a fright,' she giggled, nervousness giving the sound a brittle edge.

'Come up here. We don't want anyone to see us.' He took her hand and led her through the soft, shifting sand until they reached a sheltered hollow. His jacket was already spread there.

'I can't stop long . . .' she started.

'I know,' he whispered as his mouth found hers. Already his hand was at the buttons of her blouse. When his fingers found her hard nipples the muscles in her pelvis contracted softly, suffusing her body with a desire she hadn't known she could feel. And nothing else mattered but her need of this man. There was no need for him to coax her, she was as eager as he. When he entered her, too impatiently, too eagerly for finesse, she groaned and clasped him to her, winding her legs round him to take him more deeply into her. As he moved within her she surrendered herself completely until the convulsions which gripped him inside her shook through her body, making her cry out. Deep inside she felt flooding heat as Gray trembled in the grip of his own climax. Never, ever could she have guessed that it could be like this.

'I love you, Morag,' he groaned, sinking his face into the damp skin of her breasts. 'God help me I love you.'

'I love you too,' she whispered. 'I don't think I ever stopped loving you.'

An hour later she hurried home, slipping upstairs silently then scrubbing the sand from her body with cold water before creeping into bed beside Donny.

'You were a long time,' he grumbled, his voice thick with sleep.

'I went to the beach,' she said, glad of the darkness to hide the lie. 'It's beautiful there at this time of night.'

He grunted and moved closer to her, letting his hand rest on her breasts, his hand teasing a nipple which was still tingling from Gray's mouth. His other hand slipped between her legs where she could still feel her lover's semen seeping on to her thigh.

'No,' she pulled away abruptly, knowing she couldn't let him do this, not tonight. 'My head,' she complained. 'It's still sore.'

Donny leant over and kissed her lightly. 'Get some sleep then. You'll likely feel better in the morning.'

She didn't. Her head pounded with fear every time she thought about what she'd done. Her throat felt tight and guilt brought a rosy sheen to her cheeks. She was jumpy, nervous and bad tempered.

'Don't worry yourself about the shop,' Donny said when he came in for breakfast. 'And if you're no better in the morning you can take yourself off to the doctor.'

Morag felt as if she had a genuine fever. She burned for Gray's touch and though she spent every morning telling herself that she wouldn't see Gray again, she still met him whenever she could.

It was impossible to tell Donny she was going for a walk every night so she took to wandering along the beach on the one or two afternoons each week when Gray was not at sea or busy on the boat, leaving Donny to have his afternoon nap before the children came in from school.

The beach was long and golden, curving round the bay to the next headland. Behind it lay deep dunes where the village children played. But now, as September cooled into October with harsh winds and stormy days, it was deserted. Even so they were careful to meet a mile or so away from the village and all risk of prying eyes.

Gray watched her as she came towards him, her bright hair whipping round her head in the blustery wind and his heart contracted in sudden pain. He loved Morag so much that it was destroying his life. He felt trapped, stifled, could hardly bear to look at his good-tempered, faithful wife who trusted him so completely. There was no way out. He could never marry Morag. They were doomed to a snatched half hour here, a furtive ten minutes there when he yearned to have her with him all the time. He knew that his wife had seen the change in him; he realised too that he couldn't stand the deception for much longer, knew that he couldn't face the inevitable pain and destruction that the discovery of their affair would cause. He had taken the one escape route open to him and now he had to tell Morag what he had done.

'You can't,' Morag stared at Gray, horror written all over her face.

'It's too late. I've signed up. I leave on Thursday.'

'No . . . No . . . It's already Tuesday,' she wailed. 'I won't let you.'

'Morag. You know why I had to do this. We can't go on like this. You know we can't. We can't ever be married. There's no future for us.' He had said all this to her already today but repeated it because he had to say something to take his mind off the pain in her eyes. 'If we go on seeing each other, they're bound to find out sooner or later.'

'But you're going to war. You could be killed,' she whispered, appalled.

'No. Not me,' he assured her with a bravado he was certainly not feeling.

'Oh God, Gray. What have you done?' she sobbed into his chest.

They made love then, desperately, violently, clinging to each other in the sand and the dampness of their own bodies until exhaustion forced them to stop.

They gathered their scattered clothes and dressed, shivering in the wind that had failed to pierce them before.

'I won't see you again,' he said, kissing her tenderly.

'I can't bear it,' she sobbed.

'You're cold. Go on, home,' he croaked, starting to walk through the dunes, towards the coastal road which ran behind them.

Morag watched him until she could see him no more. Then she turned and walked slowly along the beach.

Unable to face Donny yet, knowing that she was perilously close to tears still, she huddled on a rock on the point and stared sightlessly out to sea.

'Here you are! I was getting worried.' Donny perched beside her. Her long, lonely walks had started to trouble him recently. He had even found himself harbouring some very unwelcome suspicions and had felt slightly ashamed of himself when he had set out to find her this afternoon. Even more ashamed to discover her on this cold rock doing nothing more than watching the sea.

Aware that her future lay only with this man Morag tried to smile. 'I lose track of time here.'

'Come away home, lass. Your hands are frozen. It's too late in the year to be sitting here for hours.'

'Aye,' she agreed, sadly. 'I don't think I'll come here again.'

SIXTEEN

Morag knew she was pregnant as soon as her monthly period failed to appear. And she knew it was Gray, not Donny, who had impregnated her. She and Donny had long ago agreed that they didn't need to add to their family, a decision Morag had never regretted. When she and Donny made love he was meticulously careful to withdraw. She knew he had never let her down. She and Gray had practised the same restraint, on all but two occasions. The first time, right at the start of their affair, she had been lucky. The last time, their final time together, she had not.

Now she had to tell her trusting, loyal husband that she was expecting a child; had to make him believe the child was his. Even though the mere sound of Gray's name was enough to bring tears to her eyes, Morag knew that she owed it to Donny and the children, and to Gray, to make sure the truth was never discovered. So, if she couldn't actually love Donny she would act the part so well that he would never know how badly she still bled for Gray because, if she failed now, if he doubted her, so many innocent lives would be ruined.

'Pregnant?' Donny dropped his paper and stared at her. 'Are you sure?'

She nodded miserably. 'I'm sorry, Donny,' she sobbed. 'I'm really sorry.'

'Och, lass,' he was out of his chair and at at her side

instantly. 'Don't cry. It's not so bad is it?' He stroked her hair gently.

'I don't know,' she sniffed. 'I thought you didn't want any more children.'

'Well,' he smiled slowly. 'There's a lot of braw weans around who were wee surprises. We'll love it just the same.'

He seemed to be accepting it, she should have known he would, but she had to make sure. 'I thought you . . . you know. You always pull out.'

'Aye, well, there's been times when I've maybe been a wee bit slow,' he admitted with a grin.

She managed a watery smile back. 'Oh . . .'

'I'm sorry, Morag. This is my fault.'

'No,' she stopped him guiltily. 'I was just afraid you wouldn't want it.'

'Not want it? Whatever gave you that idea? I'll be right proud,' he asserted. 'Come on, lass, dry your eyes and let's drink to the new wean.' He was already at the cupboard bringing out the bottle and glasses.

'To the bairn,' he toasted.

'The bairn,' she repeated but couldn't bring herself to meet his eyes.

Ina, at eight, was old enough to understand that she was to have a baby brother or sister and greeted the news dubiously.

'Will I still be your little girl?' she asked her mother, her eyes huge with worry.

Morag laughed and hugged her close. 'I will always love you, Ina,' she reassured her. 'And you will love your little brother or sister too.'

'I can help,' offered Maureen who, at eleven, was a mature and serious child.

'You surely can,' Morag smiled at her tiny step-daughter who was hardly taller than the gangling Ina. 'I'll be glad of that when the bairn's born.'

'What about you, lad?' Donny asked Maurice who was frowning over a school book.

The lad shrugged his shoulders. 'I'm not going to help,' he said decisively. 'Bairns are for women to look after.'

Donny guffawed. 'What would you rather have: a sister or a brother?'

Maurice pushed his book away and looked at his father seriously. He was almost thirteen and more like his father with every passing year. Big, broad and hard working, he had a studious side to his nature which Donny had never professed to having. But his real enthusiasm was saved for the bakery. Already he could competently bake bread and took especial pleasure in decorating the tiny, delicate cakes his father produced for special occasions. As with any question he thought long and hard before giving his answer. 'Whatever it is I'm too old to play with it, so it wouldn't make that much difference,' he decided at last. 'But . . .'

'But?' Donny encouraged him.

'Well, if it's a boy . . .' Maurice sounded reluctant to say whatever was on his mind.

'Go on, son,' Donny encouraged him.

'You always said I would take over the bakery from you,' the lad blurted out. 'If it's a boy will I have to share it?'

Donny frowned. 'I hadn't thought of that,' he admitted. 'But even if you take over the bakery you'll still have to look after your sisters.'

'I know that!' Maurice retorted. 'But will I still be in charge?'

'Och, aye, son. You're the oldest. You'll be in charge.'

'That's all right then,' Maurice said, pulling his book back to him. 'But maybe it had better be a wee girl. Just in case.'

Well into her seventh month, Morag strolled through the village and turned on to the Butts. The larger she got, the more uncomfortable she felt and walking was the only way she could ease the discomfort. As a rule she avoided the beach, it held too many memories for her, but today, in early April, she was tempted by the bright sun and light breeze.

The Butts was steep and unevenly setted so she trod carefully. There were fishermen's cottages, some of the oldest in the village, down one side, blank walls on the other. The spring weather had brought folk out of their homes to sit in the sun. Morag smiled and waved as she made her way towards the beach. Near the bottom, ensconced in a creaking rocking chair with a rough blanket over her old legs, sat Granny Guthrie. Morag crossed to the far side of the street. The old lady was famous in the villages and was said to have the gift of second sight. The women called her a witch and though Morag didn't believe that, Granny Guthrie did have a gruesomely frightening appearance with her hooked nose and lined face.

'Well, lass, and where are you off to in such a hurry?' the old woman called, gesturing imperatively.

It was impossible for Morag to ignore her. 'It's such a braw day. I thought I'd walk along the beach,' she said.

'Aye. It'll do you good no doubt,' the old woman nodded, closing her wrinkled eyes again.

Thinking she was asleep Morag moved away. 'You've a shock in store, Morag Archibold.' Granny Guthrie opened her rheumy eyes and peered at Morag again.

'What?'

'This war,' the old woman went on. 'So many dead. Young men dying every day. There's bad news on its way, lass. Take care how you deal with it or you'll lose everything.'

Morag stared, the blood draining from her face. 'What do you mean?' she asked in a hushed whisper.

'Och, what has she been saying to you?' Rose, Granny Guthrie's daughter, peered over the forestair at her mother then hurried to Morag's side, drawing her away. 'Take no notice, hen. She's an old woman and her mind wanders.'

'She said there's bad news coming,' Morag said, shivering suddenly.

'It's the war. It's playing on her mind, that's all. Think nothing of it. Anyway,' she said in a determinedly bright tone. 'It'll be good news for you soon, won't it? Is Jeannie Moys attending you? She's very good.'

'Aye,' Morag nodded.

'Och, you'll be in good hands then.'

'I hope so.'

'Well, off you go, lass, enjoy your walk.' As soon as Morag was out of earshot Rose rounded angrily on her mother. 'For goodness sake,' she blazed, 'could you not have left the lassie in peace?'

'She had to be warned,' the old woman retorted sharply then settled back and shut her eyes again.

Rose turned away with a worried frown on her face and watched Morag making her way along the sand. There were plenty of people in the village who ridiculed her mother and just as many who were in awe of her. Only Rose truly understood that her mother's gift for seeing into the future – glimpses of things which came to her unbidden – was unnervingly genuine.

319

Only two days later it seemed that Granny Guthrie's prediction had come true when a grim-faced Rab brought the dreadful news that Morag's brother, Davy, had been killed in the Dardanelles. Morag surrendered to a storm of tears against Rab's shoulder and emerged feeling a crushing depression which refused to lift. Inevitably her thoughts turned to Gray, fear for his safety gnawing at her stomach like perpetual cramp. For Donny's sake she did her best to put her fear and sorrow to the back of her mind but often, in the long pre-dawn hours when Donny was already at work and she was alone in their bed, she sobbed until she made herself sick.

Against Donny's wishes, Morag still spent at least a couple of hours every morning serving in the bakery. The last weeks of her pregnancy were dragging and she was glad of something to lift her mind from its clogging depression.

She still had three weeks to go when Agnes McLean and Moira Davidson came into the bakery. Moira, a McArdle cousin, had obviously been crying.

'What's wrong?' Morag asked kindly. Moira was a timid girl and this wouldn't be the first time she had come into the shop in tears after a fight with her husband.

'Haven't you heard? I thought everyone knew by now,' Agnes seemed surprised.

'Heard what?' Too late Morag realised that no minor marital tiff could have caused Moira's white face and stunned expression. The first fingers of foreboding clutched at her heart.

'It's our Graham,' Moira choked.

'Dead in Ypres,' Agnes added, fighting tears. 'And him with a wife and wean.'

'Graham?' Morag repeated, her brain flailing with the unaccustomed name.

'Aye. Gray. You know. You used to walk out with him,' Agnes went on. 'The telegraph boy came the day before yesterday to Hetty's. Och, it's awful, so it is.'

The warm smells of the bakery seemed to clog Morag's lungs. When she did manage to grab a gasping breath her head spun. She clenched her hands on the counter, fighting for control, feeling the child in her womb kick out, as if in complaint.

'Are you hearing me, Morag?' Agnes asked. 'I need a plain half, hen.'

Morag managed to take the fresh loaf from the shelf behind her and threw Agnes's money in the cash tin. When the women were safely through the door she wandered into the bakery itself and slumped in the old chair Donny kept there.

'Morag, what's wrong?' He dropped the loaf tin he had been carrying on to the table where the bread toppled out and fell to the floor with a hollow thud. 'Is it the bairn?' he asked.

She shook her head. 'No . . . no . . .'

'Then what is it? You're the colour of raw dough. Shall I get you a drink?'

'No!' She shoved his hands away and struggled to her feet. 'I just had a shock, that's all.'

'Sit down, Morag.'

'It's Gray. Gray McArdle. He's dead.' Her mouth twisted with the effort of control.

Donny's massive shoulders sagged. 'Och, I'm sorry, lass. They told me yesterday. I didn't want you to find out so soon after Davy – in your condition. I know you were set on young Gray at one time.' For a while sorrow claimed him too and he stood watching her in silence.

'Away upstairs, Morag. A shock like that is not good for you. Put your feet up for a wee while. I'll come up as soon as I can.'

She dragged herself upstairs and threw herself on their bed, giving way at last to an exhausting torrent of tears. When she could cry no more she allowed herself to drift into restless sleep.

A little later Donny crept in and covered her. She was still sleeping when he closed the shop at one o'clock. He left her in peace and went downstairs to have his own nap in the sitting room.

Morag stirred and gradually opened her eyes, feeling them gritty and sore. The heavy curtains were closed and the room seemed uncomfortably stuffy. Slowly she hauled herself into a sitting position and swung her legs over the edge of the bed but, when she tried to stand up, a sharp pain knifed into her abdomen.

Downstairs Donny heard the tell tale creak of the bed springs and went to see how she was.

'Well, lass, are you feeling better now?' he asked, relieved to see her sitting on the bed.

'I think the baby's coming,' she whispered.

'It's too soon, surely?' he said sharply, fear spearing through him.

'Three weeks just.' She tensed as another pain ripped through her.

'I'll call Doctor Stobie,' Donny was already halfway through the door.

'No,' she stopped him loudly. 'There's no need. There's plenty of time and Jeannie Moys will do fine.'

'No, I'll fetch the doctor. There's no point in taking chances,' he insisted.

'Donny. Calm down,' she managed to smile at him now. 'You see to the weans, they'll be in from the school

322

any minute now. There's stew in the pan and tatties ready peeled. Give them their tea then take them to Betty's, she'll watch them till the bairn's born. We'll see about Doctor Stobie and Jeannie later.'

He hovered indecisively for a minute then clattered down the stairs. A little later Morag heard the children's voices and the sound of Donny rattling round in the kitchen. Cautiously she got up and walked to the window, bracing herself against another pain, but it was no worse than the last. She was almost disappointed. Pain would have released her mind from its unbearable, tortured grief, if only for a few hours. No matter what she did her thoughts went back to Gray, her handsome, laughing Gray, killed in a war he had fought in because it was the only way he could escape the impossible situation he had found himself in with her. Anguish gripped her, building inside until she wanted to scream. The grip of another contraction hardly registered with her.

When Donny came back upstairs, half an hour later, she was red eyed and miserable. 'I'm going for the doctor,' he decided at once. He had watched his first wife die in agony when Maureen was born and was going to take no chances with Morag.

'No,' she sobbed. 'It's not the pain. It's Gray.'

He sat on the bed and took her arms. 'Och, lass, calm yourself. Go on like this and you'll harm the wean. I know it's sad but it's a long time since you and Gray were seeing one another.' Somewhere in his abdomen his gut twisted in a spasm of sudden jealousy. How could she still feel so strongly about young McArdle after all this time? But, he told himself, he was being unfair, it was her condition which was making her react like this. 'Lay down. Try and get some rest.'

She nodded and slipped down into the bed. Donny

was right. She could damage the baby and she would never forgive herself if something happened to Gray's child now.

All night the contractions went on, gradually building in strength and becoming more frequent. By morning she was very tired and in considerable pain.

'This time I am fetching the doctor,' Donny insisted, wiping flour from his hands as he stood over the bed.

'You'll be wasting his time. I don't think this wean's in any great hurry,' she said, rubbing her aching back. 'Why not just fetch Jeannie here for now? She'll send for Doctor Stobie if I need him.'

Ten minutes later Donny was back with Jeannie Moys, a squat, lumpy woman of indeterminate age who immediately banned him from the room. Apart from Granny Guthrie, Jeannie Moys was the ugliest woman in Kilweem. A huge nose, thinning hair and uneven teeth gave her an appearance which frightened the children. The shapeless sacks of musty black material in which she dressed herself added to their terror, as did her gruff, impatient manner. Underneath this disguise she was a kind-hearted soul and the best midwife for miles around.

'Och, you've a while to go yet, lass,' she said when she had examined Morag. 'Best to be off that bed and walking about a bit. It'll ease you. Now, I've my messages to get and I'd better set some soup on the hob ready for my lot the night. I'll call back around noon. You'll be fine until then. And that man of yours is just downstairs. I'll ask him to look in every half hour or so.'

'Aye. Off you go Jeannie. I feel right enough yet.' Reassured by the woman's brisk manner, Morag allowed her memories of Gray to reclaim her for a while, the progress of her labour barely impinging on her misery.

But, by the time Jeannie came back, the pain was so great that it had succeeding in overwhelming her. Morag was gritting her teeth and writhing in agony. Almost unnoticed her strength had been sapped and she barely had the energy to raise her head from the sweat-soaked pillow.

'It'll not be too long now before this wee one says hello,' Jeannie said brightly. 'When did you start, exactly?'

'About this time yesterday,' Morag said, tiredly.

'Yesterday?' Jeannie was shocked. 'I thought you started this morning?'

'No, but there was no point in calling you too soon.'

An hour later Morag's pains were even fiercer and she was weakening visibly, though she had made no more progress. Jeannie, becoming seriously concerned by the girl's obvious exhaustion, slipped downstairs to Donny.

'It'd maybe be as well for Doctor Stobie to have a wee look,' she said.

'What's wrong?' Donny felt panic rising in him.

'Nothing that I can see but it has been a while and the lass is getting tired. Best let the doctor see her.'

Donny had his boots on and was dashing towards Kirkgate and Doctor Stobie's house before Jeannie had time to haul her well-covered frame back upstairs.

He was back ten minutes later. 'The doctor's already on a call,' he announced distractedly.

Jeannie frowned. 'You've left a message?'

'Aye. He'll be here as soon as he can.'

'Och, don't worry, Donny. He'll likely be here in time, if not, well, I've delivered plenty weans and I dare say this one will be just fine. You get yourself over to Hetty McArdle. Ask her to come here for a while. She's seen as many bairns born as I have. I'll need help when the time comes and you're in no fit state to be any use. And this'll take Hetty's mind off her own troubles.'

It was after ten that evening before Morag finally felt the need to push. By now she was so tired that she knew she couldn't work hard enough. For two hours she strained, until she ached in every fibre but still pain lanced through her and her insides felt as if they were being ripped out. And still the child would not be born.

Sitting downstairs with only his whisky bottle for company, Donny listened to his wife's weakening groans until he could stand it no more. Shoving himself into his coat he slammed out of the house and ran back to the doctor's house where Mrs Stobie told him the doctor was still out. Back outside the bakery Donny paced up and down the road, unable to face going back inside.

Morag lay bathed in sweat without the strength to open her eyes, her whole body racked with pain.

Jeannie Moys looked at Hetty McArdle, her concern plain. Hetty, her own face still etched with grief at the death of her son, shook her head gently. She had seen cases like this before and knew the child rarely survived such a long ordeal.

'We're almost there, lass,' Jeannie encouraged her gently. 'I can see the head. Two or three big shoves will do it and then you can sleep till morning.'

Morag roused herself to strain until the tendons in her neck stood out like steel ropes. Again the head moved forward and this time it did not slip back again.

'Good lass,' Hetty encouraged her. 'And again.'

'And again,' Jeannie cried, holding her hands to accept the child at last.

Morag strained then screamed as the child left her body, sliding grey and lifelessly into Jeannie's hands.

Hetty moved quickly to cut the cord and remove the

child, wrapping it in a blanket, well out of sight, before returning to help Jeannie with the afterbirth.

'She's bleeding,' Jeannie whispered urgently. With Hetty handing her towel after towel Jeannie worked with calm efficiency to stem the steady flow of blood. After thirty minutes it stopped. 'Thank the lord,' she sighed, wiping sweat from her face.

'Where's my baby?' Morag asked, rousing slightly.

'He's over there, lass,' Hetty said.

'Can I see him?' Even the words were an effort.

'Not yet. You lie quite still until Doctor Stobie can have a look at you. You've lost a lot of blood and you don't want to start the bleeding off again.'

'That happened last time,' Morag sighed, closing her eyes on her spinning head.

'Sweet Lord! Why didn't you tell us?' Jeannie demanded, angrily, but Morag had closed her eyes and didn't hear.

Donny looked up when he heard footsteps hurrying down the street.

'What are you doing out here, man?' Doctor Stobie demanded, striding energetically into the house ahead of him, just as Jeannie came down the stairs with her pathetic bundle. Catching the doctor's eye over Donny's head she shook her head, almost imperceptibly.

'The lassie's lost a lot of blood, Doctor. I think the bleeding's stopped now but she's gey weak.'

'I'll go on up.' Stobie took the stairs two at a time.

'Och, Doctor, thank goodness you're here.' Hetty, grey-faced with exhaustion herself, jumped to her feet.

Stobie grunted, his attention all for the woman on the bed. 'Not good,' he shook his head after examining her. 'But there's nothing I can do now. Make sure someone

327

stays with her, Hetty. I'll call back first thing in the morning.'

Back downstairs Donny had his head in his hands. When Stobie came into the room he looked up. 'Where were you?' he accused bitterly. 'My son would be alive now if you'd come earlier.'

Stobie shook his head and sat down opposite Donny. 'It wouldn't have made any difference, Donny. There was nothing I could have done to save the child. Mrs Moys has done a fine job. If your wife lives it will be thanks to her efforts.'

Donny jerked to his feet as the full meaning of Stobie's words hit him. 'Morag. Is she all right?'

'She's very weak. She lost a lot of blood. We'll need to keep an eye on her for a day or two.'

Donny, with Hetty at his side, sat beside Morag's bed, watching in dismay as what he had thought was a healthy return of colour brightened into the burning flush of fever. All day they bathed her body in tepid water, working ceaselessly to keep her temperature down. But still she burned. Towards the end of the second day she opened her eyes and looked at her distraught husband.

'I want my baby,' she whispered hoarsely.

'Later, lass. Later,' Donny choked through his own tears.

'No, please. Let me see him,' she begged, struggling feebly.

Donny shot an agonised look at Hetty who looked close to collapse.

'Bring me my baby,' Morag cried, still struggling weakly.

'I'm sorry, lass. The wean died,' Donny said, knowing she wouldn't be put off any longer.

Abruptly Morag stopped struggling. For a minute

Donny thought she had stopped breathing but then she sighed and her body heaved with dry sobs. Donny's shoulders shook too until Hetty pulled him gently away from the bed.

'Get some rest, Donny. You're no good to her in this condition.'

'I'll stay here with her,' he decided, slumping into a chair on the other side of the bed from Hetty. 'You take yourself home, Hetty. You've done more than I'd a right to expect.'

Hetty shook her head. 'She needs a woman with her, Donny. We'll see her through this together.'

'You're a good woman, Hetty McArdle,' he mumbled, his words slurred with emotion.

He dozed and woke to find Hetty sponging Morag's face while she tossed restlessly, muttering to herself.

'She's delirious,' Stobie said when he called, half an hour later.

'Can't you do anything?' Donny pleaded.

'I wish I could. Just keep sponging her down. I'll call back later.'

'Baby . . .' Morag murmured, 'Baby . . .'

'Shshhh, lass. Try to rest,' Donny whispered, brushing her damp hair away from her face.

'Baby . . .' Morag croaked opening her eyes but not seeing Hetty or her husband. 'Gray! Gray! No!' she sobbed.

Hetty jerked as if she had been stabbed. The long hours with Morag had taken her mind a step away from her own grief but now it flooded back to her. 'Quiet lass,' she rasped.

'It upset her, hearing about Gray,' Donny explained.

Hetty nodded, wondering how much he knew, if he knew anything at all, about the reason for her son's sudden decision to join the army.

'Gray,' Morag murmured again, 'Gray's baby . . .'

Hetty froze then looked at Donny who sank slowly on to his knees at the side of the bed. 'No. Oh no,' he choked.

Hetty closed her eyes. She had thought it was impossible to cry more tears than she had already wept for her dead son but now her cheeks were damp with fresh grief.

'Gray's baby,' Morag repeated with a long sighing breath. And then she was silent.

Donny rose from his knees, his face a mask of pain. Silently he let himself out of the room. Shutting himself into his sitting room he took out a bottle of whisky.

Hetty, tears filling her eyes, collapsed into a chair and sat through the long night sleeping only fitfully. When dawn filtered through the curtains she eased her aching bones upright and bent over Morag, testing her skin. It was cool at last, her breathing easy and regular.

Hetty McArdle sank on to her knees, clutched the younger woman's hand in her own and wept for the girl who had loved her favourite son.

Morag recovered slowly, nursed in that first agonising week by Hetty McArdle who abandoned her own family to sit at the girl's side when it was obvious that Donny couldn't bring himself to stay with his wife.

Twice a day Donny looked into the room to see if there was anything the women wanted but so far he had not spoken one word to Morag who watched him with panic in her heart. He knew, she could see it in his eyes, in the grim line of his mouth. But how?

'Hetty?' she whispered on the fifth day, propped up on a pile of pillows, her head finally clear but still too weak to leave her bed without support.

'Lass?' To look at the older woman it seemed that she was the one who was ill. Her face was grey and her eyes deeply shadowed.

'Donny . . .' Morag choked out the single word then couldn't go on and turned her head into the pillow.

Hetty sighed. 'He knows,' she said bluntly. 'The bairn was Gray's. Donny knows.'

'Oh God.' Morag closed her eyes briefly. 'How?' she asked. 'How could he possibly know?'

'You told him yourself, lass. You were raving with the fever.'

'I didn't mean to hurt him,' Morag whispered distractedly. 'He's a good man. I'm the one who deserves to be hurt, not Donny.'

'Hush.' Hetty caught Morag's cold hand in her own dry one. 'It's too late for that now.' As ever she was blunt, but not without compassion.

For long minutes Morag stared blindly towards the window then turned back to Hetty. 'Why are you here?' she asked harshly. 'You don't even like me.'

'I never said that, lass,' Hetty responded sternly but then her own composure slipped. 'I came because Jeannie asked me to help. I would have done as much for any woman. I stayed because I know Gray loved you. He told me about you two before he left. I even wondered about the bairn.' She took a deep sobbing breath. 'He was my grandson.'

'I let him die,' Morag choked.

'Don't say that! It's not true and you know it. I should know, lass. I've lost four of my own that way.' There was a moment of real communion between the two women.

'I'm sorry. I didn't know.'

'I'm the sorry one, lass. I didn't know what it was like

331

between Gray and you. I should never have interfered and I'll regret it for the rest of my days. If I'd left well alone I'd still have my son.' Tears filled her eyes and she looked away. 'That's why I stayed with you. To tell you I'm sorry.'

Morag clasped the older woman's hand and brought it to her face. 'There's no need,' she whispered hoarsely. Then, 'What am I going to do, Hetty? Donny won't even look at me.'

'You'll have to get out of this bed and go about your life as best you can. Donny's a good man but he's hurting. You did a terrible thing, Morag, and just because you did it with my son doesn't mean I approve. I don't. And I can't help you. You're getting better and I'm going back to my own family now. You'll be on your own with him and the children so it's up to you. Maybe he'll find it in himself to forgive you. Maybe he won't.' With that she left Morag to cry her bitter tears alone.

Morag kissed the children goodnight. As soon as they were settled and Donny was back downstairs she wrapped herself in her thick dressing gown and made her unsteady way down the stairs. When she opened the sitting room door Donny looked up then looked away again.

'We need to talk,' she said, perching on the edge of a chair opposite him, her heart hammering with fear.

'You shouldn't be out of bed,' he grunted, emptying his glass in one gulp and pouring himself another measure, slopping it over the table top.

'I can't stay there forever. It's been ten days now and you even have Maureen bring me my meals, rather than face me yourself. We've got to talk.'

332

'There is nothing I want to talk about,' he growled, still not looking at her.

'I want to explain, about Gray.'

'NO!' He was on his feet, his huge frame towering over her, more angry than she had ever seen him. 'I never want to hear his name in this house.'

'I didn't want to hurt you . . .' she pleaded.

The look he gave her made her feel sick.

'Do you want me to go?' she asked, dreading his answer.

'Is that what you want to do?' he retorted. 'Do you want to run away and leave me to explain to Ina that her mother's a whore? Go on then. If you haven't got the courage to face up to what you've done to this family, go.'

'I could go to my mother's for a wee while.'

'If you leave here I will never let you come back. Nor will I let you take Ina away from her family.' Donny's hands clenched and unclenched at his sides and for a moment she wondered if he would hit her but knew that was ridiculous.

'What do you want me to do?' she begged.

'I don't care about you, Morag. Just as you don't care about me.'

'That's not true!' she interrupted him angrily. 'I do care.'

'You care about having a home and a husband to make you respectable. You don't care about me, or the children,' he accused furiously. 'My God, you were having Gray McArdle's baby! You were going to make me believe it was mine; make the children believe it was their brother.'

'You don't understand.'

'Understand? Oh, I understand, Morag.' He glared at

333

her, his eyes blazing with disgust and she knew she had hurt him too much for there to ever be any hope of a reconciliation. 'Now shut your dirty little mouth and listen to me. You can sleep here, eat here and look after the children. You will work in the shop and to anyone else we will be the same as we were before. But you keep yourself away from me. This marriage is over. If you don't want to stay here under those conditions, then go back to your mother, if she'll have you. But you will leave Ina with me.'

'Donny . . .' She lifted a hand to him, tears running down her face.

He snarled and slapped it away. 'It's over, finished. Understand? I wish to God I'd never agreed to have you come here in the first place. I loathe the thought of having you in this house, of seeing your deceitful face every day, but I have the children to think about. For their sake you can stay. Now, get back to your bloody bed.' He grabbed her arm and shoved her violently towards the door. 'Get upstairs,' he bellowed.

Morag found herself on the landing, facing three white-faced children who were huddled together on the bottom stair. She knew they had heard and understood everything. She stepped over them and climbed wearily back to her own room.

In the sitting room Donald Archibold fell into his chair and purposefully filled his glass to the brim with whisky. Another two or three shots and it wouldn't hurt any more.

Morag stayed. She had no choice. The atmosphere in the house was so cold that it was almost unbearable. The children became sullen and withdrawn.

'It's your fault,' Morag heard Maurice accuse Ina one day. 'If your mammy hadn't gone with Gray McArdle it wouldn't be like this. Now my daddy doesn't love your mammy any more.' It was deliberately cruel.

'He's my daddy too,' the little girl wailed miserably.

'He's not!' Maurice spat. 'You haven't got a daddy.'

Morag collapsed at the kitchen table and found herself beyond tears.

'What's gone wrong, Morag?' Rab asked. He and Morag were standing at the far end of the harbour wall, on the very spot where Gray had first told her he loved her.

Morag shrugged and stared into the deep, green water. Rab and Annie, with Ayleen, had come for a short visit, hoping the change would help Annie who was still mourning Davy. The air of hostility which pervaded the bakery was having the very opposite effect and they had decided to leave tomorrow, two full days earlier than planned.

'Something's wrong. Do you think your mother and me are blind?' Rab insisted. 'The man won't even talk to you. He gets blind drunk every night and you wander round like a ghost. Even the children are changed.' He waited for her to say something but when she stayed resolutely silent he asked, 'Do you want to come home, lass?'

It was too much. Morag broke down into heart-wrenching sobs. 'I can't. He won't let me. He says he'll keep Ina if I go.'

Rab was appalled. 'He can't do that!'

'He will.'

'Look, Morag, I've known Donny Archibold for a long time. He's not a bad man. Och, I know he likes a drink, but no more than any other man, so I know something pretty serious must have happened between you two. Morag, lass, it worries me to see you like this. Can't you tell me about it?' He put a reassuring arm round her trembling shoulders.

335

Morag sighed, wiped her eyes and stared out to sea, not able to look at him while she spoke, pouring it all out, sparing him nothing. Before she reached the end she was aware that he had removed his arm, could feel his eyes boring into her.

'My God!' he exploded, when she finished. 'How could you do that to him?'

'I didn't mean to hurt him. I know I was wrong.'

'Aye, lass. You were wrong all right.' There was a chill in his voice which terrified her far more than anything Donny could ever say.

'Uncle Rab, please, try to understand,' she begged.

He looked at her with those piercing blue eyes. 'I understand that you've betrayed a decent man, driven him to drink.'

'I need your help, Uncle Rab,' she pleaded.

'I can't do anything for you this time, Morag. You are not a child any more. You've brought this on yourself.' His voice was so cold it made her shiver. 'It's Donny and those poor kids I feel sorry for,' he finished, turning on his heel and marching back along the sea wall.

'Eat your dinner, Maureen,' Morag sighed. The girl shook her head.

Morag got up and knelt at her side, slipping an arm round the thin shoulders. 'What's wrong? Are you not feeling well?' she asked. The eleven-year-old had seemed listless and pale for weeks. To her despair Maureen shook her off and refused to answer. Instead she slipped off her chair and went to stand beside her father who was chewing his way through his meal in the tense silence which characterised any time when he and Morag were in the same room.

'I've a sore head, Daddy. Can I leave my dinner?'

'Aye, lass,' he agreed softly. 'You can always have something later on.'

'I'm worried about her, Donny,' Morag said quietly when Maureen had gone to her room. 'She's getting too many headaches.'

'You're worried about her?' Donny sneered. 'It's your fault! How do you think the bairns feel to know their mother's a whore?'

With one anguished look at her mother Ina got down from the table and ran after her sister.

Upstairs, in the room she shared with Ina, Maureen was lying white faced on the bed.

'Is it very bad, hen?' Morag asked her, wondering if she should ask the doctor to look at the child.

Maureen turned her head away and stared at the wall. Morag sometimes thought that Donny's children hated her almost as much as he did. And no wonder, she thought bitterly, after what they had heard and especially when their father didn't bother to conceal his contempt. It hurt her even more to see the way Ina was siding with Donny, as if all the years of love which had come before counted for nothing. She sighed. They were all so unhappy, and it was her fault.

Morag knew she would get nowhere with Maureen and turned to comfort her own daughter. 'Come downstairs, Ina,' she suggested. 'Maureen's not feeling well. Let her have a wee bit of peace.'

'Go away,' Ina screamed suddenly, her thin face contorting with anger. 'Go away. I hate you. Everyone hates you.'

Morag backed away then stumbled down the stairs and out of the house, tears streaming down her face.

She ran, not caring where she went, and found herself back on the harbour wall. Slowing now she walked along it, staring down into the cold, dark sea as it crashed against the slimy stonework, sending plumes of spray high into the air. It was dark, the moon appearing only fitfully from behind wind-driven clouds, the sort of night when sensible folk stayed indoors, snug at their own firesides. Morag shivered in her thin blouse and skirt but walked on. At the end of the wall she stood and looked back at the village, at the lights which glowed from the windows on the quayside and right up the wynds to the village itself, hinting of warmth and happy families. Tears swamped her eyes again and she turned away, looking out over the angry sea, thinking of Gray who had given her the only real happiness she had ever known.

Closing her eyes, she stepped off the harbour wall and into the sea.

SEVENTEEN

T hey fished her out. Literally.

Morag hit the water hard and came to the top fighting as the instinct for survival took over. One of the smaller fishing boats, running for shelter before the weather worsened, nosed its way into the harbour just as Morag jumped. A sharp-eyed crew member raised the alarm and Morag found herself being landed on the deck among a pile of slimy fish. Even before the boat tied up she knew she had made the biggest mistake of her life.

Physically Morag survived, returning to the bakery wrapped in blankets but miraculously unscathed, to face Donny's abusive condemnation and the inevitable gossip as the story of her suicide attempt raced round the village. She did the only thing she could, retreating to a netherworld of numbness where nothing could ever touch her again. She roamed the house with vacant eyes, cutting herself off from a reality which was too harsh for her to cope with, safe at last in a comforting emptiness in which Donny's anger, Rab's rejection and the children's hostility could never reach her.

Stobie shook his head, declared himself stumped and packed her off to hospital. Three months later they sent her home. There was nothing they could do. Love and patience were the only things which could heal her, both of which were now quite beyond Donny's capacity to offer. Appalled by what had happened to her, feeling that his own cold reaction to her confession had probably been what had pushed her over the edge of sanity, Rab took her back to Pitochrie for a month, but even he couldn't seem to get though to her. He delivered her back to her shattered husband feeling he, as much as Donny, had failed her.

Morag sank quietly back into her own little world, going about her household tasks automatically and quite impervious to those around her. Donny barricaded himself behind a precarious shield of whisky, bitterly resenting that he was tied to this treacherous, empty creature for the rest of his life. The children, confused and hurt, allied themselves with their father.

Ina had an even harder burden to bear. Even though it was more than six months since her mother's attempted suicide, Ina knew they blamed her, that it was something she had done which had made her mother try to kill herself. People still looked at her in the streets, whispered about her when they thought she couldn't hear, saying her mother had gone mad. Even the teacher at school had a special way of looking at her and talking to her.

At home it was even worse. Everyone had changed. Maurice had told her that her mother had tried to drown herself because Ina had shouted that she hated her, that they all hated her. Even her daddy wasn't nice to her any more. He hardly ever cuddled her like he used to. Her childish mind couldn't see that Donny was hurting too, that his emotions were drained, leaving very little to share among the children. She started to believe that he blamed her too, because he wasn't her real daddy. Everyone in the village knew he wasn't her real daddy. Her real daddy was dead. It hadn't mattered before because her Kilweem daddy was better than any other daddy could ever be. But now the thought made her sadder than ever. She sighed and closed the top on her cardboard case. Grandpa Rab would be here for her soon. At least she knew he loved her. Maybe, if she was extra specially good, she could stay with him.

'Ina!' Donny's tired voice echoed from the bottom of the stairs. 'Hurry up, lass. Rab's here.'

Ina grabbed her case and clattered downstairs.

'Hello there, Ina,' Rab smiled warmly. 'Are you all ready then? Look, I've brought Ayleen with me to keep you company on the way home.'

Ayleen smiled shyly.

Ina looked at her young aunt warily, feeling suddenly shabby beside her. Ayleen's hair was tightly braided and her dark red dress was clean and well fitting above a pair of brightly shined boots. Ina knew her gran would tug a brush through her own wayward blonde curls as soon as she stepped out of the cart. The blue skirt she wore had been Maureen's and was already too short and too tight, like the dingy white blouse and scuffed boots which pinched her long toes into painful blisters.

'Come on then, lass. I've to hurry back.' Rab was in no mood to linger. The atmosphere between himself and Donny had been strained since Donny's refusal to discuss Morag's condition.

The last six months had been hard for them all. The children had been badly affected, bearing the brunt of the name-calling and innuendo from their hard-hearted peers. Not unnaturally they had responded by bickering among themselves. Donny, overwhelmed by anger and bitterness, felt unable to deal with their temper and yearned for peace in which to nurse his own hurt. He knew that, of all of them, Ina's suffering was the greatest and his battered heart bled for her. In desperation he

341

had begged Rab and Annie to take her for the summer, feeling that some time in a more stable atmosphere would do her good, that, by the time she returned, he would be better able to cope.

'Be a good lass,' he told her now, pressing some coppers into her palm. 'I'll see you in six weeks.'

Ina stood looking at her feet, convinced that he was trying to get rid of her. She was glad when Rab caught hold of her hand and led her outside. At least she knew her grandpa loved her.

Donny waved as the old cart trundled along the setted road, his face a gloomy mask. He sighed heavily. It was at times like these that he wished he had a family of his own to fall back on but he was an only child and his own parents were both long dead.

In the back of Rab's cart the two little girls sat in shy silence but Rab was relieved to see they occasionally smiled at one another. By the time the day was out no doubt they'd be getting along just fine.

'Mammy!' Ayleen leapt out of the cart and into her mother's arms as if she had been away for a month. Ina followed more slowly. Though she loved her grandpa deeply she was more than a little in awe of her severe-looking grandmother.

'Out you get,' Rab laughed and lifted her easily to the ground. Ina liked the way his eyes twinkled and was fascinated by his thick beard.

'My, what a sight you are,' Annie ran disapproving eyes over the child. 'You'll need a good wash before you sleep in this house.'

The past months had toughened Ina who was quick to take offence and not afraid to stand up for herself. 'I am not dirty,' she retorted. 'I had a bath last night. And my hair was washed.'

Annie flushed slightly but Rab laughed. 'Och, leave the lassie be, Annie. She's right enough.'

'Well, get your boots off and Grandpa will clean them for you,' Annie said, turning back to the house.

'Best do as she says, hen,' Rab winked. 'Here, sit yourself on the step and I'll give them a good tug.' He hauled and the boot shot off the slender foot, releasing Ina to fall back against the door in a spluttering heap. Rab fooled around on the ground, pretending he too had fallen and they both giggled. 'That's better,' he said. 'You're a pretty wee lass and even bonnier when you smile. But, just look at your poor feet. Does that hurt lass?' he touched a broken blister lightly.

'Ouch,' Ina winced and pulled her foot away.

'You must have been doing some growing. Your feet are too big for your boots.'

'They were Maureen's boots. She's smaller than me. They never fit,' she confided. She had told her mother how much her feet hurt but she hadn't seemed interested.

'Och, well, our Ayleen's bigger and she's just had new ones. Maybe her old ones would be better for you? Would you like to try them?'

She nodded. 'Yes please.'

'Annie!' he called as they went inside, leaving Ina by the sink while he went to have a quiet word with his wife. 'See what you can do for the bairn's feet,' he told her. 'They're right sore looking. Her boots are way too small, she'll be crippled if she wears them. What did you do with our Ayleen's old ones?'

'She can't have those! I'm giving them to Finty for one of her grandweans.'

'Your own grandwean comes first,' he rasped. 'Now look here, Annie. I know how you feel about Morag but

343

this lass isn't to blame for any of that. She's just a bairn yet and God knows she needs a bit of love.'

Annie felt ashamed. 'Aye,' she said, glancing at the child who, well aware of what was going on, was gamely fighting tears by jutting her jaw out pugnaciously and scowling. 'Come here, Ina.' Annie opened her arms. 'Let your old Gran see if she's got any cream for those feet while Grandpa finds some new boots.'

An hour later Ina found herself with a whole new wardrobe of clothes which the sturdier Ayleen had outgrown. And for the first time in months her feet didn't hurt. 'That's better,' Annie laughed at the child's obvious pleasure. 'You'll need another bag to take them all home with you.'

'Are they all for me?' Ina asked.

'Aye, lass, of course they are.'

'Not for Maureen?' she needed to get this quite right.

'No, they're yours,' Annie assured her.

'And when I get bigger you can have the rest of my things too,' Ayleen offered generously.

'Aye, that's the way it's done in families,' Annie agreed.

Ina went to sleep that night, curled into Ayleen's warm back, exhausted by the day's events. When she woke in the morning she was surprised to realise that, for the first time in months, she hadn't had a single bad dream.

For the next six weeks the girls were inseparable. Ayleen had friends of her own from school but rarely did any of them venture into the forest to play with her, nor could Annie often be persuaded to allow Ayleen to go to the village on her own. But together the two girls played in the garden, explored the woods and occasionally walked to the village shop to buy messages for

Annie. One day, Rab even took them up the steep hill path to see the cottage where Morag was born. Glad of the unexpected company at her isolated home, the shepherd's wife had brought them out some freshly baked scones which they had eaten under the rowan tree, gazing down at the beautiful strath, laid out in miniature below them.

The high point for Ina came on the day Rab drew up outside the cottage in a long, black car. He was to go to Perth on a message for Lady Fraser and saw no reason why Ina and Ayleen shouldn't join him. Even Ayleen, who had been in the vehicle before, was excited as they drove through the twisting glen which linked Strathannan with Perthshire. When they arrived in the town itself Ina was beside herself, especially when Rab showed them the big shops and the river and then bought hot pies for them all to eat in the park. She had only been back in the car for five minutes when her eyes closed and she drifted into exhausted sleep. Her disappointment when she woke to realise she'd missed the return journey was comical.

'Never mind, lass,' Rab soothed her. 'Maybe I could talk Lady Katrina into letting me drive you home in it.'

Ina's face dropped at the reminder. 'I'm not going home,' she said, pathetically defiant. 'I want to stay here with you and Ayleen.'

'Och, lass, you have to go home,' Annie said, cuddling her close. 'But you can come here again.'

But Ina wouldn't be comforted. On her last night in Pitochrie she sobbed herself to sleep. In the morning she emerged white faced and puffy eyed and waited in resigned silence for her Grandpa to take her back to Kilweem.

But Ina's bleak mood and her standing among the

fickle Kilweem children were both completely restored when Rab drove her, very slowly, through the village and then back again, before finally drawing the sleek, black car to an impressive stop outside the bakery. Ina, who went back to school the very next day, lived on the glory of her stylish arrival for weeks.

Morag listened to her daughter's account of her holiday impassively. In the six weeks of her daughter's absence Morag had hardly noticed she was gone. Her own condition had improved slightly, but emotionally she was dead.

For Donny life was desperately hard. An honest, trusting man, his faith in human nature and in women in particular had been destroyed, leaving him incapable of giving his children the warmth and affection they craved. In an effort to escape from an impossible situation he spent longer and longer hours in the bakery, leaving them to fill their time in any way they could. His evenings passed in an unhappy, alcohol induced haze which left him feeling bad tempered and bleary eyed long into each morning.

While Maurice and Maureen relied on each other for support, Ina responded by developing a stubborn streak of self-reliance and actively seeking the approval of her young friends, often spending more time in their homes than she did in her own. No feat was too dangerous, no prank too wild for Ina in her desperate bid for attention. Before long she was the unrivalled leader of the gang of young children who roamed the village.

Inevitably it led her into trouble, trouble which she laughed off with a bravado even the lads envied. But there were times when her pranks were downright dangerous.

'I bet you can't,' Georgie Cameron challenged, peering over the harbour wall into the murky depths below.

With his dark hair shorn to the scalp – to combat the nits which were the scourge of his family – his dirty face, wicked grin and mischievous eyes, Georgie looked every inch what he was: an undisciplined imp. But he was blessed with an inherent charm which he utilised ruthlessly to get him out of scrapes. Ina adored him. And they were the perfect pairing. With her tousled mop of fair hair, her pale, hurt eyes and her rebellious defiance she was his perfect foil.

'Can so,' Ina retorted. 'It's you that's feared.'

'Not me. But you said first so you've got to prove you can do it.'

'It's gey cold for swimming,' one of the others said, taking a step away from the wall.

'We'll get leathered if anyone sees.'

'Feardy gowk!' Ina taunted.

'I'll do it if you do,' Georgie offered at last.

'All right,' Ina agreed, slipping her boots off and dropping her dress so that she stood shivering in her vest and knickers.

'Oy! Youse lot! What the hell are youse up to?' someone shouted from the quayside.

'Now. Quick, before he gets here,' Ina glanced at the fisherman who was lumbering along the harbour wall towards them. With a last triumphant look at Georgie she leapt into the harbour, missing the end of a boat by less than three feet.

She gasped as she hit the water. It was so much colder than she had thought it would be, knocking the air out of her lungs. At last she stopped going down and kicked out for the surface, paddling towards the slimy wooden ladder to pull herself up.

'You stupid wee bitch,' Fin McArdle growled, peering down at her.

347

Ina ignored him and stared hard at Georgie who was still standing on the wall. 'Coward,' she shrieked through chattering teeth.

Georgie looked round him at the faces of his mates and knew he would never be able to hold his head up again if he didn't prove he was as brave as Ina.

'Oh no you don't.' Fin had seen what was going on and made a lunge for the lad but Georgie was too quick for a man of more than fifty years. Slipping sideways he launched himself out over the water.

But his attention had been diverted by Fin and Georgie misjudged it. He jumped too close to the boat, cracking his head on its prow as he plummeted towards the water.

By now several other fishermen were running towards the little group. 'Stupid wee bastard jumped in and walloped his head,' Fin yelled, kicking his boots off and stripping himself of his heavy jersey and trousers.

Below them the water was ominously still.

'You can't go in there,' one of the younger men said, struggling out of his own clothes, but Fin was already in the water.

Ina clawed her way up the ladder and shivered while she watched for Fin's head breaking the surface. Three times he came up, three times he went down again. At last he resurfaced, dragging the unconscious lad with him to the ladder where other, younger hands hauled the boy to the wall.

To the watching children it seemed like an eternity before Georgie coughed, groaned and opened his eyes. Someone bundled him in a jacket and hurried him home to his mother, someone else helped the exhausted Fin. Ina, with a feeling of gathering doom, realised her friends had deserted her. Shaking with cold she slipped back into her clothes and crept home.

In the morning she couldn't raise her head from the pillow. Her whole body burned, her head thumped and her chest hurt.

'Best have the doctor look at you,' Donny decided, worried by her condition.

'Well, and I'm not surprised.' Doctor Stobie seemed short of his usual sympathy as he glared first at his hot patient and then at Donny. 'Thanks to this young hoyden I've had to put three stitches in young Georgie Cameron's head and he's laying in his bed with an even worse fever than she's got.'

'What the hell?' Donny exploded.

'Aye, and that's not the worst of it,' Stobie went on grimly. 'Fin McArdle jumped into the harbour to pull the lad out and is like to be off his work for a good few weeks the way his chest sounds this morning.'

Ina groaned. 'It wasn't my fault.'

'That's not what I heard. You dared Georgie to jump in after you were stupid enough to do it yourself,' Stobie insisted.

'He dared me first,' she protested to deaf ears.

'She's wild, Doctor, always in mischief, won't be told right from wrong,' Donny sighed despairingly. 'Surely it's not right for a young lassie to carry on like this?'

'Well, it's for you to teach her,' Stobie snapped. It had been a busy night and he was tired and irritable. 'It's lucky no one was killed.' He closed his bag and handed Donny a brown bottle. 'Two spoonfuls three times a day. She'll get over it. Fin McArdle might not be so lucky.' With that he stomped from the room.

Donny loomed over his scarlet-faced stepdaughter, his patience with her pranks finally exhausted. 'Don't think you've heard the last of this. When you're out of that bed you're going to get the hiding of your life,' he promised. 'You'll learn how to behave before I'm through with you.'

Fortune was on their side. All three invalids recovered, though not before Donny had had to fend off a stream of complaints from his doorstep.

When Ina finally left her bed she was promptly leathered and sent back to it and a diet of bread and milk for three days, during which time she was unable to put her raw behind on a chair.

Nor could Ina get any sympathy from her mother who merely told her to be a good girl and obey her father. Nursing the belief that she had been unfairly treated, after all she hadn't wanted Georgie to hurt himself, Ina retreated into resentful silence.

But, compared to what happened next, even that paled to insignificance.

Georgie and Ina, drawn even closer together by the injustice of the thrashing they had both earned for their watery prank, found themselves to be even closer friends, the uncrowned king and queen of the schoolyard. And school was a place they both loathed, Georgie because he simply couldn't absorb the lessons and Ina because they bored her rigid. It didn't take them long to realise that it was possible to escape class. The easiest way of doing that was to simply walk into the schoolyard in the morning, scurry quickly round the side of the single-storey building and hop over the railings at the back. It was then a matter of crouching in the narrow alley until the bell rang. After that they worked their way carefully through the village, keeping to the back wynds until they emerged on to the coast road. All they had to do then was race across the road and into the dunes. As the weather was mostly fine they missed the last six weeks of the school year, only putting in a reluctant appearance if it happened to be raining. Happy to be relieved of their most disruptive pupils the teachers turned conveniently blind eyes to their persistent truancy, leaving Ina and Georgie free to follow the same pattern in the new school year. But, as autumn brought stormy weather and chilly days, the beach began to lose its appeal.

'We'll have to think of somewhere else to go,' Georgie decided, wiping his permanently snotty nose on his sleeve.

'But where?' Ina asked.

For days they shivered on the beach, trying desperately to come up with some safe, warm hidey hole.

'I know,' Georgie announced triumphantly, coughing on one of the hand rolls he cadged from his brothers.

'Where?' Ina shook her head at the proffered cigarette. She had tried smoking of course but it had made her sick and earned her a thrashing from Donny when he smelt smoke on her clothes. She had no wish to repeat the experience.

'The church hall!'

'What about the minister?' Minister Porteous was one of the few people who scared Ina.

'He's never there in the day time.'

'How do you know?' she challenged.

'Because I do, that's how.'

'What if he comes in when we're there?' she asked.

'We'll hear him unlocking the door, stupid. We'll have plenty time to get out.'

'Don't call me stupid,' she hissed. 'It's you that's stupid. How are we supposed to get in if it's locked?'

'Och, shut your face!' he said, huffed. Stuffing his

hands in his torn pockets he stomped through the sand towards the village.

Ina watched him go in stubborn silence.

'Well,' he yelled. 'Are you coming to look or not?'

Grinning, she ran to catch up with him.

The church hall was on the same side of Kirkgate as the school and only a few yards away, so it would be a much more convenient place for them to spend the cold winter days. They sneaked along the wynds, slipping behind walls and into doorways to avoid being seen. The back wall of the hall was level with the adjoining kirk, the back doors of both opening on to the same narrow lane.

Morag tried the heavy door. It didn't budge. 'See. I told you. It's locked.'

Georgie gave her a withering look and hoisted himself nimbly on to the window sill. With surprising ease he raised the sash then dropped down and clambered through the gap.

'Come on,' he leant out and beckoned urgently at her. Ina scrambled over the ledge and found herself sitting on a wooden draining board.

'Best close the window in case anyone sees,' she said, dragging it down again.

They were in the back room of the hall. Two stone sinks were under the window. A gas stove stood against one wall and shelves lined another. On the fourth wall was a door.

They opened it and peered out cautiously. To their left, at the back, was another door, to the right the hall itself. Georgie tiptoed down the short corridor and opened the other door. 'Pee house,' he announced triumphantly, dragging her back into the little room. 'We'll be all right here,' he chortled, systematically riffling the shelves and finding tea, sugar, cups, plates, spoons and even a tin of broken biscuits. 'See, if it's cold we can boil the kettle for a drink.'

Ina laughed. 'Aye, we'll be just fine here,' she agreed.

And so they were. They whiled away the winter days in comfort, using the gas stove to keep them warm when the weather got really cold and helping themselves liberally to the minister's store of tea and biscuits. On the two occasions when Minister Porteous had reason to call into the hall while they were in residence they were given ample warning by the jar of his key in the front doors and were able to make a leisurely escape.

By the time the New Year had come and gone, the novelty had worn off, but the weather was still bitterly cold. Boredom set in and Ina even found herself wondering if she wouldn't rather be at school.

On a particularly frosty day in late January, Ina and Georgie lit the gas to keep the chill off the little back room then sat listlessly, waiting for four o'clock to release them from their self-imposed prison. The day dragged. By half past three Georgie had arranged himself with his back against a wall, lit a cigarette and drifted into a sleepy day dream. Ina leafed through the old newspapers the minister kept in the corner but found nothing to interest her in the interminable war news so tossed the paper untidily back on to the pile. The room was warm and stuffy with gas fumes. Ina's lids started to droop.

'What was that?' Georgie opened his eyes and blinked like a startled cat.

Ina raised her dozy head and listened. 'Footsteps,' she gasped.

Somehow they had missed the sound of Minister Porteous's key in the door. What they heard now were his steel-tipped boots clicking briskly over the wooden floor of the hall. The minister came regularly after tea to check his pipes which were inclined to freeze in the winter months. He was somewhat amazed to have escaped the annual flooding which was the usual result, especially as the weather had been so very cold over the last two or three weeks. He had been surprised too by the warmth in the little kitchen which was obviously keeping the frost at bay. Then, a couple of days ago, the mystery had been explained. Succumbing to the temptation to warm himself with a cup of tea, he had discovered the kettle held water which was still warm and his suspicions had been alerted. Fairly sure the cleaner, who called in twice at week at half past four, was helping herself to his precious stores he had decided to come early tonight and challenge her.

'Jeeez!' Georgie flung his cigarette away and clambered on to the draining board. He hauled the window open and jumped through. 'Come on,' he snapped at the dithering Ina. She looked at the dirty cups, the hissing gas and the untidy heap of papers, knew there was no time to do anything about it and leapt after him just as the door opened behind her. The minister got a fleeting glimpse of movement through the still open window but by the time he'd wrestled the back door open Georgie and Ina were long gone.

Red-faced with fury the minister stepped back inside and found himself facing a conflagration. Georgie's carelessly discarded cigarette had landed on the loosely folded newspaper. Within seconds the whole pile was blazing and the heat was starting to melt the paint on the wood lined walls. In one movement Porteous turned off the still flaring gas and grabbed the kettle, emptying the water over the flames. The effect was negligible.

With his bare hands Minister Porteous tore the flaming papers from the pile, scattering them over the floor and stamping on them. When the paper was reduced to charred ashes he beat at the still smouldering pile with his hands. Only when the fire was finally extinguished did he realise that his palms were a mess of raw skin and huge blisters.

Sneaking back to the corner of the building Georgie and Ina saw smoke pouring through the window.

'We'll have to help,' Ina said, horrified, starting to go back to the hall.

Georgie grabbed her by the hair and yanked her back. 'No! Stupid! They'll know it was us then,' Georgie yelled. 'Run for it. No one can prove it was us.' He turned and scuttled along the lane.

Ina waited, still debating whether to go and help but already the smoke was less and before she could make her decision Georgie was back, shoving her along the lane. 'Run, you stupid cow,' he bawled.

Donny, who hated having his meals disturbed, made his way bad temperedly downstairs to answer the insistent banging at his front door. Raised, angry voices floated back to the kitchen making everyone pin back their ears and listen. Two sets of footsteps clomped heavily back up the stairs. Ina, who had spent the last three hours in a state of sick apprehension, saw the uniformed policeman and knew her worst fears were about to be realised.

'Come here!' Donny bellowed, beckoning his shrinking stepdaughter.

Ina was already shaking when she stood in front of the two men.

'Were you at school the day, lass?' the policeman asked.

Ina wasn't stupid. She knew it was pointless to lie about something which could so easily be checked and, in any case, she hated lying. 'No,' she whispered fearfully.

'And where the hell were you?' Donny roared.

Ina thought quickly. 'On the beach,' she said at last. It was partially true at least. Boredom had driven her and Georgie there for an hour that morning.

'Don't you lie to me,' Donny hissed. 'You were in the church hall, weren't you?' Ina was no liar. 'Yes,' she muttered, finally raising her head and looking at the two men.

The policemen let out a long sigh. 'You are in serious trouble, lass,' he said gravely. 'Do you know what happened?'

She nodded. 'We didn't mean it,' she said. 'It was Georgie's cigarette, but it was an accident.'

Even before the words were properly said, Donny was roaring at her. 'Don't try to blame someone else.'

'I'm not!' she protested.

'Now, lass, no more lies,' the policeman said. 'I've already been to Georgie Cameron's house. You and him were the only two not at school the day so I knew where to start looking. His ma says he's been in his bed all day with a cold. The wee lad's got a right runny nose, right enough, and Mrs Cameron's an honest woman.'

'He was with me all day,' Ina cried.

They ignored her.

'I'll have to ask you to come to see Minister Porteous, Mr Archibold. He's a fair man and willing to settle this quietly, supposing you pay for the damage to the church hall. Mind you, in his place I wouldn't be so generous. His hands are a right mess. The doctor's with him now.'

As far as Ina was concerned that was the end. After

delivering the inevitable leathering a perplexed Donny decided that the only way to control her was to deprive her of all freedom. Ina was delivered to school every morning by a disgruntled Maureen and collected again by her at night, bringing the ridicule of the whole school on her head. Because of her persistent absences she was way behind the other children and spent much of her time standing in the corner nursing sore hands from repeated lashings with the tawse. After school she was confined to her bedroom and on Saturdays she worked in the bakery, giving the pocket money she might have earned straight back to Donny to help pay for the repainting of the church hall's kitchen.

The church-going women of Kilweem decided that Ina was a bad influence and forbade their offspring to associate with her. Maurice and Maureen were disgusted with her. Morag merely shook her head sadly.

Georgie Cameron, who stayed away from school for a full week in support of his claim to have a heavy cold, made sure, when he finally returned, that he kept away from Ina. Had he had the courage to talk to her, to apologise, she might have forgiven him, might even have envied him the sort of mother who would defend her child so strongly. But Georgie was too ashamed of himself even to look at her.

Ina was basically an honest child. If she did wrong she expected to be punished and accepted it phlegmatically. It would never have occurred to her to shift blame on to someone else and her sense of justice was outraged by Georgie's perfidy. On his second day back at school she sought him out in the playground and, when he refused to talk to her, launched herself at his back like a little wildcat.

All she achieved was a bruised face, another belting

with the tawse and a further tongue-lashing from the despairing Donny. Nursing a grievance against the whole human race she waited until the house was in darkness and left. There was only one person in the whole world who would understand.

It was eight o'clock the next morning before Maureen discovered she was gone.

'She'll be off sulking somewhere,' Donny decided. 'She'll be home the night.'

By three o'clock that afternoon, before Donny was even seriously worried about her, Ina was plodding into Pitochrie. It was further than she thought but, though she had walked for miles, she had been lucky in getting a lift with a farmer for a couple of hours this afternoon and he had dropped her at the road end.

She sighed and climbed on to a wooden gate for a wee rest, biting into the last of the stale bread she had brought with her. She had never been into the hills in winter before and couldn't take her eyes off them. How different they looked, smothered in snow. From where she sat she could just see the ghostly skeleton of the rowan tree and a single plume of smoke rising from the tiny cottage, snuggling in a fold of the hill. Grandpa Rab had pointed that cottage out to her before, so she knew it was where her mother had lived as a child. It looked wonderful, still and remote, away from everyone. She hadn't the experience to imagine how cold and hard life on the hillfoots could be at this time of year.

Even while she sat there, fighting weariness and cold, the light started to fade. She had been lucky last night, there had been only a light frost and by wrapping up warmly and keeping on the move, she had come to no great harm but she dreaded the idea of a second night in the open, longed to see her grandparents' welcoming cottage. Swallowing the last crust she slid off the gate and made her way through the village and on to the forest track.

It was cold in the trees where the sun never reached. The snow, now only on the hills, hadn't lain here for very long but the path was treacherous with ice. Her energy almost spent, Ina's feet dragged. Those last two miles were the longest of her life.

Rab shoved his plate away with a contented sigh and went to sit by the fireside, ready to close his eyes for half an hour. The sharp knocking on the front door surprised him. No one came way down here on dark, cold nights.

'Ina?' he said, peering at the sagging figure on his doorstep. 'My God, child, what are you doing here?'

To her chagrin Ina found she couldn't speak through the tears of relief.

'Come inside, lass. Lord, you must be frozen.' He grabbed her arm and pulled her none too gently over the doorstep.

Ina shivered in the sudden light then threw herself at him, sobbing her heart out.

'Ina, Ina, what's wrong?' Annie asked.

'Get the girl something hot to drink,' Rab said. 'She's near frozen.'

'But what are you doing here?' Annie asked. 'How did you get here?'

'Later,' Rab warned. 'Let's get her warmed up first. And bring her some dry clothes.'

Ina sat with her hands clenched round a cup of hot milk, still shuddering.

'Right, lass, we'll talk this out in a wee while, when you've warmed up, but just tell me one thing,' Rab faced her across the table, taking in the bruised face, the heavy eyes and the pale skin. 'Does your father know you're here ?'

'No,' she whispered.

'He'll be worried sick!' Annie exclaimed.

'He'll be glad I'm gone. They all will,' she said in a flat voice.

Annie and Rab exchanged frowns then Rab hauled himself into his jacket and boots. 'I'll be back in a wee while,' was all he said.

While Rab went to the castle to telephone a message to Donny, telling him that Ina was safe and would be staying with them for a wee while, Annie was wise enough to let the girl relax in front of the fire. Long before Rab came back Ina was fast asleep. Not having the heart to wake her, Annie carried her to bed.

'Aye, best thing for her,' agreed Rab who had left a message for Donny with Doctor Stobie.

In the morning a still-tired Ina blurted out her woes to Rab and Annie.

'It was wrong what you did, lass,' he said when she'd finished a catalogue of woe which had shocked him.

'I know,' she said.

'Did you tell them Georgie was there too?'

'Nobody listened. Daddy doesn't love me any more and nor does Mammy. I don't want to live in Kilweem anymore, Grandpa. I want to stay here with you and Grandma and Ayleen. I'm not bad. Not really. And I'll be good all the time if I stay here,' she was crying again, something she seldom did at home.

Annie, close to tears herself, gathered the gangling child in her arms and smoothed her hair gently.

'We know you're not a bad lass,' Rab said. 'A wee tyke maybe, but not a bad lass.' He tickled the back of her neck and got a watery smile in return.

360

'Can I stay?'

'No, I don't think you can,' he said gravely. 'Now, don't go screwing up your face again but listen to me instead.' He waited while she knuckled her eyes dry. 'Right. Now there's rights and wrongs to all things and you've been in trouble?'

'Aye, but . . .'

'Och, I don't think you meant any real harm. Maybe some folk have not been as honest as they should and maybe other folk have not been quite fair. But if you've told the truth then that's one thing you can be proud of.'

'I don't tell lies.'

'I know, lass. But you can't run away from things either. When something goes wrong you have to stay and sort it out else you're letting yourself down. See, if you stay here everyone will just think you've run away from trouble. If you go back and sort it out, well, that's the brave thing to do and maybe they'll see you aren't as bad as they thought. Especially if young Georgie owns up.'

'I don't know,' she sounded doubtful.

'Aye you do. Deep in here you know,' he insisted. 'And what about your poor mother? You're all she's got. You can't just leave her.'

'She doesn't care.' It was said with a certainty that gave Rab a clearer insight into Ina's plight than anything else she had said. 'If she cared about me she would have stuck up for me the way Georgie's mam did.'

'No, she wouldn't! Georgie's mam was wrong. There's other ways of showing you care about someone. You shouldn't tell lies.' But Rab knew life was never that simple. 'Och, lass, trust me, I'll see what I can do. All right?'

361

'All right.' The one person she did trust with absolute faith was her grandpa.

Rab Bannerman borrowed Lady Katrina's car on a very thin excuse and hurried to Kilweem, praying that his temper would have cooled by the time he got there. The first place he stopped was at the minister's house. After that he went to the school and then he had a long chat with Watty Cameron and his cheeky-faced son. Then all three trailed over the road to the bakery.

An hour later he was shaking Watty's hand. 'I'll not forget this Mr Cameron,' he said. 'And neither will you lad,' he turned to the boy with a wry grin.

'No, sir, Mr Bannerman,' said Georgie, thoroughly chastened by his meeting with this imposing man.

Rab watched Watty lead his miscreant son home, knowing the lad had had his punishment and turned, grim-faced, to Donny.

He was even grimmer when he left, two hours later, but satisfied that justice, at least, would now be done. 'She needs love, that's all,' had been his parting words. But would she get it here?

EIGHTEEN

By the time she was fifteen, in 1921, Ina had left her dark days behind her and the household was relatively peaceful. Although she was still strong willed and unconventional, her wilder antics had stopped and she had settled back at school. Like Maurice and Maureen, she had long ago relegated her mother to the periphery of her life and it was to Donny that she turned for love and support. The hurt she still carried because of what she believed to be her mother's rejection was carefully disguised under a facade of total indifference.

Over the years Morag had slowly emerged from her almost catatonic state and had gradually taken a place in the community again but as an observer rather than as a participant. She understood now how badly she had hurt Donny and only she glimpsed the continuing pain and bitterness that he was so careful to keep hidden from the children; pain he anaesthetised with the aid of a whisky bottle. Desperately trying to atone for the wrong she had done him, she did her very best to be a dutiful wife and ran his home with an attention to detail that the young people found irksome. But it was too late. Starved of all physical closeness and warmth, and with no meaningful communication between them, their marriage was a sterile coexistence of two lonely people.

Donny buried himself in his work, keeping the bakery open until tea time to meet the rising demand from housewives who no longer baked their own bread. Increasingly aware of his problem he seldom drank in front of his family but, when he made his way to bed at eight-thirty every night, the first thing he did was to retrieve a bottle of whisky from its hiding place under the wardrobe. By the time he finally tumbled into bed the bottle would be empty. When he rose in the morning, fuzzy headed and nauseous, he buried the bottle in the bottom of the bin, unaware that everyone in the household knew precisely what he was doing. Only once did Morag attempt to talk to him about it, trying to make him understand that he was ruining his health. He had rounded on her so furiously that she had backed away.

Maurice and Maureen did their best to carry on as normal. Nearly adults themselves now and both working in the bakery, they quietly assumed many of their father's responsibilities, hoping to relieve some of the strain, which they believed had driven him to use alcohol as a crutch. To their consternation nothing seemed to make any difference and it was a rare, and bad-tempered, night when Donny went without his whisky.

At twenty Maurice was a huge man and very like his father in appearance. But the similarities between father and son were superficial. In Maurice, Donny's sandy colouring and brooding disposition had been replaced by violently red hair and a temper to match. Nor was Maurice's personality redeemed by the gentle humour which had once made the younger Donny popular. Maurice, always serious beyond his years, seemed to have embraced a peculiarly puritan approach to life. He had no real friends, seldom went out and showed little interest in the day-to-day affairs of the village. Shunning the relationships with girls which occupied other boys of his age he concentrated all his efforts on learning his trade and Donny was proud to admit that Maurice was a better baker than he was himself.

Where Maurice towered well over six feet tall, Maureen was tiny, neat and birdlike. Her mind was quick and incisive, her movements sharp and precise. It was she who ran the shop, kept the books and saw to the ordering, driving harder bargains than her father had ever done. She was the one who fretted about the way the debts piled up while her father insisted on drinking half the profits. Only her clever manipulation saved them from financial ruin. In between times she was wooed by practically every lad in the village but, so far, no one had measured up to her high standard.

It was already obvious that Ina didn't have her stepsister's instant appeal. She wasn't a pretty girl. Her face was too sharp for that, her eyes too knowing, her figure too angular. What she did have was character, sharp intelligence and an intensity which some people found attractive and guaranteed her a circle of admiring friends. But there were many others who were discouraged by her quick tongue, her tendency to speak her mind, and the occasional desire to be different and even to shock.

Ina was the first woman to be seen on the streets of Kilweem with a cigarette, dangling affectedly from a long holder. Some of the girls were quick to see that she never actually smoked the thing but the older people were shocked. And where Ina was, Georgie Cameron was never far away. The pair were as inseparable now as they had been in junior school.

'That lass'll end up in trouble,' was the general consensus.

It was a sentiment often repeated by Annie. Although

she loved Ina deeply, and had long ago been persuaded by Rab that it was unfair to condemn either her daughter or her grandchild because of the circumstances of Ina's birth, she still judged the girl by her eventful childhood. Rab however was more sanguine. What he saw of Ina encouraged him to believe that she was developing into a strong and resourceful woman.

Over the years Ina had remained close to her grandparents and Ayleen. She had a standing invitation to spend part of every holiday with them. The weeks she spent in Pitochrie formed a bank of treasured memories which she would draw on with nostalgic happiness for the rest of her life. When the time came for her to spend her last holiday with them before she left school, she was infinitely sad to realise that, as a working woman, she wouldn't be able to visit them nearly so often. She said as much to her grandfather.

'Aye, well,' Rab said, rubbing a beard which was now silvery grey. 'That's maybe just as well. We'll not be in Pitochrie for much longer.'

Morag gaped. 'What?'

'It's Lady Katrina, lass. She's having to reorganise. The estate's not making money the way it should. They're felling part of the forest, setting up a paper mill. It means this house will have to come down.'

'They can't do that! I'll go and speak to her about it!' Not at all daunted by the prospect of facing a titled woman, Ina was on her feet and ready to go.

'No, lass, it's too late. It's all arranged,' Annie said, gently. 'In any case, Lady Katrina's a poor soul these days. She's an ill woman. That's why she's desperate to set the estate in order for Angus. She knows she won't be able to look after things for him for much longer.'

'But you can't let her throw you out,' their grand-daughter insisted.

'She's not throwing us out,' Rab laughed. 'Just look at this place, Ina. It was falling down when your grand-mother moved in here – when your own mother was younger than you are now. It's not even damp any more, it's wet. It's inconvenient and cold, and we've not even got gas, never mind this new fangled electricity that they're starting to get in places like Glasgow and Edin-burgh.'

'There's plenty houses in Kilweem still without gas,' Ina protested.

'Aye, maybe, but there's a lot of houses better than this. Och, I'm fifty-six years old, Ina. My bones ache with the damp. The house is no loss.'

'Can't you go back to the Lodge House?'

Rab frowned. Lady Katrina's insistence that he vacate the vastly more comfortable lodge when he married Annie still rankled. 'No, Lady Katrina keeps it for guests.'

'What about the village? Is there not somewhere there for you?' Ina asked.

'Not in this village no,' Annie said hesitantly. 'Ina, lass, we're going home. Back to the highlands.'

'You can't!' Ina was suddenly lightheaded.

'Rab's got family there still. His brother died last year and his house is there for us.'

'You've no job.' Ina tried everything.

'I've no job here!' Rab interrupted her. 'But I've the promise of a place up north.'

'But what about Ayleen? She won't want to go and live up there.'

Annie laughed. 'Ayleen is one of the reasons we've decided to go. When we went to Duggie's funeral she met a lad. Well, they've been writing, he's been here to stay, she's been to stay with his folks. They want to get wed.'

'To – what's his name – Freddy?' Ina had heard Ayleen speak about her young man but hadn't thought the relationship was serious.

'Aye, that's him,' Rab nodded.

'Why didn't she tell me?' Now she was hurt. 'She's too young.'

'Maybe,' Annie admitted. 'At least if we're living up there they won't need to rush into anything. They can afford to wait a year or so, get to know each other better.'

'So,' Ina sighed unhappily. 'It's all arranged.'

'Aye. We go next month,' Annie said.

'So soon!'

'Och, don't look like that, lass. It won't make all that much difference to you. Now that you are going to be working, you'll not get the same holidays you did at school. When you do get some time off, well, there's a train goes right up to Glendarroch and a more beautiful journey you'll never make.'

'It won't be the same,' she objected.

'It's time for us to go home, lass,' Rab told her gently.

'Grandpa, I'll miss you,' she said, falling into his arms. 'How will I manage without you and Grandma?'

'You'll manage just fine. You always were independent. You don't need us now,' he rasped.

'But I do, I do,' she sobbed. But after a minute she sat up and dried her eyes, smiling wryly. 'Sorry about that. I will miss you, very much, but I'll write, and come and see you. I promise I will. And I know you're doing the right thing, Grandpa. I understand how you feel about the mountains, you never stop looking at them.'

368

'These are not mountains, lass, they're just hills!' Rab laughed. 'You wait till you see Ben Nevis, then you'll have seen a mountain.'

Ina took a heavy heart back to Kilweem with her but she had little time to brood. Her new job and entry into the adult world beckoned.

Donny would have preferred Ina to join Maureen in the shop where he could keep an eye on her but neither girl was keen on the idea. Even though they got on well, they saw enough of each other at home and, secretly, Maureen was worried that there wasn't enough money to pay Ina the wages she would have been entitled to. It was obvious too that Ina would challenge her position of seniority and wouldn't be happy about taking orders from her.

Ina understood Maureen's reluctance and frankly admitted to doubting her ability to work harmoniously with Maureen, or Maurice who seemed to measure the value of a day's work by the degree of exhaustion felt at the end.

In the end she persuaded old Mrs Haddow who ran the telephone exchange and post office to take her on as her assistant. An increasing number of better-off families had telephones these days and Mrs Haddow was finding it hard to cope with both jobs. Donny was satisfied that Ina would be kept busy and well supervised while the villagers soon came to appreciate her efficient telephone manner, though a source of local gossip was instantly lost when Ina stoutly refused to listen in on the calls, as was Mrs Haddow's habit.

'You're lucky,' Morag told Ina. 'I would have loved the chance for a job like yours. Things weren't like that in my day. It was going into service or nothing.' How different her life might have been, she thought with a touch of envy, if she had had Ina's freedom and opportunities.

'I know.' Ina smiled at her mother, relishing this rare opportunity to communicate with a woman who always seemed preoccupied and disinterested. If only her mother and father were on better terms, if only her mother could be less remote, more involved with the things which were important to her father and less concerned about the tiny details of housekeeping which absorbed her all day to the exclusion of everything else. And if only her father could be less impatient, less critical, show her mother some warmth, some understanding. If only he could find it in his heart to forgive her, how much happier they would be. That way her mother might learn to smile again and her father might stop drinking before it killed him.

'You will have to sell the car,' Maureen insisted grimly.

'No,' Donny refused to listen and fiddled about with sacks of flour.

'Well, what do you suggest we do?' His daughter flung the letter from the bank manager at him and watched as it fluttered to the floor.

'I don't know.' He tried to force his way past her, out of the bakery, but she barred his way, planting her frail, five-foot frame between him and his escape route.

'You owe two hundred pounds to the bank and another seventy to our suppliers. If we don't do something soon they'll take you to court,' she insisted.

'Stop nagging,' he bellowed. 'Leave me alone.'

'No!' Maureen was close to tears but knew she couldn't leave it now. Things had got to the stage where they were too serious to be ignored. The debts were mounting up and Donny was drinking himself insensible every night. There were mornings now when he appeared in the bakery too drunk or too hung over to be of any use, forcing Maurice to do most of the work. When Donny was fit enough to make a contribution the bread he produced was often flawed and there had been countless complaints from disgruntled customers. On top of all this, Maureen knew the money they took more often found its way into the till at the Lobster than to the bank where a large overdraft had been arranged on the promise that it would be repaid by the end of last month. The debt remained, unpaid and growing, and had resulted in the threatening letter which had arrived from the bank manager this morning.

'What's going on?' Maurice hurried to close the shop before any last-minute shopper could come in and overhear the argument.

Maureen picked up the letter and handed it to her brother. 'Read that,' she ordered tersely.

Maurice slumped on to a chair and looked at his father, a mixture of pity and anger on his fleshy face. 'We'll have to do something, Dad,' he insisted quietly.

'Tonight,' Maureen decided. 'After dinner. We'll all talk about it then.'

'We'll have to sell the car,' Morag, asked directly for her opinion, echoed her stepdaughter's earlier words.

Donny, who had listened in aggrieved silence as his daughter enumerated their debts, rose from his chair and made for the cupboard where he kept at least one bottle of whisky to supplement the supply upstairs, hoping to fool his family into believing it was his sole source of alcohol.

Donny's cunning was incredible. No matter how vigilant

371

Morag was he always seemed to find some way of smuggling a bottle or two into the house. She resorted to searching the house every day. On one single morning she discovered a bottle under the mattress, another under a floorboard which creaked suspiciously when she stood on it, a third one in the toilet cistern and a fourth at the back of the heavy sideboard in the sitting room.

She hated what the drink did to him, feeling that it was destroying what small chance they had of repairing their ailing marriage. On the rare occasions when he was sober, Donny was still a gentle, caring man, not given to wallowing in the bellicose self-pity which claimed him when he was drunk. But when challenged he would get angry and defensive and claim he could stop drinking whenever he chose. But she knew he couldn't, not any more. The compulsion seemed beyond his control. If only he could see himself the way she did, the way his family did, and make him understand that they only wanted to help him. But, until he admitted he had a problem, acknowledged he needed their help, there was nothing more they could do.

'For God's sake, Donny,' Morag hissed, watching him retrieve a full bottle of whisky from the back of the cupboard. 'Do you have to start already? It's not even half past six.'

He ignored her and poured an even bigger measure than usual then drank it down in a pathetic gesture of defiance.

'We'll sell the car,' Maureen decided. 'Some of what we get for it will pay the outstanding bills, the rest can go towards the overdraft. You'll have to go and see the bank manager, ask him for more time to pay off the balance.'

'I'm not going begging to anyone,' Donny bellowed truculently.

'There's no other way, Dad,' Maurice insisted quietly.

'Even then we'll have to cut down,' Maureen went on. 'Maurice and I will take a smaller wage.'

'I can make do on less housekeeping money,' Morag said, eager to make them see she was willing to play her part.

'And you can have all my wages if it'll help,' Ina offered impulsively.

Maureen smiled at her. 'Thanks. Maybe you could pay a wee bit more each week but it wouldn't be fair to make you work for nothing.' She turned to her father, a half-fearful expression on her face. 'See, we can all do something to help. You too, Dad. If you drank just half a bottle of whisky every day, instead of a whole one, we would soon get back to normal.'

For a moment there was absolute, total silence in the warm room. Maureen could hear her own heart thudding, could sense the anger pulsating from her father as if he was sending out waves of actual heat. Whirling round he flung his glass at the fireplace where it shattered loudly, making them all recoil in fear.

'Are you accusing me of being a drunk?' he demanded, towering over his daughter who faced him silently, refusing to withdraw her words. 'Are you saying this is my fault? Are you?'

Maurice leapt from his seat and tried to pull his father away. 'Of course she's not.'

'Let go of me.' Donny turned his furious, bloodshot eyes on his son who stood his ground, matching his father's height and breadth.

'We've all got to do something, Dad,' he said.

'Do what you bloody well like,' Donny retorted

bitterly. 'Sell the car. I don't care. It wasn't me who wanted the bloody thing in the first place. It was your mother who wanted it, so she could get out of Kilweem. This place isn't good enough for her any more, like I'm not good enough. That's why she had Gray McArdle's bairn. Because I wasn't good enough for her.'

'Donny!' Morag gasped, the blood draining from her face. 'That's not true.'

'Dad! Please, not now.' Maurice tried to push his father away from Morag but Donny shook him off.

'It is bloody well true!' he accused her. 'I've never been good enough. Second best, that's me. Don't think I don't know what you think of me. Look at what you did, shaming me in front of the whole village.'

'NO!' she cried.

'YES!' He hammered his fist into the table. 'They all know what you did. Going with another man then trying to kill yourself as if you couldn't face another day with me. Half the village thinks I drove you to it, thinks I'm some sort of monster.'

'That was all so long ago,' she whispered, appalled by the bitterness he had kept inside himself for so long.

'It seems like yesterday,' he croaked. 'Yesterday! You never really wanted me. You needed a home, a ring on your finger, money, but you never wanted me. You weren't even interested in your own daughter. You left it to me to bring her up, and right glad I was to do it, for she's a lass to be proud of. But I don't suppose you've noticed, have you? You could have been a mother to Maurice and Maureen. God knows they deserved it. They were ready to love you when you came here but you couldn't spare a bit of yourself for your own wean. What hope did they have? I've done everything I could, Morag, but what good has any of it been? You still look

374

at me with that long, miserable face as if it's all my fault, as if I'm the one with something to be ashamed of. If I drink it's so I don't have to think about you and what you've done to this family.'

His family watched in dumb horror as he staggered from the room. They heard his stumbling footsteps on the stairs and across the upper landing. The resounding slam of his bedroom door jolted them back to the present.

'I'm sure he didn't mean that,' Maurice muttered, looking embarrassed.

Morag stood and made her own slow way to the door. 'I'm sure he did,' was all she said before following her husband upstairs and locking herself into her own room.

Much later that night, after everyone had retired unhappily to bed, there was a light tap on Ina's door.

'Ina,' Morag whispered. 'Can I come in?'

Ina slipped out of bed and opened the door. Morag wandered to the window and looked out over the darkened village. When she finally turned to face her daughter, Ina could see she had been crying.

'I've decided to leave,' Morag said hoarsely. 'I can't stay here any longer.'

Ina sat heavily on the side of the bed. 'Mam,' she pleaded, 'Dad didn't mean what he said. You know what he's like with a drink inside him. I saw him helping himself to one just after I got in from work. He was drunk before we even started our dinner. He'll not remember any of it come morning.'

'He'll remember. He's never forgiven me for going with Gray McArdle. And I've no right to expect him to.'

'That was eight years ago.'

'He's right.' Morag's voice sounded distant. 'It seems

like yesterday. I loved Gray. I still do. Even though he's dead, I still love him.' She looked into her daughter's eyes, appealing for some understanding. Ina looked away. 'But it's not just that, Ina. It's what I did afterwards, that's what Donny can't forgive.'

'You were ill,' Ina said, uncomfortable with this sudden intimacy with a woman who had seemed unassailably remote. 'You're better now.'

Morag sighed. 'He hates me, Ina. And it's true, I'm the one who turned Donny into what he is now. Och, maybe you can't remember but he used to be such a good man, so kind, so generous. Look at him now.' She stood up and wandered back to the window. 'If I stay things will only get worse. He'll kill himself if he goes on drinking like this. Surely you can see that?'

Ina couldn't see anything other than the fact that her mother was leaving her. 'You can't go. What about me?'

'Come with me, Ina.' Morag turned round suddenly, fevered excitement blazing from her eyes. 'I know I've not been much of a mother to you but I do love you. You're my daughter, you're all I've got. We'll start again, find a home of our own.'

'Where?' Ina asked doubtfully.

'Glendarroch. I'd like to be near my mother and Rab,' Morag said softly. 'I've not been much of a daughter to them. I let them down too, especially my mother. It's been hard for her but she's done her best to forget it all. I'd like the chance to be close to her again, before it's too late.'

'But the highlands! It's so far away.' And so remote. Much as she loved her grandparents and liked the hills, Ina longed for the excitement of a big town, not the claustrophobic atmosphere of another little village.

'Och, but it's so beautiful up there.' Nostalgia took

Morag back to the times, in her distant childhood, when they had made the journey to the tiny village where her parents had been born.

'But how would we manage? We've no money.' Ina turned to the practical difficulties, desperate to make her mother see that this rash plan would never work. 'I'll have to give up my job. What would we live on?'

'You'll find something else. And I could work too. We'll be all right.'

'There'll not be much work in a tiny village, Mam.'

'We'll manage,' Morag insisted.

'How?' Ina demanded. 'What are we supposed to live on until we get work? You can't expect Gran and Grandpa to keep us. That wouldn't be fair.' She was getting angry now.

'Keep your voice down. You'll waken the whole house,' Morag hissed. 'This is our chance to start again, to be happy, can't you see that?'

'It's a chance for you to start again,' Ina retorted. 'It's you who wants to go. I'm happy here. Why should I leave? I've got my Dad, Maureen, Maurice, a good job, friends . . .'

'Donny's not your father, Ina. You don't owe him anything,' Morag responded cruelly, bitterly disappointed by her daughter's reaction. 'And Maureen and Maurice are not your brother and sister. You'd soon make new friends in Glendarroch. And Ayleen's your friend, you've always been close to her. Think how nice it would be to be near your grandparents again.'

'Ayleen's getting married, Mam. She won't have time for me.' Ina sighed. 'I do miss Grandpa though . . .' For a moment she seemed uncertain but when she spoke again she sounded coldly determined. 'I won't go to Glendarroch, Mam. It's too far away from everything, too quiet. I like Kilweem. And it wouldn't be fair to Dad.'

'Your father's dead!'

For all his faults Ina loved Donny deeply, more so since she had been old enough to appreciate just how generously he had welcomed her into his family, never making any difference between her and his own children; had gone on loving her despite all that had happened between Morag and him. It angered her to think her mother could assume it all counted for nothing. Her real father was nothing more than a rarely mentioned name, someone she felt nothing for, had little curiosity about. He was dead, beyond her reach, while Donny was here, part of her life, and she knew it would be a terrible betrayal to leave him now.

'I'm staying here,' she muttered, her voice trembling with fury.

'Your place is with me,' Morag responded angrily.

'Perhaps I don't have a place,' Ina whispered with such transparent pain that Morag got a glimpse of what she had done to this girl. 'I don't care what you say, Mam. Dad loves me, I know he does. And I love him. I won't leave him.' She ended on a choked sob and turned her head away.

'So, you won't come with me?' Morag asked sadly.

Ina rubbed a hand over her aching forehead. 'You're not being fair,' she wailed, torn between love for a man who had shown her nothing but kindness and a sense of loyalty to her mother.

'I'm leaving first thing in the morning. If you change your mind . . .'

'Tomorrow!' Ina could hardly believe she was hearing this. 'It's after ten o'clock at night and you're telling me that you're leaving tomorrow morning?'

'I'm sorry.'

'No.' Ina drew away from her mother abruptly. 'It's too soon. Why can't you wait?'

'I can't. The sooner I go the better it will be for Donny. After what he said this evening you must see I can't stay here.'

Ina stood up and faced her mother, suddenly looking the more determined of the two. 'I won't come,' she said. 'This is my home.'

Morag shrugged, trying to hide her hurt. 'I'll miss you.'

'I doubt it,' Ina said, just loud enough for her mother to hear. How could her mother have come to her with such an unreasonable, selfish idea? Mixed with Ina's anger was the fear of losing her mother. But to leave so suddenly; to turn her back on her home, her family, her friends, her whole life? She couldn't.

'You don't have to go like this,' she accused. 'After all these years you could wait a week or two.'

'I'm leaving tomorrow.' It was final. 'I'm sorry.' Morag crossed to the door and opened it cautiously.

Ina swung round and glared at her mother. 'Have you told him?' she demanded. 'Have you told him or are you just going to walk out without saying anything?'

'It's better this way,' Morag answered softly.

'Coward,' Ina taunted.

'I'll write to him. Explain . . .' Morag mumbled, awed by the fury she saw in this suddenly grown-up daughter.

'Don't bother. I'll tell him. He deserves that much at least. Just go. Just bloody go.' Ina turned away and didn't look round until she heard the door close. Then she crumpled on to the bed and let the tears come.

When Ina got up in the morning Morag had already fled.

379

'Why didn't you go with her?' Donny asked dully when she repeated the essence of last night's conversation with her mother.

'I will if you want me to,' she offered immediately, refusing to let him see the desperation in her eyes.

'Is that what you want?' he countered.

'I want to stay here. This is my home. But if you'd rather I went.' She sounded defiant but she was ready to run, to grab her things and leave at the first sign of rejection.

Donny, watching her closely, saw the stubborn lift to her chin and recognised shadows of the unhappy eight-year-old who had sought trouble as a way of getting attention. His heart bled for her.

'Och lass, I just wanted you to be sure of what you want,' he said, slipping a beefy arm round her shoulders. 'It's never easy to make a choice like that. You've lived here since you were a wean. You're my daughter just as much as Maureen is, and I'd miss you badly if you went. I know it's been hard on you, the way things have been between your mother and me, but this is where you belong. Maybe it's for the best – your mother going – maybe things will be different now.'

She gave him a watery smile. 'I feel like this is all my fault. Mam would never have come here if it hadn't been for me.'

'No, lass! How can it be your fault?' He tipped her chin up with his hand and forced her to look at him. 'You were just a bairn. The mistakes, and there were plenty of them, were all made by your mother and me. You've nothing to feel bad about. You're the one who came off worst in all this.'

'And you,' she smiled at him softly.

'Aye, and me,' he agreed. 'I did love your mother, lass,

I still do though I know it doesn't show. But it's hard when the person you love, loves someone else. Your Mam and me, we'll be better apart, she was right about that. But I'm not so badly off. I've still got you and Maurice and Maureen.'

'And I've still got my Dad?' she asked, sounding like a wounded five-year-old.

'Aye, lass, you've still got your old Dad.'

At first it seemed that Morag's defection had acted as a catharsis for Donny. Without needing to be badgered by Maureen he sold the car then visited the bank manager and successfully pleaded for an extension to the overdraft. Stung by the unpleasant realisation that his family thought he was a drunkard he even made a determined effort to cut back on the amount he drank.

But it didn't last. It was so much harder than he had imagined it would be. Every evening saw his resolution shattered and each morning brought a thundering hangover which he struggled to hide from them. They weren't fooled. His condition was obvious in his bleary eyes, his shaking hands, his queasy stomach. They ached for him, pleaded with him, won his slightly pathetic assurances that he would stop, cut down at least, only to see him disappear to his bedroom at an ever earlier hour to consume a bottle of whisky in sad solitude. Eventually, unable to bear the pity and condemnation he read in the eyes of his family every morning, Donny abandoned all attempts at getting up early, left the day-to-day running of the bakery in Maurice's and Maureen's capable hands, and appeared only at mid-morning to offer advice and help which Maurice obviously didn't need. The knowledge that they were managing better without him did nothing for his ailing self-respect.

The truth was that although he had tried hard to

disguise his feelings, Donny had been shattered by
Morag's departure. He saw it as the tangible proof of his
failure. After the inevitable anger had been drowned in
several bottles of best malt he started to convince himself that it was Gray McArdle who was really to blame
for what had happened; and Gray McArdle was a dead
man and no longer a threat. Even when sober, by the
end of the first month, Donny believed that what he had
told Ina was true, he did still love Morag. With a rapidly
emptying bottle at his side he made his plans, convinced
that if he went to see her, talked to her, made her understand how he felt, promised her a better life, she
would come home. Then they would be a proper family
again, happy and secure, their problems behind them.
And then, he promised himself, shaking the last drops
from the bottle, he wouldn't need to drink.

One Sunday dinner time, about a month later, they
were all facing up to the fact that whatever else Morag
might have been, she was a far superior cook than either
her daughter or stepdaughter. Shoving the remains of an
overcooked lump of prime Scottish silverside to the
edge of his plate with a grimace, Donny announced,
'Maybe I'll buy the pair of you a cookery book for your
Christmas. Still, you won't need to cook for me next
week.'

They all looked at him with surprise. It was Maureen
who asked, 'Why?'

'I'm taking a wee trip, a holiday.'

'A holiday!' Maureen, Maurice and Ina spoke in perfect unison. The idea was so novel that they all gawped
at him.

'Aye. A holiday. Youse lot are more than capable of
managing without me. In fact, Maurice makes a better
job in the bakery that I do these days,' he admitted wryly.

'Where are you going?' Ina asked.

'Glendarroch.'

'Oh. I don't think that's much of a holiday,' Ina muttered.

'There are things your mother and me should talk about,' he explained, 'For all we've had our problems she is still my wife and I should make sure she's managing. I'd like to see Rab and Annie again too. Ina,' he turned to his stepdaughter who was looking thoughtful, 'I'm sure there are things you need to say to your mother too, lass. Why don't you come with me?'

Ina darted a quick glance at Maureen and then at Maurice, worried about their reaction, but Donny was quick to forestall any possible objection from them. 'Och, don't worry about them. They're needed here at the bakery. I can't afford to close it down.'

'Aye, and we'll not let you down,' Maurice, assured him, secretly delighted with this opportunity to prove his worth.

'Thanks but I said all I had to say before she went,' Ina smiled ruefully.

'Aye, I daresay you did, but she's your mother, you need to make things right between you,' Donny insisted.

But Ina was adamant. 'No. You go. Give her my love and tell her I'll go and see her, and Grandpa and Grandma, later.'

'If you're worried about the train fare, I could lend you it,' Maureen offered generously.

'No need for that. I'll pay,' Donny said quickly.

Ina smiled. 'Thanks but I can't, not yet.' She sighed heavily. 'I'm still too angry. It's better that I wait a while.'

'Aye, well, if that's how you feel,' Donny said easily. 'When are you going and how long will you be away for?' Maurice asked, barely able to contain his excitement.

'I'm leaving on Thursday and I'll be gone long enough for you to ruin me so make sure you look after the place properly,' Donny laughed, looking better than he had for years. 'I'll be back in a fortnight.'

It was the first holiday Donny had taken since he and his first wife, Beth Bannerman, had spent a three-day honeymoon in the very village his second wife had fled to. In the intervening years he had forgotten just how beautiful this country of his was.

Donny travelled first to Edinburgh and took a train from the smutty, depressing Waverley station to Glasgow. Here, in the Forth Clyde valley, there was nothing in the vista of blackened buildings, dull little towns and pink and grey pit bings to hold his attention. His mood dictated by the drizzle which had been falling steadily since he had left Kilweem, Donny slid into nervous preparation for his meeting with Morag, planing what he might say to her, gloomily convincing himself that his efforts at reconciliation were doomed to failure. He spent his first night in a dark and dreary Glasgow hotel where he passed the evening in the bar, watching the rain splatter down the dirty windows. When he finally boarded the train which would take him nearly all the way to Glendarroch his head was thumping and his stomach churning with the familiar symptoms of overindulgence.

The first hour, spent chugging through the grim tenements of Partick and Clydebank with the window down and smoky smuts stinging his eyes as he battled to clear his head, brought no optimism to his mood. But, as they emerged from the sprawling city and headed along the Clyde, the skies cleared, the rain stopped and the sun shone, sparkling brightly off the broad stretch of river. Donny's frame of mind responded to the brilliance of the water and increasing beauty of the scenery. By the time the train rattled into Tarbet and carried on along the shores of a spangled Loch Lomond, Donny was smiling to himself, sure he was doing the right thing. The view was so beautiful it awed him. The sky, bright blue now with puffs of ever whitening clouds, was reflected in the clear waters of the loch while the hills stood high and proud in shades of green, grey and purple.

At Crianlarich, Donny, who had enjoyed solitude in his carriage for the first leg of the journey, found himself joined by two ruddy-faced men, dressed in much the same style as Rab Bannerman. They bid him goodday pleasantly then fell into conversation in lilting Gaelic. Donny caught half-remembered words in the language his first wife had slipped back into when she was angry or excited and settled back in his seat, thoroughly at ease, to watch the highland landscape slip past. The musical cadences of the men's voices, the regular motion of the train, relaxed him. His eyes closed and he slept with a smile curving the edges of his mouth. He stirred slightly when the train drew into the station at Bridge of Orchy but fell asleep again and missed the wild bleakness of Rannoch Moor, only finally waking when the engine drew to a hissing stop at Rannoch station. His travelling companions left him with a cheerful farewell and minutes later the train continued its highland journey in a cloud of steam and a long blast on its whistle. Wide awake now Donny stared from his window, mesmerised by the magnificence of the hills ahead and to the west. He knew Ben Nevis was there somewhere, with Fort William nestling at its foot and watched, trying to pick it out as the train chugged along

Loch Treig then turned west, skirting the mountain, before finally coming into Fort William from the north east.

Fifteen minutes later Donny stood with his case at his feet and gazed down the rippling length of Loch Linnhe at the mass of mountain behind him, feeling dwarfed by the sheer splendour of it all. A breeze zipped in off the water and he shivered in the late afternoon sunshine and picked up his case again. It was getting late in the day now so, rather than going on to Glendarroch, he decided to wait until morning before embarking on what he knew would be the most spectacular part of his journey. He remembered making this trip once before. The sheer breathtaking beauty of the ride had haunted him and he was eager to repeat the experience. To make the most of it he wanted the clean morning air and blue skies which were promised for tomorrow.

Breathing in another lungful of sharp, salty air, Donny strolled into the little town to find himself a hotel for the night.

He dined like a king on fresh fish, washed down by nothing more than pure, local water, then retired to bed to wake clear headed and refreshed to a crisp, sunny morning.

The journey to Glendarroch, at the point of Loch Darroch, was spectacular. The sandy beaches and limpid, green waters in the bays of the sea lochs were quite stunning in their beauty and Donny forgot everything as he watched them go by, content to let his mind fill with images which would stay with him as memories for the rest of his life. When, in the early afternoon, he finally left the train and walked the three miles to the tiny village, he was still captivated by it all.

Rab and Annie's neat cottage was on the main road, at

the western end of the village and easy to find. Wanting his visit to be a surprise, half frightened that, if she had advance warning, Morag would refuse to see him, Donny had not told them of his plans and could only hope they would be pleased to see him.

The house was a single-storey cottage, sitting back from the road in its own little patch of neatly tended garden. Behind it, forested hills rose majestically but there was none of the darkness here which had made the Pitochrie cottage seem so dark and dank. Smiling still, Donny knocked on the freshly painted front door and waited.

'Well, you've surely chosen the most beautiful place on God's earth to make your home,' he laughed when a startled Rab opened the door.

'Donny Archibold! Well, come on in, man.' Rab's face, framed now by a silver beard, broke into a broad beam as he clasped the other man's hand and led him inside.

'Donny!' Annie, neat as ever, emerged from her kitchen, wiping her hands on a spotlessly white apron. 'Och, it's good to see you,' she smiled. 'Sit yourself down and I'll fetch you something to drink.'

Half an hour later, refreshed and at his ease with Rab in the Bannerman's sitting room while Annie tactfully withdrew to her kitchen, leaving the men to talk in private, Donny tried to explain the purpose of his visit.

'You know you're always welcome here,' Rab said warmly.

'As you and Annie will always be welcome to come and stay with me,' Donny reciprocated with equal sincerity. 'To tell the truth, although it's Morag I want to talk to, I'm glad of the chance to see you, Rab, to try and tell you what happened.' Donny forced himself to turn down Rab's offer of a wee dram and went on to explain why Morag had left Kilweem.

'Aye,' Rab admitted when he had finished. 'Morag told us most of that herself.' He didn't tell his friend how angry, how unhappy and how bitter Morag was.

'I dare say she did,' Donny agreed ruefully, understanding the rest without having to be told. 'And she had every right to be angry with me. I've had plenty time to think, Rab, and I know it was my fault. I made it impossible for her to stay. All I want is the chance to talk to her, to say I'm sorry. Do you think she'll see me?'

Rab shrugged. 'I dare say there's right and wrong on both sides,' he said slowly, reluctant to apportion blame. 'She's angry still, hurt too, but I'll take you down to her place if you like.'

Donny got to his feet, anxious to get this over with. 'Right,' he said. 'Is it far?'

Rab laughed. 'No, a couple of hundred yards, at the other end of the village. But wait a while, man. She'll still be there after you've had your dinner.'

Morag's cottage was similar to Rab's and Annie's but smaller and badly in need of a coat of paint. Rab knocked on the door and called out to her while Donny hovered in the background, his heart thumping nervously, wishing he'd taken Rab up on his offer of a wee half, if only to give him the courage for what might be a very emotional meeting.

'Come on in, Rab. The door's open.' Morag's familiar voice came from the back of the house.

'I've brought someone to see you,' Rab shouted back, ushering Donny into a small, untidy sitting room.

Morag bustled into the room her face a wreath of

smiles but, when she saw exactly who her visitor was, she stopped, her smile faded and her mouth took on the set, hard line that Donny knew so well. But it seemed to him that she looked better, had put on a little weight. There was colour in her cheeks and life in her eyes which reminded him of their early days together.

'Hello, Morag,' he said, making no move towards her.

'What do you want?' she asked coldly.

'Just to talk,' he said.

'There is nothing to talk about,' she snapped, glaring first at him and then at Rab.

'There are things I must say to you, Morag,' Donny said softly.

'If this is about Gray and the bairn I lost, you've had nine years to talk to me about that, Donny Archibold. It's too late now,' Morag retorted angrily.

'Och, Morag,' Rab intervened hastily. 'Hear the man out, will you! He's come all the way from Strathannan just for a few words with you.'

Morag hesitated then plumped herself down on one of the only two chairs and said, 'I'm listening.'

'Aye, well,' Rab ran his fingers through his still-thick beard. 'I'll be off. You know the way home when you're ready, Donny.' He escaped gladly.

'No, don't go, Rab,' Morag pleaded urgently, running after him.

'I've no wish to hear what you two have to say to one another,' Rab said, turning to her. 'This is between you and Donny, lass. It's better that you say what you have to say in private.' He walked to the gate then turned and came back to his stepdaughter. 'He's a good man. Maybe he wants you to go back to him.'

'Never,' she said.

'That's for you to decide but give him the chance to

talk with you. He's still your husband. You owe him a hearing at least.' With that he strode away into the dimming summer evening.

Morag went slowly back into her house where her husband was waiting uncomfortably in the littered sitting room.

'Sit down, Donny,' she said tiredly. 'I only moved in here a couple of days ago,' she explained the uncharacteristic mess, waving a hand vaguely round the room. 'I've not had time to get myself sorted out yet.'

'I can see that,' he forced a laugh. 'And you were always so tidy at home.'

'This is my home, Donny,' she said uncompromisingly.

'Aye.' He frowned and looked away from her, not knowing how to go on. 'Have you been staying with Annie and Rab then?' he asked eventually.

She nodded stiffly. 'Aye.'

There was a long, awkward silence which Donny broke by asking, 'And how are you managing? I mean . . . are you all right for money?'

'I'm managing fine,' she assured him.

'Have you a job?' he asked, wondering if Rab was having to keep her.

'Aye. I help out at the big house, cleaning. Three days a week. I was lucky. There's not much work round here.'

'That'll not keep you. Here.' He reached into his inside pocket and drew out an envelope. 'There's a wee bit in there for you. I'll send you something each week . . .'

'I don't want it.'

'You're my wife, Morag. I'll not see you wanting,' he insisted.

'Why are you here, Donny?'

He placed the envelope on the arm of her chair. 'I'm here to ask you to come back with me, Morag.'

She snorted. 'After what you said to me? Oh no, Donny. I'm not coming back.'

'I was wrong. I should never have said what I did,' he said miserably.

'Why not?' she challenged him. 'It was true, wasn't it? I drove you to drink. That's what you said.'

'Aye, that's what I said and I was drunk when I said it,' he admitted. 'And I was wrong.'

'I don't want to talk about it,' she insisted stubbornly.

He sighed, got up and paced restlessly round the small room. 'Do you hate me so much, Morag?' he asked suddenly.

It took her by surprise. 'Hate you? No, I don't hate you,' she admitted at last. 'That's why what you said hurt me so much.' She got up too and walked away from him, uncomfortable with the way he was watching her. 'Och, I know I was in the wrong. I know how much I hurt you. And I was ill . . . after Gray died. I don't think I knew what I was doing then. But I tried, Donny, I really tried to be a good wife to you after that. I worked hard, keeping house, looking after the children. But you didn't want me any more. It didn't matter what I did.' She turned round suddenly and faced him, her eyes flashing. 'I would have done anything to make it up to you but you didn't want to know. You had your room and I had mine. If only you had been able to put your arms round me, just once, but every time I tried to touch you, you jerked away, you couldn't even bear me near you.'

'Do you have any idea how I felt?' he demanded. 'You were in love with Gray McArdle. You had his child. It was you who didn't want me.'

'That was nine years ago and you've made me pay for it ever since!'

'I was hurt too, Morag. Och, to start with I'll admit I

was angry. I didn't want you then, but afterwards I would have welcomed you into my bed, into my life again. I tried too. I gave you everything you wanted. I looked after the family to give you time to get over it, but each time I spoke to you, you closed up, turned away. You never spoke to me first, you made it obvious that you didn't want me. You still wanted Gray McArdle. A dead man!'

'I loved him,' she said, her voice husky with the strain of holding back tears. 'I know I was wrong but I loved him.' She sank back into a chair and covered her face with her hands. 'I loved Gray McArdle, Donny. I didn't want it to be like that, it just happened. I never meant to hurt you. I tried to tell you I was sorry. So many times I tried.'

'You didn't try hard enough,' he accused her bitterly.

'How could I talk to you?' she shouted. 'You were always drunk! Do you think I didn't know you went to bed with a bottle of whisky every night? Don't you think I know that was my fault?'

'I've already told you I was wrong to say that.'

'And I've already said you were right, it's true, I made you into a drunkard.'

'Perhaps that was part of it,' he admitted sadly. 'But you know I've always had a taste for the stuff.'

'Donny,' she sighed, looking up at him with wide, green eyes. 'What is the point of all this? We're just going to make each other unhappy again. Don't you think nine years of misery is enough?'

He sat opposite her and took her hands in his. She resisted at first but then let him hold them. 'Do you realise this is the first time we've really talked in those nine years?'

'We're not talking, we're arguing.'

'And listening to one another,' he insisted. 'Maybe we should have done more of that.'

She smiled at last. 'Maybe.'

'Come home, Morag. I'll not promise it'll be easy but at least we've each said our piece. We've both done things we should be ashamed of and I'm sorry I hurt you.'

'I'm sorry too.'

'Then will you come home?'

She sighed. 'Why Donny? You're managing fine without me. The children, well, they're not children any more. They don't need me now.'

'We all need you, Morag. I love you, lass. I just didn't realise it until you went away.'

She shook her head. 'You're a good man, Donny Archibold and, believe it or not, I've missed you too. But I don't think I love you.'

'I know. I've always known that. It doesn't matter. And we've not really given one another a fair chance lately, have we? Come home, Morag. Let's put all this behind us and try again.'

'And what about the whisky, Donny? Do you want me back so I can watch you drink yourself to death? And every time you have too much are you going to turn the past on me, like you did the last time?'

'I'll try to stay off the drink,' he promised.

'I've heard that before!'

'Then come home and help me. I need you there with me, Morag,' he pleaded. 'I'll only manage to stay off the drink if you're there with me.'

She stood up, and put as much distance between them as she could in the small room, feeling the unwelcome weight of responsibility dragging at her and resenting it. 'I don't know,' she admitted. 'I'm so confused. I need time to think.'

'Are you happy here?' he asked gently.

'I like being close to Rab and Mam and Ayleen. And Glendarroch's a friendly place.'

'You've got plenty of friends in Kilweem,' he tempted her quietly.

'No, not real friends. They all remember . . .'

'Och, I'm sure they don't . . .'

She sighed and turned her back to him. 'Go away, Donny. I can't think when you're here.'

'Shall I come back?'

'How long are you here for?'

'That depends on you.'

'Give me a week to think.'

And with that he had to be content.

Donny spent the week resisting the urge to go back to plead his case again with Morag. He prowled the loch shores and spent a day in Fort William, exploring the lower slopes of Ben Nevis, returning each night to Annie and Rab who conscientiously avoided all mention of Morag's name. Friday evening found him back on his wife's doorstep.

'Come in, Donny,' she called in answer to his over-loud knock. He came into her little sitting room, his huge frame overwhelming the space. She could see he was as nervous as she was from the way his hands slid in and out of his pockets, as if he didn't know what to do with them.

'Well,' he asked, unable to contain himself any longer. 'Will you come home, Morag?'

She shook her head slowly then took his hands while she explained. 'No. Not yet, Donny.'

'But why?' he asked, his fleshy face flushing with disappointment.

'It's too soon. We're still angry with each other. We need more time apart. I have to know you really want me back, that it's not just my cooking, my housekeeping you miss.'

'I'm not angry and it is you I want, Morag,' he protested.

'But *I* am still angry,' she went on. 'Och, not as bad as I was to start with and I feel better now that we've talked. But I'm not sure I want to go back to Kilweem. I was unhappy there, Donny. Now, for the first time in my whole life, I'm independent. You've given me a choice and I have to be sure I make the right one, for the right reasons. I know I can manage on my own, just, and I want to go on managing, at least for a little while.'

'A little while? How long is a little while, Morag?' he asked, anger mounting.

'I don't know. I can't you promise anything.'

'So you're going to stay here. Is that what you're trying to say?' he demanded, disappointment giving his voice a truculent edge.

'No! That's not what I'm saying. I'm saying I won't come home with you now. But later, maybe in a month or two, I might.'

'I might not want you in a month or two!' he retorted, wanting to hurt her now.

'Fine. Then you've got your answer,' she responded instantly.

Donny groaned. 'I'm sorry, Morag. I didn't mean that. I'm just upset. Disappointed. I really thought, after the other night, that you'd come back to Strathannan with me.'

He looked so miserable, his shambling frame bent and weary, that she felt her heart tighten with pity for him. She stood so that she was almost touching him, so that her breath caressed his cheek as she ran a soft hand over the side of his face. 'Donny . . . look at me?' Slowly he raised his head and met her eyes. 'I'm not trying to hurt you any more, or punish you, or anything like that,' she assured him gently. 'I just need more time. Can't you understand that?'

'I don't know,' he admitted. 'I don't know if I even understand myself any more.'

'Go home, Donny. I'll write to you,' she promised. 'And when I'm ready to go home will you come and get me?'

He looked into the green eyes which watched him so steadily and knew she would not change her mind. 'Aye,' he agreed reluctantly. 'I'll go home, Morag, and when you want me I'll come for you.'

Donny could take no pleasure in the rest of his holiday. Unwilling to go home early and face the unavoidable explanations and equally loathe to linger in Glendarroch he simply took the train south, staring out of the window at the superb scenery but seeing nothing.

The five days he spent in Glasgow were forever lost to him. His next memory was of the hotel manager roughly ejecting him on to the street, tossing his case and empty wallet after him.

Through a wave of nausea Donny looked along the pavement through a sea of disembodied legs which parted and flowed round him and realised that he was actually lying on the ground. Some vestige of pride got him to his feet and propelled him unevenly along the road until he found a small park in which to rest his aching head for an hour or so. The first bench he staggered past held a heap of old clothes and newspapers which stirred and revealed itself as a ragged, grimy human being.

'Gorrradrink?' it asked, then retreated into the shelter of its rags, muttering a string of casual curses when it realised it was wasting its time on someone as down on his luck as itself.

Donny stumbled on and collapsed gratefully on to the next bench, lying full length in the early morning chill, resting his head on his suitcase. It was a full hour before he opened his eyes again, aware of an overpowering smell. He struggled dizzily into a sitting position, fighting his stomach and moved along the bench, trying to escape the stench. It came with him, churning his stomach until he had to stagger into the bushes where he fell to his knees and retched painfully. When it was over he felt a little better. He stood up and moved back on to the path. Only then did he realise that the smell was emanating from his own person. To his horror he realised that his jacket and trousers were covered in his own old vomit.

Now that the reason for his eviction from the hotel was obvious Donny thought to check his wallet. Apart from his return train ticket, it was empty. His pockets revealed barely enough small change for the bus fare to Kilweem and nowhere near enough to buy the hot tea and buttered toast which might have settled his tortured stomach. He would have to go home now but he couldn't hope to get on a train in this condition. Dragging his case from the bench he wandered through the small park, searching for some private place to change out of his soiled clothes. He was almost resigned to retreating furtively into the bushes when, to his relief, he saw a block of gentlemen's conveniences near the road. He made his way inside, pushing past two malodorous derelicts who were lounging idly just inside the door.

The toilet block, though new, was indescribably dirty, noisome and damp but at least there was running water. Stripping down to his underpants, Donny washed himself in cold water and doused his head under the tap, scrubbing the muck from his hair. As he raised his face he caught his own reflection in the tarnished mirror. He hardly recognised himself. The man who stared back was a down and out, just like the one on the bench, the two who were standing in the doorway. His skin was grey, his bloodshot eyes sunken in black hollows, his chin was rough with at least three days' bristly growth. Still dizzy, Donny groaned and splashed more water over himself. He then propped his case on the other sink and found fresh clothes which he draped carefully over the case while he went to relieve himself. One of the tramps, who had been watching him from their position in the doorway, followed him and stood at the adjoining urinal, muttering something. Dazed as he was, Donny didn't catch what he said and looked up. To his revulsion he saw that the man was leering at his exposed member. Donny growled and backed away, right into the arms of the second man who grabbed him from behind. Donny's bare flesh crept but it was the shock of that repulsive touch which galvanised him into action. He was a big man, a full five inches taller than either of his attackers, his upper body strengthened by work in the bakery. He jabbed one elbow back into the chest of the man who was holding him, winding him and loosening his grip, then lashed out with his right fist. A vicious punch connected with the first man's jaw, sending him sprawling on to the filthy floor where he cracked his head against the base of the urinal before finally sliding into unconsciousness. Donny turned, aimed a second blow at the other man and heard a satisfying crunch as his fist connected with a fleshy nose. One more punch sent him into oblivion on the floor with his partner.

Donny ran for his clothes, lingered only to pull on his trousers for decency's sake and fled, his shirt in one hand, his case in the other. In the relative safety of the bushes he struggled into the rest of his clothing then ran from the park. Five minutes later, and still running, he reached the railway station.

Gasping for breath he rushed into the main hall and collapsed wearily on to a wooden bench, oblivious to the travellers thronging round him. People passed, looking for an empty seat but the one beside Donny remained empty. No one wanted to sit next to the huge, untidy man who was crying in public.

TWENTY

Morag chewed at the tip of her pencil, desperately raking her mind for something to make her letter to Donny sound more interesting. It was a full five minutes before she admitted there was nothing to write about other than her day-to-day routine of shopping, chatting and working, things a man would surely find tedious and repetitive. Viewed from the outside her new life did seem boring, she thought, poking the fire to a healthy, crackling blaze. So little happened here that her fortnightly letters to Donny had rapidly become a tiresome chore. His were hardly more interesting and written in a particularly laborious and wooden way which hinted that he too found the task irksome. Nor did she look forward to receiving them because he always ended by begging her to come home, jarring her conscience. The truth was, she doubted that she would ever be able to face going back to Kilweem and all the problems which had driven her here in the first place. She found excuse after excuse to stay in Glendarroch. When the snows came a full month earlier than normal she welcomed them. For the next four months it would be impossible for her to go back to Kilweem.

The kettle sang merrily on the hob. Morag sealed the envelope and brewed herself a cup of tea then settled into her fireside chair for a restful hour before bed. This was the time of day she treasured most, a time for peace and reflection and the chance truly to appreciate her new-found happiness.

All in all, she mused, she was almost content. For the first time in her life she was her own mistress, free from the strain of constantly failing to please. Even money wasn't a problem. She had found a job, light cleaning and cooking at a local house and she supplemented her wages by taking in mending, alterations and simple dressmaking. There was sufficient money for her modest needs and it was a matter of pride that she was capable of supporting herself and had no need to beg Donny for money.

Glendarroch itself, remote and amazingly self-sufficient, was a truly wonderful place to live. The villagers, who had welcomed her warmly once they realised she was of local descent, were friendly and cheerful, not ever interfering but making it known that they were available should she need help. Their generosity was boundless, the whole village rallying to help the ill, the aged or the plain unlucky. A day rarely passed when her trip to the only shop did not result in the sharing of a pot of tea across a neighbour's kitchen table. Often she returned home with a jar of home-made jam or a freshly baked scone for her tea. And, of course, her mother and Rab were nearby, and there was Ayleen's wedding to plan.

Surrounded as it was by the most marvellous scenery, Glendarroch was a place to be savoured. In her free time Morag walked for miles, sometimes on the mountain slopes, more often along the lochside. She never grew bored with the views which could hold her spellbound for hours at a time. The exercise and the freedom from worry, added to nights of undisturbed sleep, wrought marvellous changes in her. She lost the tentative,

402

nervous manner which had haunted her for so many years. Her eyes sparkled with health, her cheeks bloomed with colour and her auburn hair shone, while the smile which had seldom been in evidence in Kilweem transformed her whole face. Rab, watching his stepdaughter blossom, saw much of the younger Morag re-emerging in this attractive thirty-four-year-old woman.

Apart from Donny, the only thing which seriously marred Morag's happiness was Ina's stubborn determination to stay in Kilweem. Morag missed her daughter's lively company more than she had ever expected to. Ina's loyalty to Donny hurt but Morag knew that there was nothing to be gained from constantly nagging at the girl. In any case, Ina was almost an adult, and capable of making her own decisions. Before long she would be fully independent, wanting to lead her own life, perhaps marrying and settling down. It was, Morag thought sadly, all part of the growing-up process and she couldn't afford to throw away her own chance of happiness on a daughter who no longer needed her. She limited her letters to Ina to chatty descriptions of her new life, careful never to let any note of reproach creep on to the untidily scrawled lines and trying not to be disappointed when Ina proved herself to be reluctant to write more than a few dutiful lines in return.

The weatherwise old timers had been looking at the sky and nodding their heads sagely for a week before the weather finally broke. Slate grey clouds forced their way inland from the west, following the course of the lochs, and gathered in the glens, obscuring the slopes of Ben Nevis, away to the east.

Morag, who had taken care to lay in stocks for the winter months, sat in the window of her cottage and gazed out over Loch Darroch. It was, she thought, as if nature was holding its breath. The air was so calm that the surface of the loch was glassily still. No moving shadows disturbed the uniform darkness of the mountains and even the birds were silent. When the first flake fluttered slowly to earth, followed by another, then more and more until the view was only seen through a dizzy white haze, it was as though time had stopped.

By morning the snow had stopped but lay almost a foot deep along the road. The sky was the sort of clear, pure blue which only comes after snow, contrasting so brightly with the sheer whiteness of the mountain tops that it made Morag's eyes water to look at it. Already her kind-hearted neighbour, Archie Ross, had shovelled the snow from her path and half a dozen lads were clearing a way along the road, whistling and laughing as they worked. Morag pulled on her warm coat and shoes, wrapped a heavy shawl round her shoulders and went outside.

'There'll be more yet,' Archie said, nodding seaward to where the clouds were starting to build again.

'And all your hard work will be wasted,' she chuckled. 'Thanks for clearing my path, Archie.'

'You're welcome, though I dare say it'll all have to be done again the morn,' he laughed. 'I've seen us digging a path through the village half a dozen times in one week. But it has to be done.' He coughed and knocked his pipe out against a wall, dislodging a small avalanche of snow over his boots.

'How long will it last?' she asked.

'The snow? Only the Lord knows that, Morag Archibold. Sometimes it's days, other years we've been snowed in for months.'

She shivered. 'I didn't realise it could be so cold.'

'Away with you, lass!' he chortled. 'It's the best time of the year. It's just a case of getting organised for winter and looking out for one another. You wait, there'll be a ceilidh every weekend. Nothing like it! Plenty good, malt whisky, old Tam on his fiddle, wee Dorry Campbell singing with that fine voice of hers and dancing enough to keep you warm all night. Och it's a braw time right enough.'

Archie was right on both counts. The snow fell again, and again, effectively blocking the road and isolating the village. Nobody seemed to mind and by the weekend word had been passed round that the first ceilidh of the winter was to be held that Friday night. Archie, a widower, asked her to go with him.

It was an experience Morag would never forget. A warm, intimate gathering round a huge fire in Roddy McLeod's house where everyone made some sort of contribution to the entertainment. There was singing and dancing, stories and more singing. The village was a Gaelic-speaking community and Morag was trying hard to master the soft cadences of the language, half-remembered from her childhood. She had been touched when, out of consideration for her, most people either spoke to her in English or patiently helped her with her own attempts at Gaelic. But tonight, though the songs and stories were in Gaelic, translations were not necessary, the meaning clear in the hauntingly pure voices and the lilting melodies. When her own turn came, Morag knew it would be insulting to refuse and, with some embarrassment, made an undistinguished attempt at a song learned years ago at school. Watching others perform she realised her self-consciousness was misplaced, that a missed note or a forgotten word mattered not at all. It was the sharing that counted, the coming together, in enjoyment and without criticism, of people who depended on one another, sometimes for their very survival, in the long winter months.

Warmed by a dram of whisky Morag allowed Archie to escort her the two hundred yards home, secure in the knowledge that this was where she belonged.

Donny Archibold read Morag's latest, scant correspondence with an angry frown. Still she wouldn't say when she was coming home and this letter hinted that bad weather might make it impossible even to get a letter to him.

He screwed it up petulantly and dropped it into the heart of the fire. He had, he decided, had enough of this. He had gone all the way to Glendarroch to sort out their differences, to try and make her understand that he did need her. What more did she want? Morag's home was in Kilweem and as soon as the weather cleared he would damned well go back to Glendarroch and make her come home.

At just after nine o'clock in the morning, Donny was the only member of the family still in the house. Ina, in a last-minute rush as always, had clattered out to work a few minutes before nine. Maurice had been at work in the bakery since four that morning and Maureen had joined him at about seven-thirty. Donny drank so much each night that he felt and looked awful in the mornings. He was certainly no longer capable of starting work at such an early hour. He didn't even get out of his bed until he was sure everyone else had left, knowing his condition would give him away. In any case, Maurice managed better without him. When Donny did put in a tardy appearance in the bakery, his son assigned him the minor tasks such as scrubbing off the table or chopping and cooking meat for the pies, though even that simple job had seemed to present problems lately. Only last week he had allowed the huge pot to boil dry, ruining five pounds of steak – as well as the pot – and then having to bear his son's wrath as if he was a recalcitrant five-year-old. It had been extremely humiliating.

Donny put the distasteful memory of his son's fury to the back of his mind and prepared to face another day. Though it was not yet nine-thirty and he had had nothing more substantial for breakfast than a cup of black tea and a slice of cold, left-over toast, Donny made his way to the cabinet, topped up his little silver flask and poured himself a tumbler full of whisky. He eyed it balefully for a moment then tipped his head back and swallowed it in two huge gulps. He closed his eyes, feeling the liquid burn its way to his belly. On an almost empty stomach it wasn't long before the alcohol had the expected effect. Donny felt the bruised tightness in his gut loosen and ease. The familiar feeling of depression, the unwillingness to face another day, receded. In its place was a pleasant lightheadedness, the conviction that nothing in the world was of any real importance. Donny grinned, confident that the alcohol had no perceptible effect on him, never realising that his family would recognise the familiar glassiness in his eyes, the exaggerated care with which he now moved, and despair for him.

His headache replaced by the comforting haziness in which he spent most of his waking hours, Donny was cheerful enough to whistle as he slipped out of the back door and hurried down to the Lobster, keeping to the back wynds. The little public house was closed, naturally, at this early hour, but he was expected. Three sharp knocks on the side entrance and Donny was admitted.

He emerged furtively a short time later and lumbered up the road clutching a brace of bottles under his jacket. He took them straight upstairs and stowed one as far under his mattress as his long arm could reach. The other he slid under a floorboard, loosened specifically for this purpose. At least Maureen, who regularly found and removed the bottle he hid under his mattress, would never think of looking there for it.

Below him, in the kitchen, Maureen looked up when she heard the unfamiliar scrape and thud of the floorboard. Frowning she went to the stairs and yelled, 'Dad! Are you up there? What's that noise?'

'What noise?' he asked innocently, emerging from his room.

'A sort of thud. Did you drop something?' she persisted, watching him closely.

'I dropped my shoe,' he extemporised blithely.

'Funny-sounding shoe,' she snapped, wondering if she would ever get him to admit the extent of his problem.

With enough liquor inside him to guarantee his good humour until at least lunch time, Donny was immune to his daughter's sniping. 'What are you doing here at this time of the day?' he asked.

'Maurice wants you to give him a hand in the bakery,' she said.

'Fallen behind, has he?' he chortled, glad to know that his son wasn't perfect after all.

'Yes, but he wouldn't have done if you hadn't let the oven go out last night. You forgot to check it, didn't you?' she accused him angrily, fed up with having to make excuses to disappointed customers.

'Course I checked it,' he answered, slurring his words slightly. 'I always check it.'

It had been agreed that since Donny was now the last

to retire, he should be the one to lock up and make a final check on the coal-fired ovens, ensuring that they would be warm and ready for Maurice in the early hours of the morning. It was something he did automatically, knowing very well that a dead fire would mean at least two and more likely three wasted hours the next morning. He must have checked the ovens last night. Of course he had.

Maureen held her temper in check, knowing there was nothing to be gained from arguing about it now. 'I've customers waiting in the shop,' she excused herself and hurried away, leaving her father to negotiate his unsteady way down the stairs and into the bakery.

'You know what happened?' Maurice greeted his father angrily as soon as he showed his face round the door. 'The bloody oven went out! I'm way behind.'

'I did check it, son,' Donny lied pathetically.

'You didn't bloody check it! You couldn't have bloody checked it,' Maurice roared, his face flushing beetroot with anger.

Donny backed away. He was no longer any match for his vigorous, bad-tempered son. 'What do you want me to do?' he asked placatingly.

Maurice glared at him, tempted to yell at him to pull himself together, to stop drinking but, separated from the shop by just a single door, he knew everything he said could be heard by his customers and it was better that the family kept this problem to themselves. He took a deep breath and counted to three before trusting himself to speak.

'I've only just finished the bread. The rolls are still in the oven. I've no cakes made, no biscuits and no pies.'

Donny rolled up his sleeves. 'I'll get going on the sponge mixture then.'

'NO!' Maurice remembered his father's last attempt to make cakes when he had used too much fat and not enough flour. By some miracle the cakes had risen but the next day every customer had returned to the bakery to complain. 'I'll do the cakes. You make the pies. The pastry's made and the meat's cooking. It should be ready by now.' He nodded at the two-handled pot simmering on top of the stove.

Knowing himself to be in the wrong, Donny was wise enough not to argue. With the dexterity of many years in the trade he rolled the pastry and soon had the pie bases ready to be filled from the pot of steak and vegetables stewing on the stove.

Behind him Maurice worked frantically to catch up on himself. His face dripping sweat in the fierce heat, he whisked a last batch of rolls out of the oven with one hand and slid a tray of sponges in with the other, clattering the hot tray down on a smaller table, close to where his father was working.

'Take those through to Maureen when you've got a minute,' Maurice ordered. 'And hurry up with those pies. They've got to be ready for lunch time. I'm just going to the store room for some more fat.' He was running through the back door as he spoke.

Donny, who was working as fast as he could, bridled at his son's tone. 'Who owns this bloody business anyway?' he asked out loud before checking quickly over his shoulder and taking a slug from the flask he carried tucked into the top of his trousers. He swallowed, pulling a face as the whisky burned his throat then took a long second gulp before capping the almost empty flask and stashing it at the back of a shelf.

'Haven't you got those rolls through to Maureen yet?' Maurice asked, rushing back into the bakehouse and immediately starting to his next task. 'She's waiting for them.'

'All right, all right.' Donny gathered the still-hot rolls, cursing when he burnt his fingers, and dropped them untidily into wooden trays ready for the shop. Three or four fell to the floor. He chuckled to himself and chased them round the floor on his hands and knees. Maurice was appalled to see his father then toss the dirtied rolls back on to the tray, a thing he would never have allowed in the past when he had been proud of his high standards.

'What the hell are you doing?' Maurice bellowed, striding to the tray and hunting frantically through four dozen rolls. 'You can't put them in there. They'll be filthy.'

Donny elbowed him aside. 'Naebody'llnotish,' he decided, grabbing the tray and hauling it through to the bakery where Maureen took it from him.

'About time too.' She sniffed suspiciously. 'Have you been drinking already?' she hissed.

Donny retreated towards the safety of the bakery, not daring to speak until he was too far away for the fumes to reach her. 'Course not,' he said, contriving to look hurt.

'Will you finish those pies or do I have to do it?' Maurice scowled when Donny came back.

'Hold on to your breeks! I can only do the one thing at a time, lad,' Donny chuckled, his bad temper evaporating as the alcoholic top up hit his blood stream.

The pie bases were ready, spread over the entire surface of the table, their lids cut and piled in the far corner. All that was needed now was the filling.

Donny turned to the stove which was behind him and dragged the heavy pan forward. It had two handles, like ears, on its sides. Donny knew they would be greasy and made sure he had a firm grip before hefting the steaming pot over to the table. When filled, as it was now, with boiling meat and vegetables for four dozen pies and another four dozen bridies with enough left over to make a passable stew for the evening meal, it would have taken two men to lift the pan safely. Donny, still strong in the arms, managed to heave it over to the table and then understood his mistake. He had forgotten to leave enough space for it to rest there safely. Undeterred he balanced the pot precariously on the edge, letting the side of it rest against his well-padded stomach. The task he was about to undertake was one which he usually managed with speed and dexterity. With the pot normally steady in its own space, the ladle, wielded by the left hand, would dip in and out of the meat, filling the pies, two from each spoonful, while the right hand flicked the lids into place, sealing them with rapid pressure round the edges. Now Donny balanced the pot awkwardly against his body and worked with both hands as usual. He managed fairly well while he filled and sealed the pies nearest to the pot but the further he had to stretch over the big table the harder it became and, to make matters worse, heat from the pot was starting to burn through to his stomach and chest. Cursing he reached away to his right, missed the pie and spilled meat and gravy over several others, spoiling the look of them, then stretched again, too intoxicated to see the danger. As he reached out for the furthest pies the pot slipped. Feeling it go, he jerked back, dislodging it altogether. The pan was over three quarters full of near-boiling, greasy meat and gravy which soaked his stomach, his groin and both his legs from thigh to ankle. Donny watched the pot go and saw the liquid soak through his clothes almost as if it was happening to someone else. He opened his mouth to shout for help but Maurice had already looked up, alerted by the crash of the pot on the concrete floor. He dashed frantically across the room to his father who, still feeling no pain, had nevertheless felt his legs fold beneath him. It was only when Donny was lying on the floor, laughing into his son's horrified face, that the pain hit him. That was when he started to scream.

It was late afternoon and two days later when Morag stepped off the bus at the tollbooth, feeling weary and grubby after the long journey. It was raining. The setts were black and shiny with water, the buildings grey and dull. Folk scurried about their business with heads and backs bent against the weather. Water had seemed to pour down sullenly from the second she had received Ina's telephoned message, telling her that Donny had scalded himself in an accident at the bakery and was asking for her. There was no way she could refuse the girl's emotional appeal, though her sympathy for Donny had waned considerably when Ina explained that he had been drunk when the accident happened. Still, maybe this would teach him a lesson, she thought grimly. For a moment she stood, letting water drench her hair, and stared at the retreating bus as if she might be considering running after it. Then she sighed heavily, straightened her shoulders and dashed across the road to the bakery.

The door was closed, the blinds pulled down and the windows empty. Sudden dread filled her stomach. The bakery never closed. Donny was proud of the fact that there had not been a single occasion when the villagers had been deprived of their bread. She reminded herself that it was Maurice who was in charge here now, not Donny. Donny was in hospital. Maurice and Maureen, and Ina, would surely be at his side. That was why the shop was closed. Slowly Morag made her way to the back entrance. She was going to let herself in with her house key but changed her mind and rang the bell instead, feeling she had forfeited the right simply to walk into a house she no longer thought of as home.

For a long time nothing happened but then a door closed somewhere inside and there was the sound of slow footsteps on the stairs. Through the patterned glass in the door Morag could make out a slight, dark-haired figure and knew it was Maureen. What sort of welcome would she get, Morag wondered? Had she been able to make them understand, in her letters home, why she had been forced to leave? Or did they see it as a personal betrayal as Ina so obviously did? When the door opened she steeled herself for possible rejection.

Pale and solemn, Maureen's expression was unreadable as she said, 'Ina told us you were coming. Come on upstairs.'

Maurice was waiting at the top of the stairs, his beefy frame filling the doorway. For a fleeting second Morag thought it was Donny standing there, so great was the resemblance to the man she had married. They regarded each other warily for a moment then Morag stepped forward and stretched to kiss his cheek. He pulled away sharply and avoided her.

'Mam, is that you?' Ina shoved Maurice aside. Morag half opened her arms in welcome but dropped them again when her daughter made no further move towards her. 'I wasn't sure you'd come,' Ina said, through what sounded suspiciously like a sob. Behind her Maureen and Maurice exchanged worried glances.

'Of course I came,' Morag answered, trying to ignore the hostility emanating from all three. 'How is Donny?' she asked. 'Is he still in hospital. Can I visit him?'

Ina made a choking sound and fled back to the sitting room.

'Maurice?' Morag stared at her grey-faced stepson in increasing horror.

'Come in and sit down, Morag,' he said grimly. 'We need to talk.'

Morag sat on a familiar chair, twisting her hands nervously, dreading what he might be going to tell her. 'Well?' she demanded when the silence had lasted for too long. 'Are you going to tell me how Donny is? Which hospital is he in?'

'They took him to Inverannan,' Maurice whispered but didn't know how to say what had to be said next.

'He died during the night,' Maureen found the words which had deserted her brother.

Ina sobbed, Maureen's face crumpled and Maurice had to go and stand at the window to hide his own tears.

Morag watched them, her head spinning with shock. Even though she had sensed that something was very wrong, had realised that Donny was more seriously hurt than she had first assumed, she hadn't expected this.

'Donny's dead?' she echoed. 'But how? I thought he was just scalded.'

No one answered, they were all too absorbed by their own sorrow. In the heavy silence the grandmother clock ticked so loudly that Morag could feel the reverberations in her eardrums.

'Best tell her the truth,' Maureen advised her brother just when Morag felt she couldn't stand their silent anger any longer. 'She has a right to know it all.'

'The burns were awful,' Maurice said, his voice flat.

'All over his legs and stomach.' He swallowed loudly and forced himself to go on. 'But that wasn't what killed him. He had a heart attack. They say it was shock . . .' Maurice turned away still badly affected by the horror of what had happened and blaming himself. After all, he had known his father was drunk that morning.

'Oh God,' Morag cried.

'It was my fault,' Maurice muttered. 'I knew he wasn't fit to be working in the bakery. I knew he'd been drinking. I should never have let him near that pan.'

'No,' Morag insisted, feeling sudden pity for him. 'We all know Donny was drinking and we all tried to stop him. I know it sounds hard but if he scalded himself because he was drunk, then that was his fault, Maurice, not yours.'

'It's easy for you to say that, isn't it? But I still feel responsible,' he said bitterly, then rounded on her, his face contorted with hatred. 'He got worse, you know, after you walked out on him. You should have come home with him when he went to Glendarroch, then this would never have happened.'

Morag blanched. 'It's not my fault that your father was a drunkard,' she whispered, containing the sudden flash of fury with a tremendous effort.

'No?' Maurice challenged her acidly. 'Well, he never drank before you came here.'

'How would you know?' Morag shot back at him. 'You were just a child!'

'Stop it!' Ina screeched. 'Stop it. Don't talk about him like that.' They all stared at her.

'Ina's right,' Maureen sighed. 'It's too late to change anything now.'

They buried Donny three days later. Maureen wept

throughout the service. At one point she swayed as if she was about to faint. Morag moved swiftly to her side only to have her offer of comfort rejected. Maurice, who was controlling his own grief with a huge effort, put his arm round his sister and held her tightly, ignoring his stepmother. Ina stood slightly apart from them, turned noticeably away from her mother, holding herself straight and tall, her face strained but tightly controlled. Morag felt excluded. She swallowed her own grief and made her way back to the house alone.

Back at the bakery Donny's friends gathered in the peculiar atmosphere common to all such sad occasions. Ina watched black-coated mourners talking of mundane things, her father apparently already forgotten while they stuffed themselves with his food and drink, and hated them all. Someone laughed, a high, artificial noise. It was too much. Pushing her way through the crowded living room she dashed upstairs and shut herself in her bedroom.

Morag watched her go, wondering whether to follow and try to comfort her. She suspected she wouldn't be welcome. Ina had remained withdrawn and sullen, turning to her brother and sister for comfort and refusing to speak to her mother unless it was absolutely necessary. It was obvious to Morag that Ina hadn't forgiven her for leaving Donny, that she, like Maurice and Maureen, held her at least partially responsible for his death.

Donny's death had changed them, Morag thought ruefully, had brought them even closer together. And they were so self-sufficient, so certain they were right, so unwilling to understand, to make allowances.

The attitude of Maureen, who had been an affectionate and caring child, was particularly wounding. In the six months Morag had been away, Maureen had matured into a woman who no longer needed a mother. She seemed less anxious to please, more sure of herself, colder. Apart from that one, understandable, breakdown at the funeral itself she had coped with the tragedy admirably, reserving her tears for the privacy of her own room.

Maurice too had altered, but in him the changes were more subtle. There was a new weight to his manner, a firmness in his tone as if he had already accepted responsibility for the household. But there was also a grimness in his eyes which disturbed Morag. Perhaps it was simply the strain of his father's death, but she felt there was more to it than that. She sighed and accepted more condolences she felt she wasn't entitled to, wondering if she would ever be allowed into the intimacy of this family group again, if there was anything she could do to help them and, if there was, whether they would accept help from her.

At last people were starting to leave. Morag knew she couldn't delay the long-overdue talk with her daughter any longer.

Ina was laying full length on her bed. Her eyes were red but dry and her face looked hot. She greeted her mother tersely, determined to make her understand that it would be a long time before she would be forgiven for the way she had run off to Glendarroch without even bothering to say goodbye to her husband and stepchildren.

Morag looked at her daughter closely, realising that Ina had changed too. Like Maureen she had matured but she was harder, stronger than she had been before. There was barely contained animosity in her manner but that was only to be expected after what had happened.

Yet again Morag attempted to explain, tried desperately to convey her own feelings, to succeed where she had so badly failed on the night before she left for Glendarroch. Ina, who was even more inclined to speak her mind now, glared at her.

'We've all had our problems,' she retorted. 'And you made them worse by running away. If you had been here none of this would have happened.'

'Is that what Maurice and Maureen think too?' Morag asked miserably.

'Of course they do!'

'You don't understand,' Morag said sadly.

Ina looked at her mother coldly, her pale grey eyes hard. 'No, I don't understand. I don't suppose I ever will. There's no point in talking about it.'

Morag stilled, horrified to realise that she had seen the identical expression, heard the same cold inflection in the voice of Katrina Fraser. This critical stranger wasn't her daughter at all. Was that why their relationship was so difficult? She shuddered suddenly, deliberately shutting the treachery from her mind.

'I'll try and make it up to you all,' she promised feeling guilt, like a cloak, settle round her shoulders.

Morag had been back in Kilweem for less than a month and from the very beginning it was obvious that she was superfluous. Despite the air of grief which hung over them all, the household had already settled back into the routine it had evolved after she had left. And it was a routine which had no place in it for her.

As the new joint owners of the bakery, Maurice and Maureen continued much as before while Ina worked on at the Post Office, helping her brother and sister after work and at weekends. In her free time she either disappeared to her own room and read or went out with Georgie Cameron.

None of them seemed to have the slightest need of Morag. Determined to do her best to make life easier for them and to show them she did care about them all, she took on all the housekeeping jobs and then asked if she could help in the shop. Maurice gruffly declined her offer saying that he already employed two local women on a part-time basis and there wasn't enough work for her too. Resignedly she confined herself to the domestic chores but even here her efforts weren't appreciated. Ina openly resented her mother invading her room to sweep and dust and even Maureen told her that she preferred to look after her own things.

Gradually she started to think that they wouldn't miss her, might even be relieved if she went away again. But she wouldn't make the mistake of simply walking out on them again. This time they would talk about it, make a joint decision.

She waited until they had all gathered for dinner the next evening.

'I have something to say to you all,' she began.

They all stopped eating and looked at her, Maureen with interest, Maurice with hostility and Ina with suspicion.

'I think it might be better if I didn't live here,' she said calmly.

Ina crashed her knife and fork down. 'I might have known you wouldn't stay,' she accused bitterly, the old feeling of rejection welling inside her.

'Do you care?' Morag rounded on her bitterly. 'Do any of you care? I've been here for more than a month now and none of you have said more than half a dozen words to me.'

'You made it bloody obvious how much you care about us when you walked out the first time,' Ina spat.

'Ina!' Maurice yelled, rapping his spoon on the table and glaring at her. 'That's enough.'

Ina subsided into sulky silence and Morag marvelled at how easily Maurice was filling his father's place. She looked up and saw him watching her.

'It's obvious,' she said, meeting his eyes squarely, 'that you all hold me at least partly responsible for what happened to your father. We can't go on living like this, it's not good for any of us.'

Maurice didn't bother to deny it. 'So what will you do?'

'I'm not sure.' Ideally she would be able to persuade Ina to go to Glendarroch with her, but she already knew what Ina's reaction to that suggestion would be. The girl was hardly likely to have altered her view about the place.

'Well, Maureen and I have to clear up the bakery. You talk to Ina about what you want to do. You're her mother after all. Let me know what you decide.' With that he rose from the table and, motioning for Maureen to go with him, left them to it.

'You do understand why I can't possibly stay here, Ina?' Morag asked.

Ina didn't look up. 'I suppose you're going back to Glendarroch,' she muttered.

'Not necessarily. I've not made up my mind yet. I wanted to talk to you about it first.' Morag gave a humourless laugh. 'I was hoping to make a better job of it than I did last time.'

'Why do you have to go all at all?' Ina asked. 'Why can't you stay here?'

'In this atmosphere! Look, Ina, Maurice and Maureen

421

have the bakery, it's their business now and their house. They certainly don't want me here. They'll be fine. It's you I'm worried about. I'd like you to come and live with me. I'm prepared to rent a place in Kilweem if that's what you want.'

'Not Glendarroch?'

'Would you come to Glendarroch if I asked you to?' Morag challenged.

'No.'

'Then, if you want me to, I'll find a place here.'

'Do you really mean that?' Ina asked. 'Would you really stay in Kilweem because of me?'

'Yes.' The unadorned statement was so patently sincere that Ina was momentarily ashamed of the doubt which had been her instant reaction. 'But how could you afford a place of your own?'

'The same way I managed in Glendarroch. I'll get a job. We'll manage.'

'You've got it all worked out.' Ina couldn't keep the edge of bitterness out of her voice.

'No!' Morag protested. 'It's up to you, Ina. God knows I've made a big enough mess of your life for you. I don't want to make things worse. If you want to live with me then you'll make me very happy but, if you prefer to stay here, then I will understand. All I want is to see you happy.'

There was too much resentment in Ina to let herself be won over so easily. 'Are you sure you don't just want someone to keep you company now you're getting older?'

Morag winced but ignored the barb. 'I meant what I said, Ina. I'll not walk out on you again. I am more than willing to stay in Kilweem. But only if you want me. I'll not stay in this house, where nobody wants me, to be

422

blamed for everything that ever went wrong between Donny and me. And I'll not stay anywhere in Kilweem if you are going to go on treating me like an enemy.'

The jibe went home. Ina got up and walked about the room, her agitation obvious. 'I'd feel really selfish if I asked you to stay here,' she admitted with rare candour. 'The fact is I've grown up, Mam.'

'I can see that,' Morag whispered.

'I don't need looking after and I like it here. I told you before, Maurice and Maureen are my family, this is my home.' She saw the blood leave her mother's face and knew she had hurt her. It was a satisfying feeling.

'All right.' Morag conceded defeat. 'Maybe if I rented a place in Kilweem so that we could see one another . . . ?'

'What's the point?' Ina demanded. 'We both know you really want to go back to Glendarroch. Well, there's nothing stopping you now.'

'What time did you come in last night, Ina?' Maurice asked a fortnight after Morag had returned to the highlands.

Ina groaned and raised her eyes to the ceiling. 'Ten o'clock.'

'It was a quarter past,' he corrected her sternly. 'You've to be in by nine-thirty the night or you'll not get out for the rest of the month.'

'That's not fair!' she objected loudly. 'Dad never made a fuss like this.'

'That's because he never knew what was going on,' her brother retorted furiously. 'This is my house now and all the time you live here you'll do as I say.'

'Yes, sir,' she yelled, storming across the room and slamming the door behind her.

423

In her mother's bedroom Ina slaked her temper by turning out the clothes her mother had asked her to send on. Grabbing the last drawer out of the tallboy she emptied it ruthlessly on the bed then sat back feeling wretched.

The truth was she resented Maurice's increasingly authoritarian manner and was missing her mother and father dreadfully. She had lost her father for ever, nothing she could do would bring him back, but there was no reason for her to remain estranged from her mother.

Ina knew herself well enough to understand that it was her own stubborn nature which had doomed her mother's attempts at a reconciliation. There was something cold and unforgiving inside herself which had stored up the hurts of childhood and made no allowances for the obvious fact that Morag had done as much as she could to heal the wounds.

Despite what she had said, Ina did understand something of what her mother had gone through with her father – the atmosphere in the house had been too bitter to ignore. Much as she loved Donny, Ina wasn't blind to his faults and knew his drinking had been a very real problem, for all of them, but especially for her mother. If any man ever treated her like that she would leave him, and a lot quicker than her mother had left Donny. So why, Ina asked herself, had she acted the way she had?

She sighed. Perhaps it was simply loyalty to her father, an awareness that it had been her mother who had started this tragic chain by betraying him with another man; that it was always Donny who had had time for her, giving her the same love and affection that he lavished on his own children while her mother had spent years locked in her own private misery, misery made worse by the way Donny had treated her. Recent events proved that her mother longed to put all that behind them. The older, wiser Ina recognised that she should try to do the same. She frowned. She was proud and obstinate by nature and had never found it easy to apologise.

Suddenly her strained expression cleared as the solution occurred to her. It was obvious really. She had some holidays due so she would use the money she had saved to go to Glendarroch. She had been invited to Ayleen's wedding which was less than a month away and it would provide the perfect excuse for her to spend a week with her mother. That should give them plenty of time to clear the air and it would be wonderful to see her grandpa and grandma again.

TWENTY-ONE

The rain and chill which had persisted throughout the winter finally cleared to bring a warm and early spring. Full of optimism now that she had resolved to try and come to terms with her mother, Ina was in high spirits as she set out to spend Sunday on the beach with her friends. There were half a dozen of them, three boys and three girls, who had been friendly since their very first day at the village school. One of them was Georgie Cameron.

Ina's friendship with Georgie had endured the upheavals of childhood and adolescence and then quietly crossed the unmarked line which made them a couple. Inevitably they kissed then fondled and, recently, Georgie had seemed determined on even more than that. Only the other night he had stormed home in a sulk because Ina, yet again, had refused to co-operate with his sexual ambitions. Not that she wasn't excited by those secret fumblings, nor did she have any moral objection to giving herself to a man who professed to love her. It was the plain fear of pregnancy which always made her draw away, leaving her young, would-be lover, hot, hard and frustrated.

Ina knew they were drifting towards marriage, they often found themselves discussing their future with the ease of two people who accepted that they belonged together. Georgie worked on the boats and as soon as he was drawing an adult wage they would begin to make serious plans. The idea suited her well enough. She knew where she stood with Georgie. Marrying him would be almost like marrying a brother, safe and reliable with no unpleasant surprises in store. He said he loved her and she supposed she must love him too because she enjoyed being with him and missed him badly when he was at sea. She certainly couldn't imagine life without his quick tongue, ready laugh and infectious humour.

It was typical of Maurice that he disapproved of the whole boisterous Cameron clan. He still remembered the time when Georgie and Ina had always seemed to be in some sort of trouble and insisted, unfairly, that it had been Georgie who had led Ina astray. As far as Maurice was concerned, the fact that Georgie had grown into a sober, hard-working young man was totally irrelevant. Ina was careful Maurice didn't discover how serious things were between her and Georgie. Time enough to meet trouble head on when they had some concrete plans.

'How long will you be away?' Georgie asked glumly as they sat in the dunes tucking into sandy pies, left over when the bakery closed on Saturday.

'I'm leaving on Tuesday and I'll be back a week on Wednesday,' she answered, thinking how beautiful the sea looked when it was as blue and calm as this. The beach too looked wonderful. A broad, golden bay, five miles long, backed by grass speckled dunes. Where they were, half a mile or so from the village, the beach was wild and practically deserted but at the foot of the Butts, which was the access point from the village, there was a small cluster of people. She let her gaze travel past them, over the rocky outcrop which formed the natural barrier between beach and harbour, until it rested on the cluster of red-roofed buildings nestling in a protective niche in the coastline. What was it about some remote, highland village, she wondered idly, that attracted her mother so much? Surely there was nowhere quite as beautiful as Kilweem? She stretched and lay back on the sand, squinting up into the clear azure of the sky. Even mountains couldn't be as wonderful as this. In a few days' time she would be able to judge for herself, she thought, smiling lazily.

'What am I supposed to do when you're not here?' Georgie demanded.

She groaned audibly. 'Stop moaning, Georgie. You've had your holiday. I didn't complain when you went off to Ayr for a week did I?' she snapped, resenting him for spoiling the day.

'I suppose not,' he conceded grudgingly.

'Anyway. It's not exactly a holiday. I'm going to Ayleen's wedding.'

'So long as you behave yourself,' he teased, the sunshine making it impossible for him to maintain his affected bad temper.

She grinned. 'What you don't know can't hurt you . . .'

'You're my lassie, Ina Archibold, and don't you forget it,' he said, only half joking.

'I don't belong to anyone, Georgie Cameron, and don't you ever forget that,' she retorted. 'I'm me. Even after we're married I'll still be me and not just Mrs George Cameron. You'll not get me cleaning your boots and running round after you like your mam fusses round your dad.'

He laughed. It was one of the things he admired most about her, this unconventional streak, the determination to have her own say, her reluctance to compromise. She'd be a handful, he could see that coming, but he'd soon sort her out.

'Don't laugh at me, I'm serious,' she warned.

'Och, Ina, shut up,' he said, silencing her by bringing his face on to hers and kissing her deeply.

For a moment she resisted, but only for a moment. When his tongue wriggled its way into her mouth and his hand slipped between the buttons on her dress she felt her blood start to race. Her nipples stiffened at the touch of his fingers and she pressed herself into him, almost involuntarily, searching for his hardness, her body longing for the release her mind would not give it.

'Ehh . . . would you like us to go away again?' Al McArdle, hand in hand with Dot Moys stood on the sand, peering down at them, grinning widely. Dot's sister, Eileen, and Bertie McLean were just behind them. All four had been for a walk along the beach.

Ina shoved Georgie away, and sat up. Looking slightly pink faced she busied herself in the paper bags and handed out the rest of the pies, feeling her breathing gradually returning to normal. Another two minutes and they could have been seriously embarrassed by their friends' return. Maybe it was just as well they had come back when they did because Ina was finding it harder and harder to resist the animal pull she felt at the touch of Geordie's strong young body. Then God knows what trouble she might get herself into.

The six friends lounged round in the dunes, laughing, talking and dozing the afternoon away before, somewhat reluctantly, starting off along the beach, heading for their various homes. Ina had no great desire to hasten her return. As soon as she stepped into the bakery she would face the inevitable grilling from Maurice who would demand to know exactly where she had been, who she had been with and where, all in tones of disapproval more appropriate to an old man than someone who was barely an adult.

They splashed along the water's edge, scrawling risqué comments in the damp sand, safe in the knowledge that the advancing tide would obliterate all trace of the words almost as soon as they were written. Nearer to the village a clutch of people still lingered, all gathered on the soft sand, as if they were part of an organised group. Some sort of outing, Ina guessed. The picturesque fishing villages were getting more and more popular with day trippers and it was becoming a common enough sight for horse-drawn carts and smartly painted motor buses to rattle down the Butts and disgorge a stream of visitors on to the beach.

In front of them three young men, in shirtsleeves and braces, their trousers rolled up, their boots tied by their laces and slung over their shoulders, cavorted noisily on the tideline, soaking each other. All three wore the cloth caps favoured by working men.

As they got closer they grinned and winked cheekily at the lasses. Their high spirits were infectious. Ina and the two other girls couldn't help smiling back. Georgie, Al and Bertie instantly moved closer to their partners, slinging stiff arms round the girls' shoulders, as if they were staking claim to them, and walked on, ignoring the newcomers.

'Is there anywhere we could buy something to eat in this village?' asked the tallest of the three young men, running through the surf alongside them, his bare legs white and strong in the clear water.

No one else seemed inclined to answer so Ina stopped, forcing the others to come to a halt too, and said, 'Not on a Sunday. Everything's closed.'

He gave an exaggerated groan and made a long face at

his companions. 'Oh no.' He was tall, brawny and dark with laughing eyes. Ina couldn't help looking at him and got a frank, white-toothed grin in return.

'Are you on a day trip?' Dot asked, emboldened by Ina.

'Come on,' Georgie snarled, gripping Ina's arm hard. 'We've got to get home.'

'Aye,' one of the other young men, a lad with violently red hair and freckles, spoke up now, his attention all on Dot who blushed and giggled. 'We've come from Craigie for the day. It's right braw here, isn't it?'

'It was,' Georgie snapped, trying to pull Ina away. She shrugged him off angrily.

'Didn't you bring anything to eat with you?' she asked, more to annoy Georgie than anything else. She hated it when he tried to take charge of her. It reminded her of the way Maurice acted.

'Well, we did but we ate it all ages ago,' the third lad admitted, rubbing his stomach ruefully.

Dot giggled again. 'Looks like you'll be hungry for a while yet then. Everything closes on a Sunday. You must have known that.'

'Don't s'pose you've got anything in those bags?' the red-haired lad asked boldly, looking pointedly at the brown paper bags which contained the remains of their picnic.

'You don't look as if you're starving to me,' Dot retorted, admiring his strong body.

'Oh but we are,' the taller one protested with a wide grin which seemed aimed specifically at Ina. 'It's a church outing, see. One piece of bread and jam, a buttered scone and a drink of warm lemonade. That's all they gave us. If there was somewhere we could get something to eat we'd be right glad to pay.'

'Well . . . I might be able to arrange something,' Ina said thoughtfully. 'It's all yesterday's stuff, mind.'

'Ina!' Georgie hissed. 'Come on home. They're not really hungry, they're just trying it on.'

Ina ignored him. 'Follow us,' she told the young men who fell into step beside the six friends.

They walked to the village and down to the bakery in absolute silence. Georgie radiated fury and stomped along with his hands in his pockets. Al and Bertie were equally bad tempered and even Dot's shyer sister, Eileen, seemed uneasy. Dot and Ina however exchanged sly grins of complicity. This little adventure was certainly adding spark to the day.

'Right. Wait here,' Ina instructed when they finally reached the bakery. 'I'll be back in a minute.' As she fumbled with her key Georgie growled furiously into her ear. 'What the hell do you think you're doing? I saw you, eyeing him up. Just tell them there's nothing left and send them packing.'

'No.' She got the door open and faced him angrily. 'You've no right to tell me what to do, Georgie Cameron.'

He flushed crimson with anger, span round and marched away. After a second or two Al and Berie followed him with Eileen running after them.

The three lads watched them go with wide grins on their faces. Ina slipped quietly into the bakery and went to the tray where yesterday's unsold items were waiting to be thrown away first thing tomorrow morning. Hurriedly she stuffed four brown paper bags with sausage rolls, cakes and biscuits. As an afterthought she grabbed three big loaves and wrapped them as best she could before going back outside with them.

She was greeted with astonished laughter. 'We're

432

hungry right enough,' the tall lad said, 'but there's enough here to feed us for a week.'

'It's just leftovers,' she explained, feeling strangely embarrassed now. 'It all gets thrown out in the morning anyway so you might as well take it. Share it with the other people on your bus. It'll be a bit stale by now, mind.'

Somehow Dot was left with the other two boys, flirting harmlessly, while Ina stood slightly apart from them with the tall lad who seemed to be their leader. 'What's your name then?' he asked.

'Ina. Ina Archibold,' she said, going pink. 'What's yours?'

'Joe Lennox,' he answered, smiling broadly.

'Joe Lennox from Craigie,' Ina repeated. 'Where is that?'

'It's on the other side of Inverannan. Just a wee village. Not half as braw as this one. Harry, he's my brother, Billy and me, we're miners.' And proud of it, his manner said.

'Miners! You work underground?' she asked, thinking that explained the strong torsos and pale skins.

'Aye. Underground twelve hours a day sometimes.' His brown eyes twinkled and his mouth twitched as if he was laughing at some private joke. Ina bridled. She hated to think she was being made fun of.

'What's so funny?' she demanded, her own eyes flashing, her mouth set stubbornly.

'Och, not you, if that's what you're thinking. I was just wondering what your boyfriend is going to say the morn.'

'He's not my boyfriend,' Ina denied it instinctively but then her innate honesty made her add, 'That is, we're not engaged or anything like that.'

433

'Ina! Ina! What are you doing? Who's that?' Maurice shoved the first-floor sitting-room window open and yelled down at her angrily. 'Get up here. Now!'

'Good God! Who's that?' Joe asked, loudly enough for Maurice to hear.

'My brother,' Ina whispered, mortified.

Dot took one look at Maurice's puce face and fled.

'Ina! Inside. Now!' Maurice bellowed.

'Maybe you'd better do what he says before he gives himself a heart attack,' Joe said wickedly.

Ina fumed and stayed obstinately where she was. 'He can't boss me around,' she declared.

'Right. That's enough. I'm coming down.' The window slammed down and she heard a door bang.

'Oh no,' she panicked. 'You'd better go.'

'I'm not frightened of him,' Joe grinned and flexed his shoulder muscles as if relishing the prospect of a confrontation.

The bakery door flew open and Maurice stormed out. 'What's going on here?' he demanded, standing directly in front of Joe and towering over him, his fists clenched. 'Ina. Inside.'

She stayed right where she was. 'It's all right, Maurice,' she said placatingly. 'This is Joe and his brother Harry and their friend Billy. They're here on a day trip. They asked if there was anywhere to get something to eat. Everywhere's closed so I gave them the leftovers from yesterday.'

'How much do I owe you?' Joe asked Ina, ignoring Maurice and keeping an impudent smile fixed in his mouth.

'Get away from here. Go back to whatever hole you crawled out of and keep your filthy hands off of my sister.' Using both hands Maurice shoved the other man hard on the shoulders, forcing him to take a step backwards.

'Stop it, Maurice,' Ina yelled. 'All I was doing was giving them something to eat.'

'You get inside and stay there,' her stepbrother bellowed. 'No decent lassie lets herself be picked up by a bunch of ruffians. I'll not have you behaving like a slut.'

With commendable calm Joe turned round and handed the bag of cakes he was carrying to Harry. Unhurriedly he faced Maurice again then, so fast that no one realised what he was doing, he drew his fist back and landed a cracking punch on Maurice's nose. 'That's for calling your sister a slut,' he said as Maurice reeled back against the wall. 'And the next one will be for insulting me and my friends.' He stood tensed and ready to defend himself but when Maurice made no attempt to retaliate, he turned away in disgust. Shoving a hand in his pocket he withdrew some coins and tossed them at Maurice's feet. 'That's to pay for the food.'

Ina was affronted to think that Maurice could so humiliate her in front of the most exciting boy she had ever met. Fiery temper overcoming common sense she rounded on him, ready to lash out with a piece of her mind. To her amazement Maurice was sagging against the wall, one hand clamped over his bleeding nose, making a thin whining sound. Nor did he move when Joe took her hand and said, 'Thank you, Ina Archibold. I'm sorry about your brother but I couldn't let him say things like that about you, could I?'

Torn between concern for Maurice on the one hand and pride in a man who would rush to defend her on the other she merely stared at him. Laughing again he squeezed her hand lightly then turned and sauntered off up the road with his friends.

Ina watched until he disappeared from sight then followed Maurice inside expecting the worst. But Maurice slammed into his bedroom and wasn't seen again until the next day when he skulked round the bakery with a purple swelling under his left eye and a hugely distorted nose.

Ina didn't dare to refer to the incident again though Joe Lennox was seldom out of her mind. He had seemed so much more alive, more interesting than Georgie, better looking too, but somehow, even after such a brief encounter, he had left her feeling sad and dissatisfied. For the first time she found herself wondering if she really did want to drift into married life with someone she knew almost as well as she knew herself. But, she told herself severely, she was being ridiculous, fantasising about a young man she hardly knew and would never see again. Her future was here, in Kilweem, with Georgie.

Georgie enjoyed sulking for a whole day then, secure in the knowledge that the miners were from the far side of Strathannan and weren't likely to come back to Kilweem, arranged to meet Ina as usual on the night before she left for Glendarroch. He too decided to say nothing more about the incident, knowing very well that any verbal contest with Ina would only end with his own defeat.

Ina thoroughly enjoyed the long journey to Glendarroch. Because she had first to take a bus to Leven then the train to Edinburgh followed by another train to Glasgow before even starting the main leg of her journey, it was impossible to make the trip in one day. It was unthinkable that she should stay overnight in Glasgow on her own, so Maurice recruited Hetty McArdle to see

Ina safely on to the Fort William train. He also arranged for Hetty to meet Ina on her return to Glasgow. As Ina didn't have enough money to meet Hetty's expenses herself, Maurice was forced to pay her from the bakery till. Ina could see that he grudged every penny.

The prospect of the stern-faced ruler of the McArdle clan acting as chaperone quite ruined Ina's anticipation of her holiday. In fact Ina was pleasantly surprised. Hetty turned out to be jolly good company, obviously enjoying every moment of her unexpected holiday and looking forward to a good look round the Glasgow shops before she went home again. There was no time for Ina to see anything of the city on the outward journey but Hetty promised to take her to see the large department stores on the return trip. She saw Ina on to her north-bound train, pressing a bulging paper bag into her hands.

'You'll need something to eat,' she said. 'And don't get talking to any strangers.'

'You sound just like Maurice,' Ina sighed theatrically then smiled.

Hetty guffawed. 'Good. That brother of yours means well, lass. He's a lot on his shoulders for a lad of his age. You should be proud of him.' She stood back as the train started to move off in a cloud of steam. 'Don't forget to give your mother my best wishes, hen,' she called. 'And make sure you have a good time.'

Ina leant out of the window, 'Thanks, Mrs McArdle. See you next week,' she called then waved until a bend in the track took Hetty out of sight.

Like Donny before her, Ina was enchanted by the scenery. She spent the entire journey gazing out of the window at the ever changing lochs and mountains, hardly noticing her travelling companions who smiled at the young girl's obvious pleasure.

At last, just as she was starting to feel cramped and tired, the train pulled into Fort William. Ina hauled her two cases on to the platform and looked round for a porter to help her with them but it seemed they had both been commandeered by other passengers. Too impatient to wait Ina humped the bags, one in each hand with her small travelling bag tucked awkwardly under her arm, out of the station.

'Ina! Ina!'

Ina recognised her grandfather's voice immediately and sprang round. Rab drew a horse and cart to a halt and clambered stiffly down.

'Sorry I'm late, lass,' he laughed, hugging her. 'This old horse is like me, past his prime. He'll only go at the one speed.'

Without further ado Ina's bags were tossed into the back and she scrambled on to the seat beside Rab then laughed as the old horse refused to move.

'Bloody animal,' he growled, jerking on the reins. The horse looked over his shoulder accusingly then plodded off at a slow but steady pace. 'It'll take us forever to get home at this rate,' Rab smiled, not at all concerned, the creases round his eyes almost meeting the vertical ones which emerged from the thick growth of his beard. The lines, Ina thought, of a man who laughed a lot. He draped the reins loosely over one arm and puffed hard to get his pipe to draw. 'Still, it'll give us time for a wee chat, lass, before the women get hold of you.'

Because of the preparations for Ayleen's wedding reception which was to be held at home, Ina had expected the house to be chaotic. She should have known her

438

grandmother better. Annie presided over the arrangements with organised calm and efficiency and even insisted on giving Ina her evening meal there before finally sending her along the street to the house her mother rented.

Rab walked along with her, helping with the cases, one of which contained some of the clothes Morag had left at Kilweem. It seemed to Ina that half the population of the village came out to greet her. By the time she reached her mother's front door her head was spinning with half remembered names and faces.

Any apprehension she had been feeling at the prospect of seeing her mother vanished the minute the door was opened. Morag was so obviously genuinely delighted to see her daughter, pulling her into a fierce hug and kissing her face, that Ina knew her task would be easier than she had any right to expect it to be.

'I'll leave you two to chat,' Rab laughed, dumping the cases inside and sauntering off again with a wave. 'We'll likely see you tomorrow. Ayleen will be in then. I know she's dying to see you.'

'Come away in, hen,' Morag ushered her into the small sitting room. Ina saw the change in her mother at once. She had gained a little weight and looked fit and even a little tanned. Gone were the darkly circled eyes and the guarded but haunted expression she had worn in Kilweem. Now her green eyes were full of laughter, her expression relaxed and warm, her whole manner that of a contented woman. So obvious were the changes that Ina marked them all in the time it took Morag to draw her into the room and settle her in a chair.

They talked far into the evening with few signs of strain between them. Her mother seemed so much more at ease here that she was like a different person, Ina thought, watching Morag's mobile face as she described the preparations for Ayleen's wedding. As Ina snuggled into her warm bed and drifted towards sleep that night she was sure her mother had smiled and laughed more in that one evening than she had done for the last five years in Kilweem. Was it just that she was no longer tied to an unhappy marriage, that her future was settled, or was it this extraordinarily friendly village which had wrought such changes in her?

The following afternoon, Ina and Ayleen wandered down to the shores of the loch while Ayleen told Ina about the boy she was marrying. Sitting on the dilapidated wooden jetty, her feet dangling in the clear but icy water, Ina listened to an ecstatic recital of all Freddy's attributes and found it hard not to yawn. It seemed to her that Ayleen was measuring herself against the envy of the other girls who would have liked to catch such a good-looking, hard-working and manly fellow. To Ina's disgust it was obvious that she deferred to Freddy in almost everything, even down to the arrangement of their furniture in the tied cottage which came with his job. By the time they parted company Ina was heartily sick of hearing 'Freddy says . . .' and 'Freddy thinks . . .' She certainly couldn't imagine herself talking about Georgie in quite such rapturous terms.

Ina didn't get a glimpse of the man himself until the wedding. Sitting with her mother in the second row of pews she was able to get a good look at Freddy McPherson as he waited for his bride to arrive. Ina thought he looked pleasant enough, in an ordinary sort of way, and full of self-assurance, showing less sign of nerves than his best man who fidgeted and coughed restlessly.

'What do you think of him then?' Morag whispered wickedly.

'He's all right,' Ina conceded. 'Looks a bit conceited though.'

Her mother suppressed a laugh. 'Aye, he's got a fine big head, that's for sure, but our Ayleen's fair taken with him and that's all that matters.'

The slightly off-key rendering of the bridal march on the elderly piano got them all to their feet. The subdued chatter with which the villagers had passed the time ceased abruptly and was replaced by oohs, aahs and sighs as the bride, supported by Rab, made her way to the altar.

Ina had to admit that Ayleen was stunningly beautiful. Seen through the shimmering gauze of her veil her face seemed serene, as though she was certain that her future happiness was assured.

Rab, in a smart new tweed jacket, his kilt swaying with the easy rhythm of his stride and with his beard trimmed for the occasion, was absolutely splendid. There was no mistaking his pride when he handed his daughter to her future husband, though the sound of a muffled sob came from the front pew where Annie was fighting a losing battle with her emotions.

The reception was a lively affair. The entire population of the village, and a good few others besides, squashed their way into Annie and Rab's house and, as it was a mercifully fine day, overflowed into the garden.

Ina was surprised to see her mother dancing, yet again, with her neighbour, Archie Ross, and wondered if there was something going on between them. She dismissed the idea immediately. Not that she had much opportunity to think about it. She was taken up to dance by one after another of the men, all anxious to see

441

that their visitor did not feel left out. She had a wonderful time until a couple of hours into the celebration when she found herself with the slightly tipsy Freddy McPherson who, to her disgust, had danced and flirted with every woman in the room. Her heart went out to Ayleen who surely had a right to her bridegroom's undivided attention on this of all nights.

'So you're Ayleen's niece?' he said, innocuously enough, gripping her tightly and pulling her close to him. 'I suppose that makes me your uncle now.'

'That's right,' she shifted a little, trying to make him loosen his grip on her waist. 'Do you mind!' she muttered.

'Not at all,' he laughed and moved his hand but not before playfully pinching her ribs.

She was tempted to slap his face and walk away but knew she couldn't cause a scene and spoil Ayleen's day. 'What do you think I am?' she hissed, her face turning scarlet with rage.

'A right braw-looking lassie,' he answered easily.

'This is your wedding day! How would Ayleen feel if she knew what you're saying?' Ina sincerely hoped that Freddy McPherson was even drunker than he looked because if this was the way he acted normally it looked as if her young aunt was going to have a very unhappy marriage.

'No need to lose your head. I was only kidding,' he said frowning. 'Forget it.'

They danced on in hostile silence. Ayleen glided past in the arms of the best man and smiled at her husband, adoration pouring from her eyes. Ina looked away and so missed the equally passionate look he gave his bride.

'Ayleen took me to see your house,' she said stiffly,

feeling she had to make an effort before Ayleen realised there was something wrong. 'It's braw.'

'It'll do, for the time being,' he replied, still angry with her for blighting what had been an otherwise splendid day.'I'd have liked that place your mother rents. It's a bonny wee house that, right on the main street. It's not right letting people like your mother, and your grandfather and grandmother, come in and take over houses like that. They've no right.'

She bridled at once. 'My mother was offered the lease on that house because it had stood empty for almost a year. Nobody else wanted it. And my grandparents were born in this village. So was my mother. They've every right to be here.'

'They lost their rights when they moved away, looking for a soft life. If everyone did that there'd soon not be any villages like this left. It's happening already in the highlands. They're full of old folk. It's young folk we need here not folk like your grandfather, coming home to die.'

Her anger at his final words was so intense that she failed to understand the fervent love of the highlands which was behind his impassioned speech. 'How can you talk about him dying?' she screeched, incandescent with rage and past caring who might hear her. She shoved him away and ran into the garden where she sat fighting tears of anger.

'And what was all that about?' Rab lowered himself on to the wall beside her.

'All what?' she asked, tempted to tell him exactly what had happened between her and Freddy.

'Look, Ina, everyone else here may be stotting drunk but I am sober enough to know there was something going on between you and young Freddy. I don't think

443

Ayleen noticed anything amiss but other people certainly did. And here you are with your eyes all red and
your nose running away as if you've been crying. Now
what did the silly sod say to upset you so much?'

'You don't like him either?' she asked hopefully.

He avoided the question adroitly. 'I'm biased. To my
mind the king himself wouldn't be good enough for
Ayleen, or for you, lass.'

'Mam thinks you don't approve of him,' she persisted.

Rab sighed. 'Och it's not that we don't approve of
him. Far from it. But I suppose you'd be better to know
the truth than go on imagining things, so I'll tell you
what happened. But no letting on to anyone else that
I've told you this, mind.'

'You don't have to tell me,' she protested.

'I think I do. I don't want you with a head full of silly
ideas. Now, why do you think your grandma and I came
back up here, lass?'

'To come home.'

'Aye, but we told you there was more to it than that.
Our Ayleen met young Freddy at my brother's funeral.
Fancied herself in love with him then, she did. We
hoped that, back home, in Strathannan, she'd forget
about him, meet someone else. Not that we didn't like
him, mind, it was just that we thought she was too
young to be settling down. But our Ayleen she wasn't
having any of that. She was all set to get married there
and then. And she would have too if we hadn't decided
to move up here so that she and Freddy could go
winching properly. At least that way she had a chance to
get to know him and maybe change her mind. As you
can see she didn't. She still thinks the sun rises and sets
in his arse.'

'Grandpa!' she giggled.

'Still, in the end it's Ayleen's choice and now she's made it I'll give them both all the support they need. That's what parents, and grandparents, are for. As far as I'm concerned he's family now and I'll not hear anyone say a bad word about either of them,' he warned her gently.

She felt suddenly choked by her love for this man and turned her face into his and kissed his bearded cheek.

'That's better.' He put an arm round her and helped her to her feet. 'If you and Freddy had words, just remember it's all an act with him. Folk who don't know him properly think he's just a loud-mouthed show-off. But I suspect it's just a way of covering up shyness. Underneath he's a decent lad and he thinks the world of our Ayleen. Come on, let's go back inside, lass. It's getting cold now and your grandmother'll go her length if I disappear for too long.'

Ina slipped a hand through his arm, thanking God that she hadn't said anything derogatory about Freddy. She knew that her grandfather had taught her a lesson in loyalty and resolved to remember it for the future.

Almost before she knew it Ina was at the end of her holiday and found herself regretting that she had to go home so soon. Although Glendarroch was too isolated and much too quiet to appeal to her as a place to live, she could easily understand why her mother and grandparents were so content to stay there. The sheer beauty of the place had worked its magic on her too and she was already planning a return visit when she helped her mother with the dinner on her last night there.

'I'd like to see this place in real sunshine,' she mused, half to herself. 'Maybe I could come back in the summer?'

'You'll be very welcome at any time, Ina,' Morag smiled. 'I know your grandparents have missed you since they've been up here.' She dried her hands and perched on a kitchen chair, seeing again that uncanny likeness to Katrina Fraser and swallowing the lump of unease it always brought. 'I've missed you too, though you might not believe it.' She softened her words by smiling. 'I'm glad you came, Ina. It upset me to think we couldn't get along.'

'Me too.' Never good at anything which involved exposing too much of her inner self and always finding great difficulty with any form of apology, Ina struggled to make herself go on. 'I don't know why I acted like I did when you came home.'

'I do,' Morag said, with a hint of regret in her voice. 'You were angry with me for leaving you all. You're very loyal to Donny, lass. I can't say I blame you for that and he deserved it. He was a very good father, to all of you. It's a pity I couldn't have been a better mother.'

Ina didn't know if there was anything she could say which was honest but not hurtful. She did the best she could. 'I used to think you didn't like me, you never took any interest in me – in any of us. I guess I was too young to understand. I think I do now.'

'No, you don't. You can't.' Morag saw the hostile expression which snapped across her daughter's face, like a venetian blind being closed. 'I'm not criticising, Ina. But how could you understand it when even I don't know why I acted like I did?' She sighed. 'Let's not go over all the sordid facts again. We both know them well enough. I'll just say I was in the wrong and, perhaps, if I hadn't done what I did . . . Perhaps that would never have happened to Donny, and you and I might have got along better. So long as you know that if I didn't behave like a proper mother it wasn't your fault.'

'I know that now. I just wish I'd realised it sooner.'

'Well, I think we're starting to understand each other at last, don't you?' But even as she said it Morag prayed that Ina would never discover the real reason for the discord in their relationship, the poisonous doubt that had clouded everything since that day, so long ago, when she had discovered that Ina was not her daughter.

'Aye,' Ina smiled warmly at her mother, mercifully oblivious to her inner turmoil. 'I think we are.'

TWENTY-TWO

Ina stared out of the window at the blustery rain. What a waste of a Sunday, she thought glumly. After being penned in the Post Office for five and a half days every week she liked nothing better in her free time than to escape into the fresh air. She loved to walk on the beach with her friends, wander round the harbour or sit in the fields above the village, looking out towards the Lothians. She thought nothing of wrapping up against cold or rain just for the pleasure of being outdoors but this sort of freezing deluge deterred even her. It was almost as if winter had come back again.

She yawned, made sleepy by the huge fire roaring in the grate which was making the room stuffy and overheated. It was so boring! Maureen, who was seeing a lad from Sauchar, further down the coast, had gone to meet him just after lunch, leaving Ina and Maurice to keep one another company. Some hope, she thought, looking at her brother who was sunk into an unattractive postprandial slumber in his fireside chair.

She worried about Maurice sometimes. He led such a lonely life. All his energy went into the bakery. Despite the long hours it demanded of him he refused to hire another baker to help him, insisting they couldn't afford it, determined to put the place on a firmer financial footing than it had been in his father's time. The result was that he ended each day in a haze of exhaustion which lifted only when he counted the takings. It was a far from normal life for a young man. He had no friends of his own age, no friends at all in fact, and, to Ina's certain knowledge, he had never taken a girl out. It was hard to believe that he was only twenty-two years old when he looked and acted just like a middle-aged man.

Ina suspected that poor Maurice was simply weighed down by responsibility – the bakery, the shop, this house to run, the money to sort out and, on top of all that, two young women to keep an eye on. She knew, because he had told them so, that Maurice felt that it was his responsibility to ensure that neither of his sisters came to any harm or had the opportunity to do something they might later regret. In consequence he was something of a martinet, setting unreasonably strict rules for both girls, though Ina knew he was even harder on Maureen than he was on her.

Only last month Maureen had brought her young man, Arthur, home to meet the family, a sure sign that things were getting serious. He seemed to be a friendly, uncomplicated and perfectly respectable lad, and had a steady job in a small boatyard, at Sauchar. Maureen had been sure that not even her brother could find anything to object to in Arthur. But, despite Ina's frequent interventions, the evening had been an unmitigated disaster. Maurice had been overbearing, critical and rude, as if he was doing everything he could think of to put Maureen's suitor off. Mortally offended but polite to the last, Arthur had gone home early. The ensuing argument was the most bitter one Ina had ever heard between Maurice and Maureen. In the end Maurice had forbidden her to see Arthur again and Maureen had fled to her bedroom in tears.

Today's date – a strict secret from Maurice who

thought she had gone to see a girlfriend – was Maureen and Arthur's first one since then and Ina, who had liked the young man, sincerely hoped that Maureen would be able to smooth things over with him.

It was easier for her and Georgie. Although Maurice knew they saw a lot of one another, he hadn't yet realised how far their friendship had progressed. Ina foresaw another huge row when he did. But somehow she didn't think it would come to that. It was as if she had gone off the whole idea of marriage lately. Certainly she hadn't felt the slightest tinge of envy for Ayleen. In fact she had returned home from Glendarroch seeing Georgie in a far more critical light. It seemed to her that he was becoming increasingly bossy, narrow minded and proprietorial, parading her to his friends as if he owned her. And he was so predictable. Boring, she thought, feeling thoroughly disgruntled. But boring seemed to be the only word for today.

She gazed out at the deserted, sodden street and gave herself a mental shake. Sitting here getting more and more depressed wasn't doing anyone any good. Georgie had asked her to go to his house after lunch. She might as well. At least the Camerons would be awake.

She tiptoed past Maurice, and opened the door carefully.

'Where are you going?' he grunted.

She froze at the sound of his voice. 'I thought you were sleeping.'

'So you thought you'd sneak out?' he asked, glaring at her.

'I didn't want to wake you,' she hedged, avoiding a direct lie.

'So where are you were going?' he repeated his question testily.

'To the Camerons. Georgie asked if I wanted to go over there this afternoon.'

'What's wrong with staying here?' he demanded.

'There's nothing to do,' she said in a long-suffering voice.

'Nothing to do!' Maurice bellowed. 'The bakery needs a good clean out. If you're so bored get down there and do some work for a change.'

'I work at the Post Office five and a half days a week and then help Maureen tidy up in the bakery every night so don't accuse me of not working,' she screamed at him, infuriated by the sheer injustice of his remark.

'You listen to me, Ina. I won't have you hanging around the Camerons. You're seeing far too much of Georgie. You'll get yourself a bad name if you carry on like this.'

'Carry on like what?' she demanded.

'Going about with boys. You'll get into trouble if you're not careful.'

'I've been going about with Georgie since I was five years old!'

'Aye, but you're not five years old any more.'

'No! Too bloody true I'm not, so why are you treating me like an infant? You've got no right to stop me seeing my friends.' There were times when she sincerely wished her mother had not gone back to Glendarroch.

'I'll not have language like that in this house!' he yelled furiously. 'And I have got every right. All the time you live under my roof you'll obey my rules.'

'All right! But I'm still going out. I'll go for a walk,' she muttered, darting through the door, grabbing her coat and running down the stairs.

The rain was easing off at last though water still dripped from roofs and puddled in the road. Still seething, she started to cross the road, heading defiantly in the direction of Georgie's house, then hesitated. She had told Maurice she was going for a walk and she didn't want to disobey him deliberately. Anyway, she wasn't really in the mood for Georgie's inane chatter today and the non-stop commotion in which the Camerons lived was more than she could cope with. Instead she retraced her steps and turned down towards the harbour. There was something incredibly soothing about watching the boats bobbing at anchor. An undisturbed hour or so there would do much to restore her temper.

'Ina!'

She was halfway down Harbour Wynd, concentrating on not losing her footing on the slippery setts when she heard someone call her name. She turned, feeling rising irritation to think that the peaceful hour she had planned for herself was about to be ruined. To her surprise a tall lad, the collar of his jacket turned up to meet his cap, waved and clattered down the brae behind her, hanging on to a pedal bike, his tackety boots striking sparks from the flinty cobbles, even in the damp. As he caught up with her she stared, half recognising him. But it couldn't be. Her imagination must be playing tricks on her; after all he had been in her mind often enough recently.

He arrived at her side, breathless but triumphant. 'I knew I'd see you sooner or later,' he laughed, water dripping from his saturated fringe and running down his face. 'You do recognise me, don't you?'

As if she could ever forget that strong-boned face. 'Joe Lennox! What are you doing here?' she gasped, unable to keep a wide grin of pleasure from her face though she would have given anything to be able to maintain a sham of sophisticated indifference.

'Waiting for you,' he answered. 'Where are you going?'

'Just down to the harbour.'

'Mind if I come along?'

She shrugged. 'If you want.'

They walked side by side, not speaking until they reached the quayside where he propped his bicycle against the wall.

'What are you doing in Kilweem?' she asked, chuckling when he took his saturated cap off and shook himself, sending droplets spraying out from his mop of curly, dark hair, just like a wet dog.

'I told you. Waiting for you,' he answered calmly, sticking his cap squarely back on his head. 'I was here last Sunday too, and the one before that, but I never saw you. And I would have come back next week if I hadn't seen you today.'

'You came all that way just to see me! You must be off your head,' she scoffed, not at all sure he wasn't teasing her. 'And if you were here before, how come I never saw you?'

'Because I sat in the little sheltered bit under that tower thing. I could see the bakery door from there. But you never so much as put a foot outside all day,' he complained.

'The tollbooth! But if you wanted to see me why didn't you just knock at the door?'

'Huh! I'm sure that brother of yours would have been delighted to see me again. How's his nose by the way?' He grinned, showing attractive white teeth. Ina's stomach knotted.

'It's okay and I suppose you've got a point.' Now that she was getting over the initial shock of seeing him here she was increasingly aware of the nearness of him. She returned his gaze frankly, not at all embarrassed to feel him watching her too. His eyes seemed to draw her. They were an unusual chestnut brown, and seemed luminous, almost as if there was a light flickering behind them. They were his best feature, she decided. His skin was so pale that, even though it was obvious he was freshly shaved, a dark shadow persevered round his chin and his nose was spoiled by a quirky bend, as if it had been broken at some time. If it hadn't been for the fact that she already knew his body was strong and well muscled, she would have thought, from looking at his face, that he was too thin. Every plane of his face was sharp and defined, his cheekbones high and prominent, the angle of his jaw square, his brow wide but softened by a wild thatch of springy, dark brown curls.

But there was something more to Joe Lennox than his striking appearance. He gave the impression of physical strength, of a strong will and, the thing she liked best, good humour. And he had a distinct air of confidence about him too, not the cocky, loud-mouthed self-assurance some of the local boys assumed, but something more basic, more natural.

'I must look a right mess,' he laughed, lifting his cap again and running his fingers through damp curling hair. 'I all but drowned getting here.'

'Did you come all the way on that thing?' she looked doubtfully at the heavy old bicycle.

'Aye. I use it all the time.'

'It must have taken ages.'

'I've got all day,' he shrugged it off. 'Anyway, it was worth it.'

She blushed, something she hardly ever did these days, and found herself lost for words, an even rarer occurrence.

The rain started to drizzle down again. Joe grimaced at the sky. 'Is there somewhere we can go to get out of this?'

She thought about it. 'Not really. I'm not sitting in the tollbooth – it smells. I suppose we could go over there.' She nodded towards the gutting shed. It was nothing more than a roof, supported by metal pillars at its four corners, but it would offer some shelter.

'Come on. I'll race you.' He was off, clattering over the cobbles. Ina followed, splashing through the puddles so that her legs were soaked. 'Over here,' he called, sinking to the flagged floor and resting his back against a pile of empty crates.

'You'll never get the smell of fish off your jacket,' she warned him, settling beside him, pleased to realise they were sheltered here, protected by the piled crates, from both the wind and the prying eyes of the folk who lived in the quayside houses.

They stayed there for an hour, just talking, while the rain battered off the corrugated roof and splattered in against the side of the crates. Every so often a gust of wind caught at a loose crate, tumbling it noisily across the cobbles. Snug and protected in their wooden nest, Joe and Ina were oblivious to the weather. Unnoticed by them the rain went off, the sun made a reluctant, watery appearance and the paths began to dry. It was the people, starting to venture down to the harbour for a breath of sea air, who finally roused Ina.

'I'd better go,' she said, recognising Hetty McArdle standing at the top of her forestair. Reluctantly she got to her feet and brushed her skirt off.

'Me too,' Joe agreed. 'It's a long ride home and Mam'll kill me if I'm late for supper.'

He took her hand, linking fingers quite naturally, and

they walked up the wynd together, laughing as he tried to steer his bicycle over the bumpy setts with his one free hand. When they got to Marketgate she wondered if he would kiss her, knew she couldn't let him, not on such a very public corner.

'See you next week then?' he asked, letting go of her hand and hopping on to the saddle.

'If you like,' she said casually, ignoring the twist of exhilaration that tightened her stomach.

'At the harbour? About midday?'

'I might not get away till nearer one o'clock.'

'I'll wait,' he told her firmly, pushing himself off and turning to give her a very wobbly wave.

She watched him pedal rapidly along the road. It was strange, but she felt as if she had known Joe Lennox for ages. How easy he had been to talk to. She could still feel the warmth in her hand where he had held it. She looked, almost expecting to see a mark there but her skin was pale and clear. She took a huge breath and let it out slowly, trying to ease the tightness in her chest. It was excitement, she knew that. All the time she had sat by him she had been aware of the heat under her skin, the feeling of hollowness in her stomach. She had longed for him to kiss her, but had dreaded it, knowing already that this would be very different from anything she and Georgie ever did. She smiled dreamily, content to know that she would see him again, that he would kiss her, in time.

'Thought you were coming over to my place?' The slightly aggrieved voice made her jump and jerked her unpleasantly out of her reverie. For the second time that day she blushed, this time with guilt.

'Maurice doesn't want me to see so much of you,' she said, her voice dismissive.

'That brother of yours doesn't own you.' It wasn't the first time Georgie had said that. 'I waited in all afternoon for you.'

Ina's eyes had slid back to the disappearing figure on the bike.

Georgie frowned and followed her gaze. 'I thought I saw you talking to someone just now! Who was that?' he demanded.

'No one you know,' she answered dreamily.

'No one I know?' he spluttered, consumed by sudden jealousy. 'Who was it then? Eh?'

She glared at him, her eyes flashing with anger. 'You're getting as bad as Maurice. What's it got to do with you who I talk to?'

'Everything! You're my lassie.' He was white lipped with anger and looked just like his father, Ina thought contemptuously.

'Don't you order me around, George Cameron,' she hissed, taking an intimidating step closer to him so that her face was only inches from his.

Faced with such naked fury, Georgie backed down. 'I wasn't . . .'

'Good!' With that she stomped away, back to the bakery.

'See you the morn,' he called after her. She really was spectacular when she was angry, he thought, with a touch of admiration. They'd make a good team once they were married, so long as she learned who was the boss.

In the neighbouring village of Sauchar, Maureen and her sweetheart, Arthur, sat side by side on his parents' sofa, taking great care to ensure that no part of them was in contact, and waited impatiently for the rain to go off. After an hour of stilted conversation and unbearable silences they finally escaped to walk along the sea front. Arthur's mother and father had made Maureen effusively welcome at their modest, overly neat house on the outskirts of the little village, but it was a welcome which she found uncomfortable by comparison to the brusque, ill-mannered treatment Arthur had received at her own home. But it was a relief to know that he didn't hold her responsible for that unpleasant afternoon.

'Best to forget it, Mo,' Arthur said when she attempted to apologise again. 'Your Maurice made me bloody angry, I'll not deny that, but he'll not be able to speak to me like that once we're married.'

Maureen resisted the impulse to let out a screech of pure excitement. Arthur had spoken of marriage before but she had been frightened that he might have changed his mind.

Arthur stopped walking and turned to look out over the choppy water. 'When'll it be then?' he asked, grinning broadly.

'When will what be, Arthur McIntyre?' she asked, also turning to look at the sea, feigning innocence, determined to have a proper proposal from him.

'When'll we get wed?' he elaborated for her.

'Get wed?' she teased. 'What makes you think we're getting wed? You've never asked me to marry you.'

'We've talked about it often enough,' he retorted sharply, his pride stung. He hadn't expected her to make a game of it. 'I can't see any point in waiting. It's not as if we need to look for somewhere to live. There's a spare room at our place and me Dad says we can have that so long as you give Mam a hand about the house.'

'Why do we have to live with your parents?' Maureen asked, her pleasure dissolving as she realised he had decided on all this, had talked it over with his parents, without even bothering to consult her. As if he took her consent for granted. 'There's much more room at the bakery and it'll be easier for me if we live there. You know I have to start work early in the mornings.'

'But you'll not be working once we're married,' Arthur said.

Maureen stiffened. 'Yes I will,' she insisted quietly.

'Don't be stupid!' Arthur laughed to disguise his straining temper. 'I earn a fair wage. There's no reason for you to work. Anyway, it wouldn't be right,' he dismissed her needs carelessly and turned back to staring out over the foaming water.

'You don't understand. Maurice couldn't manage without me.' Like Ina she understood that Maurice worked too hard. He depended on her, just as she relied on him, and she would never consider letting him down. Not even for Arthur.

'Bloody Maurice!' he exploded. 'You serve in the shop! Anyone could do that. Let him hire a woman from the village or maybe that lanky sister of yours could do it.'

'I do not just work in the shop!' she bridled instantly. 'The bakery is half mine. My father left it to Maurice and me so that we would always have a home and a job. I can't leave. I do all the book-keeping, the ordering, I run the tea shop, I pay the bills and I even help in the bakery. Anyway,' she ended, 'I enjoy it.' And that, she realised, was the crux of the matter. She did love the bakery, the responsibility it gave her, the feeling of working together for something worthwhile. And she really was very fond of Maurice, even if he was a little overprotective at times.

'No!' Arthur rounded on her furiously now. 'My wife

459

is not going to work in some bloody bakery. Your place will be at home, raising the weans and looking after my parents as they get older. We'll sell your share of the bakery and do something worthwhile with the money. I might buy into the boat yard or maybe even set up on my own.' His father reckoned there was more security in putting the money into the boat yard which had a full order book and a good name already established. Arthur preferred to imagine himself setting up in competition, showing his old boss a thing or two, stealing his customers from him, sitting in an office all day and never again slicing his hand with the chisel or ramming splinters under his nails. That would be the life all right.

'Sell my share of the bakery?' Maureen's astonished voice broke into his daydreams. 'Sell it? I'll never do that.'

'You will if you wed me,' he assured her. 'Just think of it, Maureen. You'd be married to a man who was his own boss. You'd be somebody . . .'

'I'm my own boss already,' she reminded him coldly.

'Of a shop,' he sneered. 'It's not the same.'

Maureen turned away abruptly, not liking what she saw in his face. Is that what marriage to Arthur would mean? Had Maurice been right about him after all? Could she really abandon her brother to struggle on alone and then ruin him by selling her share of the business as soon as she got the chance? Did she love Arthur enough to turn herself into the housebound drudge he obviously expected her to become?

'No,' she said, turning back to face him, 'I can't.'

'Can't what?' he asked.

'I can't marry you.'

Arthur flushed then stared at her for a long time. Finally he said, 'I never asked you to marry me, did I?'

and marched off along the road to his own home, leaving her standing alone, crying her tears into the wind.

Morag walked briskly up the steep driveway which led from the village to Glendarroch House where she now worked five mornings a week, revelling in the beauty of a highland springtime. The house was inhabited by an elderly widow who spent most of her time in her chair at the window, gazing out over the loch. Once her routine chores were finished Morag was required to do nothing more taxing than keep the old lady company for an hour or two, something which was a very definite pleasure.

Age had crippled Mrs Wishart's limbs but her mind was as sharp and clear as it had ever been and she missed very little. She had teased Morag wickedly when she sensed – and Morag still didn't know how – that she was in love. Morag, afflicted by the type of blushing she had last suffered as a teenager, was obliged to admit the truth and then to add regular updates as her affair progressed. Far from resenting the old lady's curiosity, Morag was glad of someone to confide in, especially since any confidences were scrupulously respected and never found their way on to the village grapevine where her mother might get to hear them. Not that she had any particular secrets from Annie who was well aware of the situation between her daughter and Archie Ross. Morag's problem was that from the moment Annie realised what was going on, she had been eagerly urging Morag on towards marriage, seeming not to understand what a crucial step this would be for Morag, and denying her daughter the unbiased, sympathetic ear she so needed when she considered her future. It was a role Mrs Wishart filled perfectly. Only that morning Morag had told

461

her employer that she had decided to accept Archie's proposal and it was the elderly lady who had advised her to tell Ina of her plans before allowing the romance to become common knowledge.

By the time Morag got back to her own small house her mind was already planning the sewing and repairs with which she supplemented her income. She was reminded of Mrs Wishart's advice when she discovered a letter from Ina waiting for her. These letters were regular and read with much pleasure but somehow Ina hadn't been able to assign her innermost feelings to paper and to have discussed Maureen's heartbreak would have felt like a betrayal. Instead she filled them with nothing more personal than the everyday gossip of Kilweem so Morag had no idea of the emotional torments also embroiling her daughter and stepdaughter. Smiling, Morag read through the two pages of Ina's latest epistle and then placed it carefully in the bottom drawer of the kitchen dresser, along with all her other precious papers, then went to stand at her window, looking out over the loch, wondering how best to tell Ina that she and Archie had decided to get married.

High on the hillsides Morag could see sheep as nothing more than tiny dots. Now that the weather was milder the beasts, many with lambs at their sides, had been returned to the higher slopes, giving the grass on the low ground time to grow lush and green in preparation for next winter. Somewhere up there, among the clefts and gullies, the high glens and lochans, there would be a shepherd and his dog, revelling in their renewed freedom. She smiled, remembering her own early childhood with a wistful fondness, then her face broke into a broad beam when Archie himself waved as he came up her front path.

'Come along in, Archie,' she called.

'I've brought you some wood for your fire,' he told her cheerfully. 'I'll stack it for you this evening.'

'Thanks Archie,' she said, knowing that he would no more think of kissing her at this time of the day than he would consider running naked through the village, though his seeming reticence was no indication, as she knew to her own pleasure, of his behaviour once the curtains were drawn.

She still didn't know how she had come to love Archie, her kind-hearted next-door neighbour who had lost his own wife almost three years ago. Certainly there had been no sudden explosion of feeling and, for her, the attraction hadn't been a physical one, at least not to start with. Archie was a hard-working forester, more concerned with comfort than his appearance. A small man, not much above five foot six in height, his spreading waistline was not flattered by the tired tweed jacket and baggy moleskin trousers which were his normal attire. His balding head was protected by a shapeless cap and his face, toughened by constant exposure to the weather, was rosy cheeked and deeply lined, making him look older than his forty-five years. Archie was a slow-spoken and often silent man who nevertheless had a sharp mind and a dry sense of humour. But he was also a man who derived great satisfaction from his everyday life, relishing his good fortune to have been born a Scot and to live in such a beautiful area. His contentment was obvious. Morag found him an incredibly peaceful companion.

Open-hearted and friendly, Archie had been motivated by nothing more than honest neighbourliness when he first approached Morag, anxious to do what he could to help her settle in to her new home. At first they had both been unaware of the steady growth of affection as they got into the habit of stopping for a chat in the street, then of sharing a pot of tea and, later, their evening meal. She supposed they had drifted into a relationship and had both been surprised to find themselves in love. But the slow way their friendship had matured in no way lessened what they felt for one another. If anything, they valued their relationship more than if it had been something they had openly sought.

Archie only ever spoke of his first wife, Isa, who had died just over three years ago, with deep affection. He was honest too in admitting that he missed the comforts and companionship of marriage. But Morag understood that, important though these things were to Archie, he had proposed marriage out of genuine love for her, love which had survived the retelling of her own past. On the evening he had asked her to marry him he had admitted that he had been resigned to spending the rest of his life alone and was almost frightened by his good fortune in finding love for the second time. Morag, who had believed she could never love anyone as she had loved Gray McArdle, was astonished to realise that what she felt for solid, dependable Archie was deeper, more demanding and infinitely more rewarding than anything she had experienced before. She knew that Archie loved her for herself, that she was in no way a replacement for Isa Ross and never felt her own happiness to be threatened by the spectre of a dead woman. She never knew a moment of doubt about Archie and when he proposed she accepted instantly, knowing that this marriage would bring her the happiness which had so far eluded her.

Seeing him now she felt the familiar, warm glow of contentment which made every day such a pleasure to live. She brewed Archie a cup of tea so thick that it required salt to scour the cups clean afterwards and sat in the warm sitting room with him while he drank it, more than happy with the silent companionship in which so much of their time was spent.

When he went back to work, in the forest behind the village, Morag, rather reluctantly, abandoned her sewing and settled herself at her table with pen and paper, ready to write what she knew would be a very difficult letter.

Despite the fact that Ina had met Archie, and had seemed to like him, she was so unpredictable that Morag half expected her news to provoke another bitter outburst. It was entirely possible that Ina would resent her contemplating marriage so soon after Donny's death.

Morag sighed and looked out at the breathtaking view across the shimmering loch and bracken-covered hillsides which never failed to comfort her. Her relationship with her daughter, though appearing to be better than it had been since Ina's infancy, was nevertheless a fragile thing, hampered by the sheer distance between them and the nagging secret of her birth. Morag was unhappily aware that she had let Ina down too often in the past, that the girl had suffered too much, had felt betrayed and abandoned on too many occasions. To simply write and announce that she was about to have a new stepfather was to risk destroying the fragile trust which was starting to build between them. She would have to introduce Archie's name into her letters gradually, resist announcing their plans until such time as Ina would believe she had been included in her mother's confidence, right from the beginning. That way she wouldn't feel hurt and forgotten.

Morag scribbled industriously for half an hour then read the pages through, pleased that she had struck the right note by mentioning Archie's name only once along with a gentle hint that she found him attractive which Ina was sure to pick up.

She sighed and sealed the envelope, looking again across the loch. How difficult this all was. She felt a slight resentment that she and Archie would have to delay telling everyone about their plans because of the risk of upsetting Ina. Would things have been this difficult, she wondered, if she had been able to raise the son she had given birth to? Her chest tightened and the blood seemed to pound in her ears. She stood up, busied herself with small household tasks, deliberately trying to pull her mind away from the niggle of worry which found itself into her mind with distressing frequency these days. But it persisted. What sort of person had Angus become, she asked herself? Would she have made a better job of motherhood if she had been allowed to raise her own child? She felt swamped by sudden emotion. What a mess she'd made of her life. But now she was being offered a second chance. Smiling now she looked back to the mountains as the image of Archie's gentle face filled her mind. Maybe it was all for the best. The very events which had caused her unhappiness were the ones which had brought her here. And here, with Archie, she would finally find what she had been searching for all her life. Nothing else mattered. Little did she suspect that within an hour her equanimity would be shattered.

Morag came back from posting her letter to Ina and settled herself contentedly at her sewing.

'Come away in,' she called out cheerily in response to the light tap on her front door.

Nothing happened and she looked up from her sewing, startled by the unexpected silence. The villagers, out

466

of respect for one another's privacy, always knocked but, when invited to enter, let themselves in with the ease of long habit. Hastily bundling her sewing on to the table she went to open the door herself, brushing stray strands of thread from her skirt as she went.

Unsuspecting, she threw the door wide, a welcoming smile on her face. There, on her doorstep, stood her father, just as she remembered him from thirty years ago. For a moment her head swam and she clutched desperately at the door frame. She felt his hand on her arm.

'Are you all right?' he asked, his voice soft, deep and educated.

'Yes . . . yes,' she stammered, drawing a deep breath and steeling herself to look at him again, believing her senses had been playing tricks with her mind. 'I'm sorry . . . you reminded me of someone . . .' She looked him full in the face and found herself staring into her own eyes.

'So you do recognise me?' There was such a note of raw hope in his voice that her head began to swim again.

'Oh sweet Lord,' she breathed, her heart pounding painfully as she fought to control her reeling head.

The young man hesitated. He had come here prepared for long explanations, for hostility and possible rejection. Not for one moment had he expected this instant recognition. And it was plain that she did know who he was. Obvious too that it had been a tremendous shock to her. Her face was the colour of putty and she was barely managing to stand upright.

'I'm sorry,' he offered. 'I didn't mean to upset you.'

Still she stared at him, seeming frozen with shock. Slowly she shook her head, her eyes wide and glassy, the colour of the sea in the little coastal bays. His own

467

emotions raw and sensitive, he mistook her expression for anger.

'I'd better go,' he said hastily, turning in confusion and hurrying to the gate.

She gathered her wits just in time. 'NO! Please . . . come back,' she begged, her voice cracking.

Slowly he turned. 'I'll come back later,' he offered.

Morag stepped back inside her home. 'Come in,' she said.

He followed her inside and closed the door. Morag collapsed into a chair, her eyes closed. Hastily he looked about him. In the recessed niche beside the fireplace he found a bottle of whisky and a glass and poured a small measure for her.

'Here, drink this.'

She took the glass with a shaking hand and swallowed the liquor in one gulp, gasping as it burned her throat. 'Thank you,' she smiled at last.

'You do know who I am, don't you?' he asked again, sitting opposite her.

Still she couldn't commit herself to words.

He slipped a hand inside his jacket and withdrew a yellowing paper and offered it to her.

Morag read the paper she and Katrina had signed all those years ago. 'Angus?'

He nodded. 'I know I should have written to you first,' he said, 'but I was afraid you wouldn't want to see me.'

'Wouldn't want to see you?' She gave a strangled, sobbing laugh. 'Oh Lord . . . If only you knew how often I think about you . . . How did you find me?'

'Through Mrs McManus, she still lives in a cottage in Pitochrie. She told me Mr Bannerman had married your mother. His address was in the estate records. I went to

468

see him first but there was no answer at his door so I went to ask at the Post Office, to see when he would be home. The woman there told me to ask you, said you were his stepdaughter . . . I knew it had to be you. It's taken me three months to find you,' he ended softly.

'Why?' She had to know. 'Why have you come here?' Surely he must hate her for what she had done.

He shrugged. 'I thought I should meet my mother.'

'When did you find out?' she asked. 'When did you realise Katrina wasn't your real mother?'

'When she died. Six months ago. I was going through her things and found this. It was a terrible shock.' She could see the pain, still shadowing his eyes when he spoke about it. He lowered his head and rubbed at his eyes. 'I had to see you. I have to know what happened. Why did you give me away?'

Morag had recovered some of her composure now though her voice was still unsteady when she spoke. 'Didn't Mrs McManus tell you?' she asked.

'No . . .' He looked puzzled.

'She was there. She knows more about what went on that night than I do,' Morag admitted slowly. 'Pour yourself a drink, Angus, and I'll tell you exactly what happened.'

When she had finished they sat in silence, both drained by the emotion of their traumatic meeting. Finally she touched his hand lightly with hers.

'Thank you for coming here, Angus. It can't have been easy for you.'

'I had to know,' he said simply.

'I've often thought about you,' she told him. 'It's a terrible thing to know that your child is beyond your reach. You do understand why I couldn't try to take you away from Katrina don't you? It would have been cruel, even if I had succeeded in convincing the courts that you were mine.'

'Yes,' he said at last. 'I think I do understand. And I loved my mother very much,' he added. 'I miss her.'

'I'm sorry. I didn't know she had died.'

'It was an awful shock, to discover I'm not really who I thought I was.'

'I'm sorry,' she said again, feeling inadequate.

Angus stood up and straightened his jacket. 'I'd better be going.'

'Oh! Can't you stay?' There was so much they had to say to one another.

'I need to think,' he admitted, smiling at her now. 'I expect you do too.'

She nodded, not trusting her voice, devastated to be losing him again so soon.

'Would it be all right if I came back tomorrow?' he asked.

'Yes! Yes.' Relief flooded through her.

'Stay there, I'll see myself out,' he said as she tried to make her trembling legs bear her weight. And he was gone.

Morag sat back in her chair, her mind spinning. Tears were still streaming down her face when Archie came in, an hour later.

TWENTY-THREE

I na skimmed through her mother's letter then tossed it carelessly on to her dressing table and went back to the important business of getting ready to meet Joe.

It was a treat to be able to meet him on a Saturday. His shift pattern often left him little time to make the long journey up the coast and, so far, they had done all their courting on Sundays. Today though she was going to meet him halfway, in a small coastal town with a picture house. They could spend most of the afternoon together and then watch the early evening showing before catching their respective buses home. Ina applied a fresh coat of lipstick and peered at her own reflection, pursing her lips. The colour was startling, a rich ruby red, and she saw instantly that it did absolutely nothing for her pale complexion. She rubbed it off hastily, dismayed to see the dark stain it left behind. If Maurice, who had only agreed to excuse her from working in the bakery because he thought she was going to spend the day with girlfriends, saw that he wouldn't let her go out at all. She grimaced and rubbed at her lips again. Much as Maurice irritated her with his strict rules she understood that they were only his way of trying to protect her and she hated lying to him. But what alternative did she have? He even made difficulties about her seeing Georgie. If she admitted she was going out with the lad who had given him a bloody nose he was likely to pack her off to her mother, and that was the last thing she wanted. Adding a light dab of powder to disguise the redness which stubbornly coloured her lips she threw her coat round her shoulders and crept downstairs. Luck was not with her. Maurice chose that moment to come up from the bakery for his lunch and they met on the stairs. He glared at her for what seemed like an eternity.

'Nine-thirty. Not a minute later,' he growled eventually.

'Nine-thirty!' Unwisely she chose to argue with him. 'The last bus doesn't leave until then.'

'Then you'll have to catch the earlier one.' He was uncompromising.

'That's not fair.'

'The picture finishes at a quarter to eight – I've checked. That gives you more than enough time to get the earlier bus. I'll not have you hanging around the town.'

Ina opened her mouth to argue more but closed it again, warned by her brother's angry face. 'I'll have to go or I'll be late,' she muttered, brushing past him.

'Nine-thirty,' he bawled after her. 'And not one minute later.'

Ina slammed the door and hurried along the side wynd into Marketgate. She arrived at the bus stop by the tollbooth just as the bus rattled in. By the time she found herself a seat she was smiling to herself again. Even Maurice couldn't stop her from enjoying today.

On the other side of the broad street, Georgie Cameron stood in a doorway and watched the bus pull out with a scowl on his face. Ina hadn't said anything to him about going out today. As soon as the bus disappeared round the corner he slipped into the bakery.

'Where's Ina off to?' he asked Maureen as he paid for the pie he had no appetite for.

'Ina? Och, she's away to see a filmshow with Dot and Eileen. Did she not tell you?' Maureen looked at Georgie in surprise.

'Och, aye! Right enough, I forgot but I mind of her telling me now you come to mention it,' he lied, unwilling to admit that he didn't know what his own girlfriend was up to. But as he walked slowly back to his own house his expression was black.

Georgie Cameron was a long way from Ina's mind as she and Joe sat enjoying the silent film in the back row of the picture house, holding hands in the dark.

'I've to be on the eight-thirty bus,' she admitted as they emerged into the warm evening air an hour later.

Joe groaned. 'Bloody hell!'

'I'm sorry . . .'

'Och, I know fine it's not your fault. Come on, we'll walk through the park to the bus stance.' He wrapped an arm firmly round her shoulders and led her across the road.

They both knew what they were looking for. Some secluded spot, far away from curious eyes, where they could have a precious half hour of privacy before they had to part. They found the ideal place, a grassy circle, sheltered by bushes in the farthest corner of the park. Joe spread his jacket on the ground and pulled her down on to it beside him.

Ina's heart was already beating fast, her whole body roused by two hours of romantic film with Joe sitting so close that their thighs had been touching. It was as if every nerve in her body had been stripped bare. She met his mouth greedily, accepting his warm, sharp tasting-tongue eagerly, entwining it with her own, drawing it more deeply into her as if she could never get enough of him. He pulled her to him, pressing their bodies together. Both were oblivious to the possibility of someone discovering them there, each only aware of the other. Through the layers of their clothing she could feel him hard against her belly. Flame seared through the tops of her legs and fused in the place that throbbed and writhed with longing.

Breathing hard he reached for the softness of her small breasts, slipping a hand between the buttons of her blouse and under her bodice until he found her nipples, already hard and stinging. Tenderly he lowered his face and rolled his tongue round its pink ripeness. She gasped, unprepared for the tingling sharpness of his teeth as he teased her, the unbearable sensitivity that seemed to meet and match the pulsing, the yearning between her legs. As if he sensed her need he brought his other hand up, under her skirt, and touched her there, through her underwear. She tensed, stiffened, clawed desperately at the back of his neck, tangling her long fingers in the springy hair there and finally buried her face in his shoulder as her body surged to spasms of terrifying intensity. Joe held her to him, groaning softly as his own body ached for the ease he could not give it, then stroked her face with infinite tenderness as she gradually stilled.

Still shaking with shock she gradually opened her eyes to find him watching her. 'Oh God,' she murmured, awed by the violence of her own body.

'I love you, Ina Archibold,' he whispered, kissing her gently, 'I love you.'

'And I love you,' she told him, her heart still jerking inside her, her blood singing.

They sat cuddled together until the last possible minute then had to run for the bus.

'Tomorrow,' he called after her as the bus pulled away. 'I'll meet you tomorrow.'

She screwed herself round in her seat and waved, still hardly daring to believe that this wonderful man could really be in love with her.

The bus was jolting over Kilweem's setted streets before she knew it, the journey lost in an afterglow of pleasure. When she got off, at the tollbooth, her eyes were sparkling, her happiness unmistakable.

'Where have you been?'

Ina heard Georgie's aggrieved voice before she saw his face. The smile faded from her face and her mouth set in a thin, determined line. She had known, for at least three weeks now, that she had to tell Georgie about Joe. But everyone in the village thought of her and Georgie as a couple and news of their break-up — and the reason for it — was bound to cause gossip which could very well get back to Maurice, so, with a very guilty conscience, she had put it off, avoiding Georgie as much as possible.

Meeting Joe had merely confirmed what she had already started to suspect, that she didn't love Georgie. Nevertheless she was still fond of him and dreaded the hurt and anger she knew she was going to inflict on him. Even now she didn't know the best way to tell him.

'To see a filmshow,' she said, stalling for time.

'Don't give me that!' He was scornful and already irate. 'You told your Maureen that you were with Dot and Eileen but they went up to St Andrews and I know you didn't go with them. So who were you with?'

She felt her temper flare but swallowed the furious retort that she was tempted to roar at him. 'I've been meaning to talk to you,' she started.

'You've been out with another lad, haven't you?' he yelled.

She nodded. 'Aye.'

For a moment he stared at her, almost as if he couldn't really believe it. Then, 'But you're my lassie,' he said dully.

'I'm sorry,' she repeated, not knowing what else she could say to him.

'Who is it? What's his name?' he demanded. 'I'll bloody kill him.'

'It's no one from round here,' she answered him quietly.

'Tell me who he is, Ina.'

'No, Georgie. It's none of your business.'

'None of my business!' he spluttered. 'Some bastard goes off with my lassie and you tell me it's none of my business!'

'I'm not your lassie any more, Georgie.'

'Yes you bloody well are! You've always been my lassie. Everyone knows you're my lassie.'

Ina tried to push past him. 'There's no point in saying anything more, Georgie.'

He grabbed her, shoved her back against the tollbooth wall and for a moment she thought he was going to hit her but he just held her there, shaking with fury.

'Let go of me!' she hissed.

He stared at her, breathing hard, then abruptly dropped his arm and stepped back a pace. 'You're my lassie, Ina Archibold,' he repeated, but with a catch in his voice this time. 'We're going to get wed.'

Ina sighed. 'No,' she told him gently. 'No we're not.'

'Aye we are. Don't be daft. It doesn't matter if you've been out with someone else. So long as you don't see him again. I'll take you somewhere braw the morn. We could go to St Andrews if you like.' He was almost pleading with her now.

'No, Georgie!' She glanced over his shoulder towards the bakery, knowing Maurice would have heard the bus and be wondering where she was.

He stepped back as if she had slapped him. 'It's that bloody miner, isn't it?' It had come to him suddenly as she looked past him, just as she had on another day, staring after a disappearing figure on a bike. 'A filthy, bloody miner!' There was hatred in his voice now. 'Scum! That's what they are. Dirty, filthy scum . . .' He staggered, the words bitten off in his mouth as her hand slammed into his cheek. Before he had time to react she shoved past him and ran towards the bakery.

She was shaking so much she could barely get her key in the lock. She managed it at last and ran up the stairs. Maurice was waiting for her outside the sitting-room door.

'You told me you were going to a see film with Dot and Eileen,' he said, barring her way. 'But I've just seen you at the tollbooth with that Georgie Cameron. You've been with him again, haven't you? I've already told you you're not to see him anymore.'

'I wasn't with Georgie Cameron,' she snapped back at him, still shaking with anger.

'I saw you with my own eyes!' he bellowed.

'You saw me telling him I couldn't see him any more.'

'You got off the bus with him.'

'I did not! He was waiting for me.'

'Don't lie to me, Ina.'

'She's not lying.' Maureen, drawn by the sound of argument, spoke up for her sister. 'Georgie was in the bakery this afternoon, asking where Ina was.'

Ina shot her a look of gratitude. 'Can I go to my room now please?' she asked coldly.

Defeated, Maurice stood aside and let her past and

moved again to allow Maureen to follow her. 'Just so long as you're telling the truth,' he couldn't resist bawling at her as her door crashed shut.

Maureen followed Ina up the stairs only to find the bedroom door slammed in her face. 'Ina.' She rapped on it impatiently. 'Let me in.'

Ina opened the door and allowed Maureen inside. Already her anger was fading and the happiness was welling inside her again. She longed to share her secret with someone.

'Thanks for sticking up for me,' she smiled.

Maureen shrugged. 'Well, it wasn't a lie exactly. Georgie did come in looking for you, but I know you weren't with Dot and Eileen. I saw them an hour ago.'

Ina grimaced. 'So long as Maurice doesn't know.'

'I don't think he saw them.'

'Thank goodness for that.'

'So, where were you?' Maureen probed.

'Promise you won't tell Maurice?'

Maureen shrugged. 'All right.'

'Well,' Ina sat on her bed and arranged her long limbs comfortably, 'do you remember the lads who were here on a day trip from Craigie, the ones I gave the leftovers to?'

'They were miners weren't they?' Maureen asked incredulously. 'It's not one of them?'

'Aye.' Ina answered proudly. 'His name's Joe. Joe Lennox.'

'The one that hit Maurice?'

Ina laughed. 'Aye. But he asked for it.'

'You're walking out with the lad who thumped Maurice?' Maureen stared at her sister in horror but Ina couldn't see past her own memories of the day.

'He says he loves me,' she confided happily. When

478

Maureen failed to make the expected reply she brought her eyes back into focus and frowned. 'Did you hear what I said?'

'I hope not! How could you, Ina? A miner would be bad enough . . . but that ruffian who attacked Maurice!'

'He didn't attack, Maurice. It wasn't like that,' Ina rounded on her sister. 'It was Maurice's fault. You should have heard the things he said.'

'Whatever he said he didn't deserve to be punched for it. That's what happens when all these rough folk come to the village for a day out, there's always trouble at the Lobster with folk like that.'

'Joe's not rough! He's just a working lad, that's all.'

'A miner!'

'What's wrong with being a miner?' Ina challenged, her eyes glinting dangerously.

'What's right with it? Have you seen how they live?'

'Have you?'

'I've heard about them. Filthy they are, they live in hovels. They're the dirtiest villages in the whole of Strathannan. Ask Duggie McArdle, his wife's brother went to be a miner. They've not even got running water.'

'You don't know what you're blethering about. Go away, Maureen. Leave me alone.'

'With pleasure.' Maureen stomped out of the room leaving Ina to fling herself bad-temperedly on her bed. It wasn't fair, she thought bitterly. What right had Maureen to judge someone she hadn't even met? Like everyone else, she had heard tales about the miners but she knew Joe wasn't like that. And her lovely day had been ruined.

The one good thing about Maurice was his predictability.

After dinner on Sunday he settled into his favourite chair and fell asleep, just as Ina had known he would. As soon as he was snoring gently she slipped upstairs to get ready to meet Joe.

Maureen waylaid her by the back door. 'I suppose you're sneaking off to meet your mining bully boy?' she asked nastily.

'At least I've got a boyfriend. And you're nothing more than a jealous wee lassie,' Ina retorted with equal venom, letting herself out and hurrying off towards the harbour where she knew Joe would already be waiting for her. As soon as she had turned into Harbour Wynd, Georgie Cameron and Al McArdle emerged from behind the tollbooth and followed her.

Joe was there, sitting on the edge of the harbour wall with his legs dangling over the water, enjoying the sunshine, his old bike abandoned on the ground behind him. When he saw Ina he grinned and scrambled to his feet then greeted her with an exuberant kiss. She laughed and linked her arm through his.

'Don't you get fed up cycling up here every Sunday?' Ina asked him, half scared that he might decide she was too much trouble.

'If you could see Craigie you'd know why I like to come up here,' he said, reminding her of what Maureen had had to say about mining villages.

'And I thought it was me you came to see, Joe Lennox,' she retorted.

'Och no, hen. Whatever gave you that idea?' he teased. 'Come on, let's away to the beach. It'll be braw there on a day like this.'

One hand steering his bike, the other slung carelessly round her shoulders he walked with her back up to the village and down towards the beach, careful to keep to the back wynds where there was less chance of meeting someone she knew.

'Are you ashamed of being seen with me?' he asked suddenly as they strolled down the Butts.

'No! Of course I'm not.' In fact she was proud to be seen with this good-looking young man.

'Then why are we skulking round the back alleyways?' he asked reasonably.

'Och,' she sighed. 'It's Maurice. He's so strict. He doesn't think I should be going out with lads at all, never mind one who broke his nose for him.'

'Aye, but he'll have to be told sooner or later, Ina. That's if you're serious about me, that is.' He propped his bike up against the side of the last house and set off across the sand, his hand gripping hers. 'It's not right to have to tell lies about me. And what happens when I want to take you home to meet my ma and pa? You'll have to tell him before then.'

'I will,' she promised. 'I'll just have to catch him in a good mood.'

They walked on over the sand then paddled about in the water like a pair of schoolchildren, laughing and splashing until they were both soaked through.

'We'd best go and sit in the dunes until we dry off,' he laughed at last. 'You can't go home in that state.'

In the dunes it was as if they were the only people in the world, there was no one else around for miles. They lay together, her head resting on his shoulder, their eyes closed, basking in the sunshine. Ina felt her eyes growing heavy and surrendered herself to the delicious state between waking and sleeping, aware that Joe too was relaxed and breathing deeply beside her, as if he might actually be asleep.

She let herself drift, dreaming that she was with Joe,

that he was kissing her face, nuzzling her throat, licking her ears. She murmured softly to herself, feeling the heat rising in her body, imagining she could feel him pressing into her. She smiled. He felt so good, tasted so wonderful. But then the dream stopped, quite suddenly. She stirred lazily, feeling cheated and opened her eyes sleepily.

Above her Joe was resting on one elbow and looking down into her face. 'I thought you were never going to wake up.' He bent his head and kissed the hollow in the base of her throat.

'And I thought I was having a dream,' she giggled as he tickled her ear with his tongue.

Warmed by the sun and roused by the attention he had been lavishing on her while she slept, she was more than ready for him when he unbuttoned her blouse and buried his face in the warm skin of her breasts. Almost feverishly she helped him out of his shirt and ran her fingers through the light covering of wiry hair she found on his chest, revelling in his well-developed muscles and firm flesh. When he went on to divest himself of his trousers she shivered, a strange mixture of anticipation and fear. He stood before her without shame and she couldn't stop herself reaching for him. Although she and Georgie had been on the beach, many times, they had always seemed to behave furtively, had always hidden themselves from each other, relying on touch as they learned a little about each other's bodies and they had always managed to stop themselves in time. Now, as Ina looked at Joe and he bent to help her with her clothes, she knew there would be no drawing back.

He eased her down on to the sand and leant over her, kissing her in places she had been ashamed even to touch herself and she trembled with the strain of restraint, driven by an impulse too basic to resist, her body on the point of an even more devastating explosion than the one she had felt yesterday.

'You are beautiful, Ina Archibold,' Joe breathed, moving himself on to her. 'Are you sure?' he asked gently.

'I've never been surer,' she whispered, wrapping her arms round him and moving her knees instinctively up on either side of him so that he was poised on the point of entry.

He pushed gently, then again, harder, but withdrew when he felt the barrier between them. 'I don't want to hurt you.'

'You won't,' she assured him, shifting her hips so that he slid inside her again and then rising up to meet his downward thrust, helping him to break inside her. She felt no pain, her whole being was centred on where he was, pulling him into her, holding him, gasping with the violence of her own spasming climax. It was too much for her inexperienced lover who cried out, stiffened, shuddered and filled her.

For long minutes they lay clasped damply together, too tender to move. Then his mouth again sought hers. Again he found her, again she drew him into her, making it last longer, teasing one another now as they discovered what pleased and again he flowed into her.

At last they lay sated, he cradling her head gently on his chest. 'I've never done that before,' he confided, running a finger down the ridge of her backbone.

'Me neither,' she told him, reaching for him, feeling him soft and warm, and marvelling at the miracle of his body.

'I know,' he teased, kissing her face. Then, more seriously he said, 'I do love you, you know.'

'I love you too,' she replied, gazing into the dark pools of his eyes.

'Enough to marry me?' he asked.

'More than enough for that,' she answered, feeling that it couldn't be possible to ever feel this happy again.

He clasped her to him again and she felt him grow and harden. Instant heat flushed through her and she wrapped her body round his, eager to feel him inside her again.

Secure in the privacy of the dunes they rolled together, their naked bodies gleaming with sweat, her legs tight round his waist as he drove himself into her again and again. Ina felt nothing but the desperate, intensifying demands of her own body as it responded to Joe's urgent rhythm. She felt herself tighten, felt the first tremor and threw her head back as her body tensed and shuddered around him. And there, looking down at them from the crest of a dune was Georgie Cameron and his friend, Al McArdle.

'NO!' She stiffened in horror and pushed frantically at Joe, dragging her body away from his. What had been a beautiful moment had been sullied for ever.

He froze, thinking he had hurt her. 'Ina? What's wrong?'

'Up there, behind me,' she gabbled frantically and grabbed for her clothes.

Joe growled and was on his feet in an instant, struggling into his trousers as Georgie and Al hurled themselves down the sandy slope.

'Get out of the way,' Joe ordered her tersely.

'No!' she pleaded as she saw him square up to Georgie.

'Stay out of it, Ina,' Joe yelled over his naked shoulder, half crouching, gesturing at Georgie. 'Come on, you bastard,' he taunted. 'Come on.'

Too late Ina caught a flash of movement from behind her. Al McArdle, Georgie's best friend, rushed at Joe, whose attention was all on Georgie, catching him below the knees and wrestling him to the sand. For a moment Joe seemed stunned and lay still while Al struggled to his knees and tried to get astride him and pin him to the ground. He had nearly succeeded when Joe recovered and aimed his knuckles at Al's chin, unbalancing him for long enough for him to wriggle away and struggle to his feet. Almost at once Georgie was on him, landing a heavy punch on his chin and sending him a pace or two backwards.

Now Joe was sandwiched between Georgie in front of him and Al closing from behind. Ina watched in horror, knew that even Joe stood no chance with these two brawny fishermen ranged against him. Instinctively she threw herself at the unsuspecting Al, hurling her full weight into his side. The momentum carried them both across the sand and sprawling into the side of the dune. For a second he looked surprised. Then, he regained his balance and laughed at her.

'What sort of man has to have a lassie fighting for him?' he taunted, lifting her bodily and holding her easily with one muscle-bound arm.

But Joe's reaction came with the speed of lightning. 'Leave her alone,' he growled, lunging at Al and wrenching him away from Ina. Before Georgie could come to his friend's aid, Joe aimed a furious blow at the side of Al's face. Al sagged back, blood welling from a cut lip, all desire to fight gone from him as he probed a bloody socket where a back tooth had been dislodged.

Joe sneered at him contemptuously. 'Had enough already?' he asked before turning back to Georgie. 'Come on then,' he hissed. 'You wanted a fight and now you've got one. Just you and me. One to one. Come on, lad. Or are you scared to fight on equal terms?'

Georgie howled with rage and swung wildly at Joe who ducked, turned and stood up again in time to take Georgie's second blow square on his eyebrow. Blood immediately began to pour down his face, partially blinding him and giving Georgie the opportunity to strike again, catching him a vicious blow under his ribs.

Ina screamed, sure Joe was badly injured, but even before the sound had died away Joe had wiped the blood from his face and pounced on Georgie who had unbalanced himself. In quick succession he brought his fists into the other man's face three times. Georgie turned and fled clumsily through a gap in the dunes and out on to the beach. Joe pounded after him, catching him quickly and wrestling him to the ground. Al and Ina, her skirt awry, her blouse only half buttoned, followed. Attracted by the noise several people raced across the beach towards them in time to see Joe grab Georgie by the collar and haul him upright. Georgie rose, his arms flailing wildly, his face already swollen and disfigured.

Joe managed to hold him for a second but then Georgie broke away and dived at him again, landing blow after blow on Joe's unprotected body. Joe fought back, blocking him as best he could, then managed to land one final punch on Georgie's face. It connected with his temple, making Joe stagger back with the force of his own blow.

Georgie seemed to freeze then slumped to his knees in the sand. Joe leapt on him, dragged him to his feet again. Ina watched, expecting Joe to hit Georgie again but he took a couple of steps back, wiped his face with the back of his hand.

'In future,' he said, glaring at the beaten and demoralised pair, 'mind your own bloody business. Try anything like this again and I'll knock your teeth clean out of your heads.' They believed him.

Ina stared in horror from one to the other of them. Georgie's face was almost unrecognisable, blood streamed from cuts above both eyes and from his nose. Al still nursed his mouth and stared sullenly at the ground. She turned to look at Joe who was almost as badly marked as Georgie, with blood trickling down his face and on to his shoulders. His eyes were rapidly disappearing into slits of bruised and puffy flesh and his body was a mass of angry red marks and scratches.

No one moved. Joe and Georgie were both watching her, seeming to be waiting for her to make some move.

'Are you coming with me, Ina?' Georgie mumbled, his swollen mouth making his words thick and indistinct.

She took a second to adjust her clothing then walked calmly to Joe's side, linking her arm through his.

Georgie glared at her then he and Al turned away and staggered back along the beach towards the small crowd which had gathered from nowhere. Geordie stopped just in front of them and turned back to face Ina.

'Whore!' he yelled. 'Bloody dirty little whore.' Then he deliberately spat in her direction before finally pushing his way through the gaping onlookers.

Fifteen minutes later, fully dressed and with most of the sand shaken from their clothes, Ina and Joe walked slowly back to the Butts. Ina kept her head down hoping there was no one she knew among the people still enjoying the beach but she knew they were watching her.

'I'd better get on home,' Joe said, his voice muffled by his swollen lips.

'You can't go like that,' she exclaimed, dragging out her handkerchief and attempting to clean his face.

He brushed her away impatiently. 'Don't fuss,' he grunted, swinging on to his bike.

'But you're hurt,' she cried as he started to pedal away.

He stopped then and grinned back at her, giving her a flash of white teeth from between split lips. 'Not half as hurt as those two,' he laughed.

She ran to him and he caught her in a fierce hug. 'You're my lassie now, Ina Archibold, and I'll be glad to teach anyone else who wants to argue about it the same lesson as I've taught those two. I'll see you next Sunday.'

She kissed him gently on his damaged mouth, no longer caring who might be watching, and watched him cycle away, pride and love making her heart beat like a drum in her chest.

Maureen dealt with the early morning rush with her usual efficiency. The housewives who hurried to buy hot, fresh rolls for breakfast rarely had time to stop and chat. It wasn't until after she and Maurice had eaten their own hasty breakfasts of freshly baked bread and strong tea that the gossip started to percolate back to the shop.

'My, that was some carry on with your Ina yesterday, wasn't it?' Jeannie Moys guffawed as she collected pies for her family's tea.

Maureen, busy counting change, couldn't disguise her surprise. 'Ina?' she repeated. 'What carry on?'

'Och my, don't tell me you don't know!' Jeannie exclaimed. 'The whole village is talking about it. Surely she must have told youse?'

'Told us what, Mrs Moys?'

Hetty McArdle, who was waiting to be served, tutted

loudly. 'I could have told you something like this was going to happen. You should see our Al's face. A right mess he made of it. It's not right. I don't know what young Ina was thinking of, letting a stranger do that to Georgie. The laddie's heartbroken so I hear.'

'Aye. It's a right shame. I thought Georgie and Ina would be married before long, after all, they've been sweet on each other since they were weans,' Jeannie nodded her head wisely. 'Disgusting, that's what I call it. Brawling on the beach like that. Still what do you expect from a miner?'

'Aye,' Hetty agreed. 'They're a right bad lot and no mistake. I blame Ina. She should've had more sense than to strut about with her new lad.'

'Aye. If I had seen what was going on I would have called the police. That young brute should be locked up for what he did to Georgie and Al. There was no call for that.'

'Just walking along, minding their own business, I heard,' someone else added. 'Attacked they were. It shouldn't be allowed.'

Maureen listened, her eyes going from one to the other as she tried to make sense of the conversation.

'I dare say your Maurice had something to say to that sister of yours,' Hetty asked, her attention now on Maureen who looked flustered. 'Och my, don't say you really don't know?'

Maureen gaped, her incomprehension obvious.

'Well, it was like this,' Jeannie started. 'Hetty's grandson, Al, and Geordie Cameron were off down to the beach yesterday afternoon when who should they see but your Ina and that miner she's been going about with.'

'Aye,' Hetty took over. 'Brazen as you like she was, all

489

wrapped round him in the middle of the dunes, not a stitch of clothing between the two of them. Well, it was obvious what they were up to. And on the Sabbath too. Well, poor Georgie, he didn't know where to look. And him a decent young lad. To see something like that! He didn't even know she was seeing someone else. Shocked they were, sick to their stomachs. Well, before they knew what was happening they were set upon. They say he had a rock in his hand. Must have done. No one could do damage like that with his bare fists.'

'Och aye. No doubt about that, Mrs McArdle.' Jeannie nodded again. 'The doctor'd to put stitches in the pair of them. It's a miracle they weren't killed.'

'He should be locked up. Vicious animal that he is. And as for your Ina,' Hetty finished, 'well, I don't like to gossip, Maureen, but your Maurice should be told what's been going on. Lying in the sand with a common miner she was! That lassie should be shamed to show her face in the village again.'

The two women exchanged satisfied glances. 'Well, I'd best be off,' Jeannie said. 'Betty Semple went into labour this morning and it's time I was looking in on her.'

'I'll walk up the street with you,' Hetty offered.

After that everyone who came into the shop seemed to want to talk about Ina. Maureen, her mortification growing by the minute, waited desperately for a lull in business then hurried through to have a serious talk to her brother.

When Ina got in that evening the house was empty. Assuming Maurice and Maureen were tidying up after the day's work she set about preparing the tea, rehearsing just what, exactly, she was going to say to Maurice about Joe. She had hoped to be able to chose her time, to catch him in a good mood, but she had seen the way some of the Post Office's customers had been looking at her today and knew she had to tell him the truth before the gossipmongers did it for her. He wouldn't approve, that much was certain. But somehow she had to make him understand that they were in love, persuade him to let her invite Joe to tea. If Maurice got to know Joe better he would soon see that Joe was a respectable, hard-working man and Joe would understand that Maurice's rules were only his way of trying to protect her. With the blindness of love she simply couldn't imagine that these two decent men wouldn't grow to like and respect one another.

The back door banged and she heard footsteps on the stair but thought nothing of it. It wasn't unusual for Maurice to slip out for cigarettes before tea and Maureen often went with him. She turned with a smile as the door opened. It froze on her face when she saw Maurice's thunderous expression. He marched across the room, stood in front of her, then slapped her hard across the face.

She was stunned into silence. Never before had he hit her. Tears of angry shock welled in her eyes. Her hand flew to her cheek where white welts were already forming.

'That's for being a dirty little slut. It's for what you did with that filthy miner.' Maurice was white faced with rage, controlling his own temper with a supreme effort.

She should have known the story would get back to him. She opened her mouth to defend herself. 'You don't . . .'

'BE QUIET!' Maurice roared. 'You will not see him again. Ever. You'll not set foot outside of this house unless one of us is with you, except to go to work. I'll not have you shaming the whole family like this. Do you understand?'

'That's not fair,' she protested bitterly. 'You haven't even given us a chance. I love him. You can't stop me seeing him.'

'I can! You are never to see him again, Ina. If I catch you sneaking out to meet him I'll lock you in your room until I can make arrangements to send you to live with your mother in Glendarroch.'

'No! You can't.'

'This is my house. I can do what I like. Now shut your filthy mouth and get up to your room. And while you're there think yourself lucky that I haven't thrown you out on the street.'

'So, Maurice wants Ina to come here to keep her away from this young miner of hers?' Rab asked.

'Aye,' Morag passed him the letters which had arrived together this morning, one from Maurice and the other from Ina.

'This Joe Lennox sounds like a right nasty piece of work,' Annie commented.

'Aye, he does that,' Morag agreed. 'And if what Maurice says about them is true we have to get her away from him, before she gets into trouble.'

Rab sighed and ran a hand through his snowy beard. 'What about Ina's letter? She's made it clear she doesn't want to come. And she says she loves this Joe. We've got to take that into account surely?'

'Love!' Annie snorted. 'What can a lassie of eighteen know about love?'

'If my memory serves me right I was eighteen when I first fell in love with you, Annie Bannerman. And I've not had reason to think I was wrong. And what about our Ayleen? Are you telling me she doesn't know what's best for her?'

'No, of course not. But this is different,' his wife insisted.

'Aye. The difference is that we don't know this Joe Lennox and how can we possibly judge him from way up here? But we do know Ina and she's a gey sensible lass. She'll not be doing anything wrong with her Joe. You know Maurice is right strict with both the girls. It could be he's being overprotective. Maybe we should trust the lassie, give her a chance to get to know her lad properly. If she thinks everyone's against her our Ina'll just get more and more stubborn. You know what she's like,' he said.

'And didn't we try exactly the same thing with Ayleen? Look where that got us,' Annie retorted.

'It got us a son-in-law who thinks the world of our daughter and treats her like a princess. We were wrong there, Annie,' Rab warned.

'But Joe hit Maurice!' Morag said. 'No matter what Ina says, he shouldn't have done that.'

'No, I agree with you there,' Rab conceded.

'And then this other fight. What sort of person uses his fists to win every argument. What will happen when Ina disagrees with him about something? Will he hit her too?' Morag asked worriedly.

'Aye,' Annie backed her daughter. 'I've seen it happen too often, we all have. I wouldn't want Ina tied to someone like that.'

'Neither would I,' Rab said. 'Neither would I.'

'She'll find someone else. She's an attractive lass. Maybe, when she's got this Joe out of her head, she'll go back to Georgie,' Annie speculated.

'Maybe you should go to Kilweem, Morag. Meet him, talk to Ina,' Rab suggested.

'I can't do that, Rab,' Morag objected. 'I've far too much to see to here. I can't just take time off work. Archie and I need every penny we can save for the wedding. Anyway, I don't think I'm the best one to talk to Ina about this.'

'You're her mother! Who else is better qualified to

understand how the lassie feels?' Rab retorted impatiently.

'But I've already made up my mind about this Joe Lennox so what could I possibly say to help Ina? You know how it is between us, Rab. If I went down there and tried to talk sense into her we'd only fall out over it. It would ruin everything. She'd never trust me again.'

'So, what are you going to do?' Annie asked.

'Well, I can't force Ina to come here if she doesn't want to. I'll write to them both. I'll tell Maurice I agree with him. I'll ask Ina to come up here for a wee while, to meet Archie properly before the wedding. By the time she goes home I bet she'll have forgotten all about Joe Lennox.'

'I hope you're right,' Rab muttered darkly. 'I just hope you're right.'

Ina hurried home from the Post Office and went straight to her bedroom where she shut herself in to read Joe's letter in private. She had written to him first, explaining why she couldn't meet him last Sunday and begging him to write back to her. And here was his reply, sent, not to the bakery where if Maurice or Maureen had discovered it before her they would almost certainly have destroyed it, but to the Post Office.

Joe had told her laughingly that he had hated school and been a poor student. She had wondered briefly whether he would be able to write back to her at all. After all there were plenty of hard-working and sharp-brained Kilweemers who could do little more than write their own names and some couldn't even manage that much. But here was the proof of his literacy. She studied the envelope closely, smiling at the large, heavily printed writing, trying to imagine him as he bent over the envelope, a pencil in his hand.

Carefully she broke it open and withdrew the single, coarse sheet of paper. He loved her. He had written it in his large, almost childish script, right across the top of the page. Sighing she leant back against her pillows and read down the page. When she reached the end she stayed where she was, her eyes distant and unfocused, a frown etching deep ridges in her otherwise smooth brow.

What on earth was she going to do now? Joe was coming to Kilweem on Sunday, the day after tomorrow. He would stay on the beach until it was dark, hoping she would be able to meet him. She smiled softly. It was typical of him, she thought fondly. He was so determined to get his own way. But she already knew there was absolutely no chance of her slipping away from Maurice and Maureen's careful vigilance. They watched her every move and she wasn't allowed out of the house except to go to work, unless Maureen was with her. Maureen even made a point of popping into the Post Office just to make sure she hadn't taken a sly day off and gone to meet Joe. It was horrible to know they didn't trust her any more. Still, she consoled herself with the thought that now she had written to explain things to her mother, Morag would soon be writing to Maurice to give permission for her to see Joe. There would be nothing he could do about it then.

Ina was like a nervous cat all day Sunday. She prowled the house, totally unable to sit still while she knew Joe was so close, aching to go to him. She already knew him well enough to realise that he was the sort of person who let nothing stand in his way. If the situation was reversed Joe would never have allowed a small thing like a brother's disapproval deter him. He would have contrived some way to get out. Ina's great fear was that he might think she had decided not to meet him, that he might believe she didn't love him enough to brave her family's disapproval. Well, she decided, she wouldn't let him down, she would meet him, no matter what Maurice might say about it. He was only her brother, after all, and had no real right to control her life like this. The decision made, her face lost the brooding scowl which was becoming a permanent feature. In its place was a firm-chinned, tight-lipped stubbornness as Ina settled down to wait her chance.

It came after lunch when Maureen disappeared to her room and Maurice, as usual, fell asleep. If she was very, very careful she should be able to slip out, even if it was just for an hour, and be back before they were any the wiser.

She waited nervously, hardly able to discipline herself to sit down calmly and wait until she was certain Maurice was asleep. But, at last, he was snuffling comfortably to himself and she tiptoed out of the room. Luckily it was an overcast but dry day so she had no need of a coat or heavy shoes and was able to start immediately down the stairs towards the back door, cringing every time the wooden treads creaked. She was almost at the bottom when Maureen's shrill voice froze her in mid-step.

'Ina! Where are you going?' she called from the upper floor at the top of her voice.

Instantly there was a crash and thud from the sitting room and Maurice appeared on the landing below his sister.

'I knew I couldn't trust you,' he bellowed. 'Sneaking off to meet your dirty miner, are you?'

'I was going for a walk,' she screamed back at him,

consoling herself with the fact that this was at least partially true.

'On your own?' he sneered.

'You've no right to keep me here like a prisoner.'

'You've only yourself to blame.'

'I could do with a breath of fresh air myself,' Maureen intervened quickly. 'Wait a minute. I'll put my shoes on and come with you.' Ina knew she could hardly refuse but waited with very bad grace.

'Right.' Maureen ran lightly down the stairs. 'Where do you want to go?'

Ina shrugged. 'Anywhere.'

'The harbour then,' Maureen decided, leading the way.

Ina followed, her eyes darting this way and then that, probing the doorways and side wynds, wondering if Joe was somewhere close by.

Watching and understanding, Maureen asked, 'You were going to meet Joe, weren't you, Ina?' When her sister stayed resolutely silent she added, 'Do you know everyone's talking about you? They say Georgie caught you with no clothes on.' Maureen wasn't absolutely sure whether this was the truth or just a piece of vicious gossip but Ina obviously wasn't going to enlighten her so she went on: 'I know you think Maurice is being hard on you but it's for the best really.'

'You didn't think that when he tried to stop you seeing Arthur, did you? I even helped you then, Maureen. Why won't you do the same for me now?'

Maureen's attitude to Joe angered her more than anyone else's. They had always been close, better friends than many genuine sisters, but now, as the brother and sister joined forces to stop her seeing Joe, Ina was starting to feel like the outsider she really was. It was just another wound in a long list of injuries.

498

'Maurice was right about Arthur,' Maureen admitted after a long pause. 'He wasn't really interested in me. He just wanted to get his hands on my share of the bakery so he could sell it and use the money for himself. And he's right about Joe too.'

'He is not! You're wrong, both of you.'

'Honestly, Ina, what future would you have married to a miner? Whatever was behind that fight with Georgie and Al, he certainly didn't stop at defending himself. You only have to look at the state of their faces to see that. How can you love a man who's capable of doing something like that? Especially after what he did to Maurice. He'd end up knocking you about, or your kids. Is that what you want?'

'You don't understand. You've never even spoken to him. What gives you the right to criticise him?'

'I'm your sister. I care about you, Ina. Just like Maurice does.'

'You've got a funny way of showing it,' Ina retorted.

They wandered round the harbour in hostile silence until Maureen said, 'We might as well go home,'

'No! Not yet. Look, the tide's out, let's walk down to the beach. I'm sure I heard Dot and Eileen say they were going there this afternoon.'

Maureen sighed but allowed Ina to lead the way back through the village and down to the Butts. As usual the inhabitants of this ancient row of houses were sitting out, enjoying the mild weather. No one was idle. Fishermen sat on upturned crates, surrounded by a tangle of nets as their calloused hands worked deftly to repair tears. Their womenfolk worked at their knitting, fingers flying, or sewed, using the Sabbath afternoon to catch up on household mending. As they made their way towards the sand the two girls were greeted by people eager to chat. Ina was aware that she was the subject of many speculative, and some hostile, glances and was relieved when they finally reached the beach. She immediately ploughed into the soft, dry sand but Maureen hesitated.

'Och, I'm not trailing along there,' she decided. 'My good shoes will be ruined.'

'Take them off then,' Ina suggested impatiently, her eyes scanning the beach for some sign of Joe. In the distance, a lone figure sat in the sand. He was so far away that he appeared as nothing more than a tiny, dark shape but Ina knew it was him. 'Come on. Please,' she begged, a hint of desperation in her voice.

Maureen looked at the dozen or so people enjoying the beach, most clustered close to the Butts, and then gazed into the far distance. Her eyes travelled over the solitary figure and flicked quickly back to Ina who was staring at it with raw longing on her face. 'No. There's no sign of Dot or Eileen and it's starting to get cold now. I'm going home. I've the books to do.' With that she turned on her heel and marched off back up the hill.

Ina ran a few paces into the sand and as she did so the figure rose and turned to face her. She could see nothing except the pale blur of his face, the darker shades of his clothing, knew he would hardly be able to distinguish her from the other people at this end of the beach. But, as she stood, with tears springing to her eyes, he lifted one arm high above his head in a wave of recognition. Desperately she waved back, windmilling her arms so there could be no mistake, and was actually starting to walk towards him when she felt a hand on her arm.

'Come on, Ina. It's no good. I won't let you speak to

him. If you go to him now I'll fetch Maurice down here.'

It was as if Joe could hear what was going on. While Ina stood undecided, he turned and walked away from her, his distant figure becoming more and more indistinct until he finally melted into the dunes.

Ina spent the rest of the afternoon alternating between enervating depression and bitter rage. She paced the floor of her room then threw herself on her bed to weep slow, draining tears, only to rise again and resume the restless walking. In the end she collapsed on to her bed and drifted into a heavy, unrefreshing sleep.

Something disturbed her, breaking through the torpor in her brain. She woke stiff and sticky eyed, her head pounding, her mouth dry. For a minute she lay, too unhappy to make the effort to move, wondering what had disturbed her. And then it came again. A fierce, insistent hammering on the front door of the bakery. She sat up, then ran to the window, straining to peer down into the street.

'Open this door. I know you're in there.' Joe's voice, loud and angry.

Ina struggled to wrestle the stiff sash open then leant out until she could see him.

'Joe,' she hissed. 'Up here.'

He stood back and shouted up at her, 'Open the door. I want to talk to you.'

'I can't,' she yelled. 'Go away, Joe.'

'I've come to ask you to come home with me, Ina,' he begged. 'I've told my mam and dad about us. They'll make you right welcome.'

Already folk were gathering, drawn by the din. On the other side of the road she saw Georgie Cameron emerge from his own house, flanked by his father and brother, and come running towards the bakery. Before she could answer Joe's plea she heard the heavy grating noise of the bolts being drawn.

'I want to talk to Ina,' she heard Joe say, then recognised Maurice's answering growl. Georgie and his brother came from behind and each grabbed one of Joe's arms. He made no attempt to struggle but looked up at her window and shouted, 'I love you, Ina.'

A dozen faces looked to see what her response would be. She didn't disappoint them. 'I love you too, Joe,' she called.

Georgie Cameron's father, his shirt sleeves rolled up to display the hugely developed muscles in his forearms, strode round to place himself solidly beside Maurice.

'Shall we teach him a lesson, lad?' he asked, clearly relishing the prospect.

Maurice seemed to consider it for a moment, gave the pinioned Joe a look of absolute loathing then said, 'No, I can take care of this for myself.'

Ina screamed.

Maurice was a big man, his body strong from the demands of the bakery. He brought his fist into Joe's body with such force that it lifted his feet from the ground. Joe, still supported by Georgie and his brother, sagged briefly then looked at Maurice, his defiance undimmed.

'It won't make any difference,' he panted. 'Do what you like. You can't keep me away.'

Maurice, his face the colour of the local lobsters, ran at him, butting Joe under the chin with his bull-like head and then driving his fist in under the younger man's ribs. He gathered himself for another attack but Mr Cameron dragged him back.

'Enough, lad. He's had his lesson. No need to pull trouble on your own head by killing him.'

502

Maurice subsided into menacing stillness, his whole body tensed and ready to leap again at the faintest provocation.

Joe's head snapped up and back, his body seemed to cave in at the waist and his knees buckled. The supporting hands let go and he dropped on to his hands and knees on the setts. His head drooped but then he shook it, struggled painfully to his feet and even took a staggering step closer to Maurice. 'You can beat the shit out of me but you'll never win,' he snarled.

Ina thought she might die there and then, her heart was so full of pride and love for Joe that it was a physical weight inside her. She couldn't let them do this to him, she loved him, needed him desperately, couldn't take the risk of losing him. She ran from the window, clattered down the stairs and dashed outside. Maurice grabbed her by the hair and shoved her back into the doorway, blocking it with his huge frame so that she couldn't get past. Dimly she heard the murmur of approval from the watching villagers as she hammered ineffectively at his back. 'I love you, Joe,' she screamed at the top of her lungs.

Maurice swung round and slapped her. She didn't even flinch but stared at him with hatred in her eyes. Some of the women gasped.

'You leave my sister alone,' Maurice turned back to Joe who had attempted to lunge at him in defence of Ina but was restrained again by the Cameron boys. 'Come here again and I'll bloody kill you.'

Mr Cameron had to forcibly hold Maurice back. 'Take him out of the village,' he ordered his sons. 'And make sure he doesn't come back. We'll be waiting for you if you do,' he added, prodding at Joe with a hard finger.

The Camerons dragged Joe away, surrounded by a

crowd of jeering men, all eager to uphold the pride of the village.

'I'll be waiting for you, Ina,' Joe called back. 'Don't let me down, hen.'

She saw no more. Maurice used his foot to slam the door then shoved her so hard that she fell on to the bakery floor. He towered over her, quivering with rage.

'No!' Maureen, her face bleached of all colour, screamed it at him and ran to help her sister to her feet. 'How could you?' she asked him, her eyes dark and angry. 'Why did you have to hit him? He only wanted to talk. You're as bad as him . . . animals . . .' Tears rolled down her face and she wiped them away impatiently. 'This is all your fault,' she hissed at Ina. 'If you hadn't arranged to meet that filthy miner today, none of this would have happened.'

Ina stepped away, distancing herself from them both. She held herself stiffly upright and her face, although white and strained, had a look of icy determination. 'I'll never forgive you for this,' she said, the words clear and steady. 'I'll never speak to either of you again.' Then she turned and walked away. They were still staring after her when her bedroom door slammed shut.

In her room Ina sank on to the bed and stared blindly at the window, the twin germs of resentment and rebellion rooting and growing in her angry mind. Between them Maurice and Maureen had ruined everything, she thought bitterly. Joe would never dare to come back to Kilweem now. Unless she did something positive, it was over. But she wouldn't let that happen. She loved Joe and she would find some way to go on seeing him, even if it meant turning her back on her family. But how? In despair she realised what her life would be like from now on, accounting for every minute of her time and never being allowed out if there was the slightest chance that she was going to meet Joe. After today, Maurice would never trust her again. But what right, she asked herself with a flash of spirit, had he to tell her how to live her life? Then, as if a bright light had been switched on in her mind, she knew exactly what she must do. Springing up she flung open her wardrobe door and started to drag her clothes out, then stopped, forcing herself to calm down. She was overreacting, forgetting the letter she had written to her mother. There was no need for such drastic action because, in a day or two, her mother — who of all people would surely understand — would write back and give her approval. Then there would be nothing Maurice could do to stop them meeting. In the meantime she would just have to be patient.

She was almost ready to leave for work the next morning when Maurice came up from the bakery.

'There's a letter for each of us from your mother,' he said, almost as if nothing had happened between them, as if this was just another ordinary day.

She refused to answer but couldn't help looking at his hands which held two identical envelopes, one addressed to him, the other for her, both in her mother's spidery handwriting. She took the one he offered and went to the other side of the room to open it in private. Already her heart was racing in anticipation.

She read it through once, then a second time. She couldn't believe it. Her mother and worse, her grandpa, were siding with Maurice. She closed her eyes, screwing them together in an effort to stop the dizziness which had attacked her.

Morag had done her duty in the first paragraph, forbidding her Ina to see Joe again and making it plain that she supported Maurice and Maureen in this. With appalling insensitivity she had then gone on to devote the rest of her letter to a rapturous description of her own lover, followed by the order for Ina go to Glendarroch to help plan the wedding and 'forget about this Joe person'.

'So your mother agrees with me. I knew she would.' Maurice couldn't quite keep the triumph from his voice, or the relief when he added, 'She wants you to go and stay with her for a while. You can leave at the end of the week. Maureen can go with you for a week or so. She could do with a break.'

So that was the plan, Ina thought bitterly. They wanted to pack her off to the wilds of the highlands where she would have no hope of seeing Joe. But they couldn't do that to her. This was her life, her chance of happiness and she wouldn't let them take it away from her. It *was* her life and it was time for her to take control of it. She knew there was only one thing she could do now. Her head was instantly full of the plans she had started to formulate last night; her heart was racing with excitement. But she gave no sign of it to Maurice and just stared back at him with an impassive face. He made the mistake of taking it for resignation.

'Right then. I'll telephone a message for your mother then, tell her you'll be there at the weekend. Now I'd better get back to work. You too. Hurry up or you'll be late.' He clattered off down the stairs already feeling the ease in his muscles where the weight of responsibility was starting to lift.

Ina's determination didn't waver for a second. She felt no doubt, no regret about what she was going to do. Now that she had reached her decision, she wanted nothing more than to act on it. She disciplined herself

506

to wait until she heard the bakery door slam. A second later she was in her bedroom, flinging clothes into the old cardboard suitcase her mother had left. Five minutes after that she was tearing along the back wynds, knowing she couldn't risk Marketgate where Maureen might easily glance up and see her. She made for the far side of the village, racing the bus which she had heard clanking its way towards the tollbooth. She emerged from a maze of narrow wynds on to the harbour and had to run along, dodging the horses and carts of the fish merchants, come to buy the morning's catch. Slithering on the damp setts she flew round the far corner, ignoring the surprised greeting Hetty McArdle called from her front door and panted up the hill. She arrived at the top just as the single decker nosed into view. Frantically she waved her arms and, to her immense relief, the bus pulled to a stop.

Mrs Haddow, the post mistress, waited in vain for Ina to turn up for work. In addition to housing the telephone exchange and serving the community as a Post Office, the small shop, which had once been the Haddows' front room, also sold newspapers, sweeties and bits and pieces of haberdashery, as well as stocking a good range of patent medicines. As a rule Ina managed the telephone and, in odd moments, helped her elderly employer about the shop, and even then there was seldom a minute when there wasn't someone clamouring for attention. Left on her own Mrs Haddow was soon reduced to a state of nervous exhaustion.

'I'm sorry, Hetty,' she twittered after keeping the other woman waiting for nearly ten minutes while she tried to sort out a crossed line between the doctor and the harbour master. 'I'm fair run off my feet the morn.'

507

'I can see that,' Hetty said. 'Would you like me to give you a wee hand? I can spare an hour if it would help you.'

'Och, that's kind of you, Mrs McArdle. I'd be right grateful if you could just keep an eye on things for a wee minute so I can pop across to the bakery and see what's keeping Ina.'

'Has she not told you she won't be in then?' Hetty asked, tossing her shawl over the back of a chair and rolling her sleeves back.

'No, and I'm fair angry with her. Mind you, it's not like her to let me down. She's a good wee worker. I dare say she's not well. Maureen must have forgotten to let me know.'

'Och, she's not ill,' Hetty said thoughtfully. 'I saw her myself not an hour since. On the quayside, and in a great hurry she was.'

'Well, what can have got into the lass? What with all that carry on yesterday and now this. I don't know what the young folk are coming to, Mrs McArdle.'

Hetty nodded but kept her thoughts to herself. She had spent the last hour listening to the village gossip and, for the second time inside a month, most of it revolved around Ina Archibold and the young miner she had taken up with. Nor had she missed the distracted expression on Ina's face that morning, or the suitcase she had had in her hand.

'You go and have a wee word with Maureen, Mrs Haddow. I'll look after this place for you.'

'Good morning to you, Mrs Haddow. It's a braw day.' Maureen had looked up and smiled as the elderly widow puffed into the shop. She was surprised to see her looking so flustered. Her iron-grey hair, skewered into its

508

normal scrawny bun, was breaking loose from the hair-net which usually kept it strictly in place and several strands were flopping forward on to her face. 'Is anything wrong?' Maureen asked, realising the woman looked angry.

'It's your Ina.' Mrs Haddow came straight to the point. 'She's not come into work the day and Mrs McArdle says she saw her in the village an hour ago. It's not good enough, Maureen. If she wanted a day off for something urgent she should have asked me first. I don't know that I'll be able to let her keep her job after this. What with all that other trouble . . . And I thought you were a responsible lass, Maureen. Could you not have told me she wasn't going to be in the day?'

'I . . . I thought she was at work, Mrs Haddow,' Maureen stammered. 'Look, have a wee seat there for a minute and I'll have a word with Maurice. He saw her last. Maybe he knows what's happened to her.'

'What?' Her brother nearly dropped the tray of cakes he was drawing out of the oven. Without another word he stormed upstairs and checked all the rooms. Finding nothing he went into Ina's bedroom and threw open the wardrobe door. It was almost empty.

'Oh no . . .' Maureen came into the room behind him. 'The suitcase she keeps on top of the wardrobe, Maurice. It's gone too.'

'Bloody hell!' He swore softly. Then, 'That's it. I wash my hands of her. I've got better things to do than worry about Ina.' He strode back to the bakery and Maureen heard the crash of tins as he attacked his work with new ferocity.

She stood in Ina's room for several minutes before suddenly remembering about Mrs Haddow.

'I'm sorry,' she put on her best smile as she hurried

back into the shop, 'apparently Ina had a message from her mother. She's had to go to Glendarroch. She left a note for us to tell you but neither of us saw it. I'm really sorry, Mrs Haddow.'

'Aye I mind now, Jimmy Rae told me he had letters for you from Fort William. He guessed they were from Mrs Archibold,' Mrs Haddow said, forgetting her anger as her inquisitive mind stored this new information. 'Nothing wrong I hope?'

Maureen sighed. She should have known that nothing was truly private in a village as close as this one and Jimmy Rae, their postman, was as notorious a gossip as any of the women. 'I'm sorry, Mrs Haddow. It's family business,' she insisted.

The woman's face sharpened at the snub. 'That's as may be,' she sniffed. 'But your Ina had better look for another job when she comes home.' With that she gathered her dignity and hurried out of the shop.

Barely half an hour later, Maurice placed a telephone call to the Post Office in Glendarroch, asking Morag to call him back at the bakery. In fact it was Rab who was on the other end of the line when the 'phone jangled towards the end of the afternoon.

'Is something wrong?' Maurice could hear the concern in Rab's voice, even over the echoing, fuzzy connection.

'Too bloody true,' Maurice hissed. 'Ina's run off.'

'Run off! Where to?' Rab demanded.

'I think she's maybe on her way up to see you,' he said, going on to explain the events of the last two days. 'When she arrives up there you can tell her she's not welcome here any more. I'll not have this sort of carry on in my house.'

Rab swallowed his anger, resisted the urge to tell the younger man what he thought of him. 'Are you sure she's coming here?' he asked. 'Did she leave a note or something?'

'No, nothing like that. Not even goodbye.'

'Then she might be going to her young man?' Rab suggested.

'No, surely not? Even Ina wouldn't be that stupid,' Maurice insisted. 'I think she's on her way to see her mother. It was her letter that upset her.'

'Maybe. And maybe that's exactly why this would be the last place she'd want to come. Look, if she is on her way here she should arrive tomorrow some time. I'll call you back and let you know one way or the other tomorrow night.'

It was a very worried and extremely angry Rab Bannerman who finally replaced the receiver.

In the Post Office, Mrs Haddow listened in to the call, her lips pursed in disapproval. So Ina had run off, had she? Well, that would be something to tell her customers the morn.

TWENTY-FIVE

Ina stepped off the bus in Inverannan and looked round uneasily. She had never been to Strathannan's county town before and had only the vaguest notion of where Craigie was in relation to it.

She put her small case down in the middle of the pavement and huddled her coat closer round her shoulders. It was still summer and quite warm but all of a sudden she felt chilled and lonely. She shivered but after a moment of panic she put her able mind to her problem. If a bus had brought her this far, surely another one would take her to Craigie. Logic suggested that it would leave from the same area and, looking down the road, she saw several queues of people who could only be waiting for transport. Boldly she approached the nearest woman, a stiff-backed, middle-aged matron, and asked for the Craigie bus.

The woman looked her up and down. 'Are you sure it's Craigie you want?' she asked.

'Yes. The mining village.'

The woman sniffed and turned away. 'Next one along,' she muttered.

Another woman stood at the back of the next line of people, wrapped in a thin shawl which also bore the weight of a sleeping infant. Two young and grubby children hung round her skirts. 'Is this where I get the bus for Craigie?' Ina asked her.

'Aye,' the woman nodded, hardly interested, and then slapped the dirty-faced boy who was whining for attention.

'When does it leave?' Ina persisted, trying not to stare too obviously. From a distance the bare gums, straggling hair and bent figure had all suggested a woman of thirty or more but on closer inspection, Ina realised, this was a girl, little older than herself.

'It should have left ten minutes ago. It's late,' the girl complained. 'It always is.'

'How long does it take to get there?'

The girl shrugged. 'Half an hour maybe.' She slapped the lad again then ignored his outraged screams.

'When's the next one?'

'Not 'til just after six. Och, will you stop that bloody noise!' she bawled at the tearful child.

Ina thanked her and moved away quickly, the smell of unwashed bodies thick in her nostrils.

She stared round uncertainly. There was no point in going to Craigie yet. Joe would still be at work and though he had told her his mother and father would make her welcome, she felt she needed him to be there when she arrived. So, it was a case of either catching the next bus and hanging round a small village for hours, where she was likely to draw attention to herself, or spending the time in the town. To stay in Inverannan would be the better choice, she decided quickly. She had never been here before so she could pass the time simply looking round the place and there was bound to be somewhere where she could buy herself a cup of tea and something to eat.

The street where the bus had stopped was a busy one. Buses, horse-drawn carts and a few private cars clattered past in a never ending stream. Ina hovered hesitantly for a few minutes then made a dash through a gap in the traffic, dodging the steaming piles of horse dung which littered the road, and finally reached the other side safely.

She followed the flow of people and found herself in the High Street. Only in Glasgow had she seen more shops. There was even a large department store with several different windows, displaying everything from clothes to household goods and jewellery. Next to that was a double-fronted grocer's, the male assistants all in long white aprons and crisp, white cuffs. A delivery boy brushed past her, his arms laden with boxes which he dumped in the basket of his bicycle – a smart black affair with the shop's name emblazoned under the cross-bar – then rode away up the cobbled street. Ina was amazed by the range of goods displayed in the window. Different types of tea, all in fancy tins, biscuits, canned meats, even coffee, and a selection of luxury goods that the industrious housewives of Kilweem would consider a shameful waste of hard-earned money. Next door to that was a bakery, three times the size of Maurice's, and with a startling variety of cakes on offer, including a huge wedding cake which took pride of place in their window display. She wandered on, dodging the rabbits and chickens suspended by their feet in the doorway of the flesher's and found herself staring into the window of a shoe shop. She gaped, unable to tear herself away, suddenly conscious of the scruffy condition of her own sturdy, button-strap shoes which she had always thought quite smart. Here there was a range of styles and colours that she had never imagined could exist. The little coastal towns had nothing as splendid as this to offer their inhabitants.

She managed to while away a full hour doing nothing

more taxing than gazing at the window displays, imagining what she might buy for herself if she had the money. Just when she was starting to wonder what she was going to do for the next five hours she spotted a pair of very ornate gates, set at the bottom of a gently sloping road. Curiously she made her way towards them and, to her delight, discovered the town park. It was beautiful, large enough to get lost in and designed round a deep glen which meandered through the middle of it. There were neatly tended lawns, colourful flowerbeds and even glasshouses, crammed with exotic plants. Best of all she discovered a pavilion tea room. With almost a whole week's wages in her pocket plus the three pounds she had managed to save, she felt rich enough to treat herself to a cup of tea and a buttered scone.

She stepped inside and found herself in a much smarter place than she had expected it to be. Three bored-looking musicians, half hidden by a jungle of potted palms, played soft music; the clients, almost all women, sat in wickerwork chairs round lace-draped tables. Ina smiled to herself. She had never been anywhere half as nice as this and was determined to enjoy the experience. She smiled at the waitress who subjected her to a haughty stare before turning, almost reluctantly, and leading the way to a vacant table, tucked away to the side, against a wall.

Irritated by the waitress's manner, Ina tossed her head at the offered seat, straightened her back and pulled herself up to her full height. Looking down at the girl she said, in her best voice, 'I would prefer to sit by the window. I think I can see an empty table there.'

The girl sighed loudly but decided not to argue. In her uniform of a black dress, white, lace-edged apron and a dainty little cap, she looked red faced with the heat and, to Ina's surprise, she exuded an unsubtle odour of stale perspiration. So much for the superior manner, Ina thought disdainfully. She might be a plain working girl from a small fishing village but she would be ashamed to smell like that.

She settled at her chosen table and gave her order then turned to look around her. At the neighbouring table, two middle-aged women, both smartly dressed in expensive frocks and stylish hats, paused in their conversation to stare pointedly at her. Ina caught their disapproving expressions and instinctively straightened her back again and tried to look as if she did this sort of thing every day, telling herself she had as much right to spend her money here as they did. Even so, she was glad she had worn her good coat over her working clothes and had not simply thrown her shawl round her shoulders – like most Kilweem women she frequently wrapped herself in her thick woollen shawl which was such a practical and warming garment. But it was obvious that only the poorer folk wore such a thing in Inverannan. Not that there were many of them in this park, she mused, gazing through the window. The people strolling here all looked well to do, as if they had nothing more pressing to claim their time than a lunchtime wander through the park. And that girl in uniform, pushing a high perambulator, looked very much like a nursemaid or even a nanny. She attacked her scone with relish, and settled to watch the leisured folk of Inverannan as they paraded through their park. All in all there was more than enough to amuse her for another hour.

When she felt she couldn't sit at the table any longer without ordering something else, she paid the exorbitant bill and found a bench in the sun where she could sit for as long as she liked. But now, as the day wore on, and the time for her to go to Craigie and Joe, drew ever nearer, she was starting to feel almost sick with apprehension. She hadn't really stopped to think this morning. All she knew was that she had to get away from a place where everyone seemed against her. And where else should she go but to Joe who had told her he was waiting for her, had even said his parents would make her welcome? But would they? And, if the miners were as poorly paid as everyone said they were, was it fair to expect Joe's people to take her in? Would Joe still want her after what had happened to him yesterday? The questions mired her brain as she wandered through the park, up the High Street and back to the bus stop.

Perhaps it would have been more sensible to go to Glendarroch and talk to her mother, make her understand about Joe. But her mother's letter had made it obvious that she was too wrapped up in plans for her own wedding to care about her daughter's problems and, in any case, it was too late in the day to start off for Glendarroch now. For tonight at least she would have to throw herself on the hospitality of the Lennoxes. If the worst happened she could always begin to make her way north in the morning.

At the last minute she thought to call in to a flesher's and buy a huge steak pie so that she wouldn't arrive empty handed and then she stood for a whole hour at the bus stop.

The Craigie bus wound its way through the town and out into open country. In the distance Ina could see the sparkling ribbon of the Forth but the villages they passed through were small and increasingly drab. Her heart sank as she saw that the only remaining passengers were poorly dressed and even dirty looking, with

517

miserable faces. Her mood plunged lower and lower the further they got from the town. Now the countryside was dotted with pit bings which loomed black and forbidding on the skyline. Just ahead, between the road and the river, she could see a pall of smoke hanging over a grim looking cluster of houses. In her heart she knew this was Craigie.

'This is your stop, hen,' the conductor confirmed her fears as the bus drew to a halt at the side of a narrow country road.

From the pavement she could see the village below her. It was little more than four straight lines of dark, single-storey cottages, squatting in a low indentation in the hilly landscape. Even on this summer's evening, from the lone chimney on the roof of each dwelling there issued a steady plume of grey smoke which seemed to gather and hang in the air above them. Under this grim canopy the rows of houses faced each other with not even a paved street between them. Instead there was a strip of worn and muddy grass, strung with washing ropes and littered with rubbish. Between these rows of cottages was a broken line of roughly built, shed-like buildings. Even from up here she could smell them, knew with a sinking heart that these were earth closets.

Grimly she picked up her case and walked along the road until she came to a gap in the hedge where a beaten path led down to the village itself. From close up it looked even worse and the smell made her want to gag. The houses, stark, soot-stained, butt-and-ben-type dwellings, with only one window at the front, were identical. She made her way between the first two rows, searching vainly for a street name, or even a number on the doors.

A gaggle of thin-faced, dirty urchins followed her

while their mothers sat on their front doorsteps, watching with open interest. She felt her face colour.

In the end she had no alternative but to ask for help. She picked her way carefully across the grass, dodged under some grey-looking washing and approached a woman who was sitting in her doorway, peeling tatties in the last warmth of the day.

'I'm looking for Dene Row,' she said, forcing herself to smile into suspicious and hostile eyes. 'Which one is it?'

The woman cackled. 'It's all Dene Row, hen.'

'Number twelve.'

'Who's it you're after then?'

'The Lennoxes,' Ina said, watching the woman scratch between her sagging breasts and trying not to shudder.

'Third from the end.' The woman nodded her greasy head towards the far end of the row. 'Is it Jessy you're looking for?'

'Does she have a son called Joe?'

'Got you in trouble has he, hen?' The woman cackled again, her eyes raking Ina's slender body.

'No!' Ina blushed furiously and backed away, tangling herself in what might have been a towel on the washing rope. Still dogged by the children she practically ran up the rows.

Third from the end. She counted down, located what she hoped was the right house then looked back to see the woman, standing on the grass watching her, surrounded now by half a dozen others. Ina almost lost her courage then.

'That's it, Missus,' one of the children encouraged her, pointing a filthy hand towards the nearest cottage. It looked no better, but no worse, than all the others and there, propped against the wall, roped securely in place, was Joe's old bike.

Ina took a deep breath. What if he wasn't home yet? She looked behind her again not sure whether it would be worse to walk back, through the ever-vigilant women, or to knock brazenly at this door. She was still there, undecided, when a noise behind her made her spin round.

She almost screamed with fright. The man who faced her stared at her from a blackened face, his eyes eerily white in a featureless face. He wore baggy, coal-grimed trousers with an equally filthy jacket and a shapeless cap covered his hair. Only when he smiled, revealing shockingly white teeth did she know him.

'Joe?' she whispered. Behind her a growing audience of village women was edging even closer.

He guffawed, ran towards her then stopped himself from taking her into his blackened arms just in time. 'Ina!' The delight in his voice was plain enough to chase away all her doubts.

'I had to come,' she explained weakly, feeling tears of pure relief threatening to humiliate her in front of all these avid faces. She put out a hand to touch him. He laughed and drew away.

'I wouldn't do that. Not while I'm in this state. Don't worry, you'll like me better when I've had a wash.'

Behind them someone sniggered.

'What have you been up to, Joe Lennox?' a coarse voice shouted amid peals of laughter.

'Up her by the looks o' it,' came the ribald reply.

'When's the weddin'?'

'Did naebody tell ye tae keep yer legs crossed, hen?'

Ina flushed bright scarlet and would have fled there and then if another, kinder voice hadn't spoken out at that moment.

'Don't be standing there making a spectacle of yourselves

520

for the whole village. Never mind them, they've nothing better to occupy their minds. Come on inside,' a voice ordered. Ina turned and saw a small, neat woman standing at the door.

'Come and meet Ma,' Joe said softly. 'It's all right. She's half expecting you.' He gave her a gentle shove.

'Aye, well, I know who you are, lass. Joe's told me all about you. In you come and make yourself at home.' Mrs Lennox beamed and shut the door firmly on her ogling neighbours.

Ina smiled shyly, overcome by the unexpected warmth of the welcome.

'Right, you sit yourself down there and pour yourself a cup of tea while Joe gets himself cleaned off. Mind and keep your head towards the range for he'll be naked as the day he was born.'

Jessy Lennox hefted a huge kettle from the range and splashed boiling water into a tin bath which she lifted from the back of the door, then added more water from a pail by the sink. Joe stripped out of his working clothes and stood bare skinned before his mother with a cheerful lack of self-consciousness and let her scrub at his back and shoulders before taking the brush from her hands and getting on with the more accessible parts himself.

Jessy dried her hands on a spotless towel. 'You'll get used to that,' she laughed, refilling the kettle from another bucket and sitting it back on the hob. 'If they don't wash as soon as they come in the coal dust gets into everything. Some of the women make their men bathe round the back on warm days. You never know what you might find when you go to dig the tatties. You could have waited in the bedroom,' she nodded to a closed door, 'but Shug works the nightshift and he's still asleep in there.'

'That's my pa,' Joe explained as he tipped the dirty water into the stone sink.

'You mind and rinse that sink out,' his mother ordered sternly.

'Don't I always?' he laughed.

Ina automatically turned towards him and was rewarded with the sight of his muscled buttocks. She flushed anew.

'Don't worry, lass, you'll get used to it and after all, there's nothing there to be ashamed of,' Jessy laughed.

'I really am sorry to turn up on you like this,' Ina found her voice at last.

'Joe warned me you might be coming,' Jessy said, watching Ina closely over the rim of her cup, but resisting the urge to question the girl yet.

Joe, freshly dressed in clean shirt and trousers, perched on the edge of the table and got a rap over his legs from his mother.

'There's chairs. Sit on one.'

'She's an awful tyrant, my mother,' he said, laughter in his voice, but he did as he was told quickly enough.

Ina looked at his face, devoid of all traces of coal now and gasped in horror. 'Oh God,' she breathed. 'Look at you.'

He fingered his face cautiously. 'It's not as bad as it looks.'

'Not as bad as the last time your friends set about him,' Jessy added tartly.

'I bet they looked worse,' he grinned.

'I'm sorry, Joe,' Ina said miserably.

'It wasn't your fault and it got you here so I guess it was worth it,' he said lightly.

'I wasn't sure you'd really want me to come,' she admitted to his mother with a wry smile.

522

'Joe tells me he loves you, lass. If you love him back, well, that's good enough for me,' Jessy said generously. 'Though you two seem to have made a right mess of things between you. Does your family know where you are, Ina?'

'No,' she admitted, then went on to tell them exactly what had happened.

'Well, I won't interfere,' Jessy said. 'You've got yourselves into this and you'll have to sort it out for yourselves. But you're more than welcome to stay here lass, for as long as you want. Shug's on nights and can't be disturbed while he's sleeping through the day so he and Joe can share the bedroom between them. You and I will be snug as wee mice in the box bed out here, so there's plenty of room for us all.'

'I don't want to be a nuisance.'

'You won't be, unless you expect to be waited on that is?'

'No! I'll help all I can. I'll see about a job . . .'

Jessy chortled. 'Plenty of time for that, hen. You'll be lucky to find anything round here anyway.' She stood up and took off her apron, folding it and placing it over the back of the chair. 'I'll away to the shop before it closes.'

Ina shot to her feet. 'I brought you this. I nearly forgot,' she said, offering the pie.

Jessy accepted it easily. 'Thanks, hen. That was right thoughtful and you've saved me a trip. I'll away and sit in the sun for an hour until that man of mine wakes up. I dare say you two have plenty to talk about. Put the tatties on for me in half an hour and stick that pie in the bottom of the oven, will you?' With that she was gone.

'Aye well, first things first,' Joe said, draping an arm round her and pulling her close.

She lifted her face and shivered when his mouth closed on hers. 'I've missed you,' she mumbled through his kisses.

'You will marry me, won't you, Ina?' he asked.

'Yes,' she said softly, feeling as if all her dreams were coming true. 'And I'll be right proud, Joe.'

'As soon as we can would be best then, wouldn't it? I don't think I could stand living in the same house with you and not having the chance to get close to you. Ma'll watch us like a hawk.'

She giggled. 'I'm sure we'll find a way,' she promised, feeling the delicious heat flaring between her legs, wishing there was somewhere they could go right now.

They were brought back to earth by sounds of movement from the adjoining room. 'That's Pa,' Joe moaned, moving his hand away from Ina's soft breasts with incredible speed.

As soon as Jessy came back and Ina had been introduced to Joe's good-humoured father, Shug, they announced their plans, Joe beaming with pride.

'Och, did youse not have more sense than to fall out with the whole of the lassie's family? It's not the best start is it? Still, I'm fair pleased for the both of you,' Shug said, shaking his son by the hand. 'It's not easy mind, being married to a miner, Jessy'll tell you that, lass, but if you two are half as happy as we've been then you'll not want for anything that matters.'

'Well, best see the minister right away,' was Jessy's practical response. 'Make things decent like and stop the tongues wagging. It's tempting fate to have you two living under the same roof while you're not wed. Now, you men away outside while Ina and I have a wee talk.'

She waited until the door closed behind her menfolk then turned to face Ina. 'Now, lass, I always in believe in coming right out with things so I'm going to ask you something and I don't want you to be upset with me because of what I'm going to say.'

Ina felt her heart lurch in apprehension but said, 'Go on.'

'You're not in the family way are you, lass?'

Ina thought back to that day on the beach, suddenly understanding what a risk they had taken and how lucky they had been to have escaped even more trouble. She flushed slightly then met Jessy's watchful eyes with a shy smile. 'No. It's nothing like that.' She sighed then whispered, 'But I didn't want it to be like this. I love Joe. I wanted Maurice and Maureen and my mother and grandparents to love him too. But they wouldn't even listen. As soon as they found out he was a miner they were against him. They all said I wasn't to see him again.'

'Aye, well, if you're going to marry Joe you'll soon see there's a lot of folk think just like they do. It's a hard life, lass, and you'd best be sure of the way you feel before you go and see the minister.'

'I am sure!' Ina's voice was so strong and certain, her eyes so steady and direct, that Jessy couldn't doubt her. 'I *do* love Joe, but I didn't mean to force him into marrying me by coming here. You don't think . . .'

Jessy's loud guffaw startled her. 'Och, lass, never worry about that. The lad's done nothing but talk about you since he came back from that day trip. He loves you right enough. Now then, dry those pretty eyes and smile again. Joe will take care of you lass, never fret.' She bustled away and busied herself at the stove, swallowing her own tears.

Jessy Lennox told herself that she was a very lucky woman. She had a husband she still loved after twenty-five years of marriage and two sons to make any woman proud, one already married and settled. And now there was the added blessing of a daughter-in-law she already knew she would be fond of, which was a sight more than most women ever had. There was something about Ina that had grabbed at Jessy's emotions from the very first minute she had seen her, gangling, awkward but proud, in the middle of the grass with half the village avidly at her back. Now she had had time to see that the girl was touchingly honest and it was obvious to any fool that she loved Joe. What more could anyone ask?

Later that night, after Shug had gone off to work and Jessy was dozing over her knitting, Joe led Ina to a sheltered place in the woods a mile or so from the village and spread his jacket on the ground for her. She sank on to it and pulled him on top of her eagerly. In the fading light of the summer evening they made urgent love, barely waiting to shed the necessary bits of clothing before falling hungrily on each other.

Afterwards, as they lay, still entwined, he sighed mightily. 'Thank you for coming, Ina,' he said, kissing her nose. 'I promise to make you happy.'

She snuggled against him, idyllically happy, sure that she was safe forever.

Ina and Jessy hurried through their morning chores then put on their smartest clothes, ready to walk down to the small village kirk. The minister was responsible for three villages in the area and visited one each week, in strict rotation. Jessy insisted that her family attend the service.

'We can't expect the man to marry Joe and Ina if we

526

don't even turn up at his church,' she said reasonably to Shug's muttered objections.

As it was, Minister Maitland was less than enthusiastic about being asked to marry a couple who weren't regular attenders. The earliest he could fit them in was nine weeks away, he insisted dourly, wondering, like many of the villagers, if this was another pair who had anticipated the wedded state in some back alley.

'You'll have to arrange with the registrar in Inverannan to have the banns posted,' he told them sourly. 'You'll need your birth certificates when you apply for the licence.'

Ina was impervious to the minister's sneering manner. There was nothing on earth which could mar her happiness now. And now they had the date settled she could write and tell her mother and grandparents. It would be lovely if they could be there for the service.

'That man's manner sticks in my craw,' Shug grumbled. 'Did you see the way he looked down his nose at us?'

'Never mind him,' his wife chortled. 'He's going to marry them and that's the main thing.'

While Jessy and Shug went on ahead, Ina and Joe dawdled along behind, glad of some private time together. As soon as Jessy turned into the rows she saw the two men waiting near her cottage. The nearer she got to them the surer she was that they were something to do with Ina. The burly, red-headed one was too much like Ina's description of her brother for it to be a coincidence.

'Are you looking for me?' she asked the pair who were shuffling about uncomfortably under the keen gaze of the villagers who were returning from kirk.

'If your name is Lennox then it's your son I want,' Maurice replied rudely.

'I am Mrs Lennox,' she corrected him stiffly. 'And my son isn't home right now.'

'Then I'll bloody well wait,' he said, marching towards the door.

'Not in my house with those manners you won't, Mr Archibold,' she told him firmly.

'How do you know my name?' he demanded.

'Use your head, laddie,' Shug said pityingly.

'For God's sake, Maurice,' Rab exploded. 'Have you no sense in that head of yours?' He stepped forward and introduced himself. 'Mr Lennox, Mrs Lennox. My name is Rab Bannerman. I am Ina's grandfather. I've come here from Glendarroch, that's near Fort William, because I am very worried about her. From what I hear she's sweet on your son. All I really want to know is whether she's here and that she's safe and well.'

Jessy looked into those eyes, still sharp and blue, sensed the innate goodness, and the charm, of the man and softened. 'She is indeed staying with us, Mr Bannerman, and right happy we are to have her. She and Joe have gone for a wee walk after kirk but they won't be more than an hour. Come in and take a cup of tea with us while you wait.'

'Thank you,' he smiled. 'I'd be right glad of a cup. Maurice?'

'I suppose so,' Maurice muttered ungraciously.

'Maurice is Ina's stepbrother,' Rab said.

'We know.' Shug directed a withering glance at the younger man. 'She told us about him.'

'Now look here,' Maurice said, his temper simmering dangerously. 'It was your son who started all this. He damn near broke my nose.'

'So I hear, and I believe you deserved it,' Shug, normally mild mannered, had taken an instant dislike to this hulking brute. 'Anyway, you more than got even with him so that chapter's closed. I can't say I approve of a man who hits a woman though.'

'What?' Rab choked.

'Aye, Mr Bannerman. He didn't tell you that bit I suppose? Your Ina still had the marks on her face when she arrived here.' Satisfied, Shug subsided into his chair.

Rab too accepted a seat and sat in silence.

'Och, look, this is stupid,' Jessy said. 'For the sake of the young 'uns could we not try and sort this out for them?'

'That is why I'm here, Mrs Lennox. I love my granddaughter very much. I can't begin to tell you how worried we've all been.'

'She's fine. A grand lass,' she smiled. 'You should be right proud of her, Mr Bannerman.'

Rab's eyes got their twinkle back. 'We agree about the important thing then. I wish she'd told us where she was, though.'

'I think she was frightened you'd make her go home.'

Rab raised his eyebrows. 'Aye, well, I would have been happier about all this if she'd talked it over with us first. Running away never solved anything.'

'She says she tried to tell you all how she feels, but nobody listened,' Jessy said gently. 'Och, they do love each other you know. It's lovely to see them. Fair puts me in mind of when I was winching,' she mused.

Laughter from just outside made them all turn round.

'We thought we'd walk up Tower Hill,' Joe said as he and Ina burst into the room. 'Have we got time before lunch?' He stopped abruptly when he saw their visitors and an arm went protectively round Ina's shoulders.

'Grandpa,' she whispered, going very white and moving closer in to Joe.

'I take it this is your young man?' he asked.

'This is Joe, Grandpa. Joe Lennox.'

Rab saw a tall, very young man with unruly dark hair and honest eyes. He stepped forward and extended his hand. 'I am very pleased to meet you, Joe.'

Joe jumped as if he had been kicked. 'Me too,' he stammered.

'Well, lass,' Rab turned back to Ina. 'am I to get some sort of welcome from you or are you just going to gape at me?'

She hesitated for a second, as if still uncertain then flung herself at him. 'Och, Grandpa, I'm glad you're here,' she choked. 'I thought you'd be so angry with me.'

'Well, I'm not best pleased,' he admitted. 'But the important thing is that you're safe and happy. You are happy, lass?' He watched her closely.

'Aye,' she said firmly, moving back to Joe's waiting arm. 'I am happy, Grandpa.'

'That's fine then.' He settled back into his chair and winked at her. 'We'll say no more about the past though I dare say there's a fair bit to know about the future.'

It was as if the whole house let out a huge breath of relief. Jessy produced tea and scones and they pulled their chairs in closer, making a tight, warm circle in the cosy house.

Only Maurice stayed apart, looking round him with an expression of opprobrium on his fleshy face which Jessy decided to ignore. No wonder the girl had left home, she thought.

'Perhaps you should tell your grandfather your plans, lass,' Shug suggested gently.

Joe caught Ina's hand and gave it a light, reassuring

530

squeeze. 'Leave this to me,' he whispered, but not so quietly that Rab didn't catch the words. Joe got to his feet and shuffled about for a second or two. Then he lifted his face and turned to Rab. 'I have to tell you that I'm sorry for all the trouble we've caused, Mr Bannerman,' he started.

'Hummph,' Maurice growled.

'But Ina and me love each other.' He flashed her a look that couldn't possibly be misinterpreted. 'We want to get married and we'd rather do it with your blessing than without. Either way,' he added with fierce determination. 'We've made up our minds and set a date already.'

'Aye,' Rab said. 'It's plain enough how you feel about one another but lad, can't you see, this isn't the right way to go about it? You're gey young, the pair of you. Maybe youse should give yourselves time to think about it, not rush into things. Ina, come home to Glendarroch, lass, talk to your mother. Stay a month or two. If you're still sure you want to go ahead with this, then Joe here can come up and meet the family. That'll be the time to start making plans.'

'No, Grandpa. Joe and I are getting married and there's nothing any of you can do about it.' Ina's mouth was set in a line of stubborness.

'Och, lass . . .' The disappointment was plain in his voice and suddenly he looked an old man.

Ina's heart wrenched inside her. 'I'm sorry,' she whispered.

'I knew it!' Maurice leapt to his feet, his face scarlet and beaded with sudden sweat. 'You little slut,' he spat. 'You're having to get wed, aren't you? Why else would you be in such a hurry? What they said about young Cameron finding youse two on the beach with no clothes on was true, wasn't it?'

With a great effort, Joe contained his temper. 'No, Mr Archibold, Ina and I are not having to get married. We're being wed because we love each other and that's what we both want.'

'You don't understand,' Ina cried. But how could he? How could she make someone as narrow-minded as Maurice know what she and Joe felt for each other, how could she ever hope to make him see that what had happened between her and Joe was as natural, as inevitable, as the summer sun?

'Understand?' he roared. 'Och, I understand all right. You went with him like a common whore, like a bitch in heat. Everyone in the village knows it.'

'Maurice!' Rab warned at the same time as Shug put a restraining hand on his furious son's arm.

'No!' Maurice rounded on him. 'I'll say what I have to say, Rab Bannerman, and you and everyone else in this room will hear me out.' He turned to Joe who clenched his fists but stayed resolutely still under his father's watchful eye. 'You are a right bastard. I knew it the minute I set eyes on you. Well, you can have her, filthy little slut that she is. You deserve one another. Just stay away from me. And stay away from Maureen. She's a decent, hard-working lass and I'll not have my sister contaminated by the likes of you.'

While Maurice was speaking, Jessy got up and placed herself solidly beside her son. 'I think you've made yourself quite plain, Mr Archibold,' she said coldly. 'These two are in love. Aye, it's a beautiful thing to see and I feel sorry for you if you can't recognise it. They deserve a chance as much as anyone else and they'll get it here. They don't need you so the best thing you can do is take yourself and your filthy mouth out of my house.'

Maurice stomped to the door then turned and said, 'I

mean it, Ina. You'll never be welcome in Kilweem again. When you get fed up living in this slum don't think you can come running back to me for help.'

Ina watched him with tear-filled eyes then turned back to her grandfather who had heard it through without comment. Slowly he levered himself to his feet and followed Maurice to the door.

'Are you sure, lass?' he asked at the last minute.

She nodded. 'I love Joe, Grandpa,' she told him hoarsely, her voice tight with unshed tears. 'Please, don't be angry.'

'I'm not angry, lass. Disappointed maybe, but not angry.' He patted her arm. 'Aye, well, it's your life,' he said, looking along the depressing rows, his heart bleeding for what the future would hold for her in a place like this. 'Marriage isn't something to go into lightly. Once you make your vows you're bound for life, lass. Think on that before you do anything foolish. And there'll always be a home for you in Glendarroch.'

'I'll not change my mind, Grandpa,' she said firmly, shattered by the pain she saw in his old eyes. Her heart seemed to grind within her aching chest and her head began to spin.

He shook his head despairingly. 'Och, lass . . .'

Jessy who had watched and listened saw that it was time for her to intervene. 'Away inside, lass. We've given the neighbours enough to be thinking about without you bursting into tears on my doorstep.' Gently she pulled Ina inside and put her firmly into Joe's waiting arms. 'Goodbye, Mr Bannerman. Thank you for coming. You'll always be welcome here if you should want to come and see us again. And we'll look after Ina, never fear.'

'Aye. Thank God for your good heart, Mrs Lennox,' he said, still unable to smile.

TWENTY-SIX

I na emerged from the earth closet trying very hard not to gag. The necessity to relieve herself in the primitive privy never failed to turn her stomach. She wondered if she would ever get accustomed to it.

It was nothing more than a badly constructed and drafty cesspit, shared by three other, less scrupulous, families. Despite Jessy's constant efforts with scrubbing brush and carbolic it was never truly free from smells. Ina often thought that Jessy would be better saving her energy. The very fact that their privy was comparatively clean worked against them, attracting women and children from the whole row who took shameless advantage of Jessy's high standards in preference to their own foul closets.

Ina stood on the grass for a few minutes, breathing in fresher air until her fastidious stomach settled into relative calm.

'Morning, hen.' The cheerful voice made her spin round.

'Morning, Trot,' she smiled.

Sam Trotter, the postman whose round included two of the mining villages, offered a white envelope to Jessy, who was hanging washing on the line, then hovered expectantly.

She took it from him then laughed. 'I suppose you'll be wanting a cup of tea after trailing all up here?'

'Och, that's good of you, Mrs Lennox. I'm fair parched,' he admitted, with a credible degree of surprise though, on the few mornings when there was any mail for the rows, he could usually depend on a good brew from one or other of the residents.

'Come away in, Trot,' Jessy said 'I must have known you'd be up here the morn. I've got the kettle boiling already.'

While Jessy listened to the latest gossip from Trot, Ina made her way back to the communal washhouse to collect the rest of the laundry which she and Jessy had risen at dawn to do, beating the other women for the choice of sinks and the best of the stiff old mangles.

Although Ina rolled up her sleeves and gladly took her share of the household chores, this was the one thing she really hated. The washhouse was nothing more than a long shed, lined with sinks on one side and coal-fired boilers on the other, with a line of huge mangles running down the centre. The fires, fuelled by coal grudgingly supplied by the pit owners, were only lit once a week, very early on a Monday morning. Come rain or shine the washing had to be done then, or not at all. The early risers had the benefit of clean water. As the fires died down the women worked through their loads, starting with the sheets and towels and always leaving their menfolk's blackened work clothes until last. To be late meant having to wait for someone else to finish and, worse, having to do a whole week's wash in the grey and tepid water in which another family's load had already been done. If the weather was fine, as it was today, Jessy had her laundry strung out on her ropes before ten. In wet weather there was no alternative but to hoist the whole lot aloft on the series of wooden pullies which hung from the washhouse roof. When that happened the women were obliged to stand guard over their belongings until they were dry enough to be taken home and propped round the range. To turn your back for more than a minute was to lose a pair of sheets or a good dress. When the wash was finally retrieved it always smelled of smoke, and was often grubbier than when they started.

What Ina really loathed was the way the other women gossiped about her, often within her hearing, sneering at the way she struggled with the sodden sheets, wincing as the soda in the water caused her hands to redden, blister and finally bleed. Ina knew that Doris Cree, who dominated the other women by virtue of her bitter tongue, loud voice and vicious temper, was the ringleader but, out of respect for Jessy, she had steeled herself to ignore the constant barbs and snide remarks.

Today, when she returned to the steamy atmosphere of the washhouse to collect the last two sheets which she had left neatly folded on a draining board, she found them strewn over the muddy floor.

'Who did this?' she demanded furiously, glaring at Doris Cree who was now working at the sink she had been using.

Doris shrugged and grinned at her neighbour. 'Shouldn't have left them there. There's other folk need to do their wash besides her.'

Sensing a showdown the other women fell silent.

'I hadn't finished,' Ina retorted, gathering the soiled sheets into an untidy bundle and dumping them back on the draining board, shovelling Doris's own wash on to the floor as she did so.

'Hey! What the hell do you think you're doing?' Doris screamed, running at Ina and grabbing for her hair. 'Stuck up little cow. I'll learn you not to mess with my things.'

537

'That's it, Doris,' someone encouraged as the women gathered round.

Ina screamed with rage, jerked her head away and parted painfully with a handful of hair.

'What's wrong?' Doris jeered as Ina took a couple of paces back, blinking through the tears of pain which had flooded her eyes. 'Frightened to make a fight of it, are you? Think you're too good for it, do you?'

'Scared to get her hands dirty, more like,' someone else sniggered.

'Aye, not used to hard work.'

Doris was still grinning, sure of a verbal victory, when Ina launched herself at her. They crashed to the soggy, earth floor and rolled over and over, clawing at each other's faces with ragged nails, using hands and feet to pound into one another.

Doris was in her early twenties, a big woman, larded and fleshy. Ina was only a little younger, but tall, lean and fit, quicker to react and driven by absolute blind rage. When they finally cannoned to a halt, jammed up against the unyielding, rusty legs of a mangle, Ina was on top with one hand closed firmly round the older woman's nose and the other drawn back, ready to deliver a stinging slap. Doris, her skirts crumpled up round her waist, showing patched and stained knickers, kicked out, bruising Ina's shins, then kicked again when Ina's hand connected with her face, but she was winded and gasping for breath. Sensing victory Ina tangled her hand in Doris's sparse hair, gripping near the roots and tugging so hard that the other woman's neck slewed sideways.

'Get up,' she hissed, giving the hair a vicious jerk. 'Stand up.'

Slowly Doris obeyed, her face red and sullen. 'Someone

get her off,' she yelled at her neighbours. No one moved. 'Help me,' she said, a pleading note in her voice now.

Sensing a change in the balance of power in the rows, they shuffled uncomfortably but stayed resolutely where they were. In truth Doris was deeply unpopular, a troublemaker rather than a friend to any of them, and the vast majority of the women were secretly relishing her humiliation.

Still keeping a firm grip on her opponent, Ina dragged her back to the sink, forcing Doris to bend almost double to take the strain off her fragile scalp. 'Pick my sheets up,' she ordered, trampling pointedly on Doris's scattered wash.

For a moment the older woman baulked. Ina wound her fist deeper into the hair.

'All right. All right.' She admitted defeat at last.

'Rinse them through. Get the muck out of them,' Ina persisted.

'Let go of my hair. I can't work like this,' Doris choked, her head on a level with the sink.

Reluctantly Ina disentangled her fingers but kept her hand lightly on the other woman's head, the threat obvious. 'Get on with it!'

Slowly Doris obeyed, slopping cold water over the sheets and rubbing vigorously until the marks finally came out. When she was finished she stood with her head drooping over the sink.

'The wringer,' Ina snapped, determined to see this through.

The look Doris levelled at Ina was one of pure hatred. 'I'll get you for this,' she spat.

'Just try,' Ina retorted, twisting her hand in the greasy hair.

Doris Cree gathered the sheets in her huge arms and fed them slowly through the mangle, allowing them to fall into a galvanised tub on the other side. Finally satisfied Ina picked them up and made for the door.

'I wouldn't stand there gawping, Doris Cree,' she taunted. 'You've a fair bit of work to be done on your own wash yet. Best hurry else you'll never get it dried the day.'

'Well done, lass,' someone called after Ina as she escaped back into the fresh air and she knew they had accepted her at last.

'What in the name . . . !' Jessy exclaimed when Ina got home. 'Just look at the state of your face.'

Ina hadn't given her own injuries a thought until now. Her fingers probed the scratches. 'I had a wee misunderstanding with Doris Cree,' she admitted sheepishly.

'Och, for goodness sake! Have you no more sense than to tangle with likes of her? You can't get the better of someone like Doris Cree. Best to ignore her, lass. Fall out with her and she'll give you nothing but trouble.'

Ina laughed. 'I don't think so,' she said. 'I don't think so.'

Jessy looked at Ina speculatively then said, 'Och, I almost forgot. That letter was for you.'

Ina took the envelope eagerly. 'It's Mam's writing,' she said. 'I wonder if she's going to come to the wedding after all.'

'You'll not know that unless you read it,' Jessy smiled.

Ina ripped the envelope apart and sank into a chair to decipher her mother's uneven handwriting. She smiled happily as she read through Morag's attempt to make things right between them, her assurance that Joe would be welcome in Glendarroch and her sincere wishes for their future happiness, knowing that she had her grandfather to thank for her mother's change of heart. But then, as Ina turned to the second page of scrawled writing, the smile faded and was replaced by an angry frown. Jessy, glancing up from the table where she was industriously kneading dough, saw the girl pale and her mouth tighten into a hurt, defensive line.

'She's not coming.' Ina dropped the letter on to the table.

'Och, lass. I'm sorry,' Jessy said. 'Try not to be too disappointed. It is a long way for her to come after all.'

'It's not that. She's getting married herself. She wants me and Joe to go up there and meet this Archie.'

'That's a grand idea!' Jessy enthused.

'I'm not going,' Ina insisted stubbornly. 'I can't afford it.'

'Of course you can! You've got the money you brought with you from Kilweem. You've not spent that have you?' Ina had offered it to Jessy who had refused to accept anything, feeling that it was Joe's responsibility to pay her a little extra each week to support his girlfriend.

'Aye. I've still got it but Joe and I will need it when we get married, for furniture and things.'

'Och, you'll not need that much to furnish one of these places,' Jessy chortled. 'All you'll need is a table and chairs and a mattress. If the pit manager gives you widow Graham's old house, like he says he will, she'll likely sell you her furniture for next to nothing. She's away to live with her married son, in Inverannan, and she'll not be needing to take much with her.'

'I'm glad it's her house,' Ina said, momentarily diverted. 'She keeps it braw.'

'Aye, she's a decent woman. You'll not get a better

place, not in Craigie. So, you'll have enough to spare for a trip to see your mam.'

Ina still looked doubtful. Jessy wiped her floury hands and came to sit next to her future daughter-in-law.

'Make the effort, lass. Swallow that pride of yours and clear the air with your mam. You'll live to regret it if you don't.'

'I don't know . . .' Ina sighed.

'Talk it over with Joe when he comes in. See what he thinks.'

'I agree with Ma,' Joe said later. 'And you'd like to see your grandpa again, wouldn't you?'

'I don't know why she won't come here,' Ina persisted. 'You'd think she'd make the effort for my wedding.'

'Maybe she's not got the money,' Jessy suggested. 'After all, she's not got a man to support her. I dare say she's finding it hard to manage and she's her own wedding to pay for, don't forget that.'

'I suppose so.'

'That's settled then,' Joe decided.

'When will we go?' Ina asked without enthusiasm.

'You'll have to go on your own,' Joe told her.

'On my own? But I want her to meet you!'

'I can't take the time off.'

'Just a couple of days?' she begged.

'I'll not have a job to come back to if I do that, not with me needing a few days after the wedding and all,' he laughed gently.

'It's true enough, lass. You go. Have yourself a wee holiday. It might be the last one you ever have,' Jessy insisted.

'So Joe wouldn't come and meet us?' Morag asked, a tinge of complaint in her voice.

'He can't just take time off from his work whenever he feels like it, Mam,' Ina said, trying to keep the acerbity from her own voice. The long journey had exhausted her and the welcome hadn't been as enthusiastic as she had hoped.

'Give the lass time to drink her tea before you start on at her,' Archie said, winking at Ina who couldn't help smiling back. 'Ina's right enough. A working man can't just take time off when he feels like it.'

'I was hoping you'd come to Craigie for our wedding,' Ina said, looking directly at her mother.

'Aye. I know, and I would really like to see you wed, Ina, but you must see we can't do that.'

'No. I don't see.' Ina gave in to bad temper at last.

'We can't afford it,' Morag explained. 'It's no different for Archie than it is for your Joe. He has his work to go to, just like Joe, and we've got our own wedding to pay for. It all takes money.'

'I suppose so.'

'Anyway, where would we all stay if we came now? Mrs Lennox sounds a kind-hearted woman but I doubt she could sleep four extra folk in her house. And you know fine we can't stay with Maurice and Maureen. Not now.'

'I hadn't thought of that,' Ina admitted.

'Will you come to *my* wedding?' Morag threw the challenge back to her daughter.

'Mam! You know I can't.'

'Aye, I do know,' Morag answered with a wry smile. 'So it's daft to fall out when it's the same for both of us.'

Ina chuckled. 'Aye, it is, isn't it. I'm sorry, Mam. I wish I could be here and I wish you could all come to my wedding but I don't think there's a lot we can do about it.'

'We'll save up and come to see you in the summer. I promise you. After Archie and I are married and you and Joe are settled in to your own wee house. There'll be just the four of us and we can all get to know one another a bit better.' Morag reached over and kissed Ina lightly on the cheek. 'Now, you look tired, lass. Why don't you go away to your bed and get a good night's sleep?'

'Aye. Your mam's right,' Archie insisted. 'Have yourself a good rest and in the morning we'll take the cart into Fort William and buy you your wedding present. How about that?'

'That'd be just fine, Archie,' Ina said, already knowing she was going to like him, very much. 'I'm really happy for you, Mam,' she added, feeling suddenly emotional. 'I know you two are going to be happy.'

'You too, Ina,' Morag answered. 'I can see it in your eyes whenever you speak about your Joe.' She hesitated for a second then went on, sounding slightly awkward. 'I'm sorry if I was too quick to judge him before . . . I was wrong there. Your grandpa was full of praise for him. He sounds like a fine lad.'

'He's the finest there is, Mam. I know you're going to love him too. I just wish you could meet him before the wedding.'

'You love him, Ina. That's all that matters,' Morag said, showing her through to the bedroom.

'You should be proud of her, Morag, she's a fine, bonny lass,' Archie said as he kissed Morag goodnight before hopping over the wall to his own house.

'I am,' she said softly.

'So, you're going to have to tell her the truth, lass. And the quicker you do it, the better for both of you.' He fixed his brown eyes on her sternly.

Morag shivered. 'I know. I will . . .'

The five days Ina had allowed herself in Glendarroch passed in a blur of contentment. Her mother and Archie were made for each other, that much had been obvious from the very first night. If she sometimes sensed a certain nervousness in her mother she guessed it was simply because they were practically strangers to one another and assumed it would pass with time.

And then it was her very last day. Tomorrow Rab would drive her to the station and she would go back to Craigie where, in just over three weeks' time, she would become Mrs Joe Lennox. That thought, on its own, was enough to bring a smile to her lips. Much as she had enjoyed seeing her family again she could hardly wait to get back to Joe and start life as a married woman.

'Did you find my birth certificate?' she asked her mother as they walked back from the big house where Morag had taken her to meet Mrs Wishart.

Morag blanched and her footsteps seemed to slow of their own accord. 'I meant to talk to you about that, Ina,' she choked at last.

'Couldn't you find it?' Ina panicked.

'Aye. I've it here in my bag,' Morag whispered. 'But there's something I have to tell you about it. Come and sit by the side of the loch with me for a wee while.'

Ina followed her mother slowly along the shore until they came to a low, mossy wall. They sat side by side in silence while Morag wondered how best to broach a very difficult subject. Typically it was Ina who lost patience first.

'Well, what is it you wanted to tell me, Mam?' she asked.

Morag rummaged in her bag and produced a folded

paper. 'This is it,' she said, offering the birth certificate to Ina.

'Thanks.'

'Read it,' Morag ordered in a voice so harsh that Ina jumped and stared at her. Slowly she opened up the paper and read the neat entry. The date, the place, her mother's name. And her father's.

She stared at the name, not understanding what she saw. 'I thought my father's name was Angus Patterson?' she said, still staring at the paper.

She had never had any reason to doubt the story which Morag, Donny and Rab had concocted of a romance which had been tragically ended by the premature death of Angus Patterson. By the time she was old enough to want to know more about her real father, her relationship with her mother had deteriorated beyond intimate chats and she had turned to her grandfather and stepfather for information. They had both given her necessarily vague descriptions of a Pitochrie farm worker who had died of influenza shortly before the wedding. Ina had believed them implicitly when they told her there were no relations left on her father's side of the family and had long ago accepted that there was simply nothing more to know.

Morag swallowed hard and made herself go on. 'Your father's name was Angus Fraser.'

'I don't understand,' Ina said, confusion plain in her troubled eyes. 'Why did you tell me his name was Patterson?'

'Oh God,' Morag whispered. 'I've gone over this in my mind so many times but I still don't know how to tell you this.'

'Tell me what?' Ina demanded.

'I always told you your father died before we could

get married,' Morag went on, so low that Ina could hardly hear her. 'It wasn't true. We were never going to be married.'

Ina frowned then brightened, thinking she understood. To have a child outside marriage was still considered to be a terrible, shaming thing. In her mother's day it would have been a hundred times worse. 'It doesn't matter, Mam. Honestly. Don't upset yourself about it.' She could see that Morag was shaking, looked as though she might faint at any moment.

'It does matter,' Morag insisted. 'I need to tell you about him. You've got a right to know.'

Despite herself Ina was growing curious. 'You don't have to tell me, Mam. Maybe it's your business.' Obviously her mother had fallen pregnant by this Angus Fraser who had then let her down. But all too long ago to make any difference to her now. 'But why didn't you tell me his real name?'

'Just sit there and listen, Ina. Please,' Morag pleaded.

Ina shrugged. 'If you're sure.' She wriggled to get more comfortable on the smooth stones and listened while her mother related the story of her conception. When she had finished Morag stared silently over the loch for a minute then added, 'I should have told you all this a long time ago. I'm sorry I didn't.'

Ina swallowed. 'He forced you!' Suddenly she wished her mother had kept it to herself, let her continue with the fiction of a failed love affair. But this – to discover that she was the result of what amounted to rape; that she had been conceived in hate; that her father had been a wealthy man, the owner of a huge estate. 'I wish you hadn't told me.'

'I had to.' Morag blinked back tears, feeling the weight of things still untold like lead in her stomach.

'No wonder you never loved me.' It was sad acknowledgement of what she believed to be the truth.

'How dare you say that,' Morag rounded on her furiously. 'I loved you from the day you were born. I would have died for you.' But how was she going to tell her the rest? 'Whatever else I tell you, you have to believe I've always loved you, Ina.'

'Whatever else?' Ina repeated. 'What else is there?'

'Please, Ina, try to understand.'

'Understand what?' Ina demanded, her own colour fading as she sensed something worse about to be divulged.

'I never wanted you to know about this,' Morag went on, her voice trembling. 'I would have given anything to avoid it. I never thought you would have to know.' She turned away, tears streaming down her face.

'Mam?' Ina pleaded. 'Come and sit down. Whatever it is, it doesn't matter. It's all over with.'

'I wish to God it was!' Morag choked on the bile burning her throat. 'Two months ago I had a visitor. Someone I thought I would never see again.'

'Go on,' Ina said, intrigued.

'It was your brother, your half-brother. My son.'

Ina gaped. 'My half-brother? You had another child?'

'No. I only ever gave birth to one baby. A boy, born on the same night as you were.'

Ina had the very strange sensation of knowing her brain had ceased to function. She heard the words, understood the implication, but simply couldn't comprehend how it could be possible. *She* was Morag's child, she had just seen the proof of that in the certificate which was still clasped limply in her hands. 'I don't understand,' she stammered when she could get her mouth to work.

Haltingly Morag told her about that night, nearly nineteen years ago now, when she and Katrina Fraser had both given birth.

'She was desperate for a son, you see,' she ended lamely.

'You gave your child away?' Ina was too stunned to feel anything at all.

'NO! She took him! I didn't give him away. I would never have done that. By the time I found out, it was too late. I thought you were mine. I loved you with all my heart. I wouldn't have given you back to Katrina Fraser, even if it had been possible. That's why I never told you your father's real name. Don't you see? I didn't want there to be anything to connect you with that family.'

'I'm not even your child!'

'Not my blood child, no. But in all other ways . . .'

'Why?' Ina demanded suddenly. 'Why are you telling me now? What are you trying to do? My God, you've destroyed me! Even my grandparents aren't . . .' It was too much. She turned away feeling sick.

'Rab was never your true grandfather but it never stopped him loving you,' Morag reminded her gently. 'Think what you like about me, but don't make him suffer for my mistakes. He's old, Ina, his health's failing, don't hurt him. Please.'

'Does he know about this?' she asked bitterly.

'Yes.'

'No . . .' Suddenly she turned away and vomited pitifully, feeling that her whole being was voiding itself on to the grass. 'Oh God,' she moaned.

'I'm sorry, Ina,' Morag put a tentative hand on the thin, shaking shoulders. Furiously Ina shook herself free and turned back to face the woman she had always believed to be her mother, her eyes bleak. 'Why?' she repeated. 'Why are you telling me now?'

'He came to see me,' Morag said dully. 'My son. Angus. He came to see me. I hadn't seen him since before I married Donny. Then, with no warning at all, he turned up here. He traced me through Rab. You see . . .' She shuddered. 'Katrina was frightened I might try to take him from her. We signed papers agreeing that we had no claim on our own children – years and years ago. When Lady Katrina died, Angus found her copy. Well, it was obvious, from the way it was worded, that I was his real mother. It was a terrible shock for him. He came to look for me. I suppose it was the natural thing to do.'

'My real mother's dead . . .' It was too much, Ina's head span and she leant weakly against the wall.

'I'm sorry . . .'

The hopeless words roused Ina. 'And what did you say to him, this son of yours?' she demanded, bitterly angry now. 'Did you tell him that *I'm* your daughter. Did you tell him to go away, that you didn't want to see him? Did you?'

'He's my son, Ina.' Morag spread her hands in a gesture of helplessness. 'What could I do? He's my son. I love him.'

'And what about me?'

'Nothing needs to change between us. You're still my daughter. But you have got a brother.'

'I haven't got anyone,' Ina screamed in agony.

'Yes, you have,' Morag pleaded. 'You'll like him. He's a fine young man. Come to my wedding, Ina. He'll be there. You can meet him then. I know he's anxious to meet you. And Joe,' she added hastily.

Ina stared at her. 'How can you love someone you hardly know?' she demanded.

'I'm his mother,' Morag said simply.

'But not mine. You never were my mother,' Ina spat,

starting to walk back to the village, leaving Morag staring after her.

Morag watched her go then sank back on to the wall and buried her face in her hands and wept.

Ina stuffed all her things into her bag then ran along the road to the blacksmith's workshop where there was a cart for hire. 'Can you get me to Fort William for the Glasgow train?' she asked.

'Ina.' She turned automatically to the sound of Rab's voice. 'Wait, lass.' He had seen her frantic flight and guessed what had happened.

'You knew!' she accused him bitterly. 'All these years you've known I'm not her daughter.'

'Come home, lass. Let's talk about this.'

'No! Go away. Leave me alone. You don't need me now. You've got a grandson to love instead.' Turning her back on him she threw her bag into the back of the cart and sprang up beside the smith. She didn't even look back as the horse trotted smartly from the village.

Rab watched her go then walked slowly back to his own house.

'Rab? What's wrong?' Annie hurried to his side as he lurched through the front door, his face ashen with pain, gasping for breath which wouldn't come. She tried to support him as he fell but he was too heavy for her. He was dead before his head hit the floor.

'Och, lass. I don't know what to say.' Jessy was appalled.

'It doesn't matter,' Ina insisted, wiping from her face the tears which had accompanied her blurted story. When she looked up again her expression was hard enough to bring a twist of apprehension to Jessy's stomach. 'I've got Joe and I've got you. I don't need them, not any of them.'

'Come on, let's go for a wee walk,' Joe said, his voice gravelly with anger and pain for her.

Silently she let him lead her from the house and to the woods. There, in their private place, he took her, hard, thrusting the pain from them, welding her to him. She responded with equal ferocity.

'I love you, Joe,' she cried in the violence of her climax. 'I love you.'

He collapsed on to her then took her face in his work-roughened but gentle hands. 'And I love you, Ina,' he told her, the intensity of that love plain in his dark eyes. 'I'll never let anyone hurt you ever again. We've got each other. We'll be happy. I promise.'

She trembled then wrapped her arms round him and drew his head on to her full breasts, finding some measure of peace at last.

Her new-found calm lasted only forty-eight hours. Her mother's letter was terse and cruel. Rab had already been buried.

'It was my fault.'

Knowing it was beyond his power to comfort her, Joe held her, letting her sob her heartbreak into his shoulder.

In Glendarroch, Morag and Annie grieved together.

Annie shook her head mutely, past words, past tears.

'I killed him,' Morag sobbed. 'I destroyed my daughter and I killed Rab.'

'No, lass,' Archie drew her away, took her back to the warmth of his own house. 'You can't blame yourself. Life plays terrible tricks on us all. Rab was ill, we all knew it was just a matter of time.'

He cradled her like a small child until, at last, she slept.

TWENTY-SEVEN

Gradually, very gradually, the pain subsided. Instead of a raw, weeping wound there was a constant nagging ache which caught Ina unawares, often at night, causing her to toss and turn, waking Joe who silently gathered her into his arms and comforted her in a way which brought healing with it.

Their wedding had been a subdued affair. Ina had absolutely no one to take their places on her side of the rather austere church. Out of respect for her feelings Jessy restricted the guests to the immediate family and one or two close neighbours. Joe's brother, Harry, was best man and Ina asked a little girl from two houses along who was delighted to don her best frock and act as her bridesmaid. Shug gave her away. Tears brightened her eyes when she entered the church and saw the tiny congregation and the empty front pew where her mother should have been sitting but the tears vanished the moment Joe stepped into the aisle and turned to smile encouragement at her as she walked towards him.

Considering the state his friends had delivered him home in the previous night she was amazed he could stand upright. But his voice was firm and loud when he repeated his vows and his hand steady when he slipped the ring on her finger. When he kissed her she felt such a surge of love that she was frightened she was going to cry.

Outside the church the whole village had gathered,

determined to celebrate the marriage in good style. Unknown to Ina, Jessy and her friends had arranged a light meal and dancing in the ramshackle church hall and, in the end, they had a fine start to their married life.

When the drink and food were exhausted they were escorted riotously through the village and, with much laughing and many lewd remarks, pushed through the door of their new home.

'Well now, Mrs Lennox,' Joe laughed, sweeping her into his arms as soon the door was closed. 'Let's make this house ours.'

Their new neighbours noted, with some satisfaction, that it was way past midday before the curtains were finally drawn back.

Ina settled into her new role perfectly happily. The time she had spent living with Joe and his parents before the wedding had prepared her for the realities of life in a pit village and the adjustment was less traumatic than it might otherwise have been. Even though the little house, at the top end of the rows, lacked all the basic amenities which she had taken for granted in Kilweem, she was content, happy simply to be with Joe. Like all the other women she went to the washhouse on Mondays, pumped all her water from the standpipe and relied on coal for heat and oil lamps to light the dark nights. Like Jessy she spent hours cleaning the privy, determined not to be seduced by the slovenly ways of some of her neighbours.

'Well, you're a hard worker, I'll say that for you,' her new neighbour, Mrs Rankine, praised her. 'Maybe you'll shame some of the others into keeping their own places tidy.'

But although Ina adapted without complaint to the

rigours of her new life her sense of injustice was outraged by the conditions in the village.

Wherever the women gathered, in the little shop, in
the washhouse and outside the school, their conversation was made up of complaints. But, for all their dissatisfaction, it was obvious that they were resigned. Not
one of them, not even the loud-mouthed Doris Cree,
seemed to have the will to do anything positive to improve their lot. Ina listened with growing impatience
and, before her first month as a married woman was out,
she was determined to act. Outspoken and energetic, it
was Ina who wrote to the pit owner, extracting his
promise to repair the badly leaking roofs on some of the
houses and supply coal to the washhouse on Tuesdays as
well as Mondays. It was she who stood guard on Saturday mornings and made sure the lazy, bad-tempered,
midden carter cleared all the privies. And after a toddler
was bitten by a rat she even visited every cottage in the
rows and shamed her lazier neighbours into cleaning
their own earth closets and clearing the accumulation of
rubbish from outside their homes. It was soon seen that
Ina Lennox was a force to be reckoned with.

'I don't know who the hell you think you are,' Doris
Cree sneered. 'Coming here and telling everyone what
to do. You're wasting your time. They'll soon give up
trying to make these places decent. It doesn't matter
how much you clean them up, they'll never be anything
more than hovels.'

'It's up to us to make the best of them,' Ina insisted.
'The pit owners'll not waste money on repairing the
roofs and windows if they think we live like animals. It's
up to us to show them that we deserve something better.
New houses, places we can be proud of.'

'Och, aye, we'll all polish our windows and blacklead

555

the ranges and the Strathannan Mining Company will come along and say, "Well done. Youse're all so bloody wonderful that we're going to reward you by using all our profits to build wee palaces for youse all to live in."'

Ina ignored her. It was clear that she and Doris would never be friends and the village had divided almost equally in support of one or the other of them.

Jessy, watching with detached amusement and a fair degree of admiration, could see many minor battles in store for the two women and she had no doubt about who would come out on top. The traumatic occurrences of the past months had certainly hardened Ina, Jessy thought, and that was no bad thing. In villages like these it was the women who kept the families together, welded the community into a source of support and strength, and to do that they had to be tough.

One night, soon after her grandfather's death, a grieving Ina had confided the depth of her pain to her mother-in-law and had insisted that from now on she would take responsibility for her own life so that, if things went wrong, she could blame no one but herself. And the thing Ina was most determined to do was to make a success of her marriage.

Jessy saw that Ina was proving herself to be a very different person from the apparently diffident creature who had arrived on her doorstep not too many months ago, looking as much out of place as a cat in a cage. She already knew Ina well enough to realise that pride alone would drive her to achieve what her own mother had so obviously failed to provide and she was confident that Joe and Ina would indeed be happy together.

Ina herself was aware of the change but not displeased with it. She was self-assured and confident, keen to take her place in the community and prove she could cope with the hardships of her new life.

She accepted the good-natured banter of the washhouse, and the more acidic comments, with equal aplomb, quickly learning to give as good as she got, understanding that many of the other women judged one another by this simple standard. She was no longer forced to endure the spiteful comments which had marked her first weeks in the village when she had been criticised for her soft hands, her extensive vocabulary and her softer accent. She knew the women already respected her and felt that she belonged here in this tough little community. Not for one single moment did she regret her decision to leave Kilweem.

Some three months after the wedding, Ina suddenly started to feel ill, constantly tired and nauseous at the most unexpected moments. But such was her ignorance that she couldn't be sure of the reason for her sickness until Joe, worried about her, consulted his mother.

The following morning Jessy wrapped her shawl round her shoulders and hurried to her daughter-in-law's home. She knocked then stepped inside the neat little house, pleased to see everything beautifully clean and well cared for.

Ina, who had been sitting in an easy chair with her eyes closed, jumped up guiltily, surprised to see Jessy at this early hour.

'Sit down, lass,' Jessy instructed. 'Now then, our Joe tells me you're off colour?'

Ina nodded. 'I think I might be going to have a wean,' she confided. 'But I'm not sure.'

'Well, lass, you and I will have a wee talk and then we'll have a better idea of whether there really is a bairn on the way,' Jessy beamed.

'I've never missed before,' Ina replied in response to Jessy's direct question. 'But I've not seen anything since just after Joe and me were married. I wondered if it could be a bairn but I really don't know much about that sort of thing,' she admitted.

'I'm not surprised, lass. A girl needs a mother on hand to tell her about these things. Still, from what you say I'd think you were about eight weeks gone. It looks as if I'd better get the knitting pins going on some baby things.' There was no disguising the pleasure Jessy felt as she leant over to peck Ina on the cheek. 'Well done, lass. You'll have to look after yourself now, mind. And I'll get Ma Trale to look in on you. You'll be in good hands with her.'

After Jessy had left, Ina sat on in her chair. How wonderful it would be, she thought, to be able to write to her mother and share the news with her. How pleased she would be. But almost at once, Ina's instinctive reaction was swamped under the miserable memory of their last meeting and the inescapable knowledge that Morag was not her mother at all. Why then did she still feel so emotional every time she thought about her? Why, when her mind tried so hard to deny the relationship, did her heart insist on pining for her mother? Ina picked up a pen and paper and actually started to write the letter which might repair the damage but then allowed the pen to drop from her fingers. It was no use. Her mother wouldn't want anything to do with her now. She had her son. And if she had wanted to heal the rift with Ina she could have done so in the letter she had written, explaining that, out of respect for Rab, she and Archie had decided to postpone their wedding. It had been a nothing more than a few brief paragraphs informing them of the new date, in December.

Hurt afresh by its terse tone, Ina had believed no reply was expected, or even wanted. And why should it be, she asked herself again, when her mother must hold her responsible both for Rab's death and for the delay to her own marriage plans? Sadly, Ina put the paper away.

Her spirits lifted again when Joe came home and she told him about the baby. He was almost beside himself with delight and so proud that he simply couldn't keep the good news to himself. By the end of the next day the whole village knew that the young couple would soon be parents. Ina was touched by the response of some of her neighbours.

'Leave the privy to me now, lass. I'll take care of it until after the wean's born,' Mrs Rankine said.

Similarly, she discovered friends who were more than willing to take the heavier washing from her, knowing full well that she would do the same for them when their time came round again. She was offered numerous sets of baby clothes, the loan of prams and the use of cradles, even from women she had not thought of as friends. It was a wonderful feeling to know that she was part of such a caring community.

Though Ina longed for her baby to be born she was still relatively ignorant in the ways of her body and had no experience of pregnancy and birth. It didn't take the women long to realise that she was extremely nervous about the whole thing. It seemed to Ina that every wash day brought another horror story, another tale of agonising labour, bloody death and inept midwifery. Every single woman seemed to have personal experience of excruciating pain, and the fount of all this agony seemed to be the much maligned midwife. A veteran of well over a hundred births, Ma Trale was responsible for the delivery of every child in the village. If a mother died, or the child was lost, most women accepted that it was God's will, and not something for which Ma Trale could be blamed, but that didn't hinder them from using her in their attempts to frighten Ina.

Ina returned to her house every Monday feeling sicker and sicker as her expected time approached. Not that she ever showed her disquiet in public, she was much too proud for that. It was in the long hours alone in her neat little house that the fear really got to her. 'It was like being split in half,' – she'd lost count of the number of times she'd heard that. Lost count too of the number of times one or other of the women had looked at her and muttered darkly about her narrow hips. First babies were the most difficult, they said, and she knew that was true because her own mother had almost died giving birth to – not to her, she corrected her careering thoughts, but to a son. She had heard it said that if a woman was too narrow, the midwife cut the child out, slitting from front to back, and then the things she and Joe did in bed, and which the other women giggled about, would no longer be enjoyable, perhaps not even possible, and that was if she lived through the ordeal at all. She looked at herself in the slightly tarnished mirror over the fire. She was big, very big. The women said the child would be huge, hard to bring into the world. Well, she would just have to bear the pain, anything, so long as they didn't have to cut her. She couldn't stand that.

In fact she sailed through her pregnancy with the absolute minimum of discomfort.

'It should be any day now, lass. You let me know the minute you feel anything,' Jessy warned when she felt the birth was imminent.

'It takes a while the first time, doesn't it?' Ina asked.

'Aye. It'll not be quick, that's certain. A day, maybe longer. I was nearly three whole days with our Harry. But you send for me as soon as you think you've started. You don't need to be alone.'

'I will,' Ina assured her.

Inevitably she woke in the middle of the night, not certain at first why she was awake. Even when she felt her stomach tightening she did nothing more than turn over, trying to get more comfortable. After all, this had been going on for a week now. The dragging sensation in her back was new though, she thought, drifting back to sleep.

Joe slipped out of bed and away to work, taking great care not to disturb her, so she was on her own when the first real pain shot her into instant wakefulness.

Cautiously she sat up and then got out of bed, tensed against another pain. She had time to brew herself some tea and slip her clothes on before it came. Reassured she settled into her morning routine of cleaning and cooking, confident that there was plenty of time. When Joe came in he could fetch Jessy and that would be soon enough. She was determined not to make a fuss like Mary Hood had made a month ago. Her screams had been heard echoing all along the rows for more than six hours.

As the morning progressed the pains got fiercer and came more often, forcing Ina to abandon her household chores and sink into her chair. Cold sweat beaded her face. Only a few hours into it and already she could hardly bear the pain and it would be tomorrow at the earliest before the child was born. She was tempted to knock on the wall for Mrs Rankine but what would a woman who had borne four children think of her if she

561

started making a fuss so soon? Gritting her teeth Ina nearly chewed through her lip as the pain slashed through her again.

An hour later she glanced at the clock. Another hour and a half and Joe would be in. If she could just last until then. Renewed pain wiped all thoughts from her mind which centred itself mercilessly on her agony. Like all the rest it passed, leaving her shaken and increasingly scared. And then she felt the imperative urge to visit the privy. But she couldn't, not like this. Her legs would give out on her before she was halfway across the green. Levering herself cautiously off the chair she stumbled across the floor and groped for the chamber pot in the recess under the bed. Squatting in the middle of the kitchen floor she strained until her neck bulged and her eyes felt as if they were popping out. But nothing happened. She relaxed, slewing sideways on to the floor, trying to summon the energy to creep back to her chair, wondering if she had picked up the stomach upset which was affecting some of the villagers. Then the urge was upon her again. She strained, pushing down with all her might until she felt a wild gush of water that carried something solid with it. Horrified, sure she had done herself some dreadful damage, she peered between her legs. What she saw there made her freeze in sheer terror. A tiny, greyish head protruded, half in and half out of her body. Even as she looked at it another contraction tightened her abdomen. Ina knew she had to expel the infant and allowed herself to slide gently to the floor then put every ounce of energy into giving birth to her child. She felt a quick slither then instant relief. Propping herself on her elbows she peered down to see the tiny, perfectly formed but unmoving body of her son. She didn't even know she had screamed until Mrs

Rankine burst through the door, closely followed by another neighbour.

'Oh dear Lord,' she gasped. But her shock was momentary. Even as Ina groaned with the unexpected pain of the afterbirth, Mrs Rankine cut the cord and upended the child, giving it a shake for all the world as if she was flapping a used duster. There was a gurgling noise, a weak cry and then a full-throated roar of outrage.

'There, the wee soul was all but drowned,' Mrs Rankine laughed. 'Now lass where can I find a towel for this wee man?'

'The cupboard,' Ina murmured automatically, never taking her eyes off the child whose little fists were beating the air with frantic disapproval.

By the time Jessy arrived, with Joe following – newly off shift and covered in coal dust – less than a minute later, mother and son were fresh and smiling in bed.

'Why didn't you send for me?' was Jessy's first question.

'I didn't know it would come so fast. I only started last night.'

'Last night!' Jessy was horrified. 'My,' she said with a touch of admiration, 'you're a stubborn lassie, Ina Lennox, and a brave one too.'

'It wasn't as bad as I thought it would be . . . after what the other women said.'

'Aye, well, that'll teach you to pay heed to their nonsense. I thought you knew better than to believe everything they say.' Her mother-in-law smiled, tickling the baby under its unappreciative chin. 'Look at this! There's coal dust on this wean already!' She rounded on her son. 'Get away to my house and clean yourself up and don't you come back here with your filth around a baby.'

Joe knew when he was beaten and rushed, whistling, to his mother's house where there would at least be privacy to wash in.

Jessy turned back to Ina and perched herself on the edge of the bed, a determined look on her face. She knew that a woman was emotionally vulnerable at this time and she intended to take advantage of that state to bring the girl to her senses. 'Your mother'll be that proud,' she started, watching the girl's face intently.

With bewildering suddenness, Ina felt tears flood her eyes. She shook her head, feeling confused by the conflicting emotions. 'She's not my Mam,' she whispered, the hurt all the sharper because of the warm, milky infant cradled in her own arms.

'Your mother held you to her in just the same loving way that you're holding this wee man. She always believed you were her own. Even when she found out the truth, she went right on loving you. Why else would she turn her back on her son? She chose you, lass! Surely you can see how much she must have loved you?'

Ina sobbed softly, gripped her son even closer and shook her head. 'It's too late . . .'

'It's not too late!' Jessy said sternly. 'But it will be if you don't listen to what I'm telling you now, Ina, and you'll regret it to the end of your days.' She covered the girl's hand with her own, then went on, her voice softer, 'Och, there's nothing like a new bairn to heal old wounds. You be sure and let her know, lass. It's only right.'

Ina sniffed and ran a loving finger over her son's downy head. She said nothing.

Jessy got off the bed and busied herself about the little house. But she smiled to herself as she worked, sure her suggestion had been planted in fertile ground.

'Och, but he's a wee smasher,' Joe told his tired but happy wife later that evening.

'He's going to have your hair,' she said, fingering the dark down on her son's head.

'Aye, so he is,' he agreed proudly. 'I do love you, Ina,' he added kissing her gently.

'I love you too,' she told him, as she told him every night.

'What'll we call him?'

'Hugh, after your pa, if you like.'

'No, he'll just get called Shug. I hate that.'

'So do I,' she giggled.

'Jack's a braw name,' he suggested.

'That's just John really.'

'Aye. I know. How about John then?'

'John, to be called Jack?'

'Aye.' He nodded.

'All right. But John Robert.'

'Robert?'

'Rab,' she explained softly.

'Fine by me, lass. John Robert Lennox it is then.'

'Jack Rab Lennox,' she grimaced then giggled, laid her head on his shoulder and fell, deeply, blissfully asleep.

Morag gave her mother a weak, nervous smile. 'Do you think I'm doing the right thing, Mam?' she asked.

Annie looked at her daughter with affection. 'You know you are. You don't need me to tell you that Archie will be a fine husband.'

'I know. I just want everything to go well. I made such a mess of things with Donny.'

'Hush up,' Annie ordered. 'That wasn't the same thing at all and well you know it. It's a second chance, just like I had with Rab. If you're even half as happy . . .' she trailed off. Thinking of Rab still brought a lump to her throat. She controlled herself with an effort. Today wasn't a time for tears. 'Now then, the car will be here in a minute. Are you all organised?'

'Aye.' Morag laughed. 'I'll feel right daft going to the church in a car. It's only two hundred yards along the street.'

As if on cue the door opened a fraction and a young man, still with the fresh cheeks of youth and a thatch of dark auburn hair in a shade that almost exactly matched Morag's, popped his head into the room.

'Are you ready?' he asked.

'Yes. I think so,' Morag said, smiling at him.

He offered her his arm but she hesitated before stepping out of the house. 'I'm glad you're here, Angus,' she said, feeling the now familiar surge of affection for the son of whose life she had missed so much. It was followed by a pang of grief for the daughter she had lost. Morag had been deeply hurt by Ina's failure to reply to the careful letter she had written, telling her of the new date for the wedding – a letter which b~en intended as an olive branch, avoiding all mention of Rab, or anything else which might unwittingly be perceived as apportioning blame for a series of events which she herself suffered endless guilt over. Never at ease with the written word, Morag had posted it, never realising how cold and stilted the resulting short paragraphs were. Even though weeks, then months, had passed with no reply she had held on desperately to the faint hope that Ina and Joe would arrive unexpectedly to share the celebration. Now she forced herself to face the fact that she had probably alienated herself from her daughter for ever. It cast a shadow over what should have been the happiest day of her life.

566

'Me too,' Angus told her in the deep, well-modulated voice which marked him immediately as being from a different class.

He kissed her cheek then offered his other arm to Annie who took it with as much pride as Morag had. 'You just be sure and give the right woman away when we get to the church,' she teased.

They were at the car when the red motor bike tore along the path. The boy dismounted and ran across to them. 'Telegram for Mrs Morag Archibold,' he cried.

'I'll take it,' Annie offered. 'I'll give it to the best man, he can read it out at the reception.'

Morag was about to agree but then hesitated. 'Who is it addressed to?' she asked.

'To you,' Annie said.

'Archibold?'

'Aye.'

'I want to read it now.'

'Morag, you're late enough as it is,' Annie objected.

'If it was for the wedding, shouldn't it be in my new name?' Morag asked.

'Aye . . .' Annie looked uncertain.

'Give it to me, Mam.'

'We're already late. Poor Archie'll think you've changed your mind,' Annie said, handing over the envelope reluctantly.

'I've got a lifetime to live with Archie. Another minute won't make any difference one way or the other,' Morag insisted, tearing at the envelope. 'Oh God!' she breathed when she had read it. 'Oh God . . .'

'What is it?' Angus asked, his green eyes dark with concern. 'Are you all right? Do you want to sit down?'

'I'm fine. I'm fine. Och, it's just wonderful,' Morag laughed. 'Listen. "CONGRATULATIONS ON YOUR MARRIAGE

AND ON YOUR FIRST GRANDCHILD STOP JOHN ROBERT
LENNOX STOP BORN TWELFTH SEPTEMBER STOP FOUR
PM STOP ALL WELL STOP I LOVE YOU MAM STOP" Och,'
she said, her voice choked with emotion, 'I didn't even
know there was a wean on the way. Isn't that grand?' She
mopped at the tears which were streaming down her
face.

'It's just marvellous,' Angus laughed.

'Och, they've called him for Rab,' Annie sniffed into
her lace hanky.

Morag, took a deep, contented breath and swallowed
back the tears. Then she folded the telegram and put it
carefully into the front of her prayer book where it
would be safe until she had time to read it, and cry over
it, again. 'Come on then, take me to the church,' she
smiled. 'Och what a wonderful way to start a wedding.'

'Aye, a grandwean,' Annie said, slipping into the car
beside her daughter.

'And a daughter who says she loves me,' Morag's voice
trembled with the sheer joy and relief of it. 'I never
thought to hear from Ina again.'

'Of course you would, Mother. She just needed a little time to get over the shock, just like I did.' Angus
took her hand and kissed it gently. 'You have a son who
loves you too,' he reminded her softly.

'Och, for goodness sake! Will you just get us to the
kirk, Angus,' Annie ordered, successfully defusing the
emotional time bomb. 'Poor Archie will wonder what
he's got himself into if we all walk in crying our eyes
out. This is supposed to be a happy day.'

'It is, Mam. It is. The happiest day of my life.'